Passion's Awakening

"Thank you for staying on at the Lone Star, Gena. I know it's not how you expected things to be and I'm sorry," he told her softly.

"I'm not disappointed, Scott. Not with anything." *Not with you,* said the light stroke of her palm along his jaw.

"I'm glad you're here."

He lowered his face to hers gradually, giving her the chance to refuse him. Instead, he found her lips moist and parted in welcome.

Melting beneath his heat, she lifted her arms, holding safely to his shoulders at first, then drawn inexorably to the tempting terrain of his chest.

She explored the powerful, sculpted muscle. Confronted by his strength, she felt a tremor of vulnerability. He was a rugged man who could conquer with force rather than persuade with passion. Knowing that, she felt helpless yet curiously in control. For when her hands caressed him, he moaned against her mouth as if she were molding him with her touch instead of just the opposite. The sound incited a quivering response in her, and her heart thundered with a rush of forbidden desire . . .

DANA RANSOM'S RED-HOT HEARTFIRES!

ALEXANDRA'S ECSTASY   (2773, $3.75)

Alexandra had known Tucker for all her seventeen years, but all at once she realized her childhood friend was the man capable of tempting her to leave innocence behind!

LIAR'S PROMISE   (2881, $4.25)

Kathryn Mallory's sincere questions about her father's ship to the disreputable Captain Brady Rogan were met with mocking indifference. Then he noticed her trim waist, angelic face and Kathryn won the wrong kind of attention!

LOVE'S GLORIOUS GAMBLE   (2497, $3.75)

Nothing could match the true thrill that coursed through Gloria Daniels when she first spotted the gambler, Sterling Caulder. Experiencing his embrace, feeling his lips against hers would be a risk, but she was willing to chance it all!

WILD, SAVAGE LOVE   (3055, $4.25)

Evangeline, set free from Indians, discovered liberty had its price to pay when her uncle sold her into marriage to Royce Tanner. Dreaming of her return to the people she loved, she vowed never to submit to her husband's caress.

WILD WYOMING LOVE   (3427, $4.25)

Lucille Blessing had no time for the new marshal Sam Zachary. His mocking and arrogant manner grated her nerves, yet she longed to ease the tension she knew he held inside. She knew that if he wanted her, she could never say no!

DANA RANSOM

Dakota Desire

ZEBRA BOOKS
KENSINGTON PUBLISHING CORP.

ZEBRA BOOKS

are published by

Kensington Publishing Corp.
475 Park Avenue South
New York, NY 10016

First printing: June, 1992

Printed in the United States of America

To that provoking friend
who insisted I jot down a
quick outline for this story
to send along with
the proposal for *Dakota Dawn*.
"Why not? What have you got to lose?"
Sound advice.

And for the Native Americans
for whom I've developed such a strong
respect during the researching of
this novel.

Prologue

Sound exploded within the conical walls of hide, war whoops echoing as if the entire Crow nation were swooping down out of the Hills bent on blood. Jerked from the somber tones of his dream and yet dazed with sleep, the boy responded nimbly. Instinct rather than conscious effort brought him rolling out of the bed of willow rods and skins, from that cozy burrow of warmth into frigid darkness. His hand was groping for the carbine he'd laid on the ground beside his mat when he was seized from the shadows behind him. Fingers clenched ruthlessly in his short black hair. One swift movement snapped his head back, and before he could whisper up a prayer or a curse, a cold edge of steel touched to his forehead.

For a long moment, the raw sawing of his breath was the only sound, and then came a soft chiding voice.

"Were I your enemy, I would be readying your hair to decorate my lance."

The ebb of tension left the boy weak in limb, but no shivery movement betrayed him. "Then I am lucky the enemy does not see fit to rise as early in the day as you, *tunkasila*."

The cruel grip lessened to become a gentle rumpling of the newly shorn locks. It was a fond gesture, one that took the sting from disapproving words. "Slow. You are too slow. To sleep like the dead is to become one of the dead. Have I taught you nothing, Lone Wolf? You must never let down your guard. Be alert to danger and ready to fight to protect yourself and your loved ones."

The boy, Wolf-Who-Stands-Alone, came off his knees and sat back on his sleep platform to regard his grandfather. His mouth was shaped with a rueful smile. "There is little chance of me being scalped while at the white man's school in the east."

The old man shook his head wisely. "Do not underestimate an enemy, *takoja*. It is when you think yourself safe that you are in the greatest danger."

"Then perhaps I should stay here with you."

It was said lightly but the old man knew different. He didn't need the light from a brighter fire to detail the unspoken hope etched in the uplifted gaze. An impossible hope. His answer was kind but firm.

"No, my son."

Shoulders slumped in dejection and Yellow Bear was moved to place his hands upon them. "The day is young. You should seek more sleep." There was an immediate straightening in the young form.

"No, Grandfather." The boy thought uneasily of the dark vision he'd awakened from, and he felt cold all over. "I would rather talk with you. I have years in which to sleep." His hands scrubbed over his face. His brow was damp. So were his palms. It was a sweat of terror yet lingering from the netherworld of dreams. Ordinarily, he would have spoken of it to his grandfather, who was wise in such matters and who would know how to interpret the frightening images he'd seen. But he held to worried silence. And that silence sat as bitter as a lie.

8

"You are troubled, *takoja.*"

The boy couldn't speak an untruth. "Yes." He stared hard into the final embers of last night's fire, hoping the old chief couldn't read his thoughts.

"You will do well. Your mind is clever and quick."

It took Lone Wolf a moment to realize his grandfather was speaking of the distant school. He replied easily. "I will not disappoint you. I have no fear that I will fail to stand with pride amongst the whites." No, his fears were not for himself. They were with his father's people. "But I would rather be here, standing beside you."

The sentiment was soft-spoken, a wish rather than argument. He had expended all of the latter over the last few months and he knew them to be futile.

"Your place is not here, *takoja.*"

"Why?" the boy cried, suddenly taken with a fierce anger against circumstance. "Because I am half white?" He surged up to the full arrogant height of his thirteen years to shout, "I am a man, the son of a Lakota warrior, not some weak, white child."

"Sit down," Yellow Bear admonished quietly. "You need not wake the entire tribe with that truth."

Shamefaced, Lone Wolf resumed his seat, but his fire hadn't dimmed. It burned hot in his veins, mingling with the blood of his father. He looked to the old man beside him with the passion of that heritage bright in his golden eyes. "My place is here, *tunkasila.* I would dance with our people and pray for the Messiah to come and bring with him the buffalo. I would be here to greet the spirit of Far Winds, my father, when he returns to restore the land to our people." The fervor of hope that had seized the starving Sioux raced through him, blinding him with enthusiasm to other truths.

9

"And to rid the world of the white man? Would you speak that prayer, as well?"

The boy was silent. The heat of excitement died inside him. His mind was torn from mystic promise by the images crowding his heart. His mother. His adopted father. His brother. His maternal grandfather. Could he speak the words to destroy them to save his father's people? A great division of spirit rose to torture his young soul, and understanding his anguish, the old chief put his palm against one light bronze-colored cheek.

"Go to the east. In this, your mother has found great wisdom. She is right in her want to spare you the pain of choice."

"But it's a coward's path to run from difficulty."

"It is your path. There is no shame in it. Walk it proudly."

"But—"

"Listen."

And the boy was silent.

"Our people dance and pray and wait for a miracle to return the old ways. That miracle may or may not come today or tomorrow. If it does not come, we will need the wisdom you can find in the eastern schools. This knowledge the white man denies our people, for with knowledge comes strength and power. Despite his words, he wants us to remain where we are like his spotted animals on the hoof, fenced and docile. What you learn, Lone Wolf, could bring new hope to our people, new ways to restore our dignity and our pride. The road you take will not be easy, for it is one you must walk alone. Would you step from that noble path to serve your own will?"

There was a slight pause, then a soft, "No, Grandfather."

10

The old man smiled. "I will miss you, Son of Far Winds."

With a low sound of distress, the boy turned into his embrace and hugged hard to the sinewy form, breathing in the scents of the hunt and the sky and the tall grasses that he would always associate with the chief of the Miniconjou. Not the stale, despondent smells of starvation and despair that clung to the reservation. When a tremor shook through his shoulders, the old man pushed him away.

"Tears are for women and the war whoop for men to drown their sorrows."

"I have had a dream, *tunkasila,* and I am afraid," the boy blurted out. "I saw snow falling red upon the ground. I heard the soldiers' music and the cries of children. I saw *unci* running from some great terror but she could not escape it." His breathing quickened as if hurried by his grandmother's panic. "I saw Yellow Hair, the one they called Custer, riding through our people, cutting them down with his sword. How could that be? His death came before I was born. What does it mean, Grandfather? What does it mean?"

For a moment, the old chief did not speak. Then, gently, he touched the boy's anguished face and soothed, "A dream, is all, not a vision." Lone Wolf released a great sigh of relief. "Your thoughts are troubled with fears of what is to come. Rest yourself, *takoja,* and give your mind ease. We will talk more when the sun smiles upon us." When he saw the boy's reluctance, Yellow Bear added, "Sleep well. I will sit here with you so the dark dreams will not return."

And not doubting for a moment that his grandfather could hold even the blackness of the mind at bay, the boy settled back upon the bed of hides and closed his eyes. And no dreams came to torment him.

However, as the old chief sat until the hours of dawn watching over his grandson's slumber, he had no ease of mind.

Snow falling red upon the ground.

Yellow Bear gave silent thanks that the boy would not be there to see it.

Chapter One

He told her it was a land of savage extremes. A land of glorious sunsets and magnificent distances, of limitless sky pierced by bold mountain peaks. His voice hushed into a Sunday-like reverence when he spoke of the Dakotas. Of the plains called alkali deserts that yielded millions of acres of God's finest grasslands. Of the flat monotony ending at the abrupt twisted beauty of the badlands. Of a land both treeless and endowed with great forests. Barren yet supporting a wealth of wild game and lush vegetation. With intense heat backed by bitter cold, temperature of 120° in the summer and -40° in winter. His home. And she couldn't wait to see it, to know firsthand what stirred the heart of Scott Prescott with such poetic passion.

It was all that he'd said and more. Vast, untamed, untouched. Like nothing she'd ever seen before. And never had Genevieve Trowbridge felt so intimidated and terrified as she was by the quiet infinity of the Dakota plains.

Miles and miles of nothingness. It hadn't appeared so threatening from the window of the train. Rather picturesque, she had thought at the time. Like one of the Russell paintings Scott was so fond of. But as their carriage whirred farther and farther from all evidence of civilization, a sense of foreboding settled like the shimmering heat haze that turned the acres of short grass into an undulating sea.

So hot! And it was only mid-June. There was no way to perspire daintily. It trickled uncomfortably from under her high collar and beneath the warm hug of her cashmere gown. She could feel her artfully crafted curls wilt against the back of her neck. But her mother had taught her a lady never fidgeted, so she sat still and composed with her lace-mitted hands demurely posed upon her lap. After all, she had no right to complain. She'd insisted upon coming. She'd all but forced the idea upon her fiancé. He'd argued that she could meet his parents at their wedding in October but she hadn't wanted to wait. He was going to visit his beloved Dakota and she was determined to go along. To see for herself the land that lent animation to his smile and a soft wistfulness to his gaze. Dakota. How she hated all that she'd seen so far.

Gena glanced to their traveling companions to see how they fared. No better than she, from all appearances. She took comfort in their misery. At least she was not alone in it. All four looked as unprepared for and overwhelmed by the situation as she, herself, was, yet equally determined to suffer in good grace. She felt a twinge of guilt, knowing they had come to lend an air of propriety to her trip. She had only to look upon their pinched, flushed faces to know it was not the grand adventure they had anticipated in the cool of her family's Boston parlor.

Across from her, Scott's cousin Beth seemed near to swooning. A fan fluttered incessantly in her usually languid hand, but, Gena had to admit, the heat did inspire her friend's pallid features to a more healthy glow. Her husband, Merle Armitage, was sweating at her side without apology. He was a big man, compacted into a narrow coat and corseting vest. Even his jovial temperament had flagged over the last few miles. At the opposite corner, Beth's brother, Horace Billings, sat stiff in his starched collar and strangling necktie, as if he considered it a matter of personal pride to rise above the unpleasant circumstances. When he caught her glance, his thin mustache twitched then turned up hopefully, an invitation not missed by the woman who sat on Gena's left. Caroline Davies sported Horace's large amethyst on her hand and was not about to endure any trespass upon her future fortune. Gena had to smile. As if a woman possessed of Scott Prescott would ever look elsewhere.

Gena canted an admiring eye toward the man seated on her right and was aware of an exquisite fluttering within her breast. Lounging back against the seat in his lightweight blue serge suit, her fiancé seemed to suffer from no symptoms of discomfort. He looked . . . wonderful. A feeling of pride and shy possession warmed through her; a heat much more pleasant than the sweltering afternoon clime. As if to reassure herself that it was true, she touched the diamond solitaire upon the third finger of her right hand. He was hers. The idea still amazed and thrilled her. By the year's end, a year that would bring in a new century, all that she had would transfer from father to husband. The flutters subtly shifted into an uneasy palpitation.

To distract herself from the sudden, unworthy fit of nerves, Gena pursued the study of her intended. He was looking out over the miles of green, presenting her with a sharply sculpted profile. It was a tantalizing compromise of fine lines and broad planes. Even after the years in the east, he'd never lost the deep outdoor coloring of the west. It made a stark contrast to his snowy shirt collar. Now that she'd seen his country, she could compare the two, Scott Prescott and the wild land that was both smoothly regular and boldly angular. His features were like that. Beneath the short crisp cut of his jet-black hair, equally dark brows made a lazy arch. Slanted eyes were shaped in a perpetual squint against the strong sunlight

15

of the plains, with deep creases fanning from their corners when he smiled. Eyes that fascinated because they were as purely gold as the broad wedding band he would slip on her finger in the fall; gold without a faintest trace of green or brown. A thin nose bisected the high, wide flare of browned cheeks that tapered to a strong jaw. An easy stretch of his mouth scored deep, curving valleys into that rugged terrain. It was a face that was restless even when relaxed.

She'd seen men more handsome but none as physically compelling. She'd been mesmerized from the first time she'd seen him on the polo field, watching him ride as one with his horse. Like a "wild Indian," Horace had sniffed disdainfully, but Gena had been, and was, intrigued. She'd never seen anyone move with such fluid confidence and control, and she'd been quite breathless by the time they were introduced. There was a strength and ease to his manner, a gentle drawl tugging at his words, a kiss of western gold to his features that set him apart from other men of her acquaintance. She suffered no awkwardness in his company, no tangle of shyness or nerves, perhaps because Beth's "cowboy" cousin was the most natural, honest, and unassuming person she'd ever met. For all his ruggedly framed masculinity, there was a deep quiet to Scott Prescott that never failed to calm her. And she was delighted by his leisurely court.

A perfect match, her parents claimed. The lines of the Boston branch of his family were impeccable. Horace confided that he was sent the princely sum of $1,200 annually from his grandfather, a well-known Dakota rancher, to see himself through Harvard Law School. Money he didn't use, much to his cousin's bewilderment, to buy himself a fashionable set of society friends or to squander upon the vices of gambling, debauchery, and exclusive clubs. He spent it on a few finely tailored suits and the best bit of horseflesh he could find in eastern sta-

16

bles. The rest he saved. He rode hard but he didn't bet. He played hard but he didn't drink or carouse. He was widely recognized but few could claim to know him. He pursued his education with an intensity few could match and graduated at the top of his class. A shrewd, brilliant business mind, her father boasted, one that would be an asset to his company.

But it wasn't his lineage or his moral fiber or his wealth or his business prospects or even his looks that made the greatest impression on Gena Trowbridge. She loved him for his kindness and for the way he made her feel safe and revered.

As if he sensed her scrutiny, and her need for reassurance, Scott turned to her with his easy smile. And suddenly, Gena felt very foolish in her fears. Everything would be fine. Casually, he reached for her hand, taking it in the curl of his strong brown fingers and bringing it up to hold like something cherished upon his breast. Then he looked away.

Beneath her palm, she could feel the hard, assertive pulse of his heart and the vital warmth of him. A man's warmth. And despite the heat of the day, she shivered. Her breathing altered as she concentrated upon that small hand trapped helplessly against him. Against the firm, powerful chest. Caught within the overwhelming grasp. Slowly, determinedly, she eased it free and was able to draw a decent breath once trembling fingers were laced tight together upon her lap. Scott hadn't noticed her desertion. His attention was fixed upon a mass of dark shapes dotting the low hills ahead.

"Oh, look," Caroline called excitedly. "Are those buffalo?"

The others twisted eagerly in their seat, straining to make out the animals contentedly grazing in the distance.

"Cattle," Scott corrected. "My grandfather's."

There was a noise of disappointment as the trio settled back upon the leather cushions.

"Will we be seeing any buffalo herds?" Merle asked hopefully as he mopped the rivulets from his forehead with an equally damp handkerchief.

"There are no more buffalo herds. Haven't been for a lot of years."

Merle looked sulkily out over the expanse of grass. "Darn. I did so want to see buffalo. An American institution, don't you know."

Scott smiled blandly.

The handkerchief continued to blot away. "The steward on the train told me they used to carry hunters through miles and miles of them. Shot them by the thousands from the open boxcars. Fell thick as ticks in an Indian blanket, he said."

"Oh, my," Beth exclaimed, glancing nervously out over the rolling hills. "We won't see any Indians, will we?" Her husband patted her hand and looked just as anxious.

"Not likely," Scott told them. "They're mostly northeast of here, on the reservation. Haven't heard of any scalp-raising for the last ten years or so."

Merle petted his wife's hands with more confidence, saying, "Don't go vaporish, my dear. From what I hear, they're tame as lap dogs." When she supplied a wan smile, he looked back to Scott. "Did you ever hunt buffalo?"

His words drawled in reply. "Not from a train."

Merle sighed regretfully. "Too bad they're gone. I would have enjoyed bagging a few of the shaggy beasts. What a thrill it must have been, right out in the midst of all those behemoths, just you and the charging bulls, with only a measure of gunpowder between you and sudden death."

"And a speeding train," Scott murmured. His smile was thin. "A real man's sport."

18

Beth shivered. "Oh, stop it, Merle. You're positively giving me goose bumps. Such brutish talk in front of ladies."

Her husband muttered a suitable apology, but his small, pale eyes were still aglow with visions of the chase.

"Do you suppose we could see some Indians, Mr. Prescott?"

Scott leaned around Gena to regard Caroline Davies's rapt expression. "What did you have in mind, Miss Caroline? Some introductions?"

Her hands fluttered to an agitated bosom. "Good heavens, I don't want to get that close."

"Just a little polite sightseeing, then. The rest of you want to gawk at the Indians, too?" There was eager head-nodding from all but Gena. She was looking at him, puzzled by the odd nuances in his voice. He smiled again and replied easily, "Don't suppose they'd mind any. Just hide your valuables and keep your hair safe under a hat so none of them go getting any ideas."

The ladies gasped in chorus.

"Really, Scott," Horace chastened. "Can't you see you're frightening our companions with your jest. I assure you, ladies, we will be quite safe." He reached to the floor of the carriage where his tapestried valise rested between his feet and withdrew a shiny, silver-plated derringer. "I don't think any of the savages would dare accost us."

The women and even Merle looked with wonder and repulsion at the tiny gun and, to a one, immediately felt safer. None thought to question if it was loaded or if the elegant Mr. Billings had ever fired upon anything in his cloistered life.

"Yessir, Horace," Scott affirmed. "That surely would put the fear of God into them."

With a manly puff of his narrow chest, his cousin returned the palm pistol to his bag. Secretly, he hoped one

19

of the timid redmen would make a threatening move so he would have the chance to display his prowess before Gena. And Caroline, of course.

"Look there," Merle shouted. He came half out of the seat, and the sudden shift of his bulk set the carriage rocking. Again, heads were craned to follow his excited pointing. A man on horseback was skimming a far ridge at breakneck speed. "Is that a real cowboy?"

The rider's hat knocked back to swing by its tie strings, revealing a shock of red hair that gleamed along the horizon like a setting sun. Suddenly aware of an audience, he reined in his painted stallion, bringing it up to dance on powerful hind legs. His wave brought an appreciative echo of *ooohs* and *ahhhs* from the easterners. Scott, alone, was unimpressed.

"The genuine article," he told them lazily.

Like a trained showman, the rider urged his mount into a flashy, ground-eating canter. While the spectators watched with suspended breaths, he executed a dazzling display of trick riding, using the saddle as a fulcrum to slide off either side of the heaving flanks to touch down on the ground then lightly vault back up and over.

Gena was captivated by the daring feats of horsemanship. She was unable to draw a breath until the rider crested a far hill and disappeared from sight. It was then she heard Scott mutter softly from her side.

"Danged fool."

Just then, the carriage topped a low ridge and the Bar K Ranch spread below them. Gena stared. She wasn't quite sure what she'd expected, but certainly not a large, fashionable mansion set squarely in the center of grass, sky, and cows. Sunlight glinted off prisms of stained glass set in upper-story windows and shone hot and black off the shingling of its turrets and gables. A wide wraparound porch offered an inviting shade from the merciless broil of the plains. Set off from the house were a collec-

20

tion of tidy buildings and corrals, the whole affair enclosed in a pole-and-post surround. Their carriage spun through wide gates above which the name *Bar K* was emblazoned. The driver took them right up to the front door, where they were met with a bevy of expectant house servants who quickly set upon their bags.

As Scott handed her down, Gena was aware of the sturdy figure of a man regarding them from the shadow of the porch. He made no move to come forward in greeting but waited for them with an imperious patience.

"Uncle Garth," Horace called out as he climbed the steps. "You're looking fit and fine. I can't tell you how much we appreciate you putting us up like this."

There was a low reply. Gena couldn't make out the words that sounded ever so much like rumbling thunder. On Scott's arm, she was guided up to the steps, and was the last one brought forth to meet Garth Kincaid.

"Hello, Grandfather." Scott formally extended his hand to the stocky older man. Gena could see the resemblance in the width and strength of build, but the younger man had more height and less sheer bulk of presence than the man before them. The rancher was one mass of solid power forced into the confines of a fashionable suit of clothes. From the cut of the cloth to the glitter of gold on fob and finger, Garth Kincaid spoke of affluence, but there was not one fraction of softness on his broad form. His features were hard and hewn from badlands stone beneath carefully oiled hair not yet gone to complete gray.

Kincaid surveyed his grandson expressionlessly as if he were seeing him after a week's absence instead of for the first time in almost ten years. He nodded in approval of what he saw: a dapper young man of style and substance, his daughter's son. "Looks like the east agreed with you, boy," was all he said as he took the proffered hand.

"Yessir. It had some mighty fine things to offer. And I brought home one of them." His arm lightly circled Gena's waist to coax her forward for the inspection of those granite-hard eyes. "Grandfather, this is Miss Gena Trowbridge, my fiancée."

The old man smiled. It was a gesture of courtesy, Gena felt, done without any genuine warmth or delight. "Welcome to the family, Miss Trowbridge." He leaned forward so his leathery cheek brushed by hers. Then, he turned, leading the way into the house with attention back on Horace. "How long will you be staying?"

That was all. No words of fondness. No displays of affection. If Scott was at all disappointed by his cool reception, there was no hint of it in his manner. He steered Gena into the long, cool hall and began to follow the others into the sunwashed parlor.

"Scotty!"

He'd no sooner turned than a big, handsome woman swept him into a rib-crushing embrace. He was grinning wide when she finally released him. "Howdy, Ruth. Ruth, I want you to meet Gena. We're going to be married."

Gena stood for the cursory inspection, then was enveloped in a gentle hug. Blushing slightly, she glanced at Scott, hoping he'd tell her the identity of the woman. More than servant, she guessed, but not quite an equal. Ruth stepped back, retaining Gena's hands as she beamed. "Oh, Scotty, you got yourself a pretty one. Does your mama know about this?"

"Well . . . I'm riding on over a little later on," he mumbled.

"Shame on you for keeping such a thing to yourself. You make yourself to home, Miss Gena, and if you need anything at all, you just come on out and ask for it." Her happy gaze went between them once more before she entered the parlor to speak quietly to the Bar K's owner.

22

While the two of them spoke, his big hand rested absently on her rounded hip. Gena looked away, embarrassed by the unexpected intimacy. It was really none of her affair. When the woman swept by on her way to the rear of the house, she flashed the younger woman a quick, warming smile that was by far the best welcome she'd received since crossing the Missouri.

Kincaid's parlor was a slice right out of *Godey's*. It was an impressive museum of wealth and status, much like her family's in Boston. Greenery hung in the big bow window. Matched furniture huddled about the fireplace: a sofa, a thronelike gentleman's chair, several side chairs and an armless lady's chair. Each velvet arm and back was protected by a hand-embroidered tidy of neat precise stitches. She wondered if the woman, Ruth, had made them. Side tables and curio shelves were covered with runners trimmed in macrame lace. Small and large works of art were densely arranged above furniture and hanging shelves. A favored piece, a Remington, was placed upon an easel beside an upright piano. The mantel was crowded with treasured mementos and grainy picture portraits. She couldn't tell if Scott had posed for any of them. Intuitively, she doubted it. She had felt no sense of his inclusion in this big, cold room. Nor in the regard of the big man who was his grandfather. And she wondered why.

After an hour of polite parlor talk, Gena began to feel the effects of the day's travel. Her attention lagged and the smile became fixed upon her face as she listened to Merle expound, again, upon his investment in a brand-new motorcar soon to be delivered from the manufacturer.

"It's my conviction," he announced to all, again, "that the motorcar will put an end to traffic noise in the city. Without all the clatter of horses' hoofs and the rumble of steel tires, it should be as quiet as a country lane. After all, they are smaller, so the streets will be less crowded. Next year, they estimate eight thousand will be registered. It's the future of transportation."

Beth gave an exaggerated sigh, quite bored with the topic of her husband's new toy. "Anything will be better than the smelly smokestacks of the steam locomotives. I swear, someday the foul air from the elevated railroads alone will blot out the sky."

"Just try to run cattle with those fancy contraptions," Kincaid asserted. "Give me a good horse, any day."

"Mark me, the horse will be obsolete in ten years' time."

Kincaid looked at his grandniece's husband as if he were insane, but before he could comment, Ruth appeared in the doorway to announce dinner. "Something light," she offered, "because I'm sure the ladies are weary and would like to retire early."

"You look tired," Scott observed softly as he assisted Gena to her feet. "I was thinking that I could take you over to meet my parents tonight, but if you'd rather—"

Gena was shaken by a sudden apprehension. She knew she looked far from her best, and her spirits were flagging. She'd come too far to make a poor impression. "Could we wait until tomorrow, Scott? It's been such a long day."

"Whatever you want, Gena," he told her, but she could read the disappointment in his eyes, could sense his restlessness in the way he looked toward the west through the large bowed windows.

"You go," she said abruptly. He looked at her in surprise, expression touched with guilt that he would be so willing to leave her alone on this, her first night in a strange place. But she could read the longing in his face, could see his desire to be home. "I'll be fine here. It's not as though I'm amongst strangers, you know. Go home, Scott, and see your family. You've waited too long to put

24

it off another night just to listen to Merle's soliloquies and Horace's boastings. Go. I'll make excuses for you."

"You're sure?" He may have questioned, but he was already miles away in his thoughts and in his heart.

"Quite sure." She managed a smile. "Go."

He took up her hand and surprised her totally with the warm press of his lips upon it. That bright glow was in his eyes, that flame that sparked of home and family. She recognized it with a tug of wistful envy, wondering what it would be like to be on the receiving end of such a look.

"Tell my grandfather I'm taking a horse. I'll bring my folks by in the morning."

And he was gone. She suspected only a stringent control kept him from running. As she promised, she joined the others in the dining room and made the necessary apologies for her fiancé's sudden absence. Then, despite her vow to the contrary, she sat through the long meal, painfully adrift and more alone than she could ever remember.

"What do you think, Beth?" Caroline whispered over her shoulder as they climbed the runnered stairs single file behind Ruth. "Isn't it all just too, too quaint. Your uncle is so rustic. I find him ever so amusing."

"Hush, Caro," Beth cautioned, nodding toward the housekeeper's straight back.

Caroline pooh-poohed the idea of a servant taking insult and pouted the rest of the way up to the hall. As Ruth pointed the way to their rooms, the young woman exclaimed in sudden horror, "Dear me, do say there's indoor facilities."

The housekeeper gave her a long, stoic look, then murmured politely, "Yes, ma'am. You'll find a very modern bath right to your left. We are quite civilized for all our rustic charm. I'm sure you ladies will not be too inconvenienced during your stay. Breakfast is at six in the dining room. If you prefer a tray in your room at a more

25

fashionable hour, I will do my best to accommodate you. Good evening." With a rustle of stiff taffeta, she left them on the landing.

"Why, I never."

"Now, Caro . . ."

"If one of my servants dared such insolence with me . . . Gena, you simply must speak to Scott and see what he can do about having that woman removed at once."

"Caroline, this is not his home. It would be presumptuous for him to—"

"Oh, never mind," the black-eyed beauty snapped in a peevish temper. "I should have known you wouldn't put your timid little foot down over anything so trivial as your guests' well-being."

As Gena paled, Beth spoke up on her behalf. "Caro, you are the one who's behaving badly. It's only for a week. Surely you can endure it for that long."

"A week in this godforsaken place," Caroline sniffed. "I fear I shall truly go mad if all I have for distraction are cows and a few raggedy Indians."

"I'm sure my uncle has planned a few diversions," Beth soothed, petting her future sister-in-law's arm as if she were a high-strung dog in need of calming. "You're overwrought, is all. Things will look better in the morning."

"At six A.M.? Civilized, indeed. I will take my tray no sooner than ten. And the fruit better be fresh."

Gena sighed as she listened to them moving down the hall to their rooms. Suddenly, her head ached and her spine was recalled to every bump in the long road from the train depot. She slipped into her room, finding it a grateful sanctuary for her fatigue. A bedside lamp was burning, casting a pleasant glow. Her trunk was at the foot of the big wooden bedstead and its contents already removed, shaken and hung within a corner cupboard. On first glance, she was taken by the welcoming decor. Floorboards were muffled beneath a thick wool carpet and the walls warmed by a floral-and-stripe paper, both in cool shades of prairie green. Then, even as she was thinking how pretty it was, she heard her mother's voice: *Small rugs should be in the bedchamber, as carpets absorb gases and contagious effluvia. Wallpaper harbors disease and insects fostered by the bad air in sleeping rooms. So very deleterious to bodily health. A fevered brain is tormented into a state of nervous irritability by patterns upon the wall.*

Mother, Gena thought with a sigh. So concerned that all be pure and proper. Right then, she was determined to enjoy a good night's sleep in the cozy little room. Bad air and all.

Slowly, methodically, she performed her nightly ritual, carefully folding away her clothes and slipping into her bed gown before sponging away the day's soiling at the washstand. Eighteen pins were plucked, counted, and stored in their own little box before her fingers indulged in the luxury of a scalp massage. Then, she picked up her brush and began the first of fifty strokes. Her hair was her glory, a thick pale blonde that spun past her shoulders like silky floss. What would Scott think when he saw it down and free of its daily confines? She glanced into the small mirror atop the washstand and lifted the heavy weight of it with the backs of her hands. What would it feel like, having his strong browned fingers threading through it?

The face reflected back in the glass had gone suddenly stiff and white. Unsteady hands resumed hurried pulls of the brush, then quickly worked the soft tresses into a regimented braid. She crawled beneath the covers, and even within the close confines of her high collar and long sleeves she felt a decided chill.

Soon she would know exactly what it would be like to share her most private moments with Scott Prescott.

She trembled in the center of the big bed, and despite her exhaustion, it was a long time before she could sleep.

Chapter Two

It stretched out before him between river and range: the vast running sweep of plains country. The clean, inviting scent of it filled him with a strength more potent than the most intoxicating 150-proof and did crazy, reckless things inside his head. He felt like the suit of summer Sunday best his mama packed away over the winter months, dragged out all wrinkled and stale to finally flap in a restoring breeze. He'd been breathing in old smells, his senses dulled, cramped, and idle for too long. The freshness of sun and sky burned through his nose, cleansing the mustiness from his lungs. In celebration of that wild freedom, he let loose a loud, undulating wail. It was a sound that echoed back centuries.

He rode without a saddle, feeling the churning rhythm of the horse between his thighs. Using the pressure of his knees to guide the galloping animal, he let the reins fall slack along the stallion's muscular neck. His fingers tore loose his necktie. It was caught up by the rush of wind and fluttered back, forgotten. His coat was similarly discarded without a thought to cost. The sensations were of far greater value, the feel of his fine linen shirt taut across his chest and whipping like a desert sail at his back. The cool of twilight air tugging at open collar. He would have stripped right down to his cotton drawers if he didn't

28

think he'd be mistaken for some marauding reservation jumper out to steal a bit of expensive horseflesh. With one hand on the reins and the other meshed in the snapping mane, he urged the horse on by leaning low, until their silhouettes blended into one.

It sounded like impatient thunder, but Scott's trained ear told him of another rider's approach. Fast and hard. He cast a quick glance back to see a solitary horseman bisecting the adjacent hill to his right, charging down upon him in all-out leather and lather almost right on top of him. His long-dormant instincts had nearly failed him. Bending down across the sleek neck, Scott applied his boot heels and was rewarded with an extra notch of speed. Confident he could outdistance his pursuer, he'd begun to smile when he heard a faint whoosh of something circling overhead. He had time enough to jerk back on the reins before a length of Manila settled over his shoulders and cinched up tight, pinning his arms to his sides. Without the saddle beneath him, he was plucked neatly off the stallion's back with an expert snap of the rope. And for a moment, he rode only air. Then the ground came up with a very solid smack of hard-packed earth.

He didn't move. He wasn't sure he could, at first, with all the air pounded from him along with a good piece of his pride. He lay still, eyes closed, listening to the sound of a blown horse pulled up beside him, the rattle of its rider's spurs as he dismounted.

"God above, Scotty, if I've done kilt you, I ain't never gonna hear the end of it. Don't go a-playing possum on me. Scott? You all right?"

He waited for just the right tone of panic to settle in, then with a lightning-quick move, Scott kicked out to knock the feet from under his assailant. There was a surprised *oof* as he was joined in the brittle short grass. Before the other could react, his chest was straddled, his guns plucked neatly from his holsters, and the short blade of a knife lined up beneath his Adam's apple.

"Whatcha waiting for, ya sneaking Injun?" the fallen man snarled. "If it's my scalp you want, go on and take it!"

"Dang your dirty white hide, I will."

With that, Scott seized a handful of red hair from above his victim's left ear and sliced it off with a flick of his blade. He was about to release a conquering yell, when the cowboy's elbow socked him with a breath-stealing force to the ribs. Over he went, trophy scattering in the breeze. For several minutes, the two of them engaged in a noisy, hand-to-hand grappling, grunting at the well-placed jabs of elbow and knee, cursing and panting as they rolled in a tangle of arms and legs. Finally, as if by some silent mutual consent, they pushed apart and lay gasping and groaning side by side.

"You crazy son of a bitch, you could have broken my neck!"

"Knew you could outride me, but never could match me with a rope. And I'm gonna tell Mama what you just called her."

"Then I'll tell her about your Bill Cody Wild West Show this afternoon and she'll tan you but good. You got no brains, Rory."

"You got 'em all, big brother. Me? Shucks, I'm just as dumb as an ole stump." And he sounded proud of it.

"Some mighty fine riding."

"Learned from the best. Said he were half horse, half Injun."

A soft laugh, then a sigh. "It's good to be home."

That simple sentiment brought them together for a fierce embrace after which they both looked skyward, grinning and breathing deep of the companionable scents of exertion, horse, and tangy crushed grasses.

"You shore look purty," Rory exclaimed with an admiring whistle. "Soft as one of those city sissies." His play-ful jab deflected off rock-hard middle. "Learn yourself anything in them fancy books? Or with them fancy women?"

"Enough. How 'bout you? Daddy got you riding night-hawk?"

"Heck, no. Never could sweet-talk the fillies the way you do. I'm running the range for the major. Made me his foreman last year. Could be because me and the cows sorta got us the same thinking capacity."

"Foreman," Scott echoed. A strange feeling curled in-side him. A sort of wondering resentment that things had changed while he was gone. Rory would be almost twenty, far from the gangly, hero-worshiping tag-along he remembered, but, rather, his own man. Garth Kin-caid's man. While he'd been away, his brother had sprouted like the deep-rooted blue gamma, tended by the love of family. He felt a subtle stab he couldn't quite believe was envy. In a tight voice, he remarked, "Well, what do you know." He followed that with a soft, "I'm right proud of you."

"Why, I thank you for that, Scott. Means a lot coming from you."

Rory had come up on one elbow and was looking down at him with such wrenching sincerity, Scott nearly choked on the vague lump of his jealousy. He managed to smile, then looked back up at the sky with an almost an-gry concentration. What was wrong with him? He'd been the lucky one, the one to get away and earn a college degree.

"So, which one of them sweet things in the buggy was yours? And don't try telling me you didn't have no time to do any serious spooning in that high-faluting school." The redhead grinned provokingly. "Or did they all have too much sense to get tangled up with a mangy ole sod-buster like you?"

31

"The fair one. Gena."

Rory made a low rumbling sound of male appreciation. "My, my, my. One fine-looking gal. You bringing
her all the way out here with you, she must not be as stiff
and starched underneath all them layers of steel underwear. 'Lessen what I heard about them society fillies is
true."

Scott was fired by a consuming desire to plant his fist
square in the middle of his brother's smug smile. He sat
up, fingers gripping the grass-stained knees of his suit
pants to control the urge. In a voice as cold and slicing as
a wailing blue norther, he said, "It's Miss Gena to you.
She's a lady, not one of your hurdy-gurdies, so mind your
mouth."

Rory blinked in abject bewilderment. "Why, Scotty,
you surely know I didn't mean nothing by—"

"And she's going to be my wife."

That came out through gritted teeth, even angrier
than the first. His brother stared, mouth unhinged, for a
long second.

"Well, how 'bout that. How 'bout that!" An enthusiastic palm slapped down on the rigid shoulders, beating the
stiffness from them. "I can't believe Mama didn't say
nothing . . . She doesn't know? Git up, boy. Let's git you
home. This is gonna be one helluva reunion."

"Doesn't look like I have a horse." His grandfather's
stallion was probably going through bales in the barn by
now.

"Happens I'm a-going the same way. Proud to take you
up." Rory clambered to his feet and put down his hand to
hoist his brother up beside him.

"Now, you don't go spilling it, Rory. You keep those
gums gripped."

"My word on it, big brother. My word. Lordy, it's good
to have you home!"

32

"Doesn't that boy know any speed but full out?"

Aurora Prescott gave her stew one last turn of the spoon and reached behind her trim waist for her apron strings. She glanced through the kitchen arch to where her husband of nearly twenty-three years was paring chips of hardwood into the fire grate, but he showed no sign of having heard the flurry of hoofs beating right up to their door.

"And late, too," she continued, turning down the flame on her new Sterling range. "He's just lucky this meal isn't tougher than boot soles. Would serve him right. And you, too."

Dark eyes lifted leisurely from the piece he was shaping to frame a question. "How's that?"

"Have a talk with that boy. You're letting him run wild, Ethan."

Ethan Prescott stretched long legs out toward the fire and remarked with the lazy Texas drawl he'd never quite managed to shed, "Maybe I'll just whittle this here chair leg I was fixing for you into a nice sturdy switch to birch his backside. 'Course, don't think it would do much good, seeing as how I've been wearing on his rump regular since he was old enough to crawl and it hasn't had no effect yet. Must be the Kincaid in him."

"Is that right?" Indignation lent a tart tone to her voice.

"That's right. Stubborn, every last one of 'em." He tapped the length of wood into his palm thoughtfully. "Might have done more good if I'd applied a little birching to you."

She gave a haughty sniff, as if that didn't dignify a response, and carried the kettle of stew to the table she'd laid out with her mother's best Haviland an hour earlier. Her husband smiled to himself as he eyed her nicely rounded bottom twitching sassily around the table.

"Howdy, Mama."

There was a clomp of boots across the floorboards and Aurora tried to hold to her irritation as a placating kiss bussed her temple. She swatted with the back of her spoon at the hand reaching for a biscuit. "You're late."

"Sorry, Mama," he mumbled through a bite of pilfered biscuit. "I brung home another mouth to feed. Got enough to go around."

"Rory Prescott, you have the manners of a—"

As she spoke, her son took her by the shoulders and turned her toward the door. And suddenly, all power of voice failed her. There was deafening clatter as serving spoon fell from nerveless fingers into the blue granite-ware kettle.

The years had been more than kind to Aurora Kincaid Prescott. They had developed her beauty with each gentle line, with the subtle rounding of each curve. His mother's loveliness had always been a source of pride, but seeing her now, through a man's eyes, Scott could well understand why two strong, vital men had been driven to the extremes of life and death to claim her. It was more than her beauty. It was the essence of her, the strength, the sensuality of the woman within. And that feeling of pride moved upon him to stir a great, overwhelming tide of emotion. She hadn't made a move from the edge of the table, poised there as if caught in some uncertain spell, as if not quite sure she could trust her eyes.

And for one awful moment, he thought he saw the slightest glimmer of remembered terror in that wide, astounded stare.

"Hello, Mama," he ventured softly, and that terrible starkness fled her gaze. "I've sure missed you."

"Scott." It was a whisper that became a wail. "Scott!"

With the first offer of his smile, she launched herself across the room and into his arms, where she clung and cried energetically. Scott was enveloped by the soft, sub-

34

tle scent of lavender lingering beneath those of the kitchen. The memories it evoked brought a sharp sting behind his eyes. He blinked hard and turned his face into the unfaded brilliance of his mother's hair. Even though he topped her height by nearly a head, the circle of her arms made him feel small once again. And loved. How hungry he'd been for the power of that love.

"Ora, let the boy breathe."

Aurora obeyed her husband's scolding by stepping back but not away. Glistening eyes, golden eyes she shared with her son, devoured the lean strength of Scott's features. Trembling hands stroked through the short black hair, brushing it back from his temples before her fingertips followed the deep creases cut by his smile and finally measured the breadth of his shoulders. How he'd grown, the boy into a man. Her son.

Fearing she would once again dissolve into tears, Aurora fastened upon the first distraction she could think of.

"Scott Prescott, what happened to your nice clothes?"

He glanced down, savoring each stain of green upon his white shirt and trousers and the tone of his mother's voice that made him feel twelve years old again. "Fell off my horse, Mama. Rory, here, was good enough to double me back."

Aurora frowned. Scott fall off a horse? Her son who'd been riding like a burr since he was old enough to walk? A suspicious gaze cut over to her other son, then widened.

"Rory, what did you do to your hair?"

The redhead flushed nearly as bright as those irregularly chopped locks as he stammered, "Nothing, Mama," and rumpled the freshly trimmed patch to blend it with the rest.

Not any more fooled by the guileless smiles than she'd been ten years prior, Aurora scowled between them. "I

35

don't believe either of you for an instant. This poor meal can't afford to wait another second, so wash your hands, the both of you, and get to the table."

A pair of guilty *Yes, Mamas* cut straight through the heart of her. Hands clutched in the folds of her skirt as Scott passed by her. They trembled with their want to catch at him, to hold him, to gather him close, but she felt her husband's cautioning eyes upon her and so she let him go. But it was hard. Even after all the years passed by, it was hard. Her every instinct was to grab on tight. To make sure she wouldn't lose him again.

Ethan Prescott had come up off his fireside chair to tower like one of the Ponderosa pines he'd hewn to make his ranch house. While Rory nearly matched him inch for inch in height if not yet breadth, Scott still had to look up to him, as he'd always looked up to him.

"Did you listen and learn, pard?"

Scott hesitated only an instant, then cast his arms about the neck of the only father he'd ever known. "Yessir, I surely did, Daddy," he answered with a husky thickening to his words. He felt his feet leave the floor. When he was little, being lifted into his stepfather's embrace was like soaring to the clouds. And it still was.

"We'd best be getting to the table before your mama raps us upside the head."

Scott nodded, using the movement as an excuse to scrub his damp face against the broad flannel-clad shoulder that exuded the scents of wood chips and tobacco. His expensive eastern shoes settled back upon the floor and he forced his fingers to loosen.

Plates were passed as if it was just another evening meal taken between the four of them instead of the first in almost ten years. Conversation swung between Scott's schooling, Rory's position at the Bar K, and the bloodlines of the horses Ethan was raising; things men talked of when they were together. Aurora followed in silence, her eyes leaving her oldest son for only the briefest flickers. When the spoon rested in an empty kettle, Rory sat back in his chair, his dark eyes gleaming deviltry.

"Scotty has something to tell you, Mama."

Immediately, he gave a yelp and reached for his abused shin under the table.

"Scott?"

Shooting his brother a murderous look, Scott pushed the last of his biscuit around his plate and mumbled, "I was meaning to wait until after supper, but I guess I might as well just get to it. There's a lady I want you to meet tomorrow. She came out here with Cousin Beth and Horace. Her name's Gena Trowbridge and—"

"And Scotty's going to marry up with her."

"Hang it, Rory! You got the biggest mouth!" Scott leaned across the table to cuff his brother's bright head smartly. Then, he settled back into his seat and canted a look at his very quiet mother. "And I'm going to marry her," he concluded softly.

Aurora carefully set down her coffee cup. One who didn't know her would admire her for her composure. Ethan and her two sons were getting ready to lash themselves down for the whirlwind to come.

"And when did all this happen?" she began in a deceivingly calm voice.

"In Boston. She's a good friend of Beth's and we just sort of took up together."

"I won't ask you to elaborate on that. And so, when is this event to take place? Or had you planned to keep that a secret, too, until after the fact?"

Scott took a deep breath. There was no help for it now, so he figured he may as well get the worst of it out and take his medicine. "In October. We'll want you there, of course."

"There? Meaning where?"

"In Boston. Where we'll be living. Her father owns a

big company there and he wants me to work for him as legal council. It's a real good job, Mama, with good pay and Gena will be close to her family."

Aurora's features were positively frigid. Her words had all the crackle of a spring ice break. "How very fortunate for her. And when do you plan to start this new job in Boston?"

"In two weeks."

She stared at him for a long, stony moment, then her chin gave a betraying quiver.

"Mama—"

Before his hand could touch her arm, Aurora jerked up out of her chair and began to gather up the dishes in a noisy rattle.

"Mama—"

"Let me get these out of the way. I've got fresh coffee brewing and blackberry pie. That was always your favorite, wasn't it?" Her words gave a slight hitch. With arms laden with china and her eyes glittering, she stepped wide to avoid him and hurried into the kitchen.

Scott started up, but Ethan's big hand planted him firmly to his seat.

"Think you might have been a little gentler there, boy, and just swung a ten-pound sledge between her eyes?"

Ethan's chair scraped back and he rose and sauntered into the kitchen. Rory and Scott stared fixedly at the tablecloth as the sounds of his low voice and her weeping reached them.

"I'm sorry—"

"Shut up!"

Aurora returned to the table, carrying a fresh-baked pie and coffeepot. The proud angle of her head dared anyone to comment upon the puffiness around her eyes as she poured and sliced and served in silence. Then she and Ethan resumed their chairs.

Fearing he would choke on it, Scott levered a forkful of

the pie into his mouth and chewed. It could well have been prairie dirt, but he managed to smile and say, "Just as good as I remember it."

With a soft sob, Aurora pushed away from the table. This time, Scott was quicker and he intercepted her at the doorway with hands upon her shoulders.

"Mama, don't cry." The words tore from him in a low, shaky timbre. "I wouldn't hurt you for the world. You know that."

Her eyes fixed upon his with a desperation. "Then don't go. Oh, Scotty, don't go." And she clung. Even after the promise she made to herself. She couldn't seem to help it.

He enfolded her easily in his arms, drawing her up and feeling the shiver of her tears. "That's not fair, Mama. You know it. It's the chance you wanted for me. It's what you wanted. You'll like her, Mama. She's smart and refined and pretty and pale." That last he let linger with the most significance between them. "When you meet her, you'll see. She's exactly what you wanted for me. Hush now, you hear. Keep up this carrying on and I'll move on over to the Bar K."

The quiet drawl he adopted, and the quick change of tactics, he'd learned from his stepfather. Both were effective. His mother pulled back with an angry, "No you won't. This is your home and you'll stay here." She knocked aside the wetness on her cheeks with an impatient hand and took a steadying breath. "Now, you get back to the table and finish your dessert. And tomorrow, we'll ride over to the Bar K to meet Miss Trowbridge."

"Thank you." He leaned forward to place a gentle kiss on her brow, whispering softly as he did, "I love you, Mama." Then, before she was taken by the need to hold to him again, he moved to the table.

Pie and coffee were finished in an atypical silence. As soon as the last fork was laid down, Rory stood to announce, "I'd best be getting back to the Bar K." He hesitated a moment before adding, "See you in the morning, big brother." It was said hopefully, by way of an apology between them. And when Scott nodded, his animation returned. With a rattle of spurs and a cocky swagger, he went to kiss his mother good-night and clapped his father on the back. Then Scott stood and the two of them exchanged a bone-grinding embrace.

"Big mouth." It was muttered low.

"Dumb as a stump," Rory agreed with an equal hush.

Scott wandered out onto the porch and eased down in one of the rockers to watch the dust whorls of his brother's passing settle against the vast sea of darkness. And then, all was wonderfully still. He shut his eyes and let the quiet rush over him, breathing it in, letting it calm a soul that had known so little peace. He felt before he saw Ethan's giant figure move out to the rail. They didn't speak as the big Texan tamped his pipe and sparked a small flame. As he puffed, the rich aroma wafted back to tantalize all sorts of memories.

"Mama all right?"

"She'll do. Always manages to. Told her we had to make some man talk. Can't say I liked the way you kicked the legs out from under her. That what they teach you in the east?"

"No sir."

"Learned it all on your own, did you. Proud of yourself?"

"No sir."

Ethan turned to gauge his son's misery and was apparently appeased. "Good. Shows you haven't forgotten everything I taught you."

"I couldn't lie to her."

"No. You did right. A nice quick kill. Learned that from your father's people, I reckon. And like I said, she'll get over it. In a hundred years or so."

40

Scott slumped in the chair, his insides all knotted up with frustration and guilt. But the face he presented was smooth and stoic. And his stepfather wasn't fooled. It was an old Indian trick. One that nettled him to the extreme. He never knew quite how far or hard to push to break that bland facade.

"Here. Figure you'll be needing this."

Scott looked up in question, then took the wooden flute from him. It was a *siyotanka,* a courting flagolet he'd made when he was a boy. The skillfully bored surface felt familiar in his hand. Unthinkingly, he wet his lips and blew a series of low notes.

"Seems you remember that tune a lot better than you recalled your manners."

Scott lowered the flute and gripped it in his lap. He was staring hard out into the night, expression as impassive as that blackness. The set of his teeth hurt all the way up to his hair line.

"What's eating at you, boy?" came the softly persuading prod.

Scott unbent a notch. "The way she looked at me when I came in."

"How's that?"

Another notch slipped and he nearly shook with the effort to retain the rest. "Like she saw my father standing there."

The words hung for a moment between them, heavy with meaning. Then Ethan surmised impartially, "That why you're in such an all-fired hurry to get back east?"

"Partly."

"I ain't gonna stand here all night trying to drag this outta you, boy. You got something to spill, spill it."

The dark head shook, once, with a stiff stubbornness. Like his mother.

"Maybe I ought to be making that switch," the tall Texan muttered to himself. He studied the tough, self-

41

contained figure of his wife's son, searching for some clue, some weakness. Then he watched the way the flute twisted in his hands. "You going to see him?"

Scott's gaze flashed up, for a moment naked of all but despair. It was quickly and irrevocably masked when he asked in feigned offhandedness, "How is he?"

"Better than can be expected. Tough old bird. Asks about you. Want me to tell him something, or you planning to see to it?"

"I will."

The reply was taut. Ethan waited and watched. He'd seen rattlers in the coil more relaxed. When it became obvious the boy meant to give nothing else away, he sighed. Stubborn. The same single-minded, gutsy, often-wrongheaded stubbornness that plagued his wife. And danged if he could knock any sense into either of them when they got that jaw-gripping belligerence about them. So he slickly maneuvered around it.

"Do you love her?"

A startled confusion broke through the cautious barriers. "Who?"

"Your little lady from Boston."

His stepson's gaze flashed downward, then neatly evaded. "She's a fine lady."

"And you'll be happy living with her away over there in the big city?"

His response was carefully framed. "I'll do well and make you proud." The length of wood was turning in his hands with enough friction to start a good fire.

"I know you'll do that, Scott. But that ain't what I asked you."

The sudden tense movement of muscle along the younger man's jaw told he was well aware of that. And that he had no intention of answering.

Scott gave a slight flinch when Ethan's hand settled easily on his shoulder. The pressure was firm, solid.

42

"If you need help working it out, you know where to come."

The dark head nodded once. Browned fingers covered the other's hand for a brief, crushing squeeze.

"Good night, pard. Don't let it tear at you too long."

"G'night, Daddy."

From inside, he could hear the mutter of his parents' voices: low, intimate in their exchange, Ethan's cajoling, his mother's tart, then melting into a husky pleasure. A warm, wistful ache lodged inside him. He'd grown up in this house, surrounded by the ever-present evidence of affection. Ethan and his mother were open with their displays and it had given him a good feeling when he was younger, including yet unintentionally excluding him at the same time. They loved him, Ethan with all the strength of father to son, but things were different with him than with Rory. He'd always known and accepted it without bitterness. It was just the way things were. And that hadn't changed.

And he'd hated it.

Because he wasn't Ethan Prescott's son, no matter what he might have pretended. Or wished. Because of the truth he'd discovered about his real father while he was away at school.

And while he sat rocking on the porch, listening to the quiet overtures of his parents' lovemaking in the kitchen, he felt something hard and unhappy twist inside.

Because nothing would ever change. Because he would never know what it was like to exchange those sultry whispers, one lover to another.

And it broke his heart.

Chapter Three

After a surprisingly cool night, the warmth of the morning breeze felt good enough to lure Gena out onto the porch of the Bar K. Once sleep had claimed her, she'd slept deep and soundly enough to awake refreshed when the sun spilled all golden through the lace at her eastern-exposure window. She'd hurried through her morning toilet, uncertain of when she should expect a visit from her future in-laws. This was an entirely different world, a world in which life started with the dawn, and she didn't wish to appear unduly slothful. Apparently, she was the only one to hold to that concern, for the upper story of the house was as quiet as a church when she slipped from her room and down the big front stairs. The housekeeper, Ruth, had discovered her adrift in the hall and steered her to an ample breakfast and hot coffee with an apology for her employer. He'd already been called out to attend to some matter in one of the far pastures.

So Gena dined alone at the great table. Despite the rules of etiquette which forbade it, she wished she'd been free to invite Ruth to join her. The handsome woman had a way of making her feel at home and not some bothersome intruder from a far-distant realm.

When finished with her repast, Gena carried her

44

coffee out onto the wide porch to be amazed anew by the sensation of space and isolation. Even the span of ground between the house and the outbuildings seemed intimidating. Being city-bred, she'd never had a taste of such uncomplicated, unused vastness. And it was scary. And lonely.

" 'Morning."

The sound of a human voice spoken nearly at her elbow brought her about with a gasp. Hot liquid from her carelessly wielded cup sloshed out all down the front of the big man who'd approached so silently under the guise of her deep thoughts.

"Oh — my!"

"Don't fret on it, ma'am," he said easily as he brushed at the stain. His smile was wide and imperturbable. "I'll clean up just fine. Though you probably wouldn't guess it to look at me."

And Gena looked, timidly but with real interest. His costume intrigued her; a dusty — and now coffee-discolored — checked shirt upon which a blue bandanna flowed, blue denims worn over a pair of fancy stitched boots with big silver spurs, and, slung low on his hip, a pair of deadly looking pistols that put Horace's palm piece to shame. He was a handsome young man with rugged features and friendly dark eyes. And the worst haircut she'd ever seen. It was that bright red hair that made her remember.

"Why, you're the cowboy we saw yesterday when we arrived."

"Yessum, I am that."

"Your riding was quite spectacular," she exclaimed in genuine delight.

"Why, thank you kindly, ma'am. It's nice to have one's talents truly appreciated."

He was grinning and standing close enough for her to scent the pungent odors of horse and work upon him. He

45

didn't notice when her lace-edged handkerchief fluttered out to dab beneath her nose. His entire presence was rather overwhelming, but Gena supposed that here in the west, such things were more acceptable. So, she fought her want to retreat a few steps to a comfortable distance and forced a smile.

"Do you work here on the Bar K?"

"Depends on whether you'd call punching cows a job."

Punching cows? Gena continued to smile. Because of the way he said it and the manner in which his shoulders slid back a notch, she assumed it was some important employment. She would have to remember to ask Scott exactly what the punching of cows entailed.

"And tangling with Injuns, of course." His gaze slipped to her to see if that had the desired effect. She went all over still and huge-eyed. "Ran into a right nasty one last night. Nearly lost my hair."

Gena followed the casual movement of his hand to the ragged crop of hair. Merciful heavens! Could it be true? Her panicked stare quickly swept the horizon.

Sensing he might have gone a bit far in his teasing, the young cowboy eased up beside her to confide, " 'Course, you needn't worry none with me at hand."

He was about to enfold the fragile thing beneath one protective — and brotherly — arm when the whir of carriage wheels distracted him. And he grinned. His brother always did have a second sense when it came to danger.

Gena looked to Scott's arrival with relief. She couldn't be sure if the cowboy's talk had been sincere, but it frightened her none the less. Here in this godforsaken country, anything was possible. Perhaps she'd been naive to sleep so soundly when the threat of danger could well be creeping all about in the darkness. When she'd learned where Scott was from, she'd taken a new, and covert, interest in the dime novels of the west and had been truly horrified

46

by the stories contained within. Violence as a way of life, savage Indians prowling in search of innocent victims, gunfire and lynchings to see a crude justice done. Why had she ever demanded coming on this trip?

Scott vaulted lightly from the buggy in his crisp suit sent over that morning care of a Bar K rider along with his other travel belongings. As he turned to assist his mother down, he couldn't help but note his fiancée's pallor. Nor the fact that Rory stood readily at hand wearing a devilish grin. As soon as Ethan came around to claim Aurora, he took the front steps and his lady's arm. She clutched at him with uncommon vigor and there was no mistaking the tremor of her hand. Only the welcoming lift of her gaze held him from shaking his brother soundly. That warm look kindled something inside him, something subtle and possessive, and he forgot all about Rory. Or anything else, for that matter.

His hand came up of its own accord and fingertips lightly sketched her fair cheek. So soft, so pale. For a brief instant, she allowed it, even seemed to take pleasure in it, then she drew away. It was a gracious rejection, one he'd grown accustomed to whenever his overtures extended beyond the strictly and impersonally proper. And so, he was able to betray no disappointment when he dropped his hand and gave a thin smile.

"Miss Trowbridge, I'd like to present you to my parents, Aurora and Ethan Prescott." There was a loud clearing of a throat. "And this yahoo is my brother, Rory."

Gena couldn't help the acknowledging shock from showing on her face when she looked between the two Prescott brothers. For there was simply no similarity. Rory was big, brash, and as bold as his bright hair. Scott was dark and golden, possessed of an admirable restraint. Even their features were as different as night and day; Scott's sculpted with definite lines, Rory's an arrangement of strong angles. She looked to the parents for an answer and found more questions. Rory was a definitive product of Aurora and Ethan Prescott, but Scott was possessed of qualities not found in either.

As she murmured her responses, Gena regarded Scott's parents with a polite study. Dressed in a simple but undeniably elegant shirtwaist with her flaming hair softly and flatteringly upswept away from her face, Aurora Prescott was quite possibly the most stunning woman she'd ever seen. And there were those beautiful golden eyes set in a sun-warmed complexion. Eyes that were scrutinizing her just as thoroughly. And edged with a curious challenge. Gena was taken aback and turned her attention to Mr. Prescott. He was a huge mountain of a man with deep auburn hair possessed of an unruly curl and the same angular features as his younger son partially concealed by a thick beard. But nothing in his rugged image was shared with Scott except the quiet drawling quality of his voice. And more curious still was the way Scott stiffened when aware of her puzzlement.

"I am very pleased to finally meet you, Mr. and Mrs. Prescott. Scott has spoken so often of you, I feel as if we are already family."

Aurora smiled at the younger woman's words, a smile without warmth or welcome. Her reply was coolly civil. "I'm afraid he has left us to form our own opinions of you, Miss Trowbridge. And as we have very little time in which to do so, shall we go inside." And then, she came up the steps to claim an arm from either son in a commanding escort.

Gena was stunned by the obvious snub and unsure of what she'd done to deserve it. She was rescued from her dismay by the courtly arm of Ethan Prescott. He twined her hand about the crook of his elbow and said with an easy reassurance, "Don't mind his mother none. She's as prickly as a cactus when it comes to Scott. Just smile and keep clear of the spines."

Gena was mindful of his warning as she sat posed stiff and nervous upon a parlor chair while Mrs. Prescott probed her suitability as a wife. It was only to be expected, she told herself. It was a parental duty to consider the mental and physical health of a potential mate. It was not hostility, it was obligation. And spines. It might have helped had Scott offered his support at her side, but he seemed uncommonly distracted as he stood by the fireplace in discussion with father and brother. He had not supplied so much as a heartening gaze as she readied to meet the anticipated trial.

Aurora Prescott was careful not to appear overtly antagonistic. Her questions were proper, and Gena had answers prepared for each one that would display herself in a positive light. She held before her conscious mind the model of young womanhood on which her mother had reared her: a woman was not stubborn or self-centered, she had gracious manners, respected her parents, and was of a good nature, never gossiping, slandering, tale-telling, fault-finding, or grumbling. And that as a wife, she was to conduct herself with modesty and propriety to uphold her husband's name and provide him with a happy home. And children. That echoed through her thoughts to further her agitation, but she didn't speak it aloud. One did not have to speak of the obvious. Of course she would be expected to provide heirs to the Prescott name. That was the ultimate purpose of being a wife.

It was then Gena found herself studying Scott's hands. The hands that would hold her future. Hands that would touch her hair, hands that would command her obedience and submission. And guide her through the steps of procreation. Her scalp prickled, and within the choking confines of her corset, her heart began a frantic beating.

"Miss Trowbridge?"

Gena jerked her attention back to Aurora. Spots of

heat flamed up in her cheeks as she murmured, "I'm sorry. You were saying?"

"Are you ill, my dear? You appear very pale all of a sudden."

"I'm quite well, Mrs. Prescott. Please forgive my wool-gathering." Good heavens. That's all she needed was to appear feeble of mind before Scott's mother. She forced down the shivers of panic and adopted her brightest smile. *Foolish girl,* an internal voice chided. *This is the single most important interview of your life.* Parents who disapproved could make a match impossible. She could well lose Scott to a careless word or an inattentive slight. Her hands gripped in her lap as she concentrated all her energies on winning Mrs. Prescott over.

A feat not so easily accomplished. Aurora was not a fool. She looked at the very pretty, very proper young woman in the chair opposite and wondered what on earth her son could be thinking. She looked and she saw a thin-blooded Bostonian lady, laced into her tight corseted gown just as she was laced tight into her regimented lifestyle. She was not unfamiliar with the cold civility of the east and its view of marrying for security rather than love. And Scotty deserved the love of a good woman. He would not find it among the debutantes who raised coquetry and self-interest to a studied art. He wouldn't find it with the fragile Miss Trowbridge who knew only of life what she'd been told behind the cloistered doors of her family's prosperous home. She had only to look at the demure miss, sitting so timid and terrified on the edge of the sofa, to know she could not give what Scott needed. She had only to look at the lovely features colored by a purposeful wanness to know Gena Trowbridge hadn't the strength it would take to wed a man like her son. All he would get was a pretty trinket fit for display and useless for all but cosseting. She knew women like Gena, who thought only of their own frail state of health and state of

50

financial security. She'd gone to school with them, had been friends with them, had envied them and thought to become like them until her return to the Dakotas. Until everything in her life was cruelly altered.

No, if Miss Gena Trowbridge thought she could earn her permission to marry her son by simpering prettily on a sofa and spewing out a catechism of rote responses, she was very mistaken. And Aurora meant to do everything possible to see that the travesty of a wedding would not occur. And that her son would not return to Boston.

And as she smiled and poured more coffee for the pale young woman, Aurora Prescott's mind was quickly moving to see to that purpose.

"What do you think?"

Ethan and Rory regarded the lovely Miss Trowbridge and considered Scott's question.

"Mama hates her."

Rory's bluntness made his older brother stiffen. He cast a worried glance between the two women, trying to gauge that for himself. Both were smiling and talking with the utmost courtesy, but he saw beyond that. Gena was plainly intimidated, and his mother was bearing down on her like a hawk upon a field mouse. He was pricked by a feeling of irritation at his mother. And by one of mild disappointment for his intended. He had hoped she wouldn't be so cowed by Aurora's bullying. But then the gentle Gena had not been raised to stand up in the face of tyranny. She would undoubtedly expect him to step in and shield her from any unpleasantness. And he was puzzled by his reluctance to go to the rescue.

"That's a mite strong," Ethan replied with a soothing neutrality. "You know your mama, Scott. She likes to walk all over folks who'll let her."

"Voice of experience, Daddy?" Rory taunted.

Ethan grinned lazily. "I've felt me a few boot heels in my day. Now don't you go getting all het up over it, Son.

51

She'll come around when that little gal of yours catches on and shows some gumption."

Gumption. Scott assessed his bride to be with an unfairly critical eye. Gena Trowbridge was everything a man could look for in a wife amongst the social set in Boston. She was reserved, intelligent at conversation, possessed of all that cornsilk hair and Dresden-doll blue eyes, and of a dainty manner that woke the sheltering instincts in a man. But gumption? No. She was made to serve, not lead, and suddenly he was dissatisfied by that meekness. Then he chided himself for making the comparison. After all, how many women could compare with Aurora Prescott in terms of grit and gumption? Of the things she'd given Ethan, among them was not a life of leisure or a tranquil home. He'd grown up listening to their vocal discussions. And their vigorous apologizing. Did he want that kind of upheaval in his life? Or did he desire the kind of peace Gena provided with a soft smile? He'd thought it was the latter and he was angry at himself for having doubts of it now.

"Is my mother filling your head with nonsense about me?"

Gena looked up at Scott, grateful for his intrusion. Her smile wavered but she managed a steady tone. "Oh, no. We're just getting to know one another."

Scott read the frantic plea in her uplifted eyes and couldn't in good conscience ignore it. With his hand resting lightly on his fiancée's shoulder, he faced his mother the way one would brace a mountain cat bent on a blood trail.

"Didn't I tell you you'd like her, Mama."

Golden gazes clashed.

Finally, Aurora smiled and withdrew the challenge. For the moment. "She's everything you said, Scott. If you'll excuse me, Miss Trowbridge, I'll see if Ruth has some fresh coffee ready."

Gena followed the imperious exit and couldn't help but expel a breath of relief. Then, she became very aware of the warmth of Scott's fingers through the thin wool of her summer gown. And she sidled away with a subtle shift of her shoulder.

Left with his hand resting on air, Scott forced a smile and said, "Don't let her scare you. My mother's all bluff and no bite."

Gena managed a nod, but she couldn't deny she'd felt the cut of those teeth most distinctly. "That's what your father told me, too."

"Listen to him. He's the wisest man I know." Or one of them, he corrected in his own mind.

Leaving his fiancée looking more confident with the arrival of Beth and Merle, Scott eased from the parlor to confront his mother in the hall.

"Mama," he began in a warning rumble. "You lacking something in your diet that makes you have a craving for fresh blood?"

"Why, I'm not sure I know what you —"

His severe look halted her protested innocence. And his drawling words put a panic inside her.

"We can head on back to Boston if Gena gets to feeling uncomfortable. She came all this way to meet you. Don't make her regret it."

Aurora stood her ground but was off balance in the face of such defiance. This was the son she'd loved and sheltered and nurtured. And yet, he was not. Suddenly, he was calling for conditions in their relationship. Ones she was loath to meet yet daren't disregard. So, instead of challenging the words, she attacked the attitude.

"You used to have some respect for your mother's feelings. Is that something you decided to disregard along with your family home?" She saw the faltering of his resolve and plunged on recklessly. "I'm just trying to protect you from making a mistake." She reached out to

53

clutch his arm and realized immediately that it was she who had just made one. He stiffened at her grasping touch and began to pull away.

"Mama, I'm not a little boy anymore. I don't need you to protect me from living."

"And you don't need that pallid little creature in there. Why, she'd fade on the stem over the course of a summer. And she'd never survive one of our winters."

Scott bristled at the unreasonable slurs and fought them down with one softly spoken truth. "I don't see how that matters much, seeing as we won't be living here."

Aurora went still and he knew he'd hurt her. To lessen the blow, he urged gently, "Give her a chance, Mama. That's all I'm asking. No, she's not as tough and as strong as you are. But then, she hasn't had to be, either. Trust me to know what it is I need. And right now, I need you to make Gena feel welcome. Please, Mama. Don't make me have to choose between you."

She didn't respond right away and when she finally did, it was to put her arms around the broad shoulders of the man he'd become and hold tight. She felt his resistance to the embrace but he allowed it. And so she held to him fiercely, with all the considerable strength of her mother's love.

"I want the best for you, Scott. And I want you to be happy. That's all that's ever mattered to me. If you think this girl is the one who can do that for you, then you have my blessing."

Scott brought his hands up to press briefly upon her capable shoulders, then used them to coax her to release him. He was smiling, a cautious, measured smile that told her plainly he was not naive. That he knew she was not one to change her spots so suddenly. She fit her palm to one lean, browned cheek, then looked beyond him to see her father regarding them both through impassive eyes. Upon his return, Garth Kincaid had made quick work of his range grit and was dressed impeccably to greet his guests and family.

"You go back to your Miss Trowbridge, Scotty. I want to have a word with your grandfather."

Glancing back at the big man on the stairs and wondering how much he'd overheard, Scott hesitated, then said, "I want your word, Mama."

She looked up at him, meeting the rich gold of his gaze, knowing how much he set store by the vow of one to another, and told him, "You have my word that I'll be on my best behavior."

He turned his head just far enough to press a kiss upon her palm. "Then why do I feel like I just stepped barefoot into a nest of rattlers?"

Aurora smiled as she watched him saunter back into the parlor. Then she turned to her father with a cool, calculating light playing about her eyes. The old man looked wary when she took his arm.

"Major, there's something I'd like you to do for me."

The presence of her friends from the east did much to soothe Gena's discomfort in the overstuffed Kincaid parlor. She sat back and marveled at the way Aurora warmed her younger cousin Beth and manipulated the petulant Caroline until the atmosphere was congenial. She could see the gentlemen were as enamored of the fiery-haired hostess as they were bemused by her burly husband and roguish younger son. And she was more than a little surprised by the suddenly maternal attitude Scott's mother displayed in their dealings together. Tentatively, she began to lessen her guard of reserve and even to enjoy herself beneath her fiancé's approving gaze.

"What does one do with one's time way out here in this great cow pasture?" Caroline asked with an appalling lack of tact as they sat to the table.

Gena blushed for her friend's rudeness and ventured, "Why, Caro, I'm sure the ladies in the west share many of our interests."

"Oh, intellectual pursuits, I'm sure, such as reading and sewing and domestic tasks. You should be quite in your glory, Gena. But what of social entertainments? Not all of us are so content with just our own company as you."

The censure silenced Miss Trowbridge, but it was Aurora who came unexpectedly to her rescue. She regarded the brash Miss Davies unblinkingly until the other had the good grace to look down.

"We are hardly primitive, despite appearances. If you feel rested enough after yesterday's journey, I was going to suggest an afternoon of calling upon our family's friends in the vicinity. The major has planned a small get-together in your honor for tomorrow, and it would be a good time to get acquainted with some of the guests. I'm certain there will be an enthusiastic response to the cards we leave so you will not be lacking for companionship until the time comes for your return."

The idea was met with a chorus of quick agreement, and after the ladies had freshened, they stepped up into the luxuriously sprung Kincaid carriage with their gloves, parasols, and high-button shoes and a handful of engraved cards to pass out at the neighboring ranches.

After they'd traveled for the better part of an hour and Gena still had yet to see signs of another dwelling, she asked, "How far are your neighbors?"

"Oh, a close neighbor could be considered fifteen miles. Most are farther." Aurora noted her anxiety and added, "One gets used to the loneliness."

"And are there many ranches like your father's nearby?"

"None like my father's," she stated proudly. "But there are a handful of spreads that we'll be able to visit this

56

afternoon. More, if we were to include the farmers. But I thought you would prefer to mingle with your own kind while you are here."

Gena reflected upon that for a moment, then asked, "Were the people we're to visit friends of Scott's when he was a boy?"

Aurora gave her a rather piercing look then replied carefully, "Scott was a rather solitary child. They are friends of my father's."

The silence that followed was threaded with a peculiar tension. Wanting very much to return to the easy cordiality of moments before, Gena sought to change the subject. "Mr. Prescott has a most distinctive accent. Is he from the south?"

Aurora's features warmed. "He's a Texan. Born and bred. That's something you can't take out of a man. He came up to the territory in '76 and couldn't make himself leave it. The Lone Star was a dream that flourished between us, that and our boys."

"I had often wondered over Scott's manner of speech, but I can see it was learned from his father. Odd that they should share no other similarities." The words came out innocently enough, for she was simply speaking her thoughts aloud, but Aurora Prescott underwent a sudden stiffening. She stared long and hard at the younger woman before explaining.

"That is because Ethan is Scott's stepfather. We were married when he was a baby. My first husband was killed before Scott was born. Scott has said nothing of this to you?"

Gena felt a prickle of uneasiness. *Killed* not *died.* She murmured a quick, "No, he hasn't. Please forgive me if I've caused you any distress in mentioning it."

Aurora smiled her forgiveness, but there was a chill to her gaze that didn't thaw. And then a thoughtful glint took its place. "Not unusual, I suppose. Scott considers

57

Ethan his father. He has no reason to say otherwise."

But he did. An enormous reason. And as the carriage sped on toward the first of a sprinkling of prairie mansions, Aurora wondered why he had kept the past a secret.

And she wondered how the demure Miss Trowbridge would react to the truth.

"Ah, one of the finer things of civilized life," Garth Kincaid remarked as he opened the gift his grandson brought him from the east. He looked over the twelve bottles contained in the Cellarette case, exclaiming in satisfaction at each one; claret, sauterne, Burgundy, invalid port, sherry, Plymouth gin, cherry liquor, and two each of Scotch whiskey and rye. "You say they ship these anywhere in the U.S. for only fifteen dollars?"

"Anywhere they have a railroad."

"Progress," the old man sighed. "A wonderful thing." He selected one of the bottles of Scotch and two glasses.

"I don't drink, Grandfather."

Kincaid gave Scott a brief glance and overruled him. "This time will be the exception." He poured a neat shot for each of them and extended one. "A toast. To your success."

Scott took the glass with a diplomatic smile. Conscience gave before the indescribable privilege of his grandfather's praise. It was a first in his memory, an occasion long dreamed of, an achievement to be treasured. It meant that all the sacrifice was worth it. Just to see the shine of admiration in the old man's eyes.

The whiskey burned. He tried not to gasp, and blinked the tearing from his eyes while the major sipped in appreciation. It scorched all the way down to his belly and pooled there with an unexpected warmth. He was surprised enough to venture another taste and was

58

pleased when it went down easier. It only seemed to peel the first layer from his throat.

"Fine stuff," Kincaid commented, refilling both glasses before the younger man could protest.

"The best," Scott affirmed with a slight breathlessness.

"The best my money could buy. Money well spent. As it was on you. I made a promise to your mother that you would have the best, and so you did."

Scott settled into one of the big leather chairs that sat in audience before the rancher's massive desk. He was again surprised when Kincaid chose to sit in the other instead of across the impersonal worktop. Drink and dreams went straight to his head until he was dizzy with the mixture.

It had always been a source of puzzlement to him. Garth Kincaid had never shown any fondness for him as a boy while he fawned over his brother, Rory. He knew why, of course, but that didn't make the differentiation any kinder. He'd always held the utmost respect for the shrewd rancher who'd carved an empire out of wilderness, and he'd always suffered for its lack of return. He'd tried. Throughout his younger years, he'd pushed to the limit of his abilities and beyond to gain that attention. He'd been the best rider the Bar K had ever seen, but that accomplishment only widened the gap between them. An inherited trait. He knew that was what his grandfather considered it. Which was why it held no value in his eyes. But schooling. That was different. It was a talent uniquely his own, and he'd put all the rest behind to be the best. None had been as surprised as he when Garth Kincaid offered to pay his way through one of the best schools in the East. Hard work had its reward. And at last, he was being honored for it. And it was intoxicating.

"And I hope I can repay you for your generosity."

"Perhaps in a way you hadn't considered," the major mulled over quietly. Scott was immediately all attention,

59

the pleasant fogging of whiskey pushed from his mind.

"How so, sir?"

"Progress. It can be friend or foe. Did you know they were tinkering with electric lights a county over? And with that will come the telephone. Imagine." He shook his great head in amazement, but his eyes were half-shuttered and far from overwhelmed. "Times are changing, Scott, and the man who can change with them will be the one who'll survive. When I began the Bar K, I had little more than my own ambition and a few head of cattle and the miles they called public domain. A cattleman made his own lands and enforced his own code of right and wrong. The grass was all we needed to grow the best herds in the nation. I weathered it all, boy: the Indians, the nesters, the barbed wire, the drought of '86, the blizzard of '87 and '88 and then that danged black blizzard of '89. Couldn't swallow for the dust. I had losses of nearly sixty percent. Thousands of my cattle died huddled and frozen against those illegal fences strung in the name of progress. But I survived it. And I mean to go on surviving."

At his grandfather's urging, Scott drained his glass and consented to another. The chair contoured to his form and the major's voice was a pleasant rumble from the past.

"Ranching is different now. It's more than just a man of ambition and a bunch of cows. It's business and it's politics and the big spreads are going under. I'm a last of a dying breed, Scott, and I don't mean to go gracefully when I can still fight. And that's how you can help me."

He straightened in the chair and put the glass aside before it could pickle his thinking any further. Surely his grandfather would want to deal with a cool, collected mind, not one scrambled by its inexperience with drink. "I don't see how—"

"I need a man like you, Scott. I need an educated voice

60

to speak for me in the Stock Growers' meetings. I need a powerful voice full of the fire of progress to take my part against those who'd see me busted up into a passel of grubbing homesteads. I made sure you had the best so I'd get the best. What do you say, son?"

Scott's head reeled. He cursed the liquor as he tried to summon logic to his defense. But it was a poor second compared to the invitation in his grandfather's eyes. A look that invited him for the first time to step in from the outside. How he shook with an eagerness to take that step.

But he couldn't.

"I've got a job in Boston. Miss Trowbridge and I are to be married in October." He spoke both those things sadly, regretfully, by a bond of word if no longer desire.

Garth Kincaid patted his grandson's knee and sat back in his chair. His expression was benevolent. "I'm well aware of that and I'm not asking for you to change your plans."

"But I don't—"

"Give me the rest of the summer." He played out that tempting bit of bait with all the skill of an expert trapper. Ethan Prescott would have been envious. But then Ethan hunted out of necessity. And never had he stalked helpless game. "Work with me, son. Lend me your knowledge and your advice. Help me get into the next century in one piece. That's how you can repay my debt. That's all I'm asking."

He let that settle deep and waited with a master's patience for the trap to spring.

"What do you say?"

Chapter Four

If the guests at the Bar K thought the Dakota ranch uncivilized, they were in for a delightful surprise with the coming of the next afternoon. While the puzzled company looked on, the prairie manse was draped like a forest primeval. Cheesecloth in shades of verdant splendor trimmed the mantels, the mirrors, the doorways, and the staircases of the receiving rooms inside. Lanterns were hung from posts and trees and strung along the porch. On the broad expanse of yard, Turkey rugs were laid out to form small islands upon which chairs and tables clustered. And promptly at three o'clock, carriages began to arrive. From river and rail, they came; the area's prestigious, the state's well-known. All at the summons of Garth Kincaid in response to formally engraved invitations sent out two weeks prior. A summons to a *fête champêtre;* the ultimate garden party.

Quality entertainment in any form was hard to come by in the west, so when there was reason to shake out the best frills and fancies, few would refuse despite the inconvenience of travel. Because of the isolation, most affluent ranchers chose to live in town, but none had any objection to answering Major Kincaid's call. For over an hour, arriving guests were shown into the house to deposit their wraps and freshen up. When they were ready, an impeccably garbed Ruth escorted them to a tented area where their hosts were receiving.

"How did you manage, Mama?" Scott murmured as he edged up beside the convivial hostess. She was a stunning confection all done up in the cool green shades she'd chosen for the party, a pert, plumed hat affixed over bright curls.

"Why, I couldn't let your friends think we were barbarians," she whispered back, then took a moment to greet the state's upcoming senator. She looked back to her handsome son and smiled. "Are you pleased? I chose the theme 'A Mid-Summer Night's Dream.' I took a bit of liberty with the calendar but I don't think anyone will mind. I've been following these kinds of affairs in *Harper's Bazaar* and *The Ladies' Home Journal*. I hope I did everything right. It's been quite a few years since I've mingled with society's cream. I didn't want you to be embarrassed by your humble country relations."

He brushed a light kiss upon one smooth cheek. "As if I would be. You didn't need to go to all the trouble."

"I'd say it was no trouble at all but that would be lying. Your poor grandfather will probably turn up his toes when he gets the bill for it. He shouldn't complain. I did invite every political friend and foe I could think of. He'll just consider it a business expense."

Scott had grown suddenly quiet at the direction of her words. He sought out and spied his grandfather courting some legislative bigwig and was uncomfortably called to their last conversation. He'd promised to think it over. And he'd done little else for the last twenty-four hours. The remnants of a headache didn't make it any easier. Nor did his mother's prompting.

"Where is Miss Trowbridge? I'd expected to find you at her side, showing her off to the others."

"She was still getting ready when I — there she is, now."

Aurora followed the direction of her son's gaze to the

wide porch steps. Gena Trowbridge posed upon them like a dainty spring flower upon a slender stem. Pale yellow hair was softly puffed beneath a fashionably ruched bonnet, and the S-curved lines of her corset-molded figure were swathed in fine muslin of a delicate floral print. Aurora shifted her gaze back to the young man at her side and she observed his features carefully. There was a look of appreciation etched upon them. But no fire. No rush of passion. She smiled in her relief and put a hand upon the small of his back.

"Go and fetch her, Scott. She looks dreadfully adrift."

At her compelling push, he went across the lawn, his long, fluid strides drawing many an interested glance from the ladies present. Their attention filled her with pride in him. He was handsome and dashing and every bit as elegant as any of them. And then, it began. She watched the whispers stir like a breeze across the prairie grasses. She saw the way the others beheld him, in curiosity and poorly veiled distaste. And just as panic began to rise within her, a steadying arm anchored about her waist.

"He'll do fine, Ora. Have a little faith in the man he's become."

She looked up at Ethan, and he was moved by the fear he saw in her lovely face. A fear he'd never been able to conquer with all his words and all his love and all his best intentions. He couldn't make Scott Kincaid into more than a son of name only.

"He's not a boy any longer," he soothed, following his words with the gentle trace of a forefinger along one curved cheek. "He'll handle them. Can you?"

The subtle challenge brought an immediate lift of her chin into a haughty angle. "As if I had anything to be ashamed of."

But he could see her eyes upon her son and the worry in that gaze. And there wasn't a damned thing he could do about it.

From her perch upon the stairs, Gena was also watching Scott make his way through the milling others. None of them could capture her attention quite so thoroughly. She would never lose her fascination with the way he moved. She'd gone to see a display of wild animals once. Each in its own way had paced the tiny confines of its cage with a restless grace, with an energy that couldn't be trapped within the limited area of the bars. Her companion had remarked upon the dumb savagery of the beasts who did not seem to comprehend either the fact that they were caged or the futility of their travels to and fro. But to Gena, there had been a sad poetry in the prideful creatures who refused to surrender hope. Scott Prescott moved like that, all pent-up motion distilled into an effortless control. And her gaze caressed over him, mesmerized by the easy way his hands swung close to lean hips, by the way he placed his feet upon the ground with all the light grace of a high-wire aerialist. And as he took the steps with his easy lope, a wild exhilaration shook her.

Scott wasn't sure what happened. Gena was standing prim and pretty upon the porch, with her features composed into an almost ethereal picture. Then, a languorous transformation overcame her, effusing warm color into her fair cheeks, widening her eyes until they were black and shining with what he could have sworn was desire, parting her gentle lips into a full, inviting curve that was sensuality itself. He couldn't have been more stunned had she decided to suddenly shuck out of her dainty gown right there on the porch. The effect was the same. Something dropped away from the pristine facade of Gena Trowbridge in that fleeting second and left her very bare to his startled gaze. And the man in Scott Prescott growled to life for the first time since he'd known her.

He moved eagerly toward her the way a man nearly frozen would rush to embrace the saving warmth of a fire. Attention transfixed by the unexpected simmer, he caught his foot upon the top step and nearly stumbled into her. She didn't retreat. Instead, she leaned forward, almost beckoning a contact between them. He caught at her forearms for balance. Her hands cupped his elbows. And drew him toward her. Senses stunned and passions beating with a startled vigor, he righted himself to stand so close, her hem brushed over the toes of his shoes. And all he could think while he stared down upon her entrancing face was how very much he wanted to kiss her. Not the chaste, uninvolved pecks upon the cheek she occasionally permitted but a mouth-to-mouth, tongue-tangling, right-down-to-the-tonsils kiss.

Some of what he was thinking must have displayed itself upon his face, for abruptly she blushed hot and dipped her head. But she didn't pull away. And then, he saw she was laughing.

"And what is it you find so funny, Miss Trowbridge?"

"I — I'm sorry. It's just that I was admiring the graceful way you walk and—"

"And I fall into your lap," he finished a bit sourly.

"I'm sorry. It's quite uncharitable of me to laugh." And then she proceeded to chuckle until her bosom quivered with restrained mirth. That was a sight to restore his humor, as was the vivacious glow to her features when she shyly looked up at him. And he still wanted to kiss her.

"I deserve it. I confess I was distracted."

"And what was it that so addled you, Mr. Prescott, that you could not set one foot in front of the other?"

"I shall make it my business to find out, Miss Trowbridge. Now, before everyone starts to stare, will you take my arm. If for no other reason than to hold me up should my feet become tangled again."

"Only if you promise not to drag me down with you."

Then, she must have realized how that sounded and flushed even hotter. But still, she had not moved away.

With infinite care, thinking for the first time and with some surprise, how delightful tumbling upon the ground with Gena Trowbridge might be, Scott took her small hand and nestled it into the crook of his arm. A strange effervescence tingled through him, not unlike the kick of his grandfather's Scotch but, hopefully, with less unpleasant results. Then, with more pride than he could ever remember feeling, he led her down from the porch and across the lawn to where his mother waited, masking her frown.

It couldn't have been a more pleasant day. The sun was warm and the breeze balmy. A hired band played for the enjoyment of the guests who strolled, visited, or partook in the games of croquet, lawn tennis, and archery. Punch bowls were refilled at regular intervals with lemonade and frappé for the ladies and with claret punch and Apollinaris water for the gentlemen. Extra servants added for the day shuttled silver trays carrying wine glasses to the ladies avoiding the sun upon the porch and under the trees whence they enjoyed watching the silly contests Aurora had planned to keep the younger set occupied.

"Would you like me to win you a prize, Miss Trowbridge?"

Gena looked up in surprise into the languid eyes of Horace Billings. Scott had only just left her side and it was as if he had been awaiting the chance to engage her.

"I did not know you were an archer, Mr. Billings."

"I have many talents, Miss Trowbridge. Would you like a demonstration?"

Gena felt uncomfortable with his fixed attention and sought a way to gracefully escape it. She cast about rather frantically. "Wouldn't you rather champion Caroline?"

Horace's thin mustache took a severe downward turn. "She seems quite enamored of the young congressman's converse at the moment. What do you say? Shall I give it a go?"

He looked so hopeful, she could not bear to crush him with a refusal. At her nod, he fairly beamed and took up a bow.

Archery was one of the active games considered suitable for either sex. Ladies and gentlemen took turns siting at targets placed at ten-, fifteen-, and twenty-yard intervals and safely out of the way of any wandering cattle or cowboys. Smiling confidently, Horace selected the middle distance and let an arrow fly. There was a moment's panic as the missile careened off a tree branch and neatly severed a big red satin bow atop one of the ladies' hats.

With a hand to her mouth, Gena struggled not to smile and murmured to the dejected athlete, "Oh, my. Perhaps the arrow was misshapen."

Horace brightened at that and gave her a grateful smile. "Would you like to try, Miss Trowbridge? It's really quite easy."

At his continued insistence, she finally accepted the bow and checked about for any unseemly targets. Most had moved a cautious distance upwind. She released the string and gave a yelp of surprise at a sharply stinging snap against her forearm. Before she could hug the injured limb to her, her arm was taken in a strong grasp and turned palm upward.

"No damage," Scott diagnosed as he ran his thumb over the tender spot. "Except for a probable bruise. Let me show you how to do that."

The heat from Scott's fingers, and the nearness of him as he stood almost touching along the entire length of her body, made Gena forget all about the throbbing in her arm. A more immediate pulse had begun within her chest. She remained with breath suspended and every tendon taut, as Scott fitted himself against her to direct her movements. One big hand covered the small one holding the bow as his arm encircled her shoulders to guide the other. As he instructed her to pull back, her slender form trembled like that drawn string.

His face was pressed close against her hair where her hat brim tilted, his breath a gentle whisper upon the tendrils that framed her brow. His words slid over her senses like a calming breeze.

"That's right. All the way back till your thumb grazes your ear and your little finger touches the corner of your mouth. Now hold it there."

When her pull abruptly slackened, he steadied her with his hands over hers.

"Don't be afraid, Gena. I'd never let anything hurt you. Trust me."

And she did. She trusted him and the wonderfully warm sensations taking hold of her body. In the secure fold of his embrace, she let herself lean back into the hard support of his chest and her eyes drifted closed of their own volition.

"Now turn your elbow out. Like this." His fingers slid along the length of her arm to rotate it at an awkward angle. "There. Now there's nothing for the string to snap onto. Look at your target, and when you're ready let 'er fly."

That was spoken low and so close, she could feel the hot touch of his mouth against her temple. The reaction liquefied. Her eyes squeezed tighter, sealing her into a dark, private bliss and her fingers numbly opened. It wasn't until she heard the twang of the string that she realized she'd released the arrow. Aghast, her eyes flew open.

"I hit it!"

Scott looked down at the target where her arrow shivered just shy of the outer ring. "That you did. Nice shot." Then he turned back to her, to where her huge eyes were staring upward, to where her lips were so temptingly close just a slight bend of his head would claim them. He could feel her shivering like that arrow where she curved against him, her hips into the straddle of his thighs, her shoulders upon the wall of his chest, her craned neck in the grove of his shoulder, but there was no distress in her gaze. Only a dazed sort of discovery that worked on his insides with the force of a constricting fist.

"Bravo, Miss Trowbridge."

Horace's shout was a singularly disturbing interruption. It brought the two of them apart but couldn't erase the impression they'd made upon one another in that brief, telling moment. Gena looked to the dapper gentleman with ill-concealed irritation.

"Thank you, Mr. Billings. And you were right. It is quite easy."

That gentleman flushed, recounting his own failure in her eyes, then muttered, "A pity your hit was not closer to the mark. It seems another is destined for the prize."

"Do you want it, Gena?"

Scott's crooning tones exacted a delicious quiver along her limbs. She looked up at him, into the golden eyes that suddenly seemed as fiery as the setting sun. She nodded, numbly, her thoughts far from the insignificant trinket but fixed upon a far more valuable reward.

Flushed with the want to show off for her, Scott weighed the bow in his palm and plucked one of the arrows. He was smiling at her, scarcely giving note to the target twenty yards away. His draw was smooth and powerful, filling the sleeve of his tailored coat with the bunch of contained muscle. And when his finger touched against the corner of his smile, he glanced down the length of the yard and let the string pop. Gena gave an excited gasp as the arrow buried deep into the center ring of the farthest target.

In some chagrin, Horace muttered, "What luck"— and grinning confidently, Scott set out to prove luck had nothing to do with it. He let six arrows fly, one after the other, until a pattern the size of Gena's palm filled the middle of the bull's-eye. It was then he realized the foolish price of his pride. The whispers started anew. He heard them ripple through the awed gathering that stared at the bristle of arrows in a daze of near horror. And then, those looks shifted to him. As if unaffected, he set down the bow and took up Gena's arm. The prize was forgotten in his hurry to steer her away in favor of the buffet table.

Aurora had taken the menu from the latest issue of the *Journal* and had heard nothing but grumbling from her husband and youngest son. They protested it was torture enough to endure the confines of a suit and tie without being starved in the process. She would have been furious to find they passed upon her delicacies of jellied chicken, cress with cold tomatoes, thin bread and butter, frozen strawberries with whipped cream and fancy cakes, in favor of a bowl of Ruth's stew in the kitchen. As the guests savored the dainty fare, servants bustled about to take up the soiled glasses and plates before they accumulated upon the grass.

Gradually, darkness settled over the big yard to lend an undeniable air of romance to the gathering. To supply mystery as well, and keep within the theme she'd chosen, Aurora had the guests don masks to hide their identities. For the first waltz, each was to find the partner who wore a mask of the same color.

From behind the slits of her disguise, Gena searched through the animated crowd only to have her hopes dashed. She had no trouble identifying Scott's easy walk or the fact that his mask was a startling white against the swarthy hue of jaw and throat. His partner was a nicely rounded female giggling behind a nervous fan. She felt a momentary stab of pique and was somewhat shamed to realize how much she had wanted the feel of her fiancé's arms around her once again. And was recalled to her mother's warning: *To keep a man's love you must keep his re-*

71

spect. Be ever on your guard to allow no rough freedom, no romping caresses or wayward behavior.

"Miss Trowbridge! Oh, how very fortunate for me."

She pulled her gaze from the sight of Scott with another woman on his arm to view a puffed and well-pleased Horace Billings with a strained temper.

"I see we are both blue," he announced smugly, tapping his mask.

"Indeed we are, Mr. Billings," she noted with a glum smile as the first strains of the music began and he rather nervously claimed her hand.

As her partner moved her about beneath the canopy of stars in a predictable pattern of turns, Gena's covert gaze followed the lithe steps of another. As the music progressed, lanterns winked on about the company, dispelling the magical shadows until upon the last note, masks were removed to the delight of all. All but the woman in Scott Prescott's care. Gena wasn't close enough to hear the words Scott offered her, probably a polite thank-you for the dance, but she could plainly see the dawning dismay upon that female's face. Her features grew pinched and pale, as if something undeniably dangerous had reared up in front of her. Her gloved hand jerked free with unqualified rudeness before she pointedly turned her back and hurried away. Gena wasn't the only one who noticed. Aurora took a quick step forward only to be firmly caught about the waist and whirled out by her husband to the beginning chords of the next waltz.

Distracted by the odd behavior of those about her, Gena momentarily lost sight of her fiancé. With a purposeful nod, she dismissed her smitten partner and began to wander amongst the whisperers. She paid no attention to the actual words muttered; the tone was disturbing enough. Even her friends had taken part in the gossip, for she heard Caroline's claim quite clearly.

"I never would have guessed. To think all this

time we accepted him as one of us."

"Caro, you hush this instant," Beth hissed at her. "I won't have you upsetting Gena with this malicious hearsay. You don't know if any of it is true."

"For your sake, I should hope not," she shot back wickedly. "After all, you are related to him."

For all her brave words, Beth looked stricken by that thought, then glanced up to see Gena's puzzled features. She quickly arranged her wan face into a smiling welcome. "Oh, Gena, I didn't see you there. Come join us."

"Perhaps later. I'm looking for Scott. Have you seen him?"

"I shouldn't wonder that he'd hide his face." Oh what fun Caro would have over the coming days with this delicious bit of hearsay, but for now, beneath her future sister-in-law's sharp censure, she settled for provoking innuendo. Beth was inordinately protective of her meek friend and it would not do to alienate herself in the other's eyes. Discreet nettling would have to do.

Gena tried to ignore that spiteful aside, but Caroline's words were a torment to her curiosity. What exactly was it about Scott Prescott that had everyone in hushed whispers? She wouldn't find the answer here, not amongst maligning rumor and half-truths. She would discover it from the source.

"I haven't seen him, Gena," Beth began. Why did she look so sympathetic? "Why don't you stay with us for a while. We were about to —"

"No," she cut in sharply, her agitation making her unseemingly rude. "I need to find Scott." And as she hurried away, Caroline's searing taunt dogged her heels.

"I should not be in such a hurry to rush to my ruin were I in her place."

Breathing shortened by the relentless cut of her corset, Gena was about to give up her search when a shift of moonlight brought a lone figure to her attention. He was standing apart from the rest of the guests beneath one of the tall cottonwoods. He'd shed his tie and coat, and the white of his shirt gleamed in the darkness. He was looking off toward the rolling hills and the loneliness of that expression twisted her heart. And his handsomeness made it beat faster.

He heard her approach, and turned. He didn't smile. He didn't speak.

"I've been looking for you." She nodded down to his discarded clothing. "Tired of all the socializing?"

"I've never been much at it. But you go on back and don't mind me. Horace will see you have plenty of dances."

Was that a tang of jealousy in his voice? The possibility thrilled her. She came closer to his solitary figure, not caring that they were isolated from the others. Or perhaps excited because they were. "I don't want to dance with Mr. Billings. I want to dance with you."

He seemed to consider that for a moment, then supplied a thin smile. "I'm not in the mood for it tonight."

"And what are you in the mood for?"

Scott stared at her. Could he be mistaking the soft invitation in her words? She'd never been one to encourage contact of a personal nature. In fact, just the briefest unplanned touch sent her skittering like a colt. But tonight, when he was feeling about as low and spiritless as a man could feel, she glided up with that hint of temptation. And he had to wonder why.

"Just thought I'd catch up on my stargazing. Don't see many stars in Boston. At least, not like these."

"Mind if I look with you?"

"What about your friends?"

"They won't miss me."

He gave her a thoughtful look, apparently searching for something. Then he shrugged. "Suit yourself. Kind of lonesome business, though."

She wasn't sure what it was that stirred so poignantly in that moment. Perhaps the tug of sadness at the corners of his slanted eyes. Perhaps the way he shoved his hands into his trouser pockets and squared his shoulders to prove he didn't need any of the laughter and camaraderie from the lawn above. Suddenly, she wanted to breach that isolation. Impulsively, she reached out a hand and placed it on his arm. A bold thing, considering a woman never took a man's arm unless it was first offered, and bolder still since she'd never been with a gentleman in his shirtsleeves. The fabric was thin and warmed by the heat of his flesh beneath it. With just the slightest press, she could test the swell of muscle and tautness of tendon. And she was filled with a decided wantonness, for it was an exquisite arm and she thoroughly enjoyed the sampling.

"You must be used to the loneliness," she said softly.

His gaze jerked from the dark jewellike heavens to the guileless blue of her eyes. "Why would you think that?" he demanded tightly. What had she heard? Who had told her?

"Living way out here, I mean. So far away from neighbors and friends." She felt him relax but he didn't speak. So she continued. "What was it like? Growing up out here?"

His eyes warmed to that faraway richness as he continued to stare at the stars. "I'd wake up every morning to see the sun rise. When it was warm, I went down to the river to drink water from my hands and swim. Then I'd sit on the banks and dry in the sunlight, watching the fish simmering in the slows, the birds nesting in the brush, and the hawks circling overhead. There were never enough hours in the day to tire of the pleasure of watching the world."

"How beautiful that sounds. It must have been hard to leave it behind."

Scott looked down at her sweet face and saw the goodness, the sincerity, shining there. But how could he ever explain to her? The separateness, the not-belonging, was as old as his years. He understood it; he intuited it. He knew he had no place among those dancing in the lantern light. The fine clothes were like the mask he'd worn. Underneath, nothing could change what he was. What he saw reflected back in the eyes of others. And when she knew, would he see that same silent disgust?

"I never should have come back."

That soft reply perplexed her. "But your family, your home is here. I can see how you love them whenever you speak of them."

"You can't see anything, Gena."

She winced at his sharp, angry tone because it made her sound foolish and shallow. Her hand pulled back and he felt its absence as keenly as a slap.

"Gena—"

"It's getting a bit cool. I think I should go back up—"

Suddenly, he couldn't bear for her to leave him alone in the darkness. "No. Don't go. Here."

Before she could react, he whipped his coat up off the grass and spun it about her shoulders. Its settling weight was like an immobilizing embrace. She stood, still and startled. His fingers lingered on the lapels, kneading, gathering the fine fabric into his palms until she was coaxed closer and closer to him. Her eyes dropped from his only to be tormented by the full curve of his lower lip. She looked lower and was entranced by the patch of golden skin exposed by his open collar. A pulse was throbbing there, quick, impatient. Her heart began to echo and amplify that beat.

His dark head moved slightly, lowering gradually.

"S-Scott."

"I've been wanting to do this all afternoon."

His voice was a low vibration.

He was going to kiss her.

And she was going to let him.

Admitting it to herself was no less surprising then telling him, "It's what I've wanted, too."

With an agony of anticipation, she shut her eyes and put back her head. And she felt his mouth on hers, just the faintest touch.

Warm. Dry. Soft.

"Scott . . ."

It was a wondering sigh. Enough to quicken a flame of urgent need within a guarded heart. She didn't respond to his first tentative exploration, and he realized with an aching tenderness it was because she didn't know how. He knew in that instant that he was the only one she'd ever allowed to taste the delicate offering of her kiss. And that made the fire burn hotter in his veins. He wet his lips and applied them to the cushioning luxury of hers, shaping them, teasing them, parting them. Her innocence opened the way, for she'd no reason to protest what she couldn't know was coming.

Gena was lost. Her resources were blunted by a daze of sensual discovery. Trapped tight to the hard, powerfully hewn planes of his thighs, midsection, and chest, she experienced a weak languor. It sapped the strength from her limbs, the very solidity from her bones. And even if she could, she wouldn't have moved. So this was kissing. The novel awareness whispered through sensation-drugged thoughts. Oh, it was nice. And he did it so well. The pressure of his mouth tightened and kept increasing in fervor, forcing her lips farther apart. Then she felt the light stroke of his tongue between them. The effect was devastating. Hands that had hung limply flew up to clutch his shirt, clenching, twisting, until he was inflamed by that needy desperation.

Encouraged beyond logical thought by the sudden willingness of the woman who'd held him at bay with her reserve, Scott gave before an urgent hunger. His tongue plunged deep. His breath escaped in a loud rush. A primal moan of want resounded low in his throat. And Gena panicked. He could feel the stiffness seize her body, the objection chill her lips, even before the tiny whimper wrung his conscience dry.

He let her go. He had no other choice unless he meant to continue by force. Panting and knotted painfully with frustrated intentions, he watched her race toward the safety of the house, like a moth from a dangerous flame. And he cursed low in a tongue she wouldn't have recognized had she heard it.

Gena was wheezing and clutching at her sides by the time she stumbled into the bright hall. A quick glance at the mirror built into the coat rack brought her up short in shock. She looked positively . . . lascivious. Beneath a skewed hat, her hair was mussed and torn free of its pins by her wild race through the shadows. Under the wrap of Scott's coat, her bosom was heaving at an indelicate rate. Her eyes were huge, and her mouth—her mouth was full and wet and wanting. Bruised and pouting from his possession.

What if anyone had seen her?

That single glance into the glass told her no minor reparations would restore her composure. The best thing would be to seek the sanctuary of her room and to pray, vigorously, for the wickedness to leave her. Even if she spent the hours until dawn upon her knees. And she feared that was what it would take to drive out the demon of lust Scott had called to with his kisses.

Voices.

In a frantic scramble, she darted into a dark alcove beneath the stairs and pressed flush against the wall. She squeezed her eyes shut, hoping upon hope that she wouldn't be noticed in her disheveled state. She nearly moaned in horror when she recognized the tones of

Scott's mother. Her lips gripped tightly to suppress her gasps for air and she was afraid she would surely suffocate before they moved on and opened the way to her escape.

"I'm not being ridiculous. And I'm not in the least hysterical," Aurora snapped.

Gena heard a low reply. She couldn't distinguish the words but the accent was unmistakable.

"You saw what happened. Nothing's changed for him. I was a fool to think schooling would make a difference. None of them will ever see anything but his father in him. Damn their narrow, bigoted minds."

Gena swallowed her shock and went rigid as the footsteps grew nearer.

"Ora, he did fine. What did you expect? The suit to make the man? You ought to be proud—"

"I am proud! Of the kind of man he is, of what he's managed to accomplish. It's just not fair, Ethan. It's not fair."

Gena heard a gentle murmuring and what sounded like a muffled sob. Aurora Prescott crying? The idea astounded.

"If he'd stay, he could show them all. I know he could." His mother's voice shook with conviction.

"But he's not, Ora."

"Because of *her*."

Gena recoiled from the venom in Aurora Prescott's words.

"Can't he see how unsuitable she is? There's not a spark of life in her. He might as well have a pretty fashion doll upon his arm. Oh, that's well and good at some fancy society party when all that's required are dainty manners and a shallow smile. But what about when he needs someone, someone who'll understand him? He's confused by her pedigree and her pretty face. But a pedigree isn't the same as passion. He deserves that from the

79

woman he marries. He deserves what you and I have. And Miss Blood-thin-as-mineral-water Trowbridge is not going to give it to him."

"Ora, you're the one not being fair now."

"Aren't I? Then why hasn't he told her who he is? Or rather who his father was? If he hasn't trusted her that far, why should I have any faith? And what happens when she learns the truth? She'll scorn him, Ethan, and it's going to break his heart. I can't let that happen. I won't let that happen."

That final vow faded as they continued down the hall.

Gena stood for a long time, trembling in the silence. Aurora's vehemence slashed her confidence to shreds. That and the sinister overtones haunting Scott's past.

Finally, she bolted from beneath the stairs and fled, unseen, to her chamber above. There, she curled upon the bed, fully dressed, still hugging Scott's coat about her. From the yard below, she could yet hear the strains of music and laughter but it had the vagueness of a dream. A confusing midsummer night's dream. And as she studied the pattern of stripes and flowers upon her wall, her mind was beset by one single plague.

What was the mystery surrounding the man she was about to marry?

Chapter Five

He rode slowly. It took every scrap of his control to retain an impassive face.

Nothing had changed.

For miles, there was nothing but dirty squalor. A poverty so great it stunned the senses and numbed the soul. An atmosphere of despair so prevalent it wrung the heart dry. A desolation so vast it crushed the spirit of hope.

Dear God, what had they done to the once-proud Lakota people?

In the nine years he'd been away at school, not one thing had been done to improve the lot of the Sioux. It had been talk, empty words, white man's words. The reformers with their high ideals, the politicians with their condescending smiles, the average easterner with his indifference. And he had become just like them. In nine years, what had he done?

Nothing.

And his conscience wept at the sights around him. They were starving. They were poor. They were like lost souls left to wander in an unfeeling world. A world not their own. For nine years he had blunted his spirit so as not to feel their pain. But now, confronting this—this horror, he felt the agony of each and every one of them rip through him until his heart bled.

Dear God, why had he ever come back?

He could feel their dulled eyes upon him. Suffering and circumstance had snuffed out even the mildest curiosity. He could see reflected in their eyes what they saw when they looked at him astride his fine horse, fleshed out beneath his store-bought suit. A white man. And they had seen enough fine, fat white men not to care if another chose to mingle in their midst, lording his superiority from up where the breeze blew free. Children approached him, catching at his stirrups, too aware of their hunger to know there was no pride in begging. And in the eyes of a few, the old ones, he saw a resentment spark. A hatred and mistrust as old as the mutilation of the hills, as old as the decimation of the buffalo. And he wanted to shrink from it. But he didn't dare. Pride held him upright in the saddle, pride and a respect for what had been. And so he rode without looking to the right or the left, for he couldn't shame them by acknowledging their disgrace.

He needed no one to show him the way to the home of Yellow Bear. The old chief's tipi stood in the inner circle of dwellings with its opening facing east. Its markings were the same, only made upon canvas rather than buffalo hide. He pulled in the horse and sat it for a long second before actually swinging down. He let the animal's reins trail and gave no thought to the goods lashed behind the saddle. No one would steal from him. The Miniconjous were not thieves despite all that had been stolen from them. He stood at the flap of his grandfather's tipi, on the threshold of two worlds, and he paused again. He was a white man sweating and shaking in an expensive suit of clothes, and that's all Yellow Bear would see when he stepped inside. And the old man would despise him for it. And for the promise he had broken.

"Do not stand beyond my door all day. You will find it easier to speak your words from inside."

Scott sucked in a shivery breath as the familiarity of the voice pierced his memory. The calm, knowing voice that had taught him the wisdom of the universe and the humility of man. He was full of that humility now. And it was those lessons that prompted him forward on two legs instead of crawling on all four.

"Hello, Grandfather."

Yellow Bear was seated on his bed of hides and made an attempt to rise. Scott knew he was badly lamed from the loss of his toes and from his many wounds. He quickly sank down onto one of the other platforms so the old chief wouldn't have to look up at him. It was then he suffered his first jolt.

The years had not been kind to the once-proud leader of the Sioux. It was more than the gauntness of hunger leaving skin to sag on bone. It was more than age that bowed strong shoulders. It was as if the misery of the people he loved had dimmed the bold light that once flamed in his spirit. The imprint of that tragedy lined his face like the scarring of tears. Old eyes regarded the young man beside him, eyes that had lost none of their wisdom of sight.

"It is good to see you, Scott."

Scott.

Never, never had Yellow Bear called him by his Christian name. The significance of it now had a stunning impact. As if the man in the suit and tie was not deserving of the fondness of a Lakota name from the old chief in his government-issue clothes. Words choked up in Scott's throat, damming back all the things he'd wanted to say to the old man to touch upon what they'd been to one another. Instead, he heard himself saying in a distant tone, "You look well, Grandfather."

"That I owe to your father. He has been good to come often to see to the ails of this old body."

"He's sent you a side of beef. It's bundled on my horse.

83

And my mama made some bread and raspberry jam."

Yellow Bear raised his brows at the idea of Aurora Prescott's gifts, but he murmured, "Thank them and let them know it will be distributed among those in need."

Scott looked at the loose folds of flesh and wanted to cry out in protest that the food was meant for him. Then he gripped his jaw tight. That was not the Lakota way. How had he forgotten that? All one had was divided among the many. It was one trait the greedy white man could never understand. As if to make amends, he reached into his pocket and withdrew his own gift for the old chief.

"This is for you," he said unnecessarily as he pressed it into the gnarled hand.

Yellow Bear considered the gold watch for a long silent moment, then he smiled at the well-intentioned boy. "It is a good gift. I will carry it with pride because you thought of me."

But it wasn't a good gift. Scott saw that at once. It would be nothing more than a useless trinket to a man who carried the sun and stars within his soul to tell the time of day. It hadn't been chosen well, with Yellow Bear in mind. It had been selected for what it represented: a regimented white man's world. He remembered his grandfather's scorn when he'd remarked that a white man had to look at his watch to tell when he was hungry. It was an insult to the old ways, and Scott writhed inside at his own foolishness as Yellow Bear slipped the watch into the pocket of his patched coat. He felt his face stiffen around his smile as he searched for something to say. Yellow Bear studied him through those wise old eyes as if he could look into the tormented heart of him and see his every guilt and shame.

"Your father has spoken of how well you've done in the big school in the east. He tells me you can now practice white man's law. It is an honorable thing."

The words poured out as if he couldn't speak them fast

enough to spit the bitter taste of conscience from his mouth. "I'll be working in Boston for a big company there."

"It is an important job?"

Scott hesitated. Important? He would be looking for legal loopholes and placating political powers over expensive luncheons in private clubs. He would be wearing a necktie and tight shoes while working up contracts to keep the rich rich and the poor from getting their hands upon it. Important? No. Not when compared to the plans he'd once made so boldly before this man. Plans he'd abandoned for his own selfish pursuits. He couldn't look up into the lined face.

"It is a good job."

"And will doing it make you happy?"

He stared hard at the dirt floor, swallowing down the bile of disgrace. "It is what I've chosen to do."

"Then it is good."

Disgust and guilt clenched inside him. Yellow Bear had no words of condemnation, nor did he call him back to the vows of the boy he'd once been. He seemed resigned to let Lone Wolf be replaced by Scott Prescott. And if he mourned the change, he did not betray it.

"I can't stay, Grandfather." He clambered to his feet in a sudden claustrophobic panic. The past was crowding him. He couldn't breathe. He could no longer bear to look upon the withered old man who'd once been a respected warrior. He wanted the purity of his childhood memories back and he couldn't have them. How had it gone so wrong? How had he strayed so far? How had he become so complacent in his travels of the easier path, to the point where his weak excuses were reason enough for him to continue blind?

"You will return to sit before my fire again?"

"I don't know," he confessed in an agony of shame. And when he braved a glance at the old chief, the wizened features drew into a small smile. As if he understood the pull of his convictions. As if he held no blame.

That forgiveness was too much. Scott stumbled from the tipi, nearly reeling in anguish. Never had he felt such wretchedness, such complete failure. And he had failed. His grandfather. His father's people. But he couldn't please them all. In his youth, he'd had such grand ideals, but experience had tarnished them to a dull despair. He couldn't be everything to everyone and he had made his choice.

He should never have come back.

"So when are you taking us to see the Indians, Scott?" The question was purred across the supper table.

Gena looked from Caroline's sweet smile — an expression as false as it was misleading — to her fiancé. Since he'd appeared at the Bar K in time for the evening meal, he'd been quiet and self-contained. He took the request without blinking an eye, and she couldn't miss Caroline's subtle disappointment. What reaction had she expected to gain?

"We can go tomorrow, if you like. We'll have to get an early start. It's a ways to travel and you won't want to make both trips in full sun."

As if she, too, had been anticipating something else from her cousin, Beth let out a breath of relief. Then, she looked worried. "You said we'd be in no danger. Are you sure?"

"You don't need to fret over the Sioux," Garth Kincaid supplied in confidence. "They had their backs broken back in the winter of '90. Haven't heard much more than a whimper out of them since."

"But the books and the papers back east . . ." Horace began, sounding unhappy that he wouldn't have the opportunity to brave the savage in his lair. "You couldn't

86

pick one up without hearing of the atrocities out here."

"In the early days, Mr. Billings, you wouldn't have gone within twenty miles of a Sioux camp without a regiment behind you. That was back when General George was up there stirring 'em up. They'd come sneaking down out of the hills and make off with my cattle and horses without nary a man seeing so much as a shadow. When they were in paint, a man and his family were lucky to wake up with their hair on." He stared hard at his plate for a moment, his jaw grinding as if chewing on a particularly tough memory. "Yessir, just the names were enough to scare the bejesus out of you. Crazy Horse, Red Cloud, Sitting Bull, Yellow Bear. Bad ones, every one."

"What made them that way, Mr. Kincaid?" Gena asked in genuine innocence. "Surely they had some reason. Or thought they did."

"We were taking their land from them," Scott said softly. He didn't look at anyone at the table but rather through the filmy lace at the windows, toward the vague outline of the Black Hills. "And we still are. It would rile you some, too, if a bunch of strangers who spat on your beliefs decided to build on your front yard in Boston without so much as a by-your-leave. Then they decided the yard wasn't good enough and they moved right into your house, crowding you out the back door with no place to go. Reckon they thought they had reason."

"But there are millions of acres out there," Merle put in. "And the Indians signed treaties giving up their rights to it."

Scott smiled wryly at his ignorance. "Treaties with the government lasted about long enough for the ink to dry. We made around a thousand and never kept to the terms of one of them. You see, our government never intended to keep them. They were supposed to take care of an immediate problem, then be disregarded as soon as we were strong enough to enforce a more profitable arrangement. The tribes had no legal standing. Their only recourse was to complain to the president or go to war."

"But if the documents they signed were legal —"

"You see, that's the irony of the whole thing. To an Indian's way of thinking, no man can claim to own the land any more than one chief can speak for all his people. Those are our perceptions of the law. So we pick out a friendly chief and sweet-talk him with a lot of promises he doesn't understand, get him to sign a paper he can't read, and we've got ourselves the right to do pretty much whatever we please."

"That seems hardly fair," Gena murmured. Her features were puckered with uncertainty.

"Fair?" Kincaid bellowed. "What's fair about trying to protect your loved ones?"

"Nothing."

Grandfather and grandson exchanged a long look that far surpassed the understanding of any in the group. All they could feel was the tension of beliefs clashing over the tender slabs of beef and broiled potatoes.

"So what happened to the Indians?"

Scott tore his stare from the elder rancher to glance at Gena. Her soft eyes were round with concern. It gave the harshness in his heart ease. "They were rounded up and herded like cattle onto unpleasant little plots of land where the government could imprison them in the name of progress."

"And it didn't take them long to learn how to wring the government and the eastern bleeding hearts dry, did it?" Kincaid sneered. "Always with a hand out, like mangy curs crowding on a porch at feeding time. Never had a one of them refuse to take the beef I sell for federal annuities."

"Forty years ago, the Teton Sioux were the masters of the northern plains. Since then, they've been forced onto reservations with all the symbols of their culture disappearing just as the buffalo disappeared. Government rations and annuity goods replaced the buffalo they hunted, and corrupt reservation agents, their chiefs and warriors. Their religion and customs were crushed by the programs designed to help them. They have no will to resist, no desire to change, and they'll carry their grief to the grave."

"How very sad," Gena whispered as Scott's words tugged at her vulnerable emotions. "And how cruel."

Garth Kincaid snorted. "Is it cruel to force the Indian to give up his scalping knife? Is it cruel to make him stop his barbarous dances in which he cuts and tortures his own flesh sometimes to the death? To force him to educate and marry his daughters under a civilized code of law rather than selling them at a tender age into concubinage? Is it cruel to crush the rituals that teach their young the debauchery, diabolism, and viciousness of the Indian race?"

Scott's features darkened to a deep, hot copper as he ground out fiercely, "And you would prefer installing unscrupulous agents and giving them complete power over superstitious and helpless people? Keeping them prisoners, isolated from any kind of normal, honorable life? Dominated by fear and force and made into paupers starving for the want of food that's extorted from them?"

There was a long, taut pause, then Kincaid purposefully relaxed. "I see an education has not convinced you to change your views."

Scott, too, backed down enough to admit, "What I've learned has only enforced them."

"You seem quite knowledgeable about the plight of the Indian," Caroline interjected. "How is that?"

Scott gave her a cool consideration, then drawled, "I studied the *Handbook of Federal Indian Law* at Harvard. And I've grown up next to them. I spent a lot of time in their camps when I was younger. They trusted my father enough to let him treat their sick. He was a surgeon in the War Between the States."

The woman's black eyes narrowed with interest. "And did your mother go with you, as well?"

"No." That single syllable snapped. Then, Scott smiled easily, a wide, white baring of teeth. "Guess she must have shared my grandfather's dislike of Indians."

"Well," yawned Horace, "this has all been very fascinating, but I for one am completely weary of the entire subject. And I'm not at all sure I can in good conscience allow Miss Davies near such dismal creatures."

"I've been having second thoughts, myself," Beth echoed. All the talk of desolation and disease had her nervously thinking of her own fragile health. Could any good come of exposure to dangerous and unwholesome gases that must flourish in the face of poverty? She felt positively weak just contemplating the risk.

"I should like to go." Gena's quiet claim surprised them all.

"Oh, Gena," Beth protested. "Have a care for yourself. You cannot *want* to travel all that distance just to see a few begging Indians. How very unpleasant it all sounds. Not at all romantic or adventurous. You will be in a state of depressed nerves for days. I really think—"

"And I appreciate your concern, dear Beth, but I think I will go now and see if Ruth would mind fixing a light repast for the journey. Please excuse me."

They all stared at her straight-backed retreat, and polite table conversation was impossible to resume.

The night was cool and quiet. Scott drew it in deeply to calm the fever of his thinking. Try as he would, he could not control it. He kept smelling the stale reservation smells, seeing the deadened pain in his grandfather's eyes. Feeling the shame of their meeting; one in which

90

not one word of Lakota had been exchanged. Did Yellow Bear think he'd forgotten it? It was the language of his heart, his soul, while English was the embodiment of his mind. And that heart and soul was torn now by things he'd tried to put behind him with the clear reasonings of his mind. And couldn't. Garth Kincaid was right. Eastern schooling hadn't changed his thoughts while civilizing the man. It had taught him how to deny and submerge them. How to lie in white man's fashion, to others, to himself.

But what was the truth? What could he do to keep the promise of a thirteen-year-old boy who knew nothing of the world beyond the grasses of South Dakota? He hadn't wanted to go east to leave that brave-hearted, naive-headed boy behind. But he'd gone. And he'd listened and learned about the ways of the world. And he knew he couldn't change them. He couldn't turn the tide of a nation where separateness bred ignorance, ignorance fear, fear conflict. And ironically, it was the fear the majority held of the minority that was the greater. How could he make a stand for his father's people when he hadn't been able to make a stand for himself?

He hadn't told Gena.

He'd lived a lie in Boston and had himself almost believing it. He'd thought by immersing himself in civilization, he could accept and be accepted. And he thought he'd succeeded. He'd carried the wishes of his mother and his Grandfather Kincaid as if they were his own and he'd vowed to make them proud of his choices. He'd vowed to become what they wanted and he had. He was educated, urbanized, sophisticated. And so empty inside he could hear the echoes clear through his soul. He owed it to them not to complain. Not to mourn for what he could not have. He would settle for prestige instead of pride. He would compromise freedom for financial gain. He would surrender passion for the proper. He had the perfect glossy appearance. He had the perfect job waiting. He had the perfect wife in Gena Trowbridge.

And none of them touched upon the heart of the man. None of them meant anything to him.

Desperately, he brought the image of Gena's face before him. He could love her. He knew he could. She was smart and kind and she would give him comfort if not caresses. He should be satisfied with that. So why was he so restless? Perhaps he could stir some life inside her that would make a shared eternity bearable. She'd liked his kiss, at least until propriety interfered. Would it always be like that? Him needing to give, her refusing to take. There were worse things, he guessed. But he couldn't think of what they might be.

That was the problem. He was thinking too much. He was feeling too much. He had to get away from the turmoil of the past. When he'd believed things possible. When he'd believed in love. Once surrounded by the cold compassionless east, he would forget these things. He would forget the scent of the sky and the grass. He would forget the feel of pain and pride moving inside him.

And he would make them proud.

Gena stood in the doorway. Behind her, she could hear the sounds of conversation and laughter from her friends in the parlor, but she had no wish to join them. All her attention was drawn to the lone figure sketched in twilight. He was leaning against one of the support posts at the far bend of the porch where light and the noise of merriment fell short of reaching him. She could see the powerful outline of his shoulders as they rose and fell. That melancholy gesture called her to the subtle shadows where all she wanted and feared waited.

"I was afraid you had left for the evening."

He gave no hint of surprise. He must have been aware of her presence before she announced it. She had always marveled at that uncanny sense. It was as if Scott noticed things just an instant before any one else, as if he was always alert for the slightest change. He didn't turn to her or offer any welcome. Gena plucked up her courage and made herself join him against the rail. She couldn't pretend all was the same between them as it had been in Boston. There, their court had a familiar pattern, one that was formal and — safe. During the half hour they had together within her parents' home to say their good-nights, she had never felt this particular nervousness, this twisting anticipation. Not once had he ever pushed the boundaries of propriety to the point of discomfort or censure. And she'd been sure he was as content with them as she, herself, had been. The quiet conversation, the small smiles, the gentle tuck of her hand within the bend of his arm. She'd never felt afraid of him or uncertain of what he expected. But that had changed.

Because of the kiss.

Until then, all had been calm and predictable, both in situation and inside herself. Hers was a quiet soul, unused to the rigors of emotion, trained to avoid undo excitants. She had no idea how to contain the sudden whirlwind of sensation Scott had released within her. That she'd allowed him to free. She'd fretted through a near-sleepless night, confusing in those pre-dawn hours the substance of reality and dream. She'd actually thought she heard Puck's pipes beckoning to her through the flutter of lace at her window. Coaxing her imagination the way Scott Prescott did her desires.

She stood beside him in the dusky evening, trembling with an expectant dread. What if he thought to take more liberties? An eager thrill shot through her and she saw it firmly crushed. A decent woman didn't anticipate such vulgar happenings. She prevented them with a sober, righteous, and superior behavior. Her mother had warned her about men in the unmarried state. She'd cautioned that a man without a wife becomes savage and sinful and that it was the work of a good woman to soften and refine those base impulses. She stressed the purer the woman, the more restrained and elevated the man. And Gena respected Scott. She carried enough regard in her heart to help him attain an honorable station among men. And so she could not encourage such passions within his breast, not now and not even upon their marriage. It was up to her to display control.

And so, when he turned to her in the pale half-light, she met his look with an impersonal smile and a shiver of resolve. His golden eyes gleamed in the darkness, probing hers with a disturbing intensity. She couldn't in good conscience meet that gaze. Instead, she modestly lowered hers and found it tortured by the sweeping contour of his full bottom lip. Her pulse quickened into a fever of hurried beats.

"Gena, my grandfather has asked me to stay for the summer."

Her stare flew up, wide and disoriented. "What?"

Scott looked back toward the dark swell of the hills and elaborated in a tense voice. "He wants me to work with him on certain legislations. It would take until the fall to draft the necessary proposals and present them."

"But you have a job—in Boston." Her words were edged with an unmistakable panic.

"This wouldn't be a job. My grandfather paid for my education. It would be my way of paying him back for his generosity. I'm sure your father would understand. And if he can't hold the position open for me, there'll be other jobs."

But Gena wasn't thinking about his employment. Her heart and head were consumed by another worry. A congestive anguish rose until it was all she could do to breathe. She was going to lose him. To his home. To the hills.

Scott saw the fears etched upon her quiet features, and guilt clutched fiercely. He hadn't meant to hurt her. Not by any of it. Least of all by his own confusions. He forced a reassuring smile but she failed to respond.

"It will only be for the summer."

"And the wedding?" That was spoken so faintly, it was a mere whisper.

"It will only be for two months," he restated. Still, she wasn't calmed. Dampness glittered in her big, uplifted eyes, shimmering there with prismed brilliance and pain.

"But you'll come back?"

The uncertainty quavering in her tone snapped something vital inside him. Impulsively, and a bit desperately, his arms circled her frail form to pull her close to the crashing thunder of his heart. "Yes," he insisted with a penetrating strength. "Then I'll come back."

The solidity of his embrace should have convinced her. As should have his passionate vow. But there was another disquieting shadow she could not overcome with words or deed. It was the terrible tension in the way he held her. The almost angry emphasis in his voice. His promise was more frightening than her doubts.

"I don't want to return to Boston without you." She said it softly but the statement echoed a mounting anxiety. She forgot all her earlier reservations and clutched at his coat with shaking fingers. If only he could make her believe it would be all right. If only she didn't feel so cold at the thought of separation. The pledges they'd made in the east seemed so far removed from this vast, wild land. So awfully distant. What if he changed his mind? What if he never followed? Her mind went numb with the possibilities.

"Just for two months, Gena. Then I'll be back and we'll go through with our plans. Everything will be just as we've talked about. It will, Gena. It will. I promise. I just

95

need to finish things here. I need to make my peace and put it behind me. Can you give me that time? Can you trust me that far? Please say you can."

And then it was a matter of him, not her, needing the reassurance. As if he was the one who needed — desperately — to believe. His arms were coiled tight, as if by pressing hard enough he could meld them into one. It wasn't the intimacy of the embrace that upset her. It was the frantic way his breath raced through her hair. As if he was afraid of something too horrible to speak in words. As if he could force, by sheer power of will and body, that mysterious terror to relent. And in doing so, she shared his distress most acutely. What could be so bad that he would cling to her as a means of salvation? Was it the secret he refused to share? Her uneasiness continued to grow.

His head turned so that his cheek rested upon her fragile shoulder.

"I need you, Gena."

The low, huskily spoken claim wrought an instant stiffening. Then, when he didn't pursue the words with any physical persuasion, she began to think he meant something else altogether. Something far more important than matter of the flesh. And she was recalled to Aurora Prescott's misgivings. That braced her. There was nothing Scott needed that she could not supply.

Gingerly, she lifted a hand to lay atop her fiancé's dark head. The short black hair was silken to the touch. That sleek texture fascinated because it had been so unexpected. For a moment, her fingers lost themselves to the seducing sensation and she was able to say, unequivocally, "I do trust you, Scott. I trust you and — and I love you."

Her admission fed his frenzied state. He clutched her close, painfully so, and vowed with a rumbling sincerity, "You won't regret it, Gena. You'll see. Everything will be fine as soon as I'm finished here. We'll be married. We'll honeymoon in the White Mountains. I'll work for your father. We'll have a nice house, maybe something with a little land around it. And you can have someone come in to do the cleaning and cooking. And we'll have children, lots and lots of children. Will that make you happy, Gena? Will it?"

She'd gone very still, her features frozen with a horror only the night could see. And then, she said very quietly, "Yes, Scott. That will make me happy."

Chapter Six

The sky was cloudless. The wind had not yet risen. The midmorning sun was benign, creating a basking warmth far short of noontime intensity. With her parasol tilted toward the east, Gena found the trip quite comfortable.

For the first hour, they'd seen nothing but Kincaid cattle. There were shorthorns and the stocky red-and-white-faced Herefords cropping on the rich short grasses. Mingling through them were the original range kings, the lanky Texas longhorns. Scott paid them no mind but responded to her curiosity with detailed replies. He didn't consider himself an expert on ranching, not like his brother, but he had more than a nodding familiarity with the way things worked on the range. He spoke colorfully of the trail drive that brought his father up from the Lone Star State to fall in love with the Dakotas and of the booming cowtowns that sprang up in response to the hundreds of thousands of dollars the cattle industry came to represent. And he told with less enthusiasm of how the hunger for grass and gold had cornered the Indians and seen their precious buffalo slain.

About the time he fell silent, their light buggy turned out onto the quietude of the far-reaching virgin prairie. There were no roads, only an occasional path cut by cattle en route to a pond or stream. There was nothing except the sounds of the insects in the grass and the soft melancholy cooing of mourning doves. Again, Gena felt that chill of isolation, of being stranded in a place so far removed from others that even God had forgotten its existence. How could they have stood it, those who came before her? How did women like Aurora Prescott survive the loneliness? And from all appearances, thrive? She clutched her parasol in damp hands and said a silent prayer of thanks that she would be leaving in less than a week and that Scott would soon follow. She could endure anything until then. Or so she thought. And then the buggy had crested a low hill.

Not even Scott's glum depictions over the dinner table had prepared her for the Cheyenne River Reservation. There seemed an endless forest of shabby, pointed tents rising up from desolate ground. Some of the dwellings were no more than rude brush shelters. There was no running water, no relief from the sun which now broiled down from overhead. And dust. So much dust carried on the hot, dry breeze. That and the scent of crowded humanity.

Gena put her handkerchief to her mouth to strain out the dirt and stifle her dismay.

"We don't have to go any closer."

Scott's quiet words distracted her from the grim tableau. She glanced at him, then paused to really look. His golden eyes were watchful, piercing in their study of her face. She had the feeling he was expecting something from her. There was the faintest edge of hope skirting his expression. Along with a subtle wariness. He was waiting for her response and she guessed of its importance by his silence. Determinedly, she lowered the lacy linen square. And she smiled.

"It's all right. Please go on. It's just the heat. I'm not used to it."

He probed her sincerity with a lengthy hesitation, then snapped the reins to start them forward once more. Gena took a deep breath and carefully schooled her features to display none of her shock or distress. It was important for Scott not to know how the dismal place upset her. She wasn't sure why. She just knew. And so, she sat beside him, calmly observing her first sight of Native Americans without clutching at her escort and hair.

A white woman in their midst stirred more interest than a simple man on horseback. Scott was incredibly tense beside her. She wondered anxiously if he was worried for their safety, and yet she noted that he bore no weapons. Apparently, that was not his concern. But there was something mighty preying upon his mind, for she could see the way it scored his lean cheeks and set his mouth into a thin, narrow line. Aware of the scrutiny from all sides, she cast a few furtive glances of her own at these people Scott had named the proud warriors of the plains.

She saw no warriors. No evidence of pride. Men lounged indolently in front of their lodgings or crouched in small circles engaged in games of chance. Their idleness was not carried to the women, for they were busy in their tiny garden patches, tending fowl or children or going about some household industry. They regarded her with covert curiosity, intrigued by her clothing and fair skin and hair. Most were dressed like the paupers she'd seen in the city's poor districts. All looked lean and hungry. In looking at them, she perceived no threat, only a deep current of sadness. And that was when she lost her fear. Her mother had raised her to believe that charity to the unfortunate was a virtue without equal and that it was their duty to show kindness to those in need. And never had she seen such needy creatures, even amongst the poor they visited with their philanthropic societies in the east. She knew the kindred look of despair, had seen it in the Boston slums, and she no longer saw savages before her but a people in need of compassion.

She thought of the caged wild things, restless and mourning their freedom. Only here, she saw no hope and her heart swelled in sympathy.

"I have things to deliver," Scott announced, drawing up the buggy. As he wrapped the reins around the whip base, he added, "Just stay put. No one will harm you."

"Would it be safe for me to get down?" She was looking at the gathering of brown-skinned children shyly peering in their direction.

"If you like. Just don't wander off."

When he went back to unlash the supplies he'd brought, he heard a sudden giggling and looked back up. Gena was standing beside the buggy, surrounded by the timid children. She was handing out something that made their cautious little faces gleam. As he approached, they scattered like frightened chicks.

"What's that you've got there?"

Gena blushed and brushed off her hands after returning an empty sack to the hamper in the boot. "Just some cornstarch cakes. I asked Ruth what they might like and she thought these would do." Her gaze followed the lithe youngsters, growing wistful. "Such beautiful little children." When she turned back toward the buggy, Scott could have sworn he saw moisture gathering in her eyes. It wasn't pity or distaste. Rather a tender sorrow.

And Scott's chest seized up with emotion. He tried hard to swallow and found he couldn't. He stared at Gena, at the fragile flower he'd assumed would shrink in horror when faced with such brutal conditions of life. He stared hard and saw a thread of resilient compassion woven into a fabric of care. When she'd smiled down into the expectant faces, she'd seen children, only children. It surprised him. And it pleased him more than any single thing he could think of.

When he took up her hand, Gena glanced up in question. His fingers meshed and squeezed tight. It was a needy, hurtful grasp but she didn't try to draw away. She was too caught up in the fixed intensity of his expression.

"Scott?"

"Gena, there's someone I want you to meet."

He began walking, almost pulling her alongside in his somber concentration. Gena trotted wordlessly, breathlessly, caught by his grip and his grim purpose. She almost balked when he flipped up the flap of one of the Indian tents. But the fervor of his manner, regardless of its mysterious cause, prompted her to step into the dim unknown. She was aware at once that they were not alone. An old man sat cross-legged on a hide-covered bed. His gray hair was long, falling past his stooped shoulders and twined into two thin braids. He was wearing a faded checked shirt and denim pants with leather slippers covering his feet. He regarded her through obsidian eyes, as unfathomable as his expression was severe until they slid to Scott. Then that gaze warmed like the hard-packed earth outside and all the harsh lines in his coppery face became just an old man's wrinkles.

"I am honored by your visit. Come. Sit."

The words were in English, grunted out in a deep monotone but quite clear. Gena hesitated until Scott stepped past her and lowered himself to one of the mats. Gathering her skirts to keep them out of the dirt and the fire ashes, she arranged herself beside him. The old man's study made her uncomfortable, and she kept her gaze canted down so he might not read of her uneasiness.

"Miss Gena Trowbridge of Boston, this is Yellow Bear, a great and powerful chief of the Miniconjou Sioux."

Yellow Bear chuckled. "Your praise falls like heavy rain but will not stand upon the ground. I am Yellow Bear of the Lakotas. You have traveled far. I would offer my hospitality."

102

Gena was about to speak a refusal, unwilling to take when he obviously had so little to spare, but Scott gave her a stern look and shook his head slightly.

"Thank you," she said softly.

Almost immediately, a woman appeared with a bowl and set it on the ground between the two mats. She gave Scott a warm smile and nodded shyly to his female companion before slipping out in silence. Gena glanced at the shriveled strips of what appeared to be some kind of meat, and reluctance gripped her belly. Not minding the absence of dinnerwear, Scott dipped his fingers into the dish and carried a bit of the meat to his mouth. His gaze prompted her to do the same. She stared back into the bowl. She'd seen no sign of animal life within the Sioux compound, other than some stringy dogs. Her stomach clenched.

Yellow Bear smiled wryly. "Eat. It is Prescott beef. I have heard them boast of its taste. It is not buffalo but it will do."

Forced by his tolerant humor into action, Gena picked up a small sampling and bit into it gingerly. It had a rich, smoky flavor and, despite its appearance, was chewy not dry.

"It is very good. Thank you and thank the hands that prepared it."

The old man looked pleased with her remark. His inscrutable stare went between the silent young man and the pretty pale lady from Boston and his wondering grew.

"How do you find our land, Miss Trowbridge? Is it to your liking?"

"It's very different from Boston," was her diplomatic reply.

"Ah yes. Boston. I have heard of this place from my cousin, Sitting Bull. He made many visits to the east when he was with Colonel Cody and found it, too, very different."

Gena glanced up in wonder. Who in the east had not heard of Sitting Bull, the warrior who brought down Custer. She had seen his likeness and was recalled to his haughty features beneath a great bonnet of feathers, his strong body clad in elaborately beaded hides. He had looked like a warrior, like one of the painted renegades she read about in her treasured Beadle novels of the west. But this man, the chief Garth Kincaid mentioned in the same breath as Sitting Bull, had none of that arrogant fire. She couldn't picture him leading a band of blood-thirsty savages down from the hills to scalp innocent citizens in their beds.

"I had read much about the west but this is not what I expected." *You* are not what I expected, her averted gaze told him.

"All things change, Miss Trowbridge. I was born on the prairie where winds blew free and there was nothing to make the sun a shadow. I knew every stream and wood and hunted them all like my fathers before me, and like them, I lived happily. This was my country. I did not come here to find riches and freedom; I am a part of it, as the rock and the tree and my ancestors before me. I have seen the blood of twenty million buffalo spilled. I have seen the wild horse enslaved behind the plow, the eagle shot from the sky, and the sacred mountains where my people communed with the Great Spirit violated. I have lived to see the Indian a prisoner of those who would make him into a muddy-complexed white man. And soon, our tipis once lit by buffalo oil will have electric lights and the messages we sent in puffs of smoke will race along the wires of this thing they call the telephone. I have lived to see all these changes. Perhaps, Miss Trowbridge, I have lived too long."

How had she ever thought him a spiritless old man? As he spoke, a deep flicker of life took flame and burned passionately in his words. She could feel the vital pulse of his people throb in the telling of the past. He had been a great man, a great chief. She could feel that power in him, that wisdom of life, that strength of authority. How sad it was to see it stripped away. How wrong it was, she felt within her heart. Impulsively, she asked, "And is there nothing in all this change that can be for the good of your people?"

Yellow Bear smiled grimly and shook his head. "To the white man, the Indian is no more important than the grizzly or the buffalo or the mountain lion. They have reduced us from men to children. They have taken our bows and pushed plows into our hands, saying 'Feed yourselves.' But the Lakota is not a farmer. We are hunters. Our men walked a proud path. We were warriors, shamen, protectors of our families. But the white man's laws have stripped us of our honor and have left us with no value to our families."

"But there are members of our race who would help yours. In Boston, we have an Indian Citizenship Committee."

He waved aside her good-intentioned protest. "There are men and women who would call themselves the friend of the Indian. They are convinced of the rightness of their cause and are sure their god approves. But they have never asked the Indian what he wants. They have never sought value in our customs. Their solution to the Indian problem is to do away with the Indianness and to absorb us all into their superior Christian civilization. They claim land, education, and citizenship awaits those who walk the white man's road. But it is a path we cannot take. We are men, not children, and the road is not ours."

"Then I am very sad for both our people."

Scott sat a silent observer to the deepening conversation. He was proud of the way Gena expressed herself and of the understanding rooted in her gentle soul. And he could see Yellow Bear was impressed or he would not

105

have been moved to discuss such things. He was discovering a tenacious heart within the meek Miss Trowbridge. But would that generous heart encompass him when the truth be told? His tension mounted because he knew there could be no answer until all was risked. Then it could well be too late.

"You speak well for a white woman, of what is in your heart and mind, not of what has filled your ears. Is that the way of all the people in Boston?" Yellow Bear leaned forward for her answer.

"I cannot claim it to be so," she murmured regretfully. "Though I wish it might be, someday."

"Then perhaps I will live a while longer, New Waw, and we will both see."

"New Waw?"

"White Swan. It will be your name among us, for there is grace and beauty in what I have seen." He looked to Scott at last and smiled. "You have chosen well, *takoja*."

"What a beautiful name. What does it mean?"

Yellow Bear regarded her impassively. "It means 'son of my son,' as Lone Wolf is son of Far Winds, son of Yellow Bear."

"Grandson."

As she mouthed the word, her gaze turned to Scott. She took it all in with new insight: the jet-black hair, the sculpted features, the tawny summer skin that never faded. The whispers at the Bar K. And it all made sense. A terrible, terrifying sense.

Scott didn't look away from her realizing gaze nor did he recoil from it. At least on the surface. Inside, he felt dead.

Yellow Bear looked between them with interest. He saw her surprise. He felt the dread Scott wouldn't allow to show upon his face. And he wondered how his grandson could have been so foolish to keep such a thing unspoken. Unless he had been ashamed.

"Yellow Bear is my grandfather. I am half Lakota." Scott's words were unnecessary. And too late. An inapproachable stiffness had already settled over Gena's face. In a way, she was every bit as inscrutable as the Sioux. Whatever worked behind her glassy blue eyes, she refused to put on display. But Scott had a sinking feeling he would learn of it soon enough.

Why had he come back? Why had he thought she would understand?

Scott beat himself with his mistakes. He sat rigid in his grandfather's presence, feeling the heat of his ancestors' blood color his cheeks. A blood he had been afraid to claim before all those proper whites in Boston. A blood that now tainted what he'd hoped for the future.

She would not forgive him that impurity.

"Go now, for I am weary," Yellow Bear announced with a wave of one thin hand. "You are welcome at my fire, New Waw. And you, *takoja*."

Scott rose. When he assisted Gena, he could feel the brittle censure in her stance. She drew away as soon as she gained her feet.

"I have enjoyed our talk, Chief Yellow Bear. Perhaps there will be others."

The old man nodded, and smiled blandly at his grandson. He did not envy the boy for the taming of temper to come. But he would have to learn that pride and foolishness were humbled before love. Something they hadn't taught him at his eastern school.

Gena walked directly to the buggy. There, she wrestled with her skirt and petticoat to climb up on her own. There was no emotion registered on her pretty features, just an ominous calm. Scott sighed grimly and was distracted for a moment as he gave the supplies to Red Bird, his grandfather's second wife. Slowly, he approached the buggy, dreading the long trip back to the Bar K and what it would bring. He didn't know

107

what he could say to ease the sting of truth.

He was half Indian.

What could he expect of her? She had her family to think of, her reputation, her pride. The scandal would cut her to pieces. And that he couldn't allow. She'd done nothing to deserve that kind of pain. He was the outsider. He couldn't let her be guilty by association. She was too much a lady to end it with bitterness and public accusation. He needn't fear she would disgrace him. No, she would keep her reasons to herself. She would be very civilized about it. And she would never let him know how much he'd hurt her.

He settled on the seat. She was stiff as a post beside him, looking neither to the right or left. Her small hands were resting in her lap. Clenched. He wished she would turn and have at it, with her tongue, with her fists. Maybe then he would feel better. But her glacial dignity gave him no respite. She damned him with her silence.

He urged the horse forward, guiding it between the shabby dwellings of his father's people. As he did, he tried to summon a saving anger. If only she hadn't insisted on coming west with him. If she hadn't been the only one brave enough to come to the Sioux encampment. Brave? The timid Gena Trowbridge? Yes, she was, and even braver now, sitting at his side pretending not to be devastated by the truth. If only she hadn't responded quite so warmly to his kiss, hadn't held him, touched his hair, told him that she loved him. His fury twisted, becoming a self-consuming pyre. He'd never meant to hurt her. Any of them.

From out of his glum study, the familiar caught his eye. It was a ragged brave weaving almost into his path. When the glazed expression lifted, Scott gave a cry of recognition.

"High Hawk!"

The drunken warrior stumbled to a stop. Black eyes

glared up, filled with animosity. Lips curled back into a sneer. He said a single word, then spat upon the ground before wobbling away.

"*Iyeska.*"

Mixed-blood. Half-breed.

Scott's fingers whitened upon the reins. His belly spasmed as if struck a particularly vicious blow. For a moment, he couldn't move or draw a decent breath. Then, he sucked in a long pull of air as if it pained him to do so. And he was about to urge the horse on when a second slender figure rushed out in their path, apparently in pursuit of the first. It was a young woman. At the sound of the horse's snort, her dark gaze flew up in alarm. Then, she stood frozen and aquiver, like a doe run to ground.

"Lone Wolf."

She glided around the front of the buggy and came to stand at Scott's side.

"It is you! So many summers had passed, I feared you would not return. But how very handsome you are in your fine clothes." Her hand reached up to stroke his sleeve, his thigh, and Gena began to take sharp notice.

From the pictures drawn her in the east, Gena had imagined Indian women to be ignoble squaws; squat, haggard, ugly, papoose-toting drudges who toiled endlessly as their husbands' slaves. Now, how she wished that were true. For this woman, looking up at Scott through eyes dark with liquid affection, was a startling beauty. She was willow-thin, which made the jut of firm young breasts all the more apparent. Long shapely limbs were delineated by a loose cotton blouse and a full calico skirt that swirled about trim calves and ankle-high moccasins. Her features were sharply etched from tawny skin, wide dark mouth, and coal black eyes. Bits of sparkling mica threaded through straight blue-black hair, giving off diamondlike flashes whenever she set the waist-length

109

tresses in motion with the movement of her head. She was lovely, and Gena was stricken with a purely female douse of jealousy. Who was she? Another secret from the past? She felt her jaw tighten until it ached.

"Have you been to visit your grandfather? How often he spoke of you when you were away."

"Your family, are they well?" He looked in the direction High Hawk had run, his features carefully without expression.

"They have land to the north, but my brother prefers to stay here with his friends." She lowered her eyes so Scott might not see her shame.

"Tell them I will visit as soon as I am able."

"I will tell them." She stepped back from the buggy, her gaze filled with him. "They will be waiting—eagerly."

The reservation was far behind them when Gena finally spoke. Her voice was as brittle as the isinglass that glittered in the other woman's hair. "She is very pretty. Who is she?"

"I grew up with Morning Song and her brother. They were like my . . . cousins," he replied without looking at her. His gaze was leveled straight between the horse's ears.

A very demonstrative family, she thought to herself. Morning Song. A suitably attractive name. Again, she saw the slender hand lingering along his limbs. Cousin, indeed. How simple did he think her? Though she sat straight and unbending, Gena felt tears shiver in her eyes. Very simple, came her own answer. Simple enough to deceive with things as important as his ancestry. Simple enough to fool in what other ways? She blinked hard and firmed her chin. Not so simple as to make a display of her feelings to wring his pity. Pity was the last thing she wanted. What she wanted—needed—was for Scott to explain. For him to tell her why he'd deliberately kept such a vital truth from her. She wanted him to tell her who he

110

was, about the boy he'd been when he and Morning Song had known one another. She wanted him to make her understand.

And she wanted him to hold her.

But he sat stiff and silent, holding the truth to himself. And that silence hurt her every bit as much as hearing of his past from another.

It was a long incommunicative trip. They paused long enough to share the bread, cheese, and fruit Ruth had packed; and as they ate, they looked at the far hills, at the endless green of the plains, at the unbroken blue of the sky. Anywhere but at each other. Questions tormented Gena just as the answers tortured Scott.

Why hadn't he told her?

How very much she must now hate him.

The remnants of the meal were gathered and stowed in the buggy boot. Gena was lifted gently up to resume her seat. And then they continued the silent agony over the quiet rolling hills. When the Bar K came into sight, Gena could hold to her tongue no longer. She had to speak now before the company of others forbade it.

"Why didn't you tell me?" It was a low, quivering accusation and Scott tensed beside her.

"Can't you figure that for yourself? Ask your friends. Ask any of the guests at my grandfather's party."

"I don't want to hear it from them." Abruptly, she twisted on the seat to fix her angry gaze upon him. His profile was set as if in stone.

"I was going to tell you."

A small point of fury began inside her, strengthening as she heard his flat reply. "When? Just when were you going to tell me? After the wedding?"

A muscle jerked along his jaw. "Today. I was going to tell you today."

"After I'd embarrassed myself and your grandfather?"

"I'm sorry. I didn't plan it very well."

111

"I should say you did not!" She turned away, battling a flurry of emotions. She was angered by his stoic manner, deeply hurt by his continued silence, and shattered by the gravity of what she'd just discovered. She clung to the last of her composure as the buggy pulled up at the broad porch. To her relief, there was no one in sight to witness her failed efforts. Wetness marked her cheeks in hot, punishing trails. Finally, and again much too late, he put his hand over hers.

"Gena—"

She jerked free. In a thick, tearing voice, she said, "I don't know if I can ever forgive you, Scott."

He immediately went white and rigid. He forced himself to step down from the buggy, to walk to the other side and reach up for her. His hands were steady. His heart shuddered. As she leaned forward so he could catch her slender waist and turn her down to the porch, he said low and fiercely, "I cannot change the Indian blood inside me."

For a moment, Gena stayed in the circle of his hands. Her great, shimmering blue eyes studied his face, almost with a desperation, seeing there the gentleness of the man who courted her and nothing more. Then the truth ruined that image for her. She stepped back, pushing his hands away in a very definitive gesture. She saw his features harden in harsh, angry lines and she could see it was he who did not understand.

"It's not who you are that I can't forgive," she told him quietly. "It's the fact that you didn't care enough for me to trust me with the truth."

With that, she turned and moved with an inbred dignity to the house, leaving him to stare after her in helpless confusion.

Chapter Seven

The scent of tobacco and the sound of a draw knife rasping over wood were warm and familiar. For a moment, Scott stood silent in the darkness just to savor them and the thoughts of a simpler time they evoked. A time when choices were easy. A time when the path was straight. He no longer had that luxury of clear-sightedness. Somewhere along the years, he'd lost the vision. He was running blind. And scared. And panic kept growing, compounded with the anguish that the farther off the path he strayed, the more those around him suffered for the failings of his feet.

There was a sudden scrape of wood on wood, and the arm of one of the porch rockers nudged his hip.

"Take a load off, pard. 'Pears the weight's too much to carry."

Scott shook his head at his stepfather's suggestion. He walked to the edge of the porch where he stood, still and tense, looking out over the night. Ethan took in the hard, inflexible solitude of his stance, then returned to his woodworking without comment. He shared his wife's worry over the boy, but he also knew there was no sense in prodding a Kincaid until they were of a mind to budge. And Aurora's son was very much a Kincaid. After all the years of living with and loving his tempestuous wife, he'd developed a monumental amount of patience and a tolerance for that inherited bullheadedness. Not an understanding, just a peace-preserving acceptance. And so, he waited, and would wait all night if need be, for the boy to speak of whatever was pressing so mercilessly down upon his shoulders.

"Daddy, you got some kind of cure for terminal stupidity?"

Ethan didn't look up. "That what you're suffering from these days?"

"I've made such a mess of things."

You did? All by yourself? Giving yourself an immodest amount of credit there, aren't you? Sometimes things manage to get all tangled up by themselves."

"If that's so, I've been doing my best to help them along." The magnitude of his sigh made his unbending shoulders gradually lift then drop abruptly. "I just can't sort it all out."

"Maybe you just got the wrong approach. Start by looking to your heart."

"Daddy, I'm so torn up inside, breathing causes me more pain than I can handle. Nothing seems to want to mend no matter what I try. You're the healer. What am I going to do?"

Ethan set aside his knife and gave full attention to the uncompromising brace of the younger man's form. He wasn't sure the boy was ready to listen yet — but he had asked, so he would answer.

"It's the shoes."

"Shoes?" Scott turned slightly, impatience creasing his taut features. "What have my shoes got to do with anything?"

Ethan leaned back in the chair, tipping it on the rockers. "It's like I was telling your mama. Here she's got a figure that's all rounded in the right places. Why would she want to buckle on some strangling cage of convention to change what there's nothing wrong with in the first place. Because some feller over in France or New York thinks that's the way she should look? Who are they to her? Why should she go around wheezing with her — um — assets shoved up under her chin and lungs squashed against her backbone just because some folks who aren't important to her say it should be so? Hell, I'd much rather latch on to a piece of woman than be snapped at by some steel trap."

"Daddy —" Scott was plainly irritated by the digression. The big Texan was making light of his situation. He didn't care about his mother's corsets. He knew she didn't even wear one. Said she wouldn't be caught dead suffering for the opinions of others. Then, abruptly, his annoyance stilled. And he listened.

"Now you take them shoes. They a comfortable fit? Feel like you could run a mile in 'em? Or do they pinch your toes so bad they ache clear up to your eyebrows? A body would expect to see a fancy Boston lawyer wearing shoes like that. But happen you was to take them off. That make you any less good at what you do? Is it the shoes or the man in 'em?"

Scott was silent for a moment then said, softly, "Sometimes it's the shoes."

"At first, maybe. Then, I guess it depends on whether you want to be comfortable with what's on the outside or what's on the inside."

"I'm not sure what's on the inside anymore." He angled back toward the impartial darkness to hide the evidence of his distress.

"The boy who left here knew."

"That boy was naive about a lot of things."

"What kind of things?"

"About the way he viewed his father and his father's people."

"What's changed that?"

The jaw-gripping tension came over him once more. Ethan wasn't sure what he saw most in him at that moment, his mother's independent will or his father's arrogant pride. Either way, the barriers were back up to prevent the easy flow of conversation, and he wasn't sure if he was angered by it or simply saddened. He could feel his son's hurt, could feel it pulse from him like blood from a mortal wound, but there was nothing he could do to stem the flow unless he knew the source of injury. And Scott wasn't talking.

"You want to heal yourself, boy? Then you start with the truth, with what you know in your heart is right. Start by telling it to yourself and it'll be a lot easier to tell it to those around you. And those that love you, well, that ain't going to change no matter what you say."

"But what if I disappoint them?" It was a quiet question, spoken from that battered heart.

"Then, you do. They'll get over it. You're not responsible for their expectations, Scotty. The only one you're beholden to is the man inside."

"The major wants me to stay the summer to do some legal work for him."

The sudden announcement made Ethan frown. "That ole bandit? Just make sure what he's got in mind is legal, you hear. You fixing to stay, then?"

A slight nod.

"Well, that'll make your mama mighty happy. What about your little lady? How's she feel about it?"

"She's going to go on ahead to Boston."

Ethan heard the ripping undercurrents in that statement but, for the moment, let it alone. "If she was inclined to stay on, we could make room for her here."

Scott made an improbable sound. "Mama'd have her hair lifted by the end of the first day."

"I don't know. Might do 'em both a sight of good. Consider her invited, for the summer and for dinner tomorrow night. 'Bout time we got the two she-cats in the same room to get used to each other. Might be the last chance if Miss Trowbridge leaves the day after."

Scott swiveled. "You're planning on coming to the wedding, aren't you?"

Ethan's smile was bland. "If you're fixing to go through with it, I reckon we'll be there."

If.

Scott hadn't thought of his marriage as an "if" proposition before. It had been settled and sealed with his words to Gena's father and their pledge to one another. But Boston and the vow spoken there seemed so far removed from this land of rolling green and cloudless sky. From the gaunt, despairing images that haunted his soul. A commitment that wore almost as uncomfortably as his narrow imported leather shoes.

When Scott didn't arrive to join them for dinner, Gena wasn't surprised. She was disappointed. Hurt. Upset. But not surprised.

After she'd left him with the buggy, she'd been tormented by a replay of the day's discovery. Scott had deceived her. He had hidden the fact of his Indian blood beneath a careful cloak of half-truths and her own naïveté. He'd used both to his advantage. How that bruised her confidence. How that tarnished the selfless ideal she held of him. She had loved him for his openness, for his honesty, for the way he considered her feelings. Knowing the truth, was there anything left for her to love? How her heart cried out with the pain of that betrayal. This once, she'd thought herself safe. She'd thought he would have a care for her. She'd let herself be lured from her cautious inhibitions, from her repressed fear of men. She'd let him coax her with his quiet court and disarming smile into placing faith above apprehension. And he'd shattered it most cruelly. Her first instinct had been to retreat and nurse the wounds the shredding of her belief had inflicted. But from that deep, tremulous well of anguish came a stunning jolt of anger.

How dare he!

How dare he court her with lies? How dare he have so little faith in her affection?

Nettled by these thoughts, she paced the broad-shadowed porch, berating him in her mind for his cowardice. Chafing at her own that kept her from pursuing him and demanding an answer. She was so caught up in these inner turmoils, she was unaware that she was no longer alone upon the cool veranda. When she took a sudden agitated turn, she nearly collided with an unsuspected companion.

"Oh!"

"Do forgive me, Miss Trowbridge. I didn't mean to startle you. It's just that you looked so plagued with troubles, I thought you might benefit from a friendly ear."

Gena smiled absently at Horace Billings. The idea of unburdening her heart to him was as unlikely as it was impossible. She searched for the means to dismiss him without inviting any undo curiosity.

"Thank you for your concern, Mr. Billings, but you needn't have worried. The problem is not mine. I've been unable to forget the dismal plight of those imprisoned by poverty."

Emboldened by her frailty, Horace claimed, "You should not have exposed yourself to such unpleasantness. My cousin was most remiss in his duty to protect you. While he may be familiar with the harshness of this uncivilized situation, it was quite uncaring of him to force it upon one of your delicate constitution."

Gena struggled with her annoyance. Her voice was a touch more strained then its usually soft concord. "It is not my constitution that disturbs me. It is my con-

118

science. But you would not understand, having chosen to blind your eyes to the cruelty of circumstance."

Horace missed her point completely, and his anger over the insensitivity of Scott Prescott rose to an unbearable degree. So moved was he by the gentle Gena Trowbridge's discomfort, he was provoked into an unintentioned declaration.

"Were it my ring upon your finger, this whole experience would have been spared you."

Gena stared up into the suddenly fervid pale eyes. Surprise totally blanked her to a response. He took her immobility for encouragement and continued his unexpected confession.

"Surely you must know how much I respect and admire you, Miss Trowbridge — Gena. I find you a veritable saint among womankind and I am deeply distraught by the idea of you in distress."

Finding her voice, Gena said, "If that is true, please say no more."

"But I must. I have been silent for too long. And in my silence, I have driven you into the arms of an unworthy other."

Dazed by the embarrassing absurdity of it all, Gena could only shake her head in protest.

"I know he is my cousin, but I have recently come to suspect that he is no true gentleman possessed of the standards one requires in a mate."

"Mr. Billings!"

Abruptly, he seized her hands. His thin mustache was quivering with passion. "I cannot let you continue in this unfortunate alliance. In all good conscience, I feel it my duty to warn you—"

"And I'm a-warning you, friend. I suggest you take your hands off my brother's gal afore I'm motivated to show you jus' what we folks 'round here think of them what runs another man's brand."

119

Regardless of the lack of malice in the amiable drawl, Horace Billings dropped Gena's hands as if they were red-hot. His face as bright as Rory Prescott's hair, the flustered easterner mumbled an incoherent apology and fled for the safety of the house. The young cowboy grinned affably.

"I hope you don't think I was overstepping myself there, Miss Gena, but I can't abide a coyote sniffing around a henhouse. Something about it jus' galls me something fierce. If I was intruding, I do apologize." For all his humble shuffling, there was a keenness in his dark eyes that called for an explanation. She was his brother's fiancée and he'd just interrupted her entertaining the devotions of another man.

"I feel I should apologize, Mr. Prescott. Your cousin took me quite off guard. I had no idea—"

"It's Rory, ma'am," he cut in. "Mr. Prescott's my daddy and he don't like answering to it either."

Gena began to smile her relief but was inexplicably taken by tears. Seeing the dampness well in her pretty blue eyes unnerved the cocky cowboy. While he was at home courting them, the realm of comforting a female quite terrified him.

"Now there's no call to turn on the waterworks, Miss Gena. I ain't gonna say nothing to Scotty."

Mortified by her loss of control, Gena fished for her hanky then gratefully accepted a huge linen square with which to dab at her streaming eyes.

"It's not that, Mr. Pres—Rory."

Absolved from having caused her distress, Rory immediately shored up his masculine pride with a growl of, "If that varmint upset you—"

The touch of her small hand upon his arm had an instantaneous effect. He swallowed hard and grew as red and awkward as a boy. "Ma'am, if you're fretting over what he was a-saying about Scotty, you can put your mind to rest. There ain't no finer man than my brother."

"I met his grandfather this afternoon." She surprised herself by speaking aloud, then was glad she'd done so. The burden of anguish had grown too much for her to bear in silence.

"You mean Yellow Bear. Heck of a feller, ain't he? Scotty, he thinks the world of that old man."

"Then why didn't he ever tell me about him?"

Rory blinked. "You mean to say he never told you— He went and asked you to marry him without ever telling you—" He gave a low whistle, then murmured something that sounded like, "And I thought I was the dumb one."

"Then, Scott's mother was married to an Indian."

Rory hedged and muttered, "You'd best be hearing that from Scotty."

"He won't tell me anything and I have to hear it from someone. Would you rather it be from strangers?"

Rory shifted uncomfortably, caught between his loyalty to his brother and his belief that the pretty lady had a right to know what she was asking. She was regarding him with such a gentle intensity, it made him squirm. That, combined with the fact that she was so danged fine looking, Scott really didn't have a chance in the brief war of indecision.

"I still thinks he should be telling you this," he mumbled.

"So do I, but I have no intention of waiting until I'm gray to hear about it."

Rory grinned. His gaze reassessed Gena Trowbridge. On the outside, she was all starch and stays and porcelain frailty, but he was beginning to suspect that inside lurked more than even Scott bargained on. And he anticipated his brother's surprise with a genuine delight.

"Well, Miss Gena, seeing as how you got me hogtied into it, might as well paint it proper. Sit yourself down and I'll tell you what I know."

Feeling a mix of apprehension and relief, Gena positioned herself on the edge of one of the porch's wicker chairs and waited for Rory to begin. The big cowboy ambled over to the rail and looked off toward the Lone Star as he started the telling in a low, subdued tone.

Gena listened in a horrified fascination to the story of a young Aurora Kincaid en route to the Bar K after years in the east when the coach in which she was riding was set upon by renegade Sioux. She, alone, survived the slaughter of the other passengers and was taken captive by the proud warrior Far Winds, son of Chief Yellow Bear. For a year, she endured life among the nomadic tribe as they roamed the Black Hills in search of food until, finally, the chance for escape came. Heavy with child, she found herself in the hands of unscrupulous trappers, and it was Far Winds who saved her from their mean intentions with the forfeit of his own life. It was then she was discovered half-frozen along a trail by Ethan Prescott as he was checking traplines.

"Daddy took her in and delivered Scotty in his cabin whilst a blizzard had them snowed in tight. Then he brought them down out of the Hills to the major."

Rory scuffled his feet, and Gena knew him well enough to recognize the signs of an awkward evasion. How much more to the tale was he not telling?

"To trim the fat off it, Scotty was taken back by Yellow Bear, and to bargain for his return, Mama and Daddy had to promise the chief that he'd be raised knowing his father's people. Danged if I didn't think he was the luckiest son on earth getting to run wild in the Hills like an Injun. 'Course Mama wouldn't hear of me going with him. Think it worried her something fierce every time he went up to Yellow Bear's camp, scared he wouldn't come back home."

Gena puzzled over the images his words created. She

couldn't conjure up a picture of Aurora Prescott scared of anything. Any more than she could imagine her living amongst the Sioux or giving birth in an isolated cabin. She couldn't imagine any woman surviving such ordeals. And a deep respect was fostered in that moment for Scott Prescott's mother.

"By the time we was little more than boys, all that Ghost Dance trouble started brewing and Mama was afraid Scotty'd be caught up in it. That's when she packed him off to the east. And that was the last we saw of him, till now." A quiet sadness weighed his words, a loneliness in surprising contrast to the carefree cowboy he portrayed. "I lost nine years of having my brother beside me, and it appears to be a goodly number more afore I see him again. Don't get me wrong, now. I'm danged proud of what he's gone and done for himself. Jus' wish he could have done it closer to home, is all. He's about the best friend I got in this world, and anybody thinking to make bad talk about what he is or isn't, well, they got me to deal with. And I take it right personal."

He pivoted on his heel and leaned back against one of the porch posts. Though his posture was easy, there was an unswerving directness to his dark gaze and a solemnness to his manner.

"And now that you know all this, whatcha meaning to do about it? Turn your back on him and you ain't half the woman I think you are."

His bluntness brought a blush to her cheeks, and his words, a seriousness to her soul. What was she going to do? With as much confidence as she could muster, she replied, "I have no intention of turning my back on your brother."

Rory's smile was small and not as reassured as she'd hoped. "That's right easy to say now. But what you gonna do when talk starts up in the east about what Scott is? Your daddy still gonna want him for that fine job? Your

123

friends gonna invite you to their fancy homes? Whatcha gonna do the first time your little boy comes home a-crying cuz somebody called him a half-breed?"

Gena's expression was stiff and as unconvincing as her argument, "Mr. Prescott — Rory, things are not like that in Boston."

"Beggin' your pardon, ma'am, but they's like that everywhere. Scotty's been listening to it all his life. Why do you think he was in no hurry to tell you the truth? Would you have been so all-fired up to wear his ring if you knew from the get-go that his daddy used to snatch the scalps off white women and children? That he used to ride bareback in next to nothing with his face all painted up, learning how to do the exact same thing?"

Gena's pallor was his answer. From that stark white, her huge eyes shone like big bright blue glass buttons.

"Now, I ain't trying to scare you off. I jus' think you need a passing understanding of what it's gonna be like. He's gonna count on you, and if you buckle under him, he's gonna go down hard and hurting. And I don't want that happening to him. You put your mind to it, I think you'll do jus' fine."

"Apparently you have more faith in me than your brother does," she said softly, not knowing which of them was right; Scott for his caution or Rory for his confidence.

"He brought you, didn't he? He had to know there was more than a passable chance of you finding out the truth. If he'd wanted to keep it from you, he'd a kept you safely tucked away in Boston, none the wiser. Scotty always said I got a big mouth, and I believe he's right on that. So afore I goes flapping it any further, I best be saying goodnight."

While she sat in silent thought, he came away from the rail and swaggered over to plant a quick kiss to her cheek. Her hand flew up to touch the spot, and he grinned at her surprise because there was no censure in the look.

"I think you'll prove out jus' fine, Miss Gena Trowbridge. Jus' fine."

However, as she sat in still shadow long into the hours of evening, she couldn't make herself believe him wholeheartedly.

Chapter Eight

There was nothing impressive or attractive about the town of Crowe Creek. It was named, not for the proud Indian tribe, but for a cantankerous miner, Jonah Crowe. In the belief that he'd found color in the shallow, sandy-bottomed stream that trickled through the area, he'd boasted loud and clear in a raw, rugged Deadwood about his claim to glory, only to catch the interest of a trio of greedy brothers. They followed the luckless Crowe back to the winding creek and murdered him for his fortune. A fortune they never found in thirty years of sluicing and panning. Others, intrigued by the trio's fervor, crowded into the region and the first rough buildings sprouted. The town, posthumously honoring the slain miner, continued to grow despite the fact that no trace of gold was ever brought out of the tons of sandy soil they sifted. By then, the coming of the railroad was an incentive for survival, and Crowe Creek became a valuable spur to the sprawling cattle spreads as the closest sight of civilization short of the trading centers on reservation land.

Crowe Creek had everything necessary to the needy farmer and cowboy. Its wide street sported an architectural hodgepodge of false-fronted buildings. It had three mercantiles and a dozen specialty shops, a newspaper, two hotels, six saloons, several back-street bawdies, a schoolhouse, a proud Episcopal and modest Baptist church, a doctor who filled prescriptions and sold soap out front and patched gunshot wounds in back, a barber who offered hot baths for 25 cents — soap and towel included — a blacksmith and livery. And a half-dozen lawyer shingles. It was still a relatively simple matter to gain acceptance to the frontier bar, and routine settlement of land claims earned from $100 to $1,000. Some of those practicing had little knowledge beyond the classics of the profession: Blackstone's and Kent's *Commentaries* that anchored the field from as early as '63. After speaking with several of them in the course of the morning, Scott came to the conclusion that they were, for the most part, content with those narrow limits. It was like practicing medicine with a Green River blade instead of with a scalpel, and the indifferent ignorance made him grind his teeth. There was something about the atmosphere in Crowe Creek that was as unfriendly as its founder and as inhospitable as those who had sent him to his unexpected reward.

But then, he hadn't come to Crowe Creek to pursue a career or study the competition. He'd come to visit several of the stores along the broad, shaded walk. One of the parcels tucked beneath his arm contained a pair of $10 boots. Replacing his rolled-brim felt derby, a fine $20 Stetson settled comfortably atop his ears. It was as black as his short-cropped hair and banded in silver, an unlikely accessory to his crisply tailored suit. He dipped the brim to those he passed on the sidewalk, aware that their initial smiles of greeting became puzzled stares and surly scowls directed at his back. A back he kept purposefully straight as if impervious to the prick of those barbed glares. He walked with his head high, funneling off their whispers the way he'd drain rainwater with the shaped brim of his hat. But neither outward gesture meant he wasn't bothered. He just refused them the satisfaction of knowing it.

"Yo, Scotty!"

The enthusiastic cry peeled along the covered walk like a resounding canyon echo. And those who hadn't yet made the connection between the swarthy-skinned easterner and the half-breed Prescott boy were abruptly reminded with a displeased yank of memory.

Scott paused to let Rory catch up to him. He couldn't miss the shine of pride in the younger man's eyes as he fell in step beside him.

"Nice hat. Whatcha doing in town?"

"Had to send off some telegrams for Grandfather."

"The major's right pleased that you're helping him out."

Scott could have mentioned the hefty fee Kincaid was saving his pockets but he didn't. One didn't begrudge the payment of a debt. "And what are you doing here? Shouldn't you be out at the Bar K?"

"Heading that way. Might say I had some overnight business to tend to." He grinned, and Scott shook his head in mock disapproval.

"You ought to get yourself a decent girl and quit spending all your money on cheap distractions."

"Don't see how getting the one would stop the other—and anyhow, there's nothing cheap about it. And speaking of having yourself a steady gal . . ." Rory let that trail off with a meaningful drawl. He was smirking to himself when Scott cast him a glance.

"Well?"

"Being as I'm a feller who minds his business, I can't in good conscience say."

Scott snorted at that. "Rory, you hold things in about as well as a bucket that's been kicked over. Now, what are you talking about?"

"Only if I had a pretty little gal I was fixing to marry, I wouldn't like some other jasper sniffing around her skirts."

Scott braked so suddenly Rory found himself looking back over his shoulder. And what he saw made him mighty glad he hadn't greeted his brother that first morning with an arm about his fianceé. The only comparison that came to mind when he found himself pinned by Scott's golden glare was that he was suddenly staring down into the molten center of a volcano about to blow. He'd forgotten just how lightning fast his older brother could move when fingers nabbed his shirtfront and jerked him forward nearly off his feet.

"You'd best make some quick talk, Rory, and it better not be some fancy fiction on your part."

Though secure in the fact that Scott would never do him harm, Rory had to admit to a curious alteration in his heartbeat. If he'd held any doubts as to how the other felt about Gena Trowbridge, they were answered in an instant. And he grinned in the face of monumental danger.

"You got a tolerable mean streak of temper in you, big brother. 'Less you're fixing to shuck the shirt right off my back, lemme loose. I can't make free with my tongue whilst I'm strangling in my collar."

The tension eased from Scott in slow degrees. Finally, his hand opened and Rory took a quick, precautionary step back.

"Talk." The single word cracked like a snap from the hammer of a Colt Peacemaker.

"Happen I came across Miss Gena and our cousin Horace last night. He was making some mighty sweet sounds trying to coax her off your range and onto his."

Silence. Then a deadly drawl. "And was she listening?"

Rory snatched off his battered hat and slapped it at his brother's head. Scott grabbed his new Stetson, scowling fiercely as the redhead began his berating.

"For someone with all your claim to brain, you don't show the sense of a seam squirrel. Why in tarnation would she listen to the blow and bawl of some skinny basket-tail when she's got Prescott prime on the hoof all saddle-broke and ready to ride?"

Before his brother got to looking too relieved, Rory

shuffled his feet and muttered, " 'Course it's none of my business, but she did seem a mite lathered up. Could be wrong. Did look like she'd been a-crying over something. Maybe she's just all het up about leaving tomorrow, going all that way back to Boston without you. Then, I reckon she's got good ole Cousin Horace to see she don't get the lonelies too awful bad."

Rory could have sworn he heard the crack and grind of his brother's teeth. His own jaw ached with the effort of restraining his smile. Let the fool stew in his doubts a while. He deserved that for making Miss Gena cry. Of course, it was none of his business.

"Well," he drawled out long and lazily, "guess I best be getting back to the Bar K. Anything you want me to tell the little lady for you?"

"Supper at the Lone Star at seven," Scott growled out.

Rory did grin, then. "I'll bring her on out myself."

They'd begun to walk again, Scott in a stiff, proddy stride and Rory with an easy amble. Until they passed a couple of ranch hands lounging in the awning shade outside the hotel.

"What's that stink?" one of them said loudly. "Danged iffen it don't smell like Injun. You think one of them mangy, thieving critters jumped the reservation?"

The other made as if to look alarmed, and swung his gaze about so that it lingered with insulting purpose over Scott. "Don't see any blanket Injun. Jus' this here fine city dude with his polished shoes and starched shirt. Must be your nose is wrong, Tandy."

The burly fellow shook his head and argued, "No sir. That's a smell you don't forget. Can cover it up as much as you want with cologne and hair oil and it still seeps out like something gone bad on the vine. That stink of man-killing, woman-raping, horse-stealing Injun."

Rory jerked up at that. His big hands crunched into fists as he whirled toward the offenders. The fury graining

130

his face into hard, savage lines slackened in surprise when Scott gripped his arm and said low, "Keep walking, Rory."

"What? What! You ain't gonna take that from the likes of them!" His hot gaze flickered from the sneering grins of the cowpokes to his brother's stoic expression. "Scotty, we can't just walk away."

"We can and we will." He continued on, fingers biting into the other's muscular forearm, towing him like he would a truculent mule. Rory's heels grated on the boardwalk as he twisted to glare at the smirking loungers. His breath seethed from him in quick, hard pants of disbelief.

"Tole you he was yellow. They all are, 'lessen it's fifty to one. Or agin a woman."

Rory pulled mightily, trying to break free. "Dang it, Scotty, lemme go. He can't talk to you like that. I'll shove them words so far down his throat, he'll be eating 'em for breakfast tomorrow."

By that time, they'd come to a side street and Scott yanked him around the corner. Even out of sight, the hecklers' laughter followed. It was enough provocation for Rory to round on his brother in a frustration of temper.

"What is wrong with you? How could you let them go on like that? We could have taken 'em, easy."

"Them and all the others like them? You think pounding on them would change their thinking any? If it would, I'd go at it with both barrels. But it wouldn't, Rory. It wouldn't change a damned thing."

Rory took a long look at his brother and backed his anger down. For the first time, he saw the cost of his brother's control etched in harsh angles upon his face. Rage smoldered in his gaze, but with it was a resigned futility. And it was that deep, unspoken anguish the young cowboy felt the sharpest. And it made him all the madder because it made him so helpless.

"Yeah, well, it would have made me feel a whole hell of a lot better," he grumbled.

Scott cocked a smile at his impatience. "Let it roll off you, Rory."

"That's easy for you to say."

"No. No, it isn't." It never had been and it never would be. It was the way things had to be.

And Rory understood without further words between them. He'd grown up seeing the hatred and disgust aimed toward his half-brother. When he was younger, he hadn't known why that was—but Scott accepted it, so he pretended he did, too. He didn't see a dirty, stinking savage when he looked into the bronzed face. He saw the older brother he'd gazed up at the way he did the noonday sun. The older brother who taught him how to ride and stalk game and swim and curse fluently in two languages. And it didn't matter that they had different fathers. They'd been raised under the same roof, by the same hands. He'd accepted Scott's differences unconditionally because his love for his brother blinded him to them. And he'd started fighting those who flung it in his face when he was six. By the time he was nine, he was so much bigger than the other boys, none dared whisper a reproachful word, not within his hearing, anyway. And by the time he was ten, Scott was gone and they'd forgotten. He hadn't. He never forgot the wild pleasure of swooping down across the plain, hanging for dear life onto Scotty as he leaned half off his pony, firing pretend arrows at his grandfather's cattle as if they were buffalo. He never forgot the shadow he could never stretch enough to fill.

Because there was nothing he could say to express the bitter emotion in his heart, Rory silently clapped his hand down on his brother's shoulder and squeezed. Hard.

"You'd best be getting to the Bar K before Grandfather has you mucking stalls."

Rory forced a smile he didn't feel. And words that couldn't measure the constriction seizing up inside him. "I'll see you tonight, big brother."

Scott watched him saunter off, then began to lash his purchases behind the smooth sloped seat of his saddle. His thoughts were gnashing on unpleasant images: the jeering cowboys, Horace Billings fawning over Gena, the stricken look in his mother's eyes when she'd first seen him standing in the door. His mood was as nettled as a burr beneath a blanket. Everything seemed to rub him raw. As he stepped up into the saddle, he was seized by the want to ride down upon the good-for-nothing saddle tramps to count a venomous coup, then to continue on to the Bar K to stretch Billings's mousy hair upon a hoop. Dark, unseemly savage thoughts for the man inside a civilized suit and tight shoes. Fitting thoughts for the son of Far Winds, descendant of the Miniconjou Sioux.

Instead, he headed out of Crowe Creek at a dignified lope, not needing to look right or left. Their stares crept over him like a bad rash. The moment he cleared the last building, his heels lashed back, startling his mount into a plunging gallop that sent dust and his disgust in his wake.

After a mile of headlong anger, his fury released the bit, and he eased the winded horse back into a slow trot. He was breathing just as hard and felt just as lathered. It did him good to blow. The sun was hot, broiling his brow beneath the black hat. He jerked open the stiff collar of his shirt and tore the first few buttons free. Eastern convention didn't wear well in the west. It stifled what was meant to lay bare before sun and breeze. He recalled his daddy's words with a grim smile. Smart man, Ethan Prescott. Dull man, his adopted son.

What the hell was he going to do about the complicated turns his life was taking? He wished it was as easy as changing shoes. Or as simple as shedding skin. Both were pinching tight and would give him no relief. But it wasn't.

What the hell was he going to do?

Distracted by his dire musings, he almost didn't see the figure afoot until nearly trampling over it. Or rather her.

133

In some surprise and a good deal of delight, he recognized the slender maiden Morning Song. He reined in quickly and was warmed by her expression of welcome.

"Lone Wolf."

"What are you doing way out here, by yourself and on foot?" From the added height of horseback, Scott scanned the ridges but could see no sign of a broken-down conveyance or lamed horse.

Pushing a strand of damp hair from her forehead, Morning Song smiled. "I am on my way to work. I clean for a woman in Crowe Creek twice a week."

He examined her dusty moccasins and damp blouse. "But that's a good twelve miles one-way."

She pinked at his concern. "I get a ride as far as the crossroads. It is only four miles. Not far for one in good health and strong limb. And it pays two dollars that my family needs."

Impulsively, Scott cleared one of his stirrups and put down his hand. "Today you ride all the way."

Morning Song took a step back and shook her head. She eyed the fine fabric of his suit. "No. That would not be good. You should not be seen with—"

"With whom? The sister of one of my oldest friends? I will take deep offense if you do not accept. Would you make me walk when you could offer me a ride?"

"No . . ."

He stuck out his hand again and waited. Finally, reluctantly, she slipped hers inside it and was brought, with one quick pull, up in front of him, as his parcels claimed the back. She settled sideways upon his thighs, one arm casually circling his waist and the other hand grasping a handful of mane. For a moment, Scott was stunned by his awareness of her unfettered female form. No layers of convention cased her willowy figure. It was thin fabric over pure woman; soft, warm, encouraging flights of imagination. And he knew exactly why his daddy preferred his mama without corsets. Feeling uncomfortably sensitized to the molding of her rounded bottom and the brush of her breasts against his chest and arm, Scott urged the horse forward, both dreading and anticipating the distance to Crowe Creek.

He'd been thirteen when he'd last seen Morning Song. He'd been old enough to be a warrior but not an adult in other senses. He remembered the sister of High Hawk as being thin as a stick in her butter-soft elkskins, with long, swift legs that could carry her faster than most of the boys. She'd had a vivacious smile and flashing dark eyes. He remembered thinking that they would one day marry. And that summer before he'd gone away, he'd followed her down the path where she walked alone to gather water from the creek and had tossed pebbles to distract her. Always before she'd stopped to talk with him, but on that last time she'd continued, walking even faster until the tears in her eyes made her stumble. He caught up to her and in a frustration of adolescent panic had kissed her with longing, and what he hoped would pass for experience. The taste of her mouth was sweet, just as the memory was yet sweet when he recalled it. And to pull himself from the thoughts of that kiss and the feel of the woman she'd become, he began to talk.

"You said your parents no longer live in the circle of the people."

"My father took an allotment of land which we now farm. Someday, the land will belong to him and no other can claim it. Is this not a good thing?" She sounded unsure, as if she was hoping he could tell her.

"It is the way of the white man," was his noncommittal response.

"When the land is his, then he will be a citizen of the United States. This is a good thing, too. Then we will not be Indians. We will be Americans."

135

"Is that what your father wants? To be an American instead of a Lakota?"

Morning Song sighed deeply. Her chest rose, rubbing the exquisite shelf of breasts along his body. "He wants to be a free man. Free of the reservation. Free of the white man's charity. High Hawk thinks he is a fool and has told him so to his face. You have been in the white man's world, Lone Wolf. Is my father a fool to hold such hopes?"

Scott spoke quietly, from the heart, where he, too, still held such hopes. "No. No man is a fool for wanting freedom or for doing what must be done to have it. It is each man's right to live with respect and dignity. There is none upon the reservation. Perhaps he will find it on his own ground."

Abruptly, she twisted toward him. She was so close, he could see himself reflected in the dark centers of her eyes. "The woman who was with you the other day, is she yours?"

"Yes." He had no want to expand upon that when her lips were scant inches from his own, but it was that, or lose himself to the temptation. "Yes. Gena and I are to be married in the east. That is where we will live and I will work."

She turned her head away but not before he saw the disappointment etched in her features. "I had hoped you would stay this time."

He didn't want to talk about leaving his home. Instead, he asked, "And you, Morning Song, have you a man who calls you his own?"

"I am still *winyan cokabti win.*"

A woman living among other women. It didn't seem possible. She was so lovely, too lovely not to have taken the notice of the tribe's young men. He could picture her standing outside her tipi at sunset, chaperoned by an elder female friend while eager bucks by the score formed a queue and waited for the chance to exchange words and hopefully gain favor. But she said

136

she had no one and he thought it must be by her choice.

In a voice so soft, it was like the whisper of the breeze, she said, "I had often wondered how it would be to dance the *nasloham wacipi* or the *hanwaci* beneath the blanket with you. Do you still remember the steps? And there were nights when I thought I could hear the sound of your *siyotanka* playing. But it was only the wind."

Scott was silent. Had he stayed, would he be dancing the Dragging Foot and Night Dances with Morning Song? Would he be playing her song upon the flagolet? Was that how it would have been if he hadn't gone east? Morning Song instead of Gena about to become his wife?

The irregular buildings of Crowe Creek had risen up before them. Morning Song began a disturbing wriggle upon his lap as she loosened her arm from about his middle.

"Put me down here, Lone Wolf."

It was still a walk to the edge of town and he knew she was thinking of how it would look, the two of them, together. The fact that she would have to worry made him irrationally angry.

"I'll take you right to the door."

"No," she protested, twisting toward him. Her slender palm fit to his cheek in a wordless entreaty. "Please. You would only make it more difficult. For both of us."

Considering her distress, Scott reined in. It shouldn't have to be this way. The unfairness of it growled through him but he held his words inside.

"If it's what you want, Morning Song."

She looked relieved and happy. The hand touched to his face moved in a lingering caress, charting the golden terrain in unashamed expectation. Then, while his breath sucked in in sudden anticipation, she leaned toward him. Her smooth cheek brushed his. Soft wisps of her hair caught on his mouth and tickled where his shirt collar was open. Around her slender form, his forearms had grown rock hard in an effort not to tighten about her. She leaned back, but only a few agonizing inches, far enough to claim the focus of his gaze within the dark, sensuous sphere of her own.

"Thank you for the ride," she said in a low, breathy way that made each syllable caress over his skin in the same enticing manner. Then, she began to slide and he shook himself free of her enchantment long enough to ease her down to her feet. She stood there, close, her breasts pressed to the swell of his leg, her fingertips grazing his knee. "Good-bye, Lone Wolf. Come visit us. Soon."

He sat his stallion, his eyes mesmerized by the belling dance of her short skirt about trim calves as she walked quickly toward Crowe Creek. Morning Song, who at one time might have been his.

Gena sat nervously beside an unusually quiet Rory Prescott as their buggy spun toward the Lone Star. The fact that she would be sitting at Aurora Prescott's table would have been intimidating under any circumstance. With the uncomfortable wedge between she and Scott, she looked upon it with all the anticipation of the condemned. Tomorrow, she would leave South Dakota and Scott Prescott behind. And perhaps all her plans and hopes, as well. So much needed to be resolved before she stepped upon that train and she knew not where to begin.

He was half Indian. Gena had all night to think on what that might mean to her future. The consequences were frightening. Her blustery confidence about Boston's enlightenment was more for her and Rory's benefit than it was spoken with any degree of truth. The Massachusetts elite were wrapped in a social circle of snobbery that made what she'd experienced at the Bar K garden party trifling in comparison. She'd seen decent, likable individuals blackballed from polite company by the merest whisper of scandal — never mind the truth of it. One cultivated equal or superior associations, never ones that would lower the standards of acceptability. The tiniest flaw in bloodlines ruined a prospective suitor. Scott's was not a tiny blemish. It was a major stain.

While Indians were considered romantic subject matter in the east, no one would actually encourage their presence in the parlor. Opinion was distorted by the colorful dime novels which presented the red man as either a noble savage or a bloodthirsty heathen. Not the sort one would want to marry one's only daughter. She remembered Yellow Bear's skepticism about the honorable Friend of the Indian and was then recalled to a conversation in their very parlor room. One of the proponents of supposed equality of the populace had said that the intermingling of one half grain white to one hundred grain Indian was the element needed to improve the western savage. And had gone on to claim that ten grains of Indian to one hundred of white would be most injurious to the quality of the white race. She'd thought those numbers quite ridiculous then, but now they took on an ominous meaning. What kind of danger would they see in Scott Prescott with his full fifty percent Sioux blood?

What would her parents say? It was unlikely that her friends could be counted upon for their silence. The temptation for salacious gossip was too great. There would be no lucrative job at her father's company. No fine house in which to entertain their friends. No gracious social minglings. Worst of all, there could well be no marriage. By the time Scott returned to Boston, would she even be allowed to see him? Or would her parents insist she send him back his ring and all mementos impersonally through the post? She couldn't imagine them permitting the match once the truth was known. Did she have the strength to defy them on this very important matter? Should she?

Conflict caused an intense throbbing through her temples. She could feel, acutely, each of the eighteen pins securing her hair in high style. The boning of her collar rose imperiously to the line of her jaw, preventing her frantic swallowing while the tight strangulation of her corset contained her need for a cleansing breath. She clung to the hope that Scott would purge all doubts and fears. That somehow he held the magic to wipe away her anxieties. And she strained to see him as the buggy turned into the Lone Star yard, yearning for that sight of the familiar to dispel all panic.

And then she saw him highlighted upon the porch by the light from within. His dark head was bare, hair gleaming black like satin above his swarthy features. The stark white of his seven-button bib-fronted shirt accentuated the deep bronze of his complexion. Its long tails were tucked into a pair of blue Levi Strausses. Denim hugged to the powerful length of his legs right down to the shiny toes of new Cuban-heeled boots. He looked just like one of the lethally handsome heroes drawn onto the cover of *The King of the Lariat, Deadly Eye and the Prairie Rover, Bigfoot Wallace,* or any of the other tawdry dime-library titles she'd covertly read. And Gena knew a terrible dread. For this was not the man she'd been about to marry. This was the half-caste son of Aurora Kincaid.

Chapter Nine

After the overstuffed grandeur of the Bar K, Ethan Prescott's Lone Star Ranch was a subdued understatement. Its two stories, additions, and fronting porch were made of hand-peeled Dakota log. Its interior was rustic and sparse, settled by handcrafted furnishings that hunkered down comfortably before a wide-throated stone fireplace. The only embellishments were two paintings: a Remington and a Russell, both gifts from Scott. And on the wide mantel beam were three photos in wooden frames; one of a stiffly posed Ethan and Aurora Prescott in what she assumed was wedding finery and one of each son. Both were fairly recent, and Gena was momentarily bemused by the difference. Even oiled and slicked, Rory Prescott exuded deviltry. Scott's was his commencement picture. She carried a smaller likeness. He was smiling slightly and his eyes held that faraway longing as if he was thinking of home and family when it was taken. And now that she had seen both, she could understand the wistful look.

The Prescott home was — different. As different from the Bar K and her own showpiece dwelling as the Dakota buttes from Boston's hilly streets. It was an unfamiliar atmosphere, inviting a casual relaxation and unpretentious conversation. And surprisingly, she found she liked it. As much as she liked Ethan Prescott and his big redheaded son. Both were about as easy as a rope hammock strung in summer sunshine, coaxing her to sit a spell with her feet up. Scott's mother, on the other hand, was as restful as a seat atop her Sterling range. And the temperature just kept rising.

Aurora was dressed simply in a silk shirtwaist and un-bustled skirt. With her fiery hair brushed back into a casual knot, she presented a picture of capable, domestic beauty; and in comparison, with all her stiff ruchings, rasping satins and dainty point-lace, Gena felt ostentatious and useless for all but display. She wondered if Scott, too, made that unfavoring match, for there was a notable lack of expression when his eyes assessed her. She knew at once that she'd been foolish to try to impress the Prescotts with her expensive and frivolous wardrobe, not when they valued substance over show. This was the image they would retain of her after tomorrow: pretty, proper, and superfluous. How to change that in an evening? Or should she try? Was there no more to her than what they saw? An extravagant luxury in a utilitarian home. As unsuitable in their midst as a cluttered shelf of fragile bric-a-brac.

Suffering from that sense of displacement, Gena assumed the chair Rory pulled out for her at their table. Then, after she'd arranged the sweep of her skirts and settled, his broad fingers pressed lightly upon her shoulder, briefly, expressively, approvingly, to hearten her mood. When she glanced up, he gave her an audacious wink and her smile crept out in a helpless response. Then, it faded when she found herself facing her somber fiancé across the tabletop.

Scott had not so much as spoken a word beyond their initial greeting. His gaze was guarded and remote and she could take no encouragement from it on this, their last night together. It reminded her at once of their words on the Bar K porch, of the dissension of doubt that had settled

142

between them. She was no longer angry with him, but hurt and confused. And as a lady of the near twentieth century, she'd been taught the rules regarding etiquette rather than emotion. Uncertain of how to react, she relied upon the polite veneer of manners ingrained since she was old enough to sit at an adult table. Her smile was fixed, her pose demure, and inside she shook with a most discomposed terror. Because the teachings that served in the homes of governors, in the parlors of Boston's elite, made her appear vain and superficial in the present company. And she could feel Scott withdraw.

"So," began Aurora Prescott with a long, piercing stare, "what time do you leave tomorrow, Miss Trowbridge?" As if she couldn't wait to hurry her to the train and out of her son's life.

"Sometime before noon." She couldn't make herself look up at Scott. *Coward,* she chided, but her eyes simply would not move upward from the table linen.

"I'm certain you'll be glad to shake the dust off your hem and return to what you're used to. You must find all this quite tedious after the gaiety of Boston."

She knew the woman was subtly baiting her, and suddenly, she could not resist an equally silky retort. Girding her resolve, she glanced at the disapproving matriarch of the Lone Star household and murmured, "Did you, Mrs. Prescott?"

Aurora caught her frown and replied, as if to a child, "Of course not, my dear. But then, I was raised in the west and love it despite its discomforts. Or maybe because of them. However, I'm sure it all seems quite inconvenient for you, being city-bred and all. And dreadfully dull."

The three Prescott men had their gazes glued to their plates but Gena could feel their attention. None of them were willing to come to her rescue, and she was disinclined to let them see her flounder and sink beneath the tidal surge of Aurora's civility.

"Oh, no. It is quite different from what I'm used to but fascinating, too. I have the feeling there's not enough time in the day to see all of nature's wonders." Purposefully, she did not meet Scott's glance when he recognized the use of his sentiments. She didn't want the distraction from her cautious duel with his mother, intuiting that a single slip could mean disaster. Aurora Prescott would be merciless toward any show of vulnerability. She could feel the older woman tensing, ready to pounce and finish the kill. And for all her trepidation, Gena was not of a mind to be added to the menu.

"I do regret not having the opportunity to know Scott's grandfather better."

"My father —"

"Excuse me, Mrs. Prescott. I wasn't referring to Mr. Kincaid. I meant his paternal grandfather."

There was immediate silence. To speak of Yellow Bear at the Prescott table was to throw kerosene onto an already dangerous fire. Aurora sucked in a lethal breath, but before she could expel her venom, Ethan chose the moment to make his casual announcement.

"The opportunity's yours if you want it, Miss Trowbridge. Like I was telling Scotty, if you're of a mind to stay on for the summer with him, we'd be happy to put you up. You could have Rory's room. 'Tain't much in the way of comfort, but it's there if you'd like to use it."

All pretended not to hear Aurora strangling on her surprise. Purposefully, Ethan paid full attention to the roll he was buttering and refused to meet his wife's murderous stare.

"That's very kind of you, Mr. Prescott," Gena murmured. She looked across the table to a very stiff and uncommunicative Scott, trying to discern if he was for or against the idea. It was like trying to read a foreign language. All was written there, plain to see, but she didn't know how to decipher it.

Finally finding her voice, Aurora said smoothly, "I'm sure Miss Trowbridge is anxious to get home to her family and friends."

Gena swallowed hard to dislodge the sudden blockage in her throat. "Yes," she whispered. "Of course." Her gaze fell to her plate, to the meal she knew she could not force beyond the constriction that knowledge wrought. Home. Where her mother and father waited. Where she would return to them, alone. Where she faced the possibility of a future beneath their roof, beneath her father's control if Scott should not return. She was suddenly cold all over, her will to spar with Aurora Prescott gone.

Sensing her victory, Aurora relaxed and turned the conversation to the members of her family. Gena listened, excluded and only partially attentive while they talked of things she knew nothing of: ranching, horses, local politics. If it was Aurora's intention to make her feel excruciatingly isolated from the warmth of their close-knit unit, she was successful beyond her wildest hopes. And when the meal ended and Gena offered her help in the kitchen, Aurora looked at her as if she'd be about as welcomed as diphtheria.

"No thank you, dear," she all but oozed. "I wouldn't want you to dirty your pretty dress. I can handle it perfectly well on my own."

Dismissed and dispirited, Gena found herself out on the Prescott porch, drawing in the pure prairie air and trying her best not to cry. She heard him before she saw him, sensed him the way she would a sudden hot breeze or a gathering storm.

"We need to talk."

She nodded, unprepared and suddenly frightened of what would pass between them. Gone was the sense of ease she'd had with the quietly intense Harvard student, and she wondered desperately how to reclaim it. But the wide-open grasslands and even the clothes he wore this

145

evening stood as a barrier to the familiar. Why had she ever insisted upon coming? She'd lost the very man she pursued. Standing beside her was a silent stranger in stiff denims, cowboy boots, and bronzed skin. A stranger who forced her to confront a plethora of stunning truths. About him. About herself. And a gaping stretch of uncertainties.

Everything had been so perfect in Boston. She'd been on the threshold of realizing her every dream. Scott Prescott with his gentle strength; handsome, considerate, kind beyond words. He was going to take her from her life of unfulfilled repression and nurture her to a fragile bloom. He'd calmed her fears with his lazy smile and tamed her with a tender, respectful touch. And oh, how she loved him and longed to become his wife. Then, they'd come here and the Black Hills had cast a cold shadow over her dreams. Here, he was subtly different. He hadn't changed so much as he had shown more of what he was. And that "more" disturbed the placid nature of her existence. Here, she had recognized in him a wildness and passion never expressed in the east. Here, he'd let the acceptable surface charm slip to show a completely altered face. One that was dark with mixed blood and mixed loyalties. One that held a savage heritage and threatened the stability of what they would build together. A facet of his nature that was foreign and frightening and stirred forbidden responses within her pure heart. How could she have felt so comfortable with a man she knew not at all? How had she come to the point of marriage to someone so completely different than her expectations? She'd thought she knew Scott Prescott, but what she understood was as shallow as the cool reflection atop a deep and dangerous pool. Since arriving in the Dakotas, she had slipped by degree beneath that glossy, pleasing surface only to have the undertows of knowledge pull and threaten. Her balance precarious, she was afraid to venture further but, yet, unable to retreat. And Scott, himself, was no help. He offered none of the support that would give her solid purchase. And so she struggled alone against the tides of truth and, as he came to stand beside her, in imminent peril of being swept away.

She felt it immediately, that undercurrent of unsettling emotion. This wasn't the reserved, restrained gentleman who'd used their five minutes alone each night to court her with poetic words. This was the potent, aggressively masculine man who had tempted her to open her mouth to his kisses and her thoughts to wanton desires. He was no longer a safe, nonthreatening symbol of home and security. He was a blatant, virile, overwhelming male. She'd felt the power of him through his shirtsleeve. She'd experienced the dark passions of him while in his embrace. And she was very, very afraid that what she had was as unpredictable and uncivilized as the broad plains that alarmed with their vastness.

Gena glanced down at the rail of the porch and saw his browned hands resting there. A nervous quiver shot through her when she thought of those same big hands on her body, holding her, stroking her passions into a shameless frenzy of emotion. He never would have touched her like that on her father's veranda or in their cluttered parlor. He never would have made such demands upon her heart, upon her mind, were they yet in Boston. It was this land, this part of him that she didn't know and didn't understand, that was blocking her hope for happiness. In Boston, the temptation would be removed, submerged and controlled. And she wouldn't feel so horribly agitated by the simple sight of her fiancé's bronze fingers. In Boston there was safety in the staid rote of propriety. She knew at all times what to expect, what to ask for. Here, she was lost and panicked.

The truth, the truth he'd kept from her, was going to ruin all her hopes for the future. The taint of scandal was going to spoil the life she longed to share with the silent figure beside her. Why did she have to find out? Why did he have to threaten all her dreams with that single damning truth? How could you, Scott? she thought wildly, irrationally. How could you destroy everything I wanted, I needed? How could you take away my only chance? A hot, blaming anger clogged her reasonings. Why did he have to be less than what he pretended? Why couldn't it have been the way it was in Boston? Why hadn't he kept it to himself, at least until they were safely wed? How could you, Scott? How could you risk everything now?

Because anger was an unacceptable expression, she forced it down and replaced it with a desperate clarity of thought. No one could know. No one could suspect until after the marriage. But Horace knew, or he'd intimated as much. And what of Beth and Caroline and the conversation she'd overheard between them? If they returned home and Scott remained behind, rumors would fly without check. Even without fact, the harm would be done. Her parents would forbid the marriage when Scott returned. If he returned. It was then she remembered the slender hand upon his sleeve, upon his thigh.

"Scott, you have to come back to Boston with me."

She said it softly, in a tone that defied the magnitude of the request. Deep inside, minute shivers of anxiety began. She clenched her belly and her limbs in an effort to still them, but they just kept building as the silence between them built. If he would say yes, there was a chance. Together, they could beat down the rumors. With Scott beside her, she could face them all with a dignified composure. If he would come, the threat would fade and be forgotten. At least that's the hope she clung to as she waited for him to speak. And when he did, that frail hope shattered.

"I can't."

Gena squeezed her eyes shut. Panic and pressure had her heart beating hard enough to burst her eardrums.

148

Don't make me have to beg you, Scott. Don't make me have to explain. She dry-swallowed the coppery taste of terror and whispered hoarsely, "Scott, please."

His voice was brusque, almost impatient. "Gena, we've gone over this. I thought you understood."

"I don't." On that shaky note of truth, she turned to him, uplifted eyes shimmering with distress. "You have to come back with me. So things can be the way they were."

His expression was very still, very quiet. "Can they, Gena?"

Her big blue eyes grew frantic and, unthinkingly, she reached out to clutch his wrists. Faintly, she registered his resistance to that desperate grasp but she couldn't afford to pay it heed.

"They can. They will. If you'll come with me. Tomorrow."

Gently, firmly, he twisted from her shackling hold. "What is it, Gena? Are you afraid of the truth my cousins carry back with them?"

"Yes." That was true. She was afraid. But deeper, an unspoken fear cut through her confidence, the fear that he would not follow. That once she was gone, the thrall of this land and of his father's people would not let him go. She couldn't face the possibility. It wasn't the disgrace. It was the desolation. How could she make him see that he was her salvation? That he alone could rescue her from what she couldn't bear to return to.

She saw a flicker of disappointment in his eyes and knew she'd let him down with that selfish claim. He took a step back, shutting her out even as he shuttered his expression. She was losing him. Frantic to cling to her fast-fading hope, she did the foolish, the unforgivable.

"If you love me, Scott, you'll come with me."

She saw his devastating answer even before he spoke it. "I'm sorry, Gena."

"You're not," she cried with a damning certainty.

149

"You're not sorry at all."

He stood stiff and silent, watching as she fled from the porch to the shadows of the yard beyond. Knowing she was right brought a terrible twist of guilt. But not terrible enough to change his mind. In that moment, Scott recognized his relief. He was glad not to be going back. Glad to be able to hold the scent of open spaces and independence in his lungs. If only for a little while longer.

But he wasn't sorry. Because he didn't love her.

He wished he did. How easy that would make things. How clear-cut, how convenient. Pretty, fragile Gena with the pedigree to offset the smear upon his own. Proper, innocent Gena, who had never suspected she was being deceived. He writhed with shame because he had used her, used her the way some did their fortunes, to buy their way into respectability. He'd picked the flawlessly serene Miss Trowbridge to appease his mother and his grandfather, to buy his way into the white world, to calm Aurora Prescott's fears and to win Garth Kincaid's approval.

He stared at her straight back and bustled behind and saw the rigidity of both form and female. Maybe he should go with her. Maybe if he ran far and fast, the scent of green grass and clear sky would leave him. Maybe he wouldn't be haunted by the sad spectacle of his father's people, by the shame he suffered beneath his grandfather's gaze, by the wistful longing for the past the sight of Morning Song quickened. Maybe he could escape these things. But should he? Should he settle for a shadowed half-life with a woman who woke no sustaining passion in his breast?

He was staying. He had no other real choice. It was more than his promise to Garth Kincaid. It was the shadow of one made by a cocky young man filled with fire and fierce pride. He needed that fire, that pride. He needed time. And he would never have any of them if he stepped on that train tomorrow. This could well be his last chance to rectify his wrongs, to resolve the dichotomy of

150

spirit at war within himself. His only regret was that Gena should suffer for it.

Slowly, heavy of heart, he crossed the yard.

"Gena."

Light from the house shimmered upon the quiver of satin as her shoulders shook. She would not turn around, so he took hold of her arms and brought her to face him. She was so pretty and pale, but it was pity not passion that moved him. Guilt teethed and tore at him as her great, grief-pooled eyes lifted. How in God's name had he allowed himself to bring such misery into her tender-spirited gaze. Gently, feeling wretched inside, he drew close. She hesitated, holding back, then let him gather her to his chest.

Just once, once, he wished she would come to him spontaneously, as if each small concession didn't cause a bartering of her mortal soul. He wished he could find within her a constant promise of delight and desire, that she would give as he longed to give, with unfettered feeling. But she could not and she would not. And the idea of dragging a response from her or pleading for just a scrap of affection left him barren inside. How could he have pledged himself to such a bleak future? One in which he would never know the kinship his parents shared. How badly he wanted that now, now that it was too late. Too late because he'd given his word and made himself responsible for Gena Trowbridge. Whether he loved her or not. Because she didn't deserve to be hurt. Because she couldn't be blamed for what she was or wasn't any more than he could be.

He held her, feeling the shiver of her misery, excluded by the hard curve of her corset, and was suddenly angry. Angry because this was all he would ever have, a stiff, reluctant shell of propriety within his arms. Angry because he had nothing but emptiness to return to in Boston, a loneliness so deep he despaired of it to the depth of his

151

soul. Because he couldn't please them all and still have some happiness of his own.

Abruptly, he held Gena away. He studied her wan features, her slender artificially shaped figure and tried hard to summon a lasting sentiment. Some feeling that would keep him from straying into the supple embrace of another after she had gone. He'd felt it spark once beneath his grandfather's cottonwood tree, but she'd refused to let it flame. Maybe now, now that time was running down to a handful of hours, she would relent and let passion reign. She would give him reason to hope.

Love me, Gena. Save me.

As if recognizing his need, a trembling hand was lifting to his face, fingertips shyly touching, awkward in their invitation. But it was an invitation. There was no mistaking it. And he responded, lowering his head until their breaths mingled, until their lips brushed, until a warming tongue of want tangled and teased and encouraged.

"Gena."

It was a low, anguished growl, promising excitement and threatening danger. She was tempted by both into putting her arms around his neck, into hugging close to the hard frame of his body, into meeting the hurried assault of his mouth with the tremulous part of her own. He crushed her face between his rough palms, ravaging her lips and beyond with an urgent inquiry. And though her stomach knotted and her flesh broke into a rash of apprehension, Gena made herself allow his increasingly bold caresses. His hands roamed across her shoulders and back and skimmed beneath her arms until her bosom was cradled in the vee of thumbs and forefingers. Her startled heart thrust against her ribs with a frightened bruising vigor.

Stop. Stop.

Let him or you'll lose him.

His hands were shifting, giving her a moment's respite

152

before plunging her straight to hell. Through the padded layers of skirt and petticoat, his fingers hooked about the backs of her thighs. In one impatient jerk, she was pressed flush into the hard proof of his intentions. Her shock was monumental. For a moment, she forgot to struggle as his arousal pushed against her belly and his head bent farther, bringing the hot sear of his mouth to command the puckered crest of her left breast.

"Don't!"

It was a fractured whisper but she might as well have screamed it. Both hands shoved him by the shoulders, and though she hadn't the strength to free herself from his embrace, he released her, not having the will to force it upon her. Breathing hard and teetering on the edge of control, Scott met her glazed expression. He'd expected reproach, even distaste, but never the shiny-eyed terror she confronted him with. It was more effective than a slap in cooling his unexpected ardor, confusing him enough to make him step away. And hurting him enough to tinge his words with anger.

"You better go, Gena, before something else happens that we'll regret."

Her heart was hammering, locking the words of apology in her throat. But before she could explain, or try, he had possessed himself of her hand and was towing her back toward the house. She had barely enough time to compose her features as he nearly jerked her up the steps to holler inside, "Rory, Miss Trowbridge is ready to go."

Then, there were quickly murmured thank-yous to his chill-eyed mother and perplexed stepfather and Scott was pushing her up into the buggy. He moved back far enough to cast his face in shadow, but even without seeing it, she could hear the awful finality in his tone.

"Good night, Miss Trowbridge. I'll be by to say my farewells in the morning."

Then, she was carried away from him into the night.

153

Rory kept his eyes straight ahead and his opinions to himself while Gena fought for a modicum of dignity. It was silent out on the plains, with only the distant yipping of the coyotes and lowing of Kincaid cattle to disturb the peace. That and the occasional hitch of breath from his passenger. After several suspicious snifflings, he fished into his pocket to produce his handkerchief.

"Thank you," Gena mumbled, then with a flat attempt at levity said, "I seem to be taking all your linen lately."

He muttered an appropriately vague response. *Scott, you incredible idiot. What did you do?* While uncertainty tightened in his chest, he kept his hands on the reins and prayed that she wouldn't start bawling. Mercy, what was he to do if she did? He urged the horse to a faster pace and looked ahead for the rescuing lights of the Bar K.

They hadn't gone far when the sound of rapidly approaching hoofbeats reached them. Knowing no one else who could ride in the dark with such all-out recklessness, a relieved Rory pulled in the horse so his brother could catch up.

"Mind changing places with me?" Scott asked, glancing over at Gena's averted profile.

"Not in the least," Rory replied in complete sincerity. He stood so Scott could step from stirrup to seat, then passed him the reins. "I'll have your horse cooling at the Bar K." He wasted no time scrambling up into the warm saddle and applied his heels. His grin lit the darkness like a brilliant new star.

Scott settled into the seat and started the buggy off at a leisurely turn. Though his gaze canted frequently to the side, he directed his attention to the business of guiding them along the smooth ridges and hollows. Each time he saw the flutter of white lift to muffle a snagging gasp, he felt a notch more dismal. As much as he'd tried to steel his heart against it, he hadn't been able to let her go without

154

some last effort to ease the hurt he'd caused her. To repair some of the raveling shreds of their relationship, as stiffly impersonal as it might be. He knew she was not without feeling and was equally aware of how he'd bruised them. He owed her a return of the knight gallant he'd played in Boston with such detachment. Only it was harder now, for some reason to pretend that indifference. Maybe because it had felt so good to kiss her. Finally, he let the horse find its own way and turned on the seat to regard her. Sensing his scrutiny, Gena shifted to present him with her back, where tiny pearl buttons trailed down from prim lace collar. He found himself staring at the web of spun-sugar hair pulled from her neat coif. He supposed his fingers had done the damage. Just as his actions had disheveled her spirit.

"Are you all right? Do you want to talk?"

With a surprising amount of stubbornness, she squared her shoulders and shook her head.

He continued to stare at the taut pull of satin, feeling her rebuff. Chafing at the rub of guilt, he snapped, "Dammit, Gena, look at me."

Slowly, she swung her knees about until they nearly brushed his. If he hadn't known her so well, he would have sworn her expression was positively mulish. But the moisture dotting her cheeks was self-explanatory.

"I'm sorry if I upset you." He reached up to scrub away those blaming tears, but her head reared back sharply in avoidance of his touch. He let his hand drop, working it in a helpless fist upon one denim-clad thigh. "I didn't mean to spoil our last night."

Our last night.

The words echoed through the great cavern of her remorse.

Scott sat, dismayed, while she doubled over, burying her face in his brother's bandanna. She sobbed with a force that had her shoulders jerking like a pump handle. A

155

jolt of emotion slammed through him. He assumed it was guilt but it felt like hell.

"Gena, don't cry."

Her response was a gusty wail. It dwindled down to a series of hiccuping sobs, and still she wouldn't look at him. She drew an immense breath in an effort to halt the weeping, but it spilled over into tiny, broken shivers of sound. He could only watch, torn and miserable, afraid she would reject any offer of comfort.

"Take me to the Bar K, S-Scott," she pleaded, straining the words through the square of damp cotton. "Please. I don't w-want you to remember me like this."

He felt an incredible pressure in his own throat at her pitiful attempt at bravery.

"I-I'm sorry. I don't mean to c-cry." But she did, on and on, until her entire frame shook with the mournful spasms.

"Gena . . . Gena, don't . . . hush now . . . don't cry." Gingerly, he put his hands upon her arms. When she came toward him with a limp gratitude, he folded her into a tender embrace. One big hand cupped her head, drawing it beneath his chin.

Gena wept until her entire body ached. She sobbed while the image of Morning Song's hand upon Scott's leg burned through her mind and tortured her heart. She cried when she recalled Scott's look of disappointment when she'd pushed him away. And she quite simply wanted to die from the battering echo of his words. *Our last night.* And how was she spending it? — sniveling on his shirtfront instead of enjoying his kisses. Terrified of the one thing that might bring him back to her.

She was near exhaustion. The grief abated in favor of a listless fatigue. Her arms dangled loosely over his shoulders. She could feel his cheek against her hair and his hand moving gently upon the back of her neck. With her breathing almost under control, she said chokily, "Oh,

S-Scott. I'm so sorry. I don't mean to be such a b-baby."

"Don't be sorry," he crooned quietly. He continued to hold her because she seemed disinclined to leave. There were no further words of consolation he could give her, so he gave the silence of his respect.

An achy heaviness had settled in Gena's chest. She knew it wouldn't help to hold to him. It wouldn't help to plead with him. He wasn't going back to Boston. Not now, with her on tomorrow's train. Not later, at the end of the summer. He didn't have to tell her. She wasn't sure he'd even thought that far ahead. But she could feel it. She'd known it in her heart the moment he'd looked out over the barren grasslands. She'd sensed it the minute they'd ridden through the Sioux encampment. The Dakotas would never surrender Scott Prescott.

"Everything will work out fine. You'll see. It's just for the summer, Gena. Just for the summer. Then things will be the way they were."

He spoke the words, the soothing lie neither of them really believed. Things would never be the same. Because he'd seen the fear in her eyes when she pulled from him in his parents' yard. Things would never be the same because she would never see him in the same way. What she saw now was not quite good enough to marry. Not good enough to bring before her parents with the truth.

He should have broken it off then, but he wanted to spare her the embarrassment of admitting it was her wish. It would be easier through the mail. Less personal. Not that they had ever been all that personal with one another. When he thought on it, this was the closest they'd ever come to true intimacy, with her sagging, tear-drained body upon his chest and him cuddling her tenderly like a cherished child. Her arms no longer hung loosely but had inched up to curve about his shoulders with an unconscious ease. It was the first time he could remember her ever being content to remain in his arms. And it felt good,

157

however brief. Even now, as she curled against him, he knew she would be hot with shame when she realized what she was doing and she would withdraw behind that cool, excluding reserve. Sadly, he wondered why she was unable to love him, why she couldn't respond to him with the same unrestrained honesty Morning Song had displayed that same day. If she had, perhaps he would be more confident they could weather the truth together. Perhaps he wouldn't let her leave without him. Perhaps things could work out.

But even as he considered it, he felt her tense within his arms. The small circles at the base of her neck had become a more insistent caress as his fingers continued on with his thoughts. Her skin was soft and warm along her throat and he could feel her frantic swallowing. What would it take to make her throw off the proper, to make her embrace passion's potential the way she had the night of his grandfather's party? He could make her want him. He knew he could. He could make her feel the same hot jets of longing shoot down her extremities the way they did his own. In an instant of sheer frustration, he thought of tightening his embrace, of tipping up her lovely face to kiss it into a wet and willing surrender. But she was pushing, lightly, determinedly, against his shoulders, levering for an impartial distance. His arms slackened. He let her sidle away on the seat to compose herself into the familiar rigid lines.

And he knew right then that any chance he might have had to stir a need inside her had died the moment the truth was known. No blueblood from Boston was going to allow liberties to a half-breed from the plains.

Expression set in inscrutable shadow, Scott lifted the reins and steered the buggy toward the Bar K.

Chapter Ten

It was late. Not even the camp dogs stirred when a silent shadow slipped by them. There were distant voices, slurred and drunken, and from somewhere the wailing of an infant. The outsider who moved among them added nothing to the evening sounds. He stepped lightly, gracefully, on feet as quiet as a cat's despite the awkward boots. He strode with a purpose and anyone seeing him would not have interfered.

Pausing outside the tipi of Yellow Bear, the stranger called, "Matogee, do you sleep?"

"Come."

The old man sat up on his sleeping mat, and after one glance at his visitor's face, he shook the sleeping woman at his side awake. She blinked groggily up at him, then to the still silhouette clad in white man's clothing. With a gasp, she straightened, then gave a sigh of relief when the figure moved into the light.

"Leave us, Red Bird," the old chief ordered.

Not arguing that it was the middle of the night and yet cool outside, his second wife wrapped a robe about her shoulders and slipped out to leave the two men alone.

"Sit. Talk."

The first Scott complied with easily, sinking down onto one of the willow frames and tucking his feet in La-

159

kota fashion. The second didn't come so easy. The words crowding his heart continued to swell into a pounding ache. He stared into the low fire as a huge pain welled inside him, choking him, bringing the sting of sorrow to his eyes. Yellow Bear waited, watching, knowing, as anguish strained and tightened the younger man's features. Finally, the old man spoke.

"It is not good for a man to hold such grief within his heart. Like a poison, it must be lanced so it can heal. Speak, Lone Wolf. For whom do you grieve?"

"I grieve for myself," came the hoarse, emotion-clogged truth. "I grieve for the loss of one who sat before you as a boy, speaking of honor and pride. I have not walked in pride. I have shamed you and my family. My soul cannot hold this sadness any longer."

"Free it, *takoja*. I will listen. Tell me of this shame you bear alone."

"I made you promises, *tunkasila*, but they did not sustain me. I was not brave."

"You were a boy of thirteen summers," Yellow Bear chided gently.

Scott's gaze lifted then, bright and glittering with misery. "I was old enough to claim a warrior's heart. And I allowed it to be broken by my fear."

"Tell me," the old chief urged softly.

Hurt piled upon hurt as Scott dragged back the memories, the stifling terror, the horrible aloneness, like nothing he'd ever suffered before. "The city was so big, so vast. So many white men and none of my own kind. There was no one there who knew about the grass and sky, none who had seen an eagle fly, none who had slept beneath the stars. There was so much hatred, so little understanding of our people. I — I was afraid to feel their hate. I was afraid to be alone and different. I pretended to be like them so they would embrace me as their own kind. I let them believe Ethan Prescott was my father,

160

and I put those things of the Lakota behind me so I might walk as a white man while among them."

"But you are white, *takoja*."

"But that is not all I am! I let them tear the pride for my father's people from my heart. I allowed them to strip the language of the Lakota from my mind. And when the news came of Wounded Knee, I could not grieve with honor for you, for *unci*, for my people. I had to hide my tears where no one could see them because I was ashamed for them to know I mourned."

He was silent for a moment, his head hanging, his heart breaking, his eyes dry and stinging even now for the tears he had not shed. The betrayal hurt. No, it tortured. As viciously, as mercilessly within his soul as his ancestors had inflicted pain upon their enemy. His face burned. His eyes burned. His chest burned. And his conscience scalded. He gulped back the sorrow that thrust inside him, swallowing it down because he was unworthy to express it here before this man he revered. He continued his confession in the tongue of the Sioux, in the language of his soul.

"I have strayed far from the path of my people. I am walking like a blind man. Help me to see where I am going, *tunkasila*. My weakness has brought you great shame. I would understand if you banished me from your lodge and from your heart. I await your judgment." He bent forward, the heels of his hands digging into his eyes, his rounded shoulders offering to bear the scourge of his failings. But it didn't come.

"Sit up," the old man barked. "A man does not breathe in the dust from others' feet."

Scott straightened, but his gaze remained upon the ground.

"You are without pride, Lone Wolf, if you come to me to have the guilt beaten from you. I cannot and I will not be your judge. No man who walks upright can rule over the acts of another. You are your own judge. No man can shame you but yourself." His voice gentled with affection. "You have not failed me, *takoja*. My heart is strong with pride when I see what you have accomplished. The fault is not yours for the difficulty of your path. You have always straddled two roads, but now they part and you must choose. I do not envy you that, nor can I choose for you. You must look to what beats within your own heart."

"That is what my mother's husband said."

"A wise man."

"A wise man knows what road to travel. I have not been granted that sight. Neither road holds anything that I can see. One would have me as half a man, living on lies. The other is like a sad shadow of the past with no hope for the future. The white man's path gives me no joy and the despair of my father's people makes me want to hide and pretend it does not exist. I am afraid to move forward yet I cannot stand still. Have you no knowledge to share with me so that I might see where I am to go?"

"Pray, Lone Wolf. Pray to the God of your heart and soul. And listen for what he would tell you. Do not be impatient. When I was a young man of your years, I went to a high hill. I cut the flesh of my chest, sang and chanted brave songs. I showed the sky the blood flowing from my body and prayed until dreams came. That was the old way. Release the shame that binds the truth and wait for it to come. It will come."

Scott took a great cleansing breath and nodded wearily.

"What of New Waw?"

Scott's sigh was expressive. "She leaves tomorrow to return to the east."

"You will let her go?"

"She holds no place in my heart."

"Is there another?"

He thought of Morning Song, of her dark inviting

eyes, but he shook his head.

"Yet you brought the pale one to me. I found her to be of brave spirit, of good heart."

Scott said nothing, the significance lost to him. Gena was leaving in the morning. He was staying. Between the morning and the end of summer, he had to find the right path in the midst of his confusion. Maybe then. He didn't know.

"You will share my lodge tonight, *takoja*. Sleep and free the demons in your soul. I will keep watch so they will not trouble your rest."

Scott smiled, remembering when similar assurances had comforted a boy about to embark on a frightening journey. And he remembered the dream. The dream that had come so terrifyingly true. He eased out of his new boots and settled upon his side. And he found himself reassured by the old man's presence just as he had been as a child. Gradually, his eyes closed and slept without dreams.

"I for one will be so glad to get back to civilization."

Caroline voiced her opinion loudly as their trunks were being toted downstairs. Beth didn't agree in so many words but she, too, was glad to be going. Gena trailed the two women at a slower, somber pace. They were anxious to get back to Boston but she had nothing to look forward to. The long summer months ahead. The endless anxiety, waiting to see if Scott would honor his promise. The countless nights she would lie awake wondering if he would have returned if only she had allowed him to make free with her in his parents' yard. Why had she pulled away? Why had she kept him from the link that would bind more eternally than the band upon her finger? How was she to stand firm for all those separate months, championing him before her parents?

163

Never had she felt quite so fatigued, quite so forlorn.

How was she going to survive his absence not knowing?

Beth had been all clucking, silent sympathy for her since breakfast. Her gaze oozed compassion, and her bolstering pats to her arm had Gena ready to scream in annoyance. *I'm not widowed,* she wanted to shout. *Don't treat me as if he died.* But they watched her, waiting, expecting her signs of mourning, ready to comfort, ready to fuss. And she would have none of it.

Caroline finally spoke up, never one for tact or diplomacy. "Gena, dear, if I were you, I would be most grateful he decided to stay. You will be spared the embarrassment of shunning him in public."

Gena turned to her. "I beg your pardon? Whatever are you talking about?"

"Why, Scott, of course. You can't seriously believe that he will be received anywhere once people hear."

"Hear what?"

The crackling tone brought Miss Davies's black brows into soaring arcs. She sighed heavily and reached out as if to pat her hand. Gena snatched it away. "Why, Gena, sweet, Gena. Ever the naive. I cannot believe you haven't heard the gossip." She leaned forward to confide maliciously. "They say he is half . . ." She let the suspense play out dramatically. "Indian!"

Gena stared at her, then let loose a long and hearty laugh. Caroline and Beth gawked at her as if she were quite mad. "Oh, Caro, really," she chided when her mirth had died down to a rib-clutching chuckle. "How very ridiculous. I thought you had better breeding and better sense than to listen to silly rumor. I met Scott's grandfather just the other day and he was no more a ruthless savage than — why, than you are. Oh, Scott will be so amused when I tell him. But then, maybe it's best I don't. I wouldn't want him to think poorly of you."

Caroline frowned, uncertain. Gena's gaze was direct and steeped in sincerity. And she knew the simple Miss Gena Trowbridge lacked the imagination to spin and carry off such a lie. Finally, her delicate lips pouted, and with a sniff, she went to give the straps on her band boxes another check, hiding her pique that the salacious bit of information should prove false. She could, of course, spread the whispers regardless of fact, but as they concerned her fiancé's cousin, perhaps she would be wiser not to slur the name. How boring the entire affair had become, providing not the least scrap of entertaining scandal.

Gena felt her knees quivering beneath the hug of her fashionable checked travel gown. She hadn't spun a fabrication since childhood. She couldn't recall the excuse she'd invented to explain the tear in her skirt. But when her mother had discovered the damage was done in a pushing match with a neighbor bully, Gena had never forgotten the punishment or the lesson. *Proper ladies never lie.* It had confused her then, for wasn't concealing one's true feelings the same as telling a lie? Apparently not, for her mother was an expert at that deception. One of the inconsistencies of being well-reared.

She hadn't meant to lie. But then, it hadn't been a bald untruth. Just misleading enough to keep Caroline from mangling Scott's reputation. That was worth one small sin. Yes, it was. She was rather surprised by how easily the prevarication had sprung to her lips and how guiltless she now felt. Perhaps, the situation could be salvaged after all. If the truth was contained within their small group, no one in Boston need ever know. Perhaps things would be all right, after all. Hope lifted her heart for one brief instant, then plummeted again when she saw the empty yard.

If Scott would only come to Boston.

She heard the jingling of spurs and turned to give

Scott's flame-haired brother a warm smile. Without warning, he swept her up into a gentle bear hug and pressed a firm kiss to her flushed cheek.

"It shore has been a pleasure, Miss Gena. I'm looking forward to having you in the family."

Her arms tightened around his broad shoulders, clinging to him and that hope. "Thank you, Rory." She could feel the prickle of moisture behind her eyes and denied it with a few quick blinks.

He settled her feet carefully upon the porch boards and whispered, "Don't fret none. He'll be here." Then, he strode to the pile of luggage and began to oversee its positioning in the carriage.

Pasting on a face that didn't betray her turmoil, Gena stood upon the porch and watched her bags being loaded. Loaded and readied for her return to Boston. Alone. Her resolve trembled. *Oh, Scott, please be here to at least say good-bye.*

Then he was there, standing at the foot of the steps, black cotton shirt pulled taut across his chest in the morning breeze, black Stetson angled down to shade all of his expression except for an unsmiling mouth. He raised one hand and gradually eased the dark brim back, revealing golden skin and golden eyes, also unsmiling. He was so handsome, for a moment Gena forgot to breathe. Then, that feeling of suspension was replaced by a sudden panic and a heartbeat so vigorous she feared it would shake her hairpins loose.

Scott.

All the warm, innocent pleasure she'd derived from their Boston conversations came back to her. Quiet, easy, mannerly Scott Prescott who'd lounged on their veranda and asked her to be his wife. He hadn't kissed her that night. He'd lifted her hand and slipped his ring on her finger, then had stood looking at it for a long time before he smiled. That same impassive stretch of

166

the mouth that touched his lips now.

Lone Wolf, son of Far Winds, son of Yellow Bear.

The magnetic, exciting, intimidating man who had helped himself to her body's curves and who'd said, just feet from where she stood, *I need you, Gena*. Then, just as clearly, she recalled his mother's words. *He needs someone who'll understand him. She'll scorn him and it will break his heart.*

Was it true? If he needed her, was he suffering as much pain over her leaving as she was in going? She had nothing to go home to. What was she running from? The truth about his heritage? Or from the anticipation of his desire? She admitted it. There seemed so little control here in the wilds, not like in Boston where he'd been satisfied to hold her hand. Their escalating intimacy struck a pure terror in her soul and she wanted to run from it, now, as she had the night before. But as he climbed the steps with his confident, oh-so-male stride, she held her ground and managed to smile.

" 'Morning, Gena."

"Scott."

They stood for a moment like awkward strangers, taking the measure of one another while tension and temptation simmered.

"I'm sorry about last night," he began, but she cut him off with the shake of her head.

"No, don't say it." She took a deep breath and glanced at the bags they were even now strapping in the carriage. This could well be her last chance. Fighting to keep the tremor from her voice and not quite able to meet his gaze, Gena stared at his top shirt button and murmured, "Could we speak inside for a moment? Alone?"

"Sure."

He took her elbow in a light, considerate grip and steered her away from the others. The parlor was empty and cast in cool shadow. All activity was centered out in the midmorning sun. Scott doffed his hat and began tapping it nervously against his thigh. He looked uncomfortably about the room, gaze taking in the bric-a-brac, the expensive clutter of furnishings, anything but the woman before him. As if afraid of this moment and what she might say. He needn't have worried. She didn't plan to say anything.

Gena turned toward him, hesitated for the briefest instant, then goaded herself to take the impulsive step. *Give him a reason to come back to you.* She took a deep breath and closed her eyes. And, before she could talk herself out of it, whipped her arms up around his neck to pull him down to her. He had time to emit a startled gasp. His hat fell from nerveless fingers, forgotten. Then she was kissing him. Hard.

It was wrong. As wrong as it had been the night before when he was the aggressor. Scott felt the driven desperation in her embrace. It wasn't motivated by want or need or love but by fear, plain and simple. The squirming tightness in his chest eased and gave at that thought. How frightened she must be to lunge so completely out of character. How rightly insecure. And what an utter bastard he was for pushing her to such an anxious extreme.

"Gena." He levered his face away to say her name, softly, kindly. His hands were on her shoulders, not holding but rather prying her away.

The realization knocked the wind from her. It was too late. Too late to sacrifice her staid conscience. She'd already lost him. Flaming with humiliation, she choked out, "I'm sorry," and turned to escape him and the embarrassment of failure. But he wouldn't allow her a dignified retreat. He caught her arms and roped her into the gentle circle of his embrace, holding her easily but irrefutably while her body jerked with violent spasms of shame. Irrepressible tears welled in her eyes, filling them, sparkling there like crystal clear lakes of blue. Then a single

168

large drop rolled from one corner. Her misery knew no bounds.

Then he spoke, in a husky cadence that quieted her external shivers and woke them all through her insides.

"If you want to say it, say it like this."

He bent toward her and Gena held her lips still. But his mouth didn't settle there. She knew a moment of fluttery confusion as his lips brushed away the dampness upon her cheek.

"And like this."

His warm breath grazed her temple, sensitizing the spot before pressing a whisper soft kiss. Gena stood, transfixed, her eyes closed, her pulse drumming crazily. Afraid to move. Afraid to breathe. Afraid not of him but of what he was doing. Of the forbidden havoc he was stirring within.

"And this." A scintillating rumble.

His lips trailed exquisitely across her forehead then touched lightly upon each quivering eyelid and the tip of her nose. By then, her own lips were moistened, parted and anxiously awaiting like attention. Again, to her frustration, he passed them by, wringing a moan of disappointment as his kiss dropped to her chin. And then to a scented spot on her neck, just below her ear. The contact was electrifying, sparking through her system, accelerating her heartbeats to a frenzied speed, draining her body's energy to support that hurried pulse. Of their own accord, her hands lifted to the back of his head, feeling the ridge his hat had made there, then erasing it with their restless movement. She was tingling. Everywhere. Alive in every nerve and pore. So alive, it hurt.

And as his mouth nibbled along the line of her jaw, a revelation occurred in the far reaches of her mind. This was what her mother had warned against. She'd never understood before. This was the enticing lure beckoning down the path of carnal Sin with a capital S.

And it was marvelous.

And there was no way or will to resist it.

Yes, Scott. Yes. Unable to wait any longer while he teased and tempted, Gena's palms scooped around to capture the strong line of his jaw, holding him still so she could seek out the taste of his mouth. But his hands moved, too, cupping her face, preventing her from satisfying that tremulous need. Anchoring her just fractions from the paradise she sought.

Her eyes flickered open. Her gaze was desire-drenched. And pleading. In agonizing answer, he touched the part of her lips, lightly, devastating, with just the tip of his tongue. Gena shuddered helplessly and expelled an expectant breath. Her eyes drifted shut and her mouth widened, inviting him in.

An embarrassed throat-clearing from the doorway was followed by Ruth's regretful call of, "Miss Gena, they're ready to leave."

Gena's forehead dropped against Scott's shoulder. She went limp, as if exhausted by the pulls of passion. His arms enfolded her trembling figure and he held her, close to where his heart chugged like an overtaxed freight engine. He waited, tensing, expecting her to gather her reserve like a suit of shielding armor. But she didn't. She leaned upon him, face burrowed into the hollow of his throat, her light, panting breaths stroking along his bared skin.

Finally, she stirred with the utmost reluctance. She eased back from the solid support of his chest and met his stare without a trace of shyness. The hands that hadn't left his face moved slowly, in lingering circles, trickling down until her fingertips rested upon the seam of his lips. Then, wordlessly, she turned and hurried from the room to where the others waited.

Scott stood in the empty parlor, stunned right down to his Cuban heels. His hands hung at his hips, opening, closing, opening, trying to defy the way the shakes beset them. What in God's name had happened? His insides were quaking. He'd meant to stir her up a bit, to see if he could start a fire, but he hadn't expected the agitation to burn through him like dry tinder. Slowly, still stupefied, he groped about for his hat.

They were piled inside the carriage and impatient, all but Horace, who stood awaiting her on the porch. Gena moved toward them with a hazy sense of the surreal. Her awareness was blunted by the incredible wash of Scott's appeal. Her limbs were still unsteady, her heartbeat still erratic. And then there was the unfinished prospect of ecstasy in the kiss they hadn't shared. She couldn't seem to catch her breath. She couldn't make her step carry her any closer to her departure. And so, Horace came to get her.

"Come along, Miss Trowbridge," he said with a possessive familiarity as he took her arm. "We've a train to catch. And don't you worry, Scott. I'll take good care of her."

Scott jerked up in the doorframe. He felt the wind suck out of him as a fierce fist of jealousy slammed into his gut. His teeth set in a grinding grip as his gaze assessed the sight of Gena's hand tucked upon his cousin's sleeve. Logic whispered to him. Leave it alone. She was better off with a man like Horace. With a man who could give her what she deserved without the taint of shame. And he stood poised in a whorl of uncertainty.

Then Gena looked over Horace's thin shoulder, snagging his heart with a gaze of complex yearning. And he experienced that curious quaking all over again. He wet suddenly dry lips and started forward, irrationally pursuing something beyond the logic of the moment. But then, she turned away and he checked his stride.

Gena suffered from the extremes of doubt in that jarring instant. She'd watched with a hungry fascination as

171

his tongue scrubbed over his mouth and knew a perfect fear to her very soul. That was the danger of Scott Prescott, that promise of pleasure and panic. The carriage waited, ready to take her back to the solidity of her uneventful life. Where there would be no torment, no terrifying temptation. She risked another quick glance back, recognizing her folly as the compulsive longing catapulted from constricted chest to aching throat. A whole summer. Months in which to chafe over the fulfillment his stare suggested. Months in which she would be in Boston in the solicitous care of Horace Billings and he would be here, alone, with the sensuous Morning Song.

"Do come along, Gena," Caroline called peevishly from the carriage. Her fan was snapping back and forth as she eyed her fiancé's attentiveness toward the other woman.

Horace began a subtle pulling, urging her to take reluctant steps away from the inscrutable figure at the door.

Scott, do something. Say something.

But he stood motionless, his swarthy features expressionless, his eyes hot as molten gold.

Gena felt the edge of the steps beneath her toes and her heels dug in with sudden, unexpected fervor. Unbalanced, Horace teetered and regarded her in bewilderment. But she wasn't aware of it. She only knew she was upon a precipice and that an unwise step would cast her straight to oblivion.

"Rory, would you please take down my bags. I've decided not to go, after all."

Rory sent a quick look between her and his brother. He'd seen the way she'd come out of the house, all red-lipped and shiny-eyed. *Ataboy, Scotty.* "Yes, ma'am," he replied cheerfully as he turned to free her luggage from the stack bound for Boston.

"Gena, have you lost your senses?" Beth cried in disbelief.

"No, Beth. I don't believe I have," was her calm response.

"But what about your parents? They'll be expecting you."

In a voice that was more than a little breathless, Gena said, "Tell them I've decided to accept the Prescotts' invitation to stay on and that I'll wire them later." Once that was spoken, she felt a giddy relief, a wonderful sense of freedom. Seeing her friend's doubtful expression, she came down off the steps to the side of the buggy so they could embrace.

"Oh, Beth, don't worry," she whispered. "I know what I'm doing."

Beth looked past her to where her cousin stood, a dark, dangerous threat to a gently reared lady's innocence. "I hope so, Gena. I hope so."

Chapter Eleven

It wasn't until the carriage containing all her ties to the east rolled from the yard with Garth Kincaid riding escort that Gena realized the magnitude of what she'd done.

Rory stood over her bags, grinning. "My, oh, my, won't Mama be surprised," he drawled with incredible understatement. "Think I'll jus' hitch up a wagon so we can get on home." Still grinning, he ambled toward the barn.

Consequence sank deep and dire: Gena wasn't sure which confrontation inspired the most dread, Aurora Prescott or her eldest son. Slowly, clutching for courage, she turned to face her fiancé. His features hadn't altered, but his eyes had cooled to chips of amber. He gave nothing away, not pleasure, not disapproval. Apprehensively, she tried a smile and her spirits sank at his lack of response.

"I'll go help Rory with the horses."

With that brusque statement, he strode past her and headed after his brother in a ground-eating, stiff-legged gait, leaving Gena to steep in her dismay.

Rory glanced up from buckling the hames and breaststraps and allowed himself a low chuckle.

"That must have been some mighty motivating argument you gave her up at the house."

Silence.

Rory paused in his straightening of the tugs and cast his brother a curious look. "So how come you ain't smiling?" More silence, prompting him to lean his elbows against the horse's warm flanks and cock an eyebrow. "Don't tell me 'tweren't your idea."

"Mama's gonna chew my ass ragged." Scott reached by him to give the reins a proper adjustment while Rory's grin just kept getting wider.

"Seeing as how Daddy did the inviting, if there's any butt biting to be done, seems likely he'll be the one to suffer it."

Scott reached down to run the quarter strap from the breeching under the belly up to loop around the neck yoke. He gave the redhead a hard bump with his shoulder, growling, "If you're not going to help, get outta the way." Rory took a few paces back and watched the efficient workings of the straps and buckles. He picked up a blade of hay and absently sucked it between his teeth.

"Cain't understand you, Scotty," he ruminated. "You got yourself this pretty little thing and allst you seem to want to do is chase her off. Why is that, d'you suppose?"

Scott paused a second, then fed the strap he was threading through its fastening so quick it hissed like a whip. "If it was any of your business, which it isn't, her being here is just complicating things I was hoping to sort through."

It was getting interesting. Rory pitched the bit of straw away. "What sorta things?"

Scott glared at him across the horse's broad back, grasping for a way to shut him up. "Hang it if you not the nosiest son of a—" He leaned forward then, as if

175

about to impart a confidence. "Man-woman things. Stuff you don't know nothing about."

"Ha! I might just surprise you, big brother. If there's something you want to know, just come right on out an' ask me."

"I'll keep that in mind," he drawled sarcastically as he finished with the second horse.

"Now, if you was having trouble getting her to lift those fancy skirt — oww!" He jumped as Scott sent the rein ends popping across the backs of his thighs. "Dang it, Scotty, you don't have to go getting so all-fired unfriendly about it."

Scott ignored him and led the team from the barn with its buckboard filled with goods intended for the Lone Star. To them, he added Gena's bags, then silently offered her his hand up to the wide unsprung seat. While he took up the reins beside her, Rory vaulted up lightly to assume a place on her left. At Scott's questioning scowl, he smiled and said, "I wouldn't miss this for the world. 'Sides, Mama's making dumplings for supper." He sprawled out comfortably, stretching his arm along the seat back so it encompassed both Gena and his brother in an easy loop. And he grinned to himself the entire trip, thinking on the mouth-watering dumplings and how their mother was going to tear off a goodly chunk of his brother's rump and serve it as a second course.

Aurora Prescott took in the sight of Gena Trowbridge wedged between her sons and the added baggage in the wagon bed, missing none of the significance. To her credit, no trace of misgivings touched her expression as she stepped to the edge of the porch to greet them.

"Miss Trowbridge, it would seem you've decided to accept our invitation."

"If it's no trouble . . ."

176

Aurora looked to her youngest son without acknowledging the timid overture. "Rory, please take Miss Trowbridge and her belongings upstairs and see she's settled. I need a word with your brother."

Sure he was going to miss all the fireworks, Rory muttered a sulky, "Yes, ma'am," and jumped down from the wagon. He reached up to catch Gena about the waist, and swung her to the ground, then began to gather up her things. Laden like a pack mule, he staggered up the porch steps. "Come on, Miss Gena. I'll tuck you in."

Gena hesitated. Feeling courtesy dictated another attempt, she looked to Aurora Prescott, but the older woman's attention was riveted upon Scott. "It's very kind of you to—"

The golden eyes flashed to her in annoyance. "Yes. Of course. Do make yourself at home. Dinner is at seven."

Aurora turned away, dismissing her guest with an imperious tip of her red coif. Gena swallowed back the thought of any further pleasantries and followed Rory into the Prescotts' log house.

Scott took his time getting down from the wagon and coming around the team to face his mother. He stood at the base of the steps, looking up, expression without apology, without humility. But out of respect, he did sweep off his hat so it wouldn't shadow his eyes when he spoke. "I appreciate you taking her in, Mama. I know you don't have much use for her, so I'll keep her out of your way."

Aurora nodded as if the matter was of trifling importance, and Scott frowned. If it wasn't about Gena, what then? He could read his mother's agitation as clearly as a track upon the ground. Her stance was lodgepole rigid, her smile as thin as January sunshine. And about

177

as cool. He was expecting the quick snap of her temper, not this icy cut.

"Mama? Something wrong?"

"There was a young woman here looking for you earlier. A Miniconjou."

That explained it; the stiff posture, the taut lines, the chill voice. At Ethan's insistence, she hadn't interfered in his Sioux upbringing but she had always drawn the line at her front door. Whatever was Indian stopped at the boundaries of the Lone Star. It was a long-unspoken rule and he had obeyed it without question or conflict. It was her home and she would not have it invaded by the past. Usually, he was sensitive to her enmity, but on this occasion, he was impatient. If Morning Song had come all the way to the Lone Star, she must have had some vital reason.

"Did she say what she wanted?"

"I didn't ask."

He turned on his heel and started for the corral.

"Scott?" The call was high, edged with upset. He didn't pause or look back.

"Be home for supper."

She watched him single out one of her husband's fine horses and shove a bit between its teeth. Taking no time with a saddle, he seized a handful of mane and rolled up lithely onto the animal's back, guiding it with the expert pressure of his knees. Aurora watched and battled her fear. With one woman newly installed beneath her roof, he was racing full out to rendezvous with another. And of the two, Aurora realized grimly, the proper eastern puppet was much more to her liking than the thought of the sleek Sioux maiden. Perhaps she'd been wrong in wanting her son at home. For his home ranged far beyond the Lone Star into territories that filled her with dread. Maybe Boston was the best place for him. It would be easier to suffer the loss of his presence then the loss of his heart and soul.

From the upstairs dormer, Gena's attention waned from Rory's expansive gabbing to the sight of Scott Prescott riding pell-mell across Lone Star land. He rode bareback, crouching low, and she was mesmerized all over again by the powerful beauty of his oneness with the horse. *Like an Indian.* Heading where in such a hurry?

Morning Song's family lived on an allotment of land good for nothing but the cultivation of dust. Most of its lower acres were too barren to support decent prairie grasses, let alone the spindly blades of corn wilting in uneven rows. They lived in a structure thrown together with what looked like the remnants of packing crates with flattened tin cans nailed down to form a poorly pitched roof. Warped wood left gaps big enough to pass a dinner plate through. It would allow a nice circulation of air in the summer months, but he couldn't help considering the blowing snow of a harsh Dakota winter. How would they withstand it? Living within walls that swayed with the slightest provocation. In circumstance so desperate it disarmed him completely of all but despair. It was difficult not to display that horror, to look beyond it so as not to show insult. But he did, to honor White Cloud and so not to embarrass Morning Song; they had both come out to greet him.

"Ho, Mahpiya Ska," he called to Morning Song's father as he stepped down from his horse. The last time he had seen White Cloud, he'd been a big, hefty-set warrior on his way to join a hunt party. The man who extended his hand in white fashion was a slim ghost of that memory clad in reservation-issue with only the

179

length of his braided hair to claim his heritage.

"You are welcome on my land, Son of Far Winds."

Scott glanced about him and smiled tightly. He saw through two sets of eyes. The white in him said no good crops would grow, no fat beef would thrive. The Lakota mourned, for it would support no game. But he would not shame White Cloud with those observations.

"I am honored to be remembered," he said in the language of his father's people. "And I would repay it with a gift from my heart." He took the reins of his father's blooded stallion and pressed them into the older man's hand. When White Cloud would protest, he covered the gnarled hand and the reins with both of his, squeezing insistently.

"It is a noble gift, Lone Wolf, but I have no use for a horse not fit for plow or wagon."

Scott wanted to suggest Morning Song use the mount to carry her the distance to Crowe Creek, but it was not his place to do so. Nor did the surroundings indicate that they could afford to grain such a sleek animal. Instead, he murmured, "Do what is best with it. Sell it if you like. I will leave you papers of ownership so none will question."

White Cloud hesitated, stroking the magnificent creature's neck, weighing the value and what it would provide his family against the rebellion of pride that called such a gift charity. "You are too generous—"

"No. You are the one who was generous for all the nights I sat down to your food, for all the times of joy I found within your lodge, for the wisdom and friendship of a father that you have given me. This gift is too little. It would please me for you to accept it."

Pride neatly circumvented, White Cloud nodded and gave the reins to his daughter.

"I would ask a ride home of you."

Morning Song looked up at him, her eyes shining with gratitude. "I will take you when you are ready." She gave him a speaking glance, then led the horse to their dilapidated well. He puzzled over that look. It was as if she wanted to talk of whatever concerned her while alone.

Scott followed his host inside the tiny single-room dwelling where he, his wife and daughter, and their four younger children all ate and slept crowded together in cheerless poverty. Again, he was forced to choke down his pity and accept part of the meager meal they were sharing. So little. He looked at the pinched faces of the small ones, and each mouthful went down like dust. But he could not offend them with a refusal. White Cloud talked of his crops, of his plans, of his pride in the children who attended the reservation day school, while Scott nodded and made appropriate noises. The children stared. They didn't know him and looked bashful when he attempted to draw them out in their native tongue. Finally, when the scant meal was eaten and a respectful amount of visiting was concluded, Morning Song caught his sleeve.

"I will see Lone Wolf to his door." Her grip was compelling.

Scott said the proper good-byes, guilty and grateful to be putting the place behind him as he slipped up behind Morning Song on the tall stallion. She didn't attempt words until they were hidden by the hills from the eyes of her family.

"Thank you for the gift, Lone Wolf," she began softly. "You cannot know what it means to us."

"Why did you come for me today, Morning Song? What can't you speak of in your father's house?"

She sighed, and the hands he'd rested lightly upon her trim waist rose and fell with the movement. "I do

181

not wish to dishonor or be disobedient to my father, but I did not know what else to do. I thought of you with your white man's knowledge and hoped you would have some answer."

"I'll do whatever I can. You know that without asking."

She touched his hand briefly, just a warm press of fingers more expressive than words. "You have seen the land. You have seen how we live. My father has much pride and refuses defeat. To feed us and to pay for seed, he has been cutting wood from our higher ground and selling it. Now, the BIA agent has told him he must stop. He has threatened to take the land because of what my father has done. The words have frightened him and they frighten me. We do not know if he can do these things. You have read the white man's law. Can you tell us? Can they take the land the government has told us is ours? Can they forbid us from using what grows upon it? These things confuse and we do not know where to go for help. Can you help, Lone Wolf?"

Her desperation prodded Scott to anger. There was no hesitation in his reply. "I don't know, but I will find out."

Morning Song reined in the horse and with one lithe move swung her leg over its neck and slipped to the ground. When she walked several feet away, Scott was prompted to follow. He stood slightly behind her, not touching but letting her feel him there. She hugged her arms about herself as she spoke in desolate tones.

"I have tried to pretend things will be better for us doing as the white man says. I have tried, but I do not see things changing to the better. I see my father humble his pride to dig in parched dirt, tearing the spirit of the land. I hear my mother crying in the night. I watch my brother seek his dreams within a bottle and see my little brothers and sisters torn between two worlds. I do not know who suffers more, we who have seen the old ways or the young who will never taste its freedom."

She took a deep, uneven breath and Scott found his hands drawn to her strong shoulders, kneading when they would slump in despair.

"It is hard to see the confusion in the children," she continued. "They are *wojapi*, all mixed up. In the home, they are Lakotas listening to old Inktomi stories at the feet of our grandparents. At the school, they must adopt white ways and are punished for speaking or even thinking as an Indian. I have listened to them crying because of the taste of their teacher's soap and have seen their little hands scarred from the sting of the ruler. They are afraid. Would you talk to them, Lone Wolf? Would you teach them how to be strong? You have learned in their schools and you carry their wisdom. We are told that by educating the young ones they will go from being American Indians to Indian Americans. But my brother, High Hawk, he says the schools take away the pride of our people and give nothing back. Who is right?"

"I don't know, Morning Song. I wish I was that wise." He was lost for a moment, suffering the guilt her words encouraged. How could he be an example to the young Lakotas when he had forfeited pride for progress? How could he tell them that after enduring the isolation, the stripping of identity, they would be any better off within the white man's world? He shared her confusion, her frustration, her anger, in that long moment of communion. To distract her from what he could not do, he turned their subject to what was within his realm.

"Who is this man who threatens your family?"

"His name is Garrick. He works for the bureau and has charge of our district. He does not like my father,

183

and I feel he would like to see him fail. Many others who have tried to make good on their land have had misfortune fall upon them. They have been forced or convinced to lease their lands through Mr. Garrick and are paid only a small share of what is reaped upon it."

"Who does he lease the lands to?"

"I do not know. The others, they will not speak of it. I think they are afraid. But you are not afraid." She turned suddenly to face him; standing so close, their bodies brushed together. Her dark eyes gleamed with admiration. "You will ask and you will find the truth."

"Yes." That one word came out a croak. She was too close. It was too easy to fall into the liquid embrace of her stare. Too easy to feel the temptation of the lush form beneath thin cotton. Too easy to be charmed by the honest attraction glowing in her uplifted features. Scott took a hasty step back, fighting the pull of their shared past, but she would not release him from it. Nimbly, she wound her arms about his neck and hugged him, bringing her supple form against him in a way no man was meant to ignore. He felt her warm lips at his throat, at his ear, on his cheek, and finally upon his own.

It was a lusty kiss, deep, promising — everything. For a moment, he responded, to the passion, to the attraction, to the dusky mating urge that had nothing to do with proper court or stuffy parlors or chaste glances. It was a raw, basic, fulfilling sense of want, and for just a moment, he thought, *What the hell. Why not?* Here was the answer to the tension Gena stoked and refused to savor. Here was a woman who would understand and satisfy. No games. No ties. Just plain, drop-down-on-the-ground, roll-around sex with a partner who'd enjoy it every bit as much as he would. His body enthusiastically endorsed the idea. And it was mighty appealing.

184

Until she whispered huskily, "You are a good man, Lone Wolf."

He disengaged her arms and looked apologetic in the face of her disappointment. "Not all that good."

The rest of the ride to the Lone Star was in silence. Not awkward, only thoughtful. There was no embarrassment over what had happened. Morning Song was too open, too natural, to force the situation. She'd felt his response and she'd also recognized his refusal, and though it confused her, she would honor it. Either it was not the right time or she was not the right woman. She would wait to see which way it was with Lone Wolf, son of Far Winds, son of Wadutah of the scarlet hair.

It was dusk when he asked her to pull up a hill away from his mother's house. Lost in his bittersweet musings, he'd forgotten all about dinner at seven and a fiancée adrift in a hostile home. Even as he scooched off the rump of the horse he'd given away without a thought, he was in no hurry to crest the hill to join his family. He was breathing in the cool approach of evening, experiencing it in ways he hadn't for a lot of years. And he was reluctant to lose it.

"Thank you, Lone Wolf." She put down her hand and he took it unthinkingly. A slender hand, more accustomed to labor than leisure. Their fingers laced for a long moment while they shared the silence of the night. Then Scott pulled away.

"Good night, Morning Song."

There was a flash of trim calves as she nudged the stallion into an easy canter. Her loose black hair filtered back on the breeze. And he found himself standing knee deep in Prescott grass watching until the darkness embraced her.

* * *

Gena could not remember a more difficult after-noon. She spent hours trapped in the small upstairs room trying to garner the courage to go below without Scott as a buffer. She waited at the window, watching, but he didn't come.

Rory's room was spartan and overwhelmingly mas-culine. Her frilly clothes hung beside his winter gar-ments in the big cupboard, creating an uncomfortable sense of familiarity. She couldn't bring herself to re-move her underthings from her trunk to lay them inside the lower drawers. That seemed all too intimate. Her brush, comb, and hand mirror were placed upon the washstand meant to serve a man for shaving. Besides a single rough-hewn chair, the big bed was the only other piece of furniture. Made from the same split and peeled log as the chair, she supposed by Ethan Prescott, it was covered with a woolen spread of a deep green and black checked pattern, the same design that draped the win-dow. There were no pictures or shelves upon the wall, and studying them, Gena found a distinct and attrac-tive beauty in the variation of the logs that was as pleas-ing as any papering. She could feel Rory Prescott in the room, his exuberance, his energy, and she was also acutely aware that Scott would be spending his nights in the bed right across the hall. Apparently, Aurora and Ethan's room was downstairs in the original part of the house.

The thought of being alone with Scott, away from the hearing of others, created a tingle of apprehension, especially after what had passed between them in the Kincaid parlor. She'd felt his desire for her in those electrifying seconds and was aware of her own re-sponse. As was he. Would he expect a greater latitude now that she'd encouraged his attentions? Now that she'd forgone the proper to stay behind with him? How

186

much meaning would he attach to that fact? Would he consider permission given for more of the aggressive groping of the night before? She shivered and walked to the window again, rubbing her arms with damp palms. Where was he? She knew the afternoon hours had passed. Ethan and Rory were out in one of the barns. That left only Scott's mother below. An invitation that held all the appeal of the lion's den to Daniel. And she had not his faith to sustain her.

Where was Scott?

Finally, because remaining in hiding any longer would appear rude and cowardly, Gena freshened her gown and repaired any fair stragglers from their hairpins, then took the long, trepidant trip downstairs. The front door stood open, allowing a wonderful breeze inside to mingle with the delicious scents from the kitchen. She could hear Aurora humming to herself, and approached the room with caution.

For all the rustic appeal of the rest of the house, the kitchen was thoroughly modern with the exception of running water. A hand pump still supplied that service. The walls and open shelves were painted in bronze-green enamel with a spotless oilcloth covering on the floor. White muslin hung airily at the big central window. There were two tables, one for food service, the other for preparation, both covered with enameled cloth. A large Hoosier cabinet commanded one wall. It was there Aurora was working dough upon the zinc tabletop with easy access to its sugar and flour bins. Three strong chairs and a comfortable rocker were arranged out of the flow of movement between cabinet, range, and icebox. It was a welcoming, efficient room. She could imagine the Prescott family gathered there on cold winter nights watching Aurora push and fold dough. It was a warm picture, unlike any she could conceive of within her own austere home. There, a stranger tended their bread for hire and no one was inclined to linger.

Sensing she was no longer alone, Aurora turned. There was flour on her hands and upon the cuffs of her shirtwaist where they were pushed up to the elbows. There was also a smudge of it on one tanned cheek. That white streak of domesticity somehow made her less threatening, and Gena ventured a small smile.

"Is there something I might do to help? You look as though you have your hands full and Rory would be sorely disappointed if the dumplings suffered for it."

Aurora stared at her for a long assessing moment. Then she returned to the dough. "Linens are in the chest of drawers." It wasn't the friendliest overture, but at least it was an inclusion in the family affairs. It made her feel less like a burden to be doing something. She dressed the table with care, thinking as she did of how it must have been, the four of them sitting down together when Scott and Rory were young. She found herself daydreaming over the pieces of Haviland china, thinking of how much laughter and love must have gone along with the meals they held. And she envied the Prescotts the simplicity of their home and the affectionate harmony of their lives. When the three of them had dined alone, often as not, her father had used the time to sort his daily correspondence and her mother to critique their friends and neighbors, and Gena ate in silence lest she become the topic of her mother's fault-finding.

She was shaken from her musings as Ethan and Rory stomped in, smelling of horses and hay and pipe tobacco. Before following his father into the kitchen, Rory paused to lean over her shoulder, cuffing her upper arms with his big hands.

"Everything looks mighty fine in here, Sis. A man could get used to such an attractive table."

Because it was Rory Prescott, instead of coloring up in offense, she trod back on his toe and chastened, "Mind your manners, Mr. Prescott."

He laughed and bussed her cheek with a quick kiss. "I don't mind 'em if you don't." Then he sauntered toward the rear of the house with a holler of, "Something smells mighty good in here."

Listening to Ethan's rumbling drawl, Rory's warm laughter, and Aurora's good-natured scolding made Gena feel a strange longing from her isolated spot in the main room. How she wished she was free to join in their close-knit circle, and for the first time, she really saw how different things were in her own upbringing, how much caring and openness she'd missed, the quick, fond touches, the ribald humor, the earthy joy of living.

And that was how Scott found her when he stepped in from his ride with Morning Song: standing at their table, one of his mother's plates clutched to her chest, with tears glistening in her eyes.

Chapter Twelve

He stood for a long time in that doorway, feeling another woman's kiss on his mouth, feeling a terrible weight of guilt upon his heart. All the buoyancy of spirit he'd enjoyed in the knee-deep grass sank in that miserable moment when Gena caught sight of him and he was certain she could see the imprint of Morning Song all over him. And then she smiled, just the faintest welcome. Enough to stagger him with a mule kick to the conscience. He saw the wet traces on her cheeks. He'd been locked against another's lips and she'd been here, in his house, waiting for him in an agony of upset. God knows what she'd suffered in his mother's care. He hadn't cared. He hadn't thought of it once since racing from the yard.

"Gena, I'm sorry—"

She set the plate down and a hand fluttered to her face, quickly rubbing it dry as she continued to smile at him. Something in that wistful look escaped him. It wasn't blame or anger or anything like it. He could almost swear it had nothing to do with him at all. So why was she standing over his table all glassy-eyed with tears if not because of his abandonment and subsequent disloyalty? She gave no clue of cause to that thread of sad emotion.

"It's all right," she interrupted quietly, sincerely. "You're just in time for dinner. I'll take that while you wash up and get ready."

She came to him and reached for his hat. The sweet-tart scent of lemon verbena was a surprise. He'd expected something more subdued, more civilized. She had to take the Stetson off his head. Then, when he remained immobile, she put her palm to the small of his back. And pushed, actually propelling him toward the kitchen.

"Go on. Don't make your family wait." It was a soft chiding familiarity that stunned and soothed in turn, like the punch of his grandfather's liquor.

"I'm sorry," he mumbled a second time. And he meant it. He meant it right down to the tortured soul.

"There you are, Scotty," his brother called from the kitchen. "Dang. Thought I was gonna get your helping, too."

Tension at the table was as thick and smooth as Aurora Prescott's gravy. Ethan and Rory did their best to carry the conversation while Gena sat in awkward silence and Aurora's stare stabbed through her older son. Scott never lifted his eyes from his plate and then as soon as he was able, he slipped out onto the porch.

The tangy fragrance gave her away immediately. Scott braced against the rail, waiting. Here it comes. The demand to know where he'd been all afternoon when he should have been at her side, making her comfortable in his home. He put on his most stoic face so he wouldn't betray himself in expression as he almost had in fact. Then he felt it, the gentle brush of her fingertips along the taut line of his shoulder. It was a fleeting caress, jerked back the moment she realized what she was doing. A shock of expectation leaping up

191

collided with shame sinking down as he continued to stand silent, tense, waiting for her to twist the blade of blame.

But she didn't. She never even mentioned it.

"We haven't had the chance to talk since this morning," she murmured quietly. She was talking about her decision to stay. He was by turn relieved then disturbed.

"You took me by surprise. I had no idea . . ." He trailed off helplessly.

Gena's face grew hot with discomfort. "If that wasn't an invitation in your grandfather's parlor, what was it?"

"It was meant as a good-bye. I guess I didn't say it very well."

Gena swallowed down the lump of agitation that remembering woke within her. "You said it just fine. Too well, if anything." She fell silent, touching her lips with the tip of her tongue, wondering how it would have been had he kissed her. How far the moment would have carried them had they been alone. Like they would be upstairs. Tonight. And every night for the length of the summer.

"I just wish you would have said something to me first," he finished lamely.

Then, it struck her.

"You're angry with me."

He hadn't wanted her to stay. She'd mistaken his intentions in the parlor. It was to have been good-bye, perhaps forever. And now, here she was, forcing herself upon him, pushing herself into his home where she was, at least to Scott Prescott, uninvited. The longer it took him to respond, the deeper that dreadful knowledge seeped. He hadn't wanted her here and now he was stuck with her underfoot, responsible and reluctant. She was mortified and wounded to the quick.

"No. No, I'm not," he said at long last and just a heartbeat too late for sincerity. "It's just that I'm going to be real busy and I won't have much time to spend with you. You'll be alone a lot and I don't want to be the cause of you being unhappy."

Too late, Scott Prescott. It's already done. She ached with an awful loneliness even as she stood beside him. Because he hadn't wanted her to stay. For whatever reasons he might give. With all the saving dignity she could manage, she told him, "It wasn't my plan to trap your attentions. I shall do just fine on my own." Then her proud voice snagged. "And there are other trains bound for Boston. If you'll excuse me, I think I should like to go upstairs now."

He heard the melancholy whisper of her petticoat as she turned to go inside. He thought of following, of explaining. But, though Gena was naive, she was not stupid. The more he talked, the more she would suspect. The matter was best left alone, at least for this night. She was here, and he would do his best to see she had no reason to regret it. Noble sentiments, already failed.

"Scott?"

His resolve stiffened, for he knew his mother would not be in as charitable a mood as his fiancée. "Just putting some thoughts together, Mama. Be in in a minute."

But she didn't withdraw. He could feel her stare, her questions, her agitation. And he closed his eyes. *Not tonight, Mama. Not when I'm feeling about as low as a man can feel without digging a hole.*

"You were gone a long time. Did you get things taken care of?" Her words crunched like boots on bottle glass.

"Partly."

"You came in on foot. Where's your horse?"

"I gave it to White Cloud."

"You gave your father's horse—"

"To feed his family, Mama. It's not like we'll suffer the loss."

"That's not the point," she said with a low, depthless exasperation. Then her mood gentled and her hands settled upon the rigid brace of his shoulders. He allowed it for a moment then shifted uncomfortably. Her fingers tightened. "You are not responsible for them, Scott."

His silence refuted her.

With a resigned sigh, Aurora stroked her son's black hair. "I don't suppose Ethan will mind about the horse. Just be careful of how much you give away."

They both knew she wasn't speaking of property.

She squeezed his shoulders, then let her palms trail down his back, thinking of how different he was from his brother, Rory, who was quick and eager with his smiles and his hugs and his feelings. Scott had never been generous with them. Rory, who ran carelessly like a bubbling stream. Scott, who was dammed up tight, from whom emotion flowed in a controlled and guarded trickle. Scott, who never seemed to need her but whom she'd always want to hold close.

Because of the difference.

"I'll leave you to your thoughts."

She started toward the house.

"Mama?"

Aurora turned. "Yes?" She waited.

"I was—It was nothing. Nothing. Never mind." He rushed through that and shook his head as if to scatter whatever he was about to ask. His shoulders were slumped, but the hands clenching and unclenching at his sides said plainly that whatever was on his mind was far from being nothing. That restless, jerky movement was picked up in the tempo of his breathing. It sounded harsh and fast as if he was running a race against what he held inside.

"Scott?"

He shook his head again, then, contrarily, fast as a shot, mumbled, "I wanted to ask about you and my daddy, is all."

"About me and Ethan? I—"

"No." The dark head gave a small negating move. "No. About you—about you and my father."

Understanding stunned all but a vague "Oh" from her. His tension became hers.

Scott hurried on, afraid that if he paused, she would stop him from getting out what he had to say. It had been roiling around inside him since she'd stared at him, aghast, at her door. No, even before that. Too long for him to force it down quietly.

"There were so many things I wanted to ask, things that I didn't understand when I left for school. The time just never seemed to be right. You never told me much of anything, except that you lived for a year with the Sioux, that you were married to him, and that he died before I was born. It was enough when I was little. It's not any more, Mama. I need to know."

She was so still, he was convinced she wouldn't answer, that she would brush aside his questions as she'd done when he was young, with a firm yet vulnerable refusal that always managed to disarm him. This time, however, she asked at last, "What is it you need to know?"

Scott stood, struggling with the emotional cartwheeling of his thoughts and a tremendous reluctance to learn the truth. He hesitated, anxiety making him balk. "I don't want to drag up things to upset you, Mama."

"It's all right," Aurora told him softly. And she thought, studying the compression of suspense and agitation his stance betrayed, this time, it was. She took a bolstering breath and steadied herself for the cost of going back. "What do you need to know?"

Scott was looking out over the thick Prescott grasses, his eyes searching the twilight for the dim outline of the Hills. It was costing him, too, to let it play out slowly, in regimented degrees. Anguish rose up with the force of a spring flood; cold, swamping, swallowing his best intentions to stay calm. His voice thickened with it. His insides knotted with it as he thought of the woman standing in shadow behind him. "Ethan's always been the best kind of daddy to me. And I love him for it, Mama, I really do. But something was always missing. There was this big hollow I could never get filled. My father, he was like the stuff of Lakota legends. I grew up hearing of him, picturing him as brave and honorable and good and I dreamed of being with him, walking with him, learning from him. I wanted so much to know him, the man, not the legend. I wanted to ask him if I was making the right choices, if he was proud of me, if I was the kind of son he'd wanted."

"Scott —"

"Don't." That was said harsh and sharp, then immediately he softened. "Let me finish."

Aurora's hands went up to her face, to hold in the pleas for him to stop, to hold back the desire to reach out with an offer of inadequate comfort. She stood, helpless, while her son suffered all the pain she'd tried to protect him from. She prayed for the courage to hear him out and for the wisdom to answer. For him to have the strength to hear the truth.

"I had you and Ethan and Rory and I tried so hard for that to be enough. But part of me was proud of being the son of Far Winds. Part of me was in love with the idea that I was the son of a great Lakota warrior.

196

Being with Yellow Bear made him come alive for me and I worshiped the man I wanted my father to be. I was sure you must have loved him the way you do Ethan. Or you wouldn't have been able to love me."

Aurora took an instinctive step toward him, then made herself stop. She forced herself to let him continue the rending of his heart. And hers.

"You know who told me? Rory did. Just before I left. He'd been telling Grandfather Kincaid how much he wished he was me. You know Grandfather." Scott gave a tight, convulsive laugh. "He set him straight right quick. I hit Rory. I called him a liar. And I kept on hitting him until he was crying and saying how he was sorry, that he'd made it all up. I wouldn't believe what he'd said. I couldn't. And I couldn't go to you and ask, because I was afraid you'd tell me it was true." His voice broke. Breath ripped from him, aflame. He still felt it. All the hurt and confusion of a boy confronted with a complexity beyond his years. The terrible panic of being pushed from the only home he knew into a world of uncaring strangers, wondering with unrequited agony if his mother had sent him away because she couldn't bear the sight of what he represented. His jaw clamped down on that question, the one he still feared to ask. And he recalled his vow to become someone who would not be repugnant in his mother's eyes. Someone who was white. It proved a vow too difficult to keep. Broken like the treaties with the Sioux. Broken like his heart.

"In Boston, I heard stories—stories about whites captured by the Lakotas. About white women taken prisoner. How it was thought better for them to end their own lives than to be taken. In my soul, I knew it was not true, not of the people I grew up among, not of my father. But my head listened. And I began to doubt. The more I heard, the more I began to believe.

197

When I learned of things between men and women, I couldn't stop the wondering. Wondering if I'd been conceived in love or in unspeakable cruelty. And when I came home and you looked at me through eyes that saw my father, I knew." He paused. His breathing grew strong and fierce. "And I wished that he still lived so I could kill him for what he did to you."

"No. Scotty, no."

He flinched beneath the touch of his mother's hands. Inside, he quaked with violent despair. He hated himself for reminding her of what his father was. He hated the fact that he had worshiped an animal, that he'd been fooled by an image of perfection. That even now, he wished she would tell him it wasn't so.

"Mama, please. Tell me how it was between you and my father. I need to know. I have to know."

And so, she told him, glossing over no detail, as gently, as honestly, as she could manage. He wouldn't let her see his face to read the effect her words were having. From beneath her hands, she could feel his tension, his torment, and she wished for some way to give it ease. But only the truth would suffice. She owed him that. He deserved to hear it, not from distorted secondhand telling, but in her own words. When she'd finished, there was a pause, a long, climactic silence.

Then in a deadened monotone, Scott told her, "I'm glad now that I never knew him. I've never hated anyone so much in my life."

Aurora gripped his chin and compelled him to look at her. His face was hard. His eyes cold and intense. Never had she seen him look so much like the father he claimed to despise. "Don't hate," she ordered softly. "Hate is what twisted your grandfather until it was all he had to feed upon. I won't let that happen to you. I won't, Scott."

"You expect me to just accept what he did? That filthy son of—"

"Stop it." Her hand clamped over his mouth, shoving back the words but unable to stem the blaze that had taken fire behind his stare. A wild, ungovernable flame. "Listen to me. Your father was brave and honorable and good." Her son's eyes rolled in angry disbelief. "He was. And I respected him."

Scott tore away, panting, furious. "How can you say that?" he cried hoarsely. "After he—after he—hurt you?"

"He didn't." She caught his arm before he could whirl away, caught it and held firm. "Scott, what hurt me was the way things were, then. The way things were between my people and your father's. It wasn't just him or me, it was the anger and the hatred tearing the land apart." And in her anxiousness to convince, she finally believed it herself. "You're not a boy now and you're not a fool, so I won't try to tell you that I was with Far Winds by choice. He offered a way for me to survive in a very ugly, very cruel time. And I took it. Some still say it was the wrong decision but it was one I have never, ever regretted. I was his woman, and by Lakota law his wife, but he never mistreated me. I was not his whore. I was not his slave. He gave me as much dignity as the situation allowed. Twice, he gave me the chance to live in the face of death. And he gave me something so valuable, I'm grateful to him to this very day."

Scott had turned his head away. She could see him fighting to understand, to accept what offended his every sensibility. In those feelings, he was white in every way. When she paused, he mumbled, "What?" with a dull sort of curiosity.

Her palm soothed over the stiffness of his cheek, bringing him back to face her.

"He gave me you."

Scott drew a great, noisy pull of air. All the hostile fury liquefied in his gaze. He ducked his head and twisted to the side, still struggling, still hurting.

"Oh, Scotty, I'm sorry. I should have told you a long time ago. Far Winds was a fine man, a man worthy of your respect. He was a lot like Ethan, or he would have been if he'd had the chance. They were friends, you know. That's why Ethan loves you so and almost gave up his life so we could keep you."

At last, from deep within his soul, came the wrenching cry. "Mama, why did you send me away?"

Aurora was stunned by the question, and because she didn't know quite what to answer, she asked, "Why do you think?"

He swallowed down the jerking breaths and straightened with a courage that made his mother's bosom swell with pride. His reply was quietly spoken, without rancor, without blame. "I figured you had Ethan and Rory and that I was a reminder of something you wanted to put behind you and forget."

"Dear God," she breathed in shock. "Scott, how could you think that?"

His silence said he could. And did. And Aurora realized in that instant, to her vast dismay, why he would quite logically make that horribly wrong assumption.

"Scott," she murmured, slipping her arms around his unyielding form. He'd grown tall enough for her head to rest upon his shoulder though it seemed it had been the other way around only yesterday. "If there's something I'd like to forget, it's my own selfishness. I sent you away to keep you safe, to protect you from a threat I thought would ruin you. Since you were born, I've been trying to shut out the Indian in you, not because I was ashamed but because I was scared."

That was enough of a surprise to tear his attention

from his own grief. His arms came up to enfold her in an instinctively protective circle. "Scared of what, Mama?"

"Of losing you. Of losing you to the half I couldn't reach. Every time—every time you went to stay amongst the Sioux, I was afraid you wouldn't come home. At first, I feared they'd keep you. Then, I was afraid you would want to stay."

Scott's embrace tightened, feeling guilt that her worries touched so near to the truth.

"I wanted the best for you, Scott. I was afraid if you stayed you wouldn't choose our world, that you'd be hurt by the suffering of your father's people. I didn't want you to see it. I didn't want you to be a part of it. I wanted you to have a chance to be the best that was inside you. And to do that, you had to break away. Far away. Far enough that the Sioux couldn't reach you. I told myself I was doing it for you. Ethan knew better, but he didn't interfere because he wasn't your father. Maybe he should have. Then maybe I would have seen that I was doing it for myself. They were the things I wanted for you—success, acceptance, knowledge, a chance to stretch and achieve. The Lakota half would have held you back, and forgive me, but I couldn't bear for that to happen. I wanted you to have all the advantages of being my son, of being a Kincaid."

"I'm sorry, Mama. I tried. I had you and Ethan and Rory and it should have been enough. But it wasn't."

"I know. I know and I don't want you to be sorry. And I don't ever want you to be ashamed. You are a Kincaid and a Lakota and a Prescott. And in those three names there is more pride and more backbone and more cussed arrogance than you'll find anywhere."

She felt him smile against her hair, and hugged him hard before stepping away. "You do whatever's right for you, Scott. The doors are open. You choose. But don't you ever, ever feel that we won't be proud of that choice. If it's in Boston with Miss Trowbridge or in the Hills with White Cloud's daughter, I won't love you any less."

And from the open window above the porch, Gena reeled back in a shock of distress while her fiancé murmured softly, "I love you, too, Mama."

She hadn't meant to eavesdrop. Upon returning to her room, she'd been upset by her conversation with Scott, or rather by the lack of it. Doubts over whether she'd done the right thing in staying behind drove her to a desperate agitation. Unable to properly pace or throw herself prostrate upon the bed in the confines of her staid gown, she quickly shed the yards of binding fabric and unhooked her corset to allow herself the freedom of a full-bodied sob. Had she made a dreadful mistake? In remaining here? In loving Scott Prescott so much she'd stepped beyond the rules of convention? It had been an impulsive act, one of the very few in her regimented life. In the single second upon Garth Kincaid's porch, things had been so clear to her. She wanted Scott, not the things awaiting her in Boston. None of them mattered. Not the way the taste of forbidden passion did. It had rocked her. No. It had bowled her over. She hadn't known emotions could run so deep, so strong. So dangerous. Her mother told her a real woman views a man not as a lover but as a stepson toward whom she has a motherly tenderness. There had been nothing maternal in the way she'd waited openmouthed for Scott Prescott's kiss. Was it wrong, then? Had her sudden unwholesome, prurient desires led her astray? Was this anguish she suffered now her punishment? She wished for her mother's counsel. Margaret Trowbridge was never at a loss when it came to proper behavior. She would have offered some calming rationale to direct her daughter's wayward passions. Or suggested the excitement of life had brought on the same malady from which she suffered.

Overwrought by the very idea, Gena had gone to the window to draw in the cleansing evening air. It was then she had heard Scott and his mother talking below. She'd meant to withdraw at once so as not to invade their privacy. But the content of their conversation caught her and she'd been unable to move. She'd been enthralled by the dark emotions unfolding between mother and son. She sank down into the single chair before the window with tears in her eyes in witness to the terrible pain in her fiancé's voice. She wanted to weep for him, to comfort him in a compassionate embrace. And then, once she'd heard the concluding sentiments of their speech, all those gentle emotions crumbled before a devastating despair.

He'd spent the day with Morning Song.

And as he claimed his love for Aurora Prescott, she was stunningly aware of a greater desolation.

Had Scott ever once told her the same?

She sat, drained and despondent. Had Scott ever said he loved her? Gena's thoughts flew back to his proposal, to their conversations before and after. Surely he must have. Surely he would have if it were true. And it had to be true. Why else would he have asked her to be his wife? She twisted the ring on her finger, a symbol of his love. No. That wasn't true. It was a symbol of possession. The ring said, *I own you.* His lips had said, *I need you.* His hot golden stare claimed, *I want you.* But none of them meant the same as *I love you.* It shouldn't have mattered. Any of the three should have been enough to placate her. Love had little to do with marriage. That was a contract of security. Security was what she had in her own home. She wanted more from Scott. When he'd seduced her passions in the Bar K parlor, he'd brought to her an awareness of how things could be between a man and woman, and being amongst the Prescotts let her observe the deep affection family life could hold. Because love made all the difference. A difference that was beginning to come to life inside her. And it hurt. And it excited. And it scared her. But she wanted it with the desperation of one long denied.

She wanted to hear him say those three words and mean them.

And she would. She vowed it to herself. She would hear them before he placed a second band of gold upon her finger. She would hear them before he placed another kiss of temptation upon her lips.

But what if she did not?

What if he did not?

She heard his tread upon the stairs, that light, quiet step. The urge to jerk open the door and demand the truth from him was almost overwhelming. But she stayed where she was. Such an outburst was highly vulgar.

Such an outburst might bring her an answer she couldn't bear to hear.

And so she sat by the window, listening to her frantic heartbeats, listening to the soft closure of his door across the hall, listening to the whisper of her own doubts.

"Is everything all right?"

Ethan Prescott's question made her jump in surprise, as if they'd been directed to her instead of to his wife on the porch below.

"Oh, Ethan, why do things have to be so hard for him? I wish I could make them easier."

The sound of her sigh wafted up on the breeze.

"You can't."

"I know."

"C'mere."

Gena blushed hot. She'd never been privy to what went on between married couples, other than her own mother and father, of course. And they never behaved as Ethan and Aurora Prescott did. There was something fascinating and forbidden in what she imaged was going on in the shadows of the porch. She could picture them embracing, and a strange tightness clutched her chest. She felt properly embarrassed but still couldn't draw away.

"Did I do the right thing in sending him to Boston?"

"You thought so at the time."

"I'm not so sure now. And I don't know if I like him working for the major. Even if it was my idea."

"Was it? I should have guessed as much. You don't mind about Rory."

"It's not the same and you know it."

"You won't be able to change his mind. Unfortunately, he admires the old bastard."

"Ethan! You are speaking of my father."

"I know it and I know him and he ain't changed one damn bit. Good thing Scotty's got a smart head on his shoulders. He's got the sense to see things clear. Must have learned that from me."

"Very amusing, Mr. Prescott."

"Well, then, Mrs. Prescott, do you want to spend this whole glorious evening talking about Scotty and your black-hearted daddy?"

"Ethan." Then the sharpness left her voice and it became a satisfied rumble. "Ethan, you stop that. We have company."

"Well, I didn't marry so I'd have to sneak around in my own house."

Her laughter was pitched low. "I don't recall it slowing you down much even before then."

"Who's slowed down?"

His soft sensual chuckle and Aurora's purring response stirred an insidious panic in Gena. Her strict upbringing painted such blatant interaction even within the bounds of wedlock as indecent. There was nothing subdued or restrained in the suggestive sounds they made between them: contented murmurings, husky laughter, and the subtle shifting of material. Gena's face burned. Her stomach shivered. Was this the example Scott grew up to? Was this, then, what he would expect?

"Come on inside, Mrs. Prescott. We got some business to attend."

"Shore 'nuf, sweet thang," Aurora drawled in a saucy imitation of her husband's Lone Star twang. "You jus' lead the way."

That was followed by her surprisingly youthful giggle and the slam of the front door.

Tentacles of shock and thoughts ripe with excitation brought hot blotches of color to her cheeks as Gena continued to sit at the window. To wonder how it would be to have Scott Prescott carry her inside, giggling, to a shared room, to shared secrets.

Suddenly chilled, she rose to shut out the evening air. Nightdress in place, she huddled down in Rory Prescott's bed and tried to shut out the image of his brother across the hall. Of Ethan and Aurora below. Of Morning Song and her slender hand upon her fiancé's thigh.

And she was unsuccessful in all three.

Chapter Thirteen

Scott and Ethan were both gone by the time Gena came downstairs in the morning. She hadn't slept well and was aware of the late hour by the intensity of the sun. Off to a wonderful start with Aurora Prescott, testifying to a slothful nature. The dining table had already been cleared of linen. A good sign that she'd missed the first meal of the day with the Prescott family. The scent of fresh-ground coffee drew her into the kitchen along with the sounds of industry. There, she found Aurora working the last of the whites through a hand wringer.

Aurora's cool golden eyes touched upon her, then returned to her task.

"Good morning, Miss Trowbridge."

"Mrs. Prescott. I do apologize for oversleeping so dreadfully. I am usually an early riser."

"We run by a different clock out here. It takes some getting used to." It was a statement, not an acceptance of her humble words. "Help yourself to some coffee and anything else you might like. I'm afraid I didn't have time to keep the rest warm for you."

Gena flushed at that subtle censure. "Coffee's fine." She poured and searched for some means to make amends and to start fresh with Scott's mother. She watched the woman twisting shirts with a strangling strength and couldn't help but contrast that stern capability with the giggling seductress of the night before. Her blush deepened when she thought of it. Her awkwardness intensified with that intimate knowledge of her forbidding hostess. To relieve some of her discomfort, she asked, "Where has Scott gone this morning?"

"To Crowe Creek. He had business there."

Gena hurriedly pushed aside thoughts of the business that had drawn the redhead inside in her husband's arms. "I wish I'd known," she blurted out.

"Well, it wasn't a secret. He told us at the breakfast table." *You would have known had you been there,* was the silent summation.

"I should have liked to do some shopping," Gena mumbled.

"I'm afraid you won't find anything like what you're wearing in Crowe Creek."

Gena fingered the ruffle of mousseline de soie that edged her jacket. The gauzelike silk muslin would have been the perfect morning wear in Boston. But in Aurora Prescott's kitchen, it was glaringly pretentious. "I was hoping to find something a little more serviceable, actually."

Aurora made a sound acknowledging the sense in that. "I'm sorry I don't have the time to see you there today myself." She didn't sound sorry. She sounded tired, and Gena found herself weighing the pile of laundry stacked beside the washtubs.

"Could I help you, Mrs. Prescott?"

"Wouldn't you much rather enjoy a book or something in the shade of the porch?"

Yes, in truth she would. Nothing was more appealing when compared to the heat of the kitchen, from both boiling pot and simmering hostility. "Please. It's not my intent to be a useless guest. Let me start the next load while you hang those."

Aurora paused, and pushed a strand of damp hair off her brow. She frowned slightly as she studied the younger woman. "If you like. Have you ever done wash before?"

"Of course. Many times." She'd watched. Once. Her mother sent the washing and ironing out every Monday.

Slapping the wet shirt atop the rest in a willow basket, Aurora grasped the handles and lifted. "The calicos and ginghams. The water's ready on the stove."

Alone in the humid kitchen, Gena turned to the task with a determined sigh. She would change Aurora Prescott's opinion of her. She would show her that she'd make Scott a good wife. For the next minutes, she sorted and dropped the appropriate garments into the first tub's soapy water. After working up an agitated froth with the hand plunger, as well as a damp ring of effort beneath each arm, she laid the clothes in the bottom of the second tub and dippered hot water over them. She added what she considered a proper amount of soap, covered the tub, and put it on to boil. By the time she sagged back upon her chair, her coffee was cold and she was overly warm.

Aurora returned with an empty basket. She checked the fire and was apparently satisfied, for she began to go through the stack of woolens for signs of wear and tear. She paused at the pair of trousers Scott had worn the night he'd surprised them at the door. The knees were grass-stained and ripped. Fell off his horse, indeed. She smiled to herself, thinking with fond exasperation of her rough-and-tumble sons. That much hadn't changed. Her fingers clutched in the expensive nap. How simple things had been then. The worst she'd had to repair was a bloodied nose or gashed elbow. Now their hurts weren't so easily mended. They were growing apart, Rory toward her father's vast cattle empire, Scott in search of his way between two worlds. Neither came to her any longer with their hurts, their tears, or their troubles. They were

209

off in pursuit of their lives, unaware of how empty that left hers.

Gena puzzled over the other woman's strange shift of mood. She stood with a pair of Scott's suit pants dangling from her hands, staring out the window across endless miles of memory. An incredible sadness softened her expression. Unwilling to intrude, Gena moved silently to drain the hot print fabrics and to rinse them in clean water and bluing.

Never again would Gena take a freshly laundered frock for granted. It was arduous work, hand-scalding and back-breaking work. For the better part of the day, she scrubbed and dipped and boiled and wrung and toted wet clothes. She marveled at Aurora's uncomplaining fortitude and was rather pleased with her own. While theirs had not been a companionable day, at least the stiffness seemed to have washed and rinsed out of it. While Aurora was starting supper, she was unpinning the dried contents of the last basket from the sagging side-yard line. The sun was angled but still warm enough to raise a prickle of sweat beneath her collar. She draped the final garment over her shoulder and paused to rake back her hair and loosen the top buttons. Flapping the open bodice over her flushed skin, she reached for the last piece of clothing and gave a startled gasp.

"What are you doing in my long johns?"

With one hand, she clutched her neckline together beneath her chin. In the other, she was dismayed to discover she did, indeed, hold Scott's long underwear. Her cheeks turned just as pink.

He had come upon her with that silent cat-walk of his and had been watching her dainty shoes dance back and forth beneath the edge of his mother's quilts and his daddy's denims. He tried to dislodge the lump of feeling that sight had settled in his throat but the way she colored up so rosily at his turn of humor made the clog more insistent. How pretty and fresh she looked with her pale hair in tumbled disarray, with her cheek hot and a dew of moisture upon bared skin. Almost as if she'd been tumbling in the sheets instead of hanging them. He watched her blush and handle the flannels in her hands as gingerly as if he'd been inside them. A thoroughly warming thought on this sultry afternoon amid the crisp scent of clean wash and new grass. She had picked them up by the drop seat, and in realizing it, went crimson to the roots of her hair. Scott snatched them up before they hit the ground, and he slung them carelessly over the stack in the basket.

Acutely conscious of her untidy state, Gena couldn't say she was glad to see him. Especially not in the middle of manipulating his underclothes. As fingers hurried up the row of bodice buttons, she stammered, "I was just finishing the laundry."

Scott took in the blotches of exertion on her inappropriate dress, the unnatural redness of her hands, and the way her shoulders winced away from movement. And he frowned. "Mama put you to work washing clothes?"

"Oh, no." She smiled fetchingly. "Silly me, I offered."

They stood for a moment, listening to the snap of the remaining quilts and hearing the words exchanged in last night's shadows. Neither quite knew how to end the silence. Until she wiped a sleeve across her beaded brow.

"If you want to feel a hundred percent better before dinnertime," he suggested, "you might try a dip in the stream." He gestured to a grove of cottonwoods behind the far outbuildings.

"Outside?" Even as the idea shocked, it enticed her bedraggled spirit. Cool water. A luxurious thought.

"Sure. We use it all the time in the summer." Seeing her modesty tugging back her enthusiasm, he grinned wryly. "You don't need to worry. There's nothing but a few horses and maybe a jackrabbit that's going to see you.

Daddy's mending harness and I'll be up on the porch going through some of my lawbooks. It'll be as private as an indoor bath, which you may have noticed we don't have."

Yes, she had, after making a cold, dark run in the middle of the night to the backyard privy. She felt just rumpled and wilted enough to cast off all propriety. "All right. It sounds wonderful." And rebelling against the gasps of her modesty, she snatched up a freshly laundered towel.

And it was wonderful. The water was deep and clear. And cold as winter melt. From behind the screen of trees, she laid out her fresh gown and stripped off the stained one. As daring as she felt, she wasn't quite brave enough to strip to the skin. In her cotton combinations, she waded out into the swirl of water and sank down with a chattering sigh. She shook out her hair and lathered it with the fine milled soap she'd brought from Boston, then, when it lay wet and heavy down her back, she began to work the grime and aches from the rest of her. Feeling lazy as an otter in the late afternoon sunlight, she lingered in the stream, forgetting time, forgetting place, as it soothed her into a blissful lethargy.

She thought it was the wind in the trees overhead. At first. Then, as it grew louder, she realized the sound was coming from the grassy knoll running parallel to the stream. Horses. In a hurry. Her eyes snapped open in alarm going first to the far bank where her clothes were laid out on the rocks then to the opposite incline in an agony of suspense. Too late. She sank down in the water, hugging her knees up to her chest as the horses topped the hill and the initial terror struck her.

Scott sat in one of the porch rockers with a heavy law tome opened across his knees. He tried to concentrate on finding precedents among congressional decisions, something to aid White Cloud and his family. But all he could focus on was the image of Gena Trowbridge splashing in the shallows like a shimmering panfish. Half a dozen times, he'd thought of strolling over to join her. And he'd fantasized a half-dozen receptions, some sweet, some sizzling. But the truth held him on the porch. If he violated her trust, he would be met with no scintillating welcome. She would probably shriek her head off and aim straight for Boston. Knowing that put a dampening check on his mood but his mind continued to prowl. Why couldn't she have half the free-spirited attitude of Morning Song? Or a trace of Aurora Prescott's impetuous passion? Had she either, he would have been yanking off his boots even now.

He forced his attention back to the book but in a matter of minutes was wandering again. He was remembering the softness of her cheeks and slender white throat. He was remembering the excitement stirred by her rapid little gasps for breath and control. The feel of her fingertips in his hair, along his face, on his lips. Impossibly aroused, he gave up the dry dirge of legal terminology and was about to give himself a thorough ducking in the horse trough when he heard her cry.

"S-S-Scott."

The short hairs rose along his nape and crawled on forearms.

"Scott! Scott!"

He was up off the chair, off the porch, running before the book crashed to the ground. A terrible fear gripped him, making it hard for him to breathe, to think of anything beyond reaching Gena.

He was unarmed.

It wasn't far to the creek but it seemed like miles, hours, before he was charging through the cottonwoods, skidding down the bank and into the water. One look told him everything. There was no need for panic. But he couldn't get his senses under control. Fright had driven logic to its knees. And in its place was a wild, killing fury.

Gena sat shivering in the water, her hair slicked back

and eyes huge, looking scared as a half-drowned pup. He had no time to offer her any lengthy reassurances. Just one. Curt and to the point.

"It's all right, Gena."

And she believed him. Instinctively. Without question. And because he was by far more fearsome than the trio of red men staring down stoically upon them.

One of the Indians separated from the others. He led a horse behind him. Scott stiffened in recognition of both man and animal. The brave was High Hawk and he was trailing the horse he'd given to his family. Only this pathetic-looking creature in no way resembled the fine mount he had left with White Cloud. No Lakota would purposefully ruin good horseflesh but the intent was no less clear. The animal's coat was dulled and caked with mud and excrement, its mane and tail matted with burrs. When close enough, High Hawk threw the reins down into the water, a sneer upon his haughty face.

"Take back your pity, *iyeska*. We would rather starve than be called *wagluhe*. Or have you been living in their walls so long you've forgotten what it is to have pride?"

The insult was insurmountable. First, the abuse of the horse, then the slur of half-breed, and topped with the disdainful insinuation that he was treating his friend's family as if they were the indolent loafers who hung around white men for handouts. High Hawk wheeled his horse around, putting his back to Scott, casting a further slight, as if he were no one to be feared or taken seriously.

With a low snarl of rage, Scott jerked off his water-laden boots and flung them to the bank, followed by the swirl of his Stetson. Then he was running, barefooted, bareheaded, after the retreating brave. High Hawk guided his horse at an angle up the steep embankment toward where the others waited. By racing straight up, Scott was able to intersect him. With a loud cry, he launched himself at the startled Lakota, snagging him around the neck and snatching him off his horse. They fell in a tangle of arms and legs and, suddenly, steel.

"Oh, my God," Gena moaned as sunlight glinted off the blade of a knife. She surged up and began to heedlessly splash through the water. Not toward the bank where safety had arrived in the form of Ethan Prescott with a Colt revolver and Aurora capably slinging a Winchester. But frantically downstream toward danger and Scott.

The two men grappled for the blade. They were evenly matched for size and strength and for the anger pushing them to fight. They had wrestled often as children, neither gaining a notable advantage. But then, they hadn't been hungry to do each other harm. The slant of the hillside brought them tumbling down into the water, blinding them, making a firm hold difficult on a slippery opponent. Adrenaline pumped by the sound of Gena's terror, Scott forgot that he was struggling with a lifelong friend. And when he won control of the Lakota's knife, he sent it streaking down toward the other's throat.

High Hawk lay panting beneath him, situation helpless but eyes still spitting hatred. The wicked blade was steady in Scott's hand. His brain was fueled with the memory of his fright, with the sting of insults, with the hurt of losing a friend. His blood sang fierce and hot, the blood of his father and his father's people, demanding retribution. Demanding pain for pain. His arm jerked up, fist white-knuckled about the hilt of High Hawk's knife.

"Scott, no!"

Gena's horrified cry snapped the sudden madness. With a raw growl of frustration, he plunged his arm downward, burying the blade deep in the stream's soft bank. He was breathing hard, exhausted in body and spirit.

"I give you your life."

"And I should thank you?" High Hawk snarled up at him. "You do me no favor, *iyeska*. Why should I choose to see my people raped all over again by the white man? To see you shame my father and sister with your useless promises? Leave them alone. Leave me alone. We want no part of your lies."

He began to squirm. Scott brought his knees down on his ribcage, hard, crushing the rebellion from him. "Listen to me, fool. If you want to do something for your family, crawl out of your bottle. Don't speak to me of shame when you wallow in it. If you want to help them, help me. I was and will always be your friend, even now, when there is no pride in claiming it. Get on your horse. Go back home or go back to your drinking. If you want to walk like a man again, you talk to me when you're sober. If you don't, then stay the hell out of my way."

Scott staggered up and backpedaled, giving High Hawk room to gain his feet. The beaten Lakota jerked his knife free and, without a word, stalked up the hill to where his companions held his horse. And then, they were gone.

Slowly, Scott turned and was surprised to see Gena standing so close. And stunned by how she looked, all white and wet and outlined to exquisite perfection in the damp cling of her cotton combinations. All wrought up by that unexpected jolt of attraction, and breathing still labored from the fright she'd given him, he struck out at her in reflexive anger.

"Witkowin!" he shouted. "Crazy woman! Haven't you the sense to know you were in no danger from them? I ought to beat you for the scare you gave me."

Gena went even paler. Scott Prescott flushed by indignant anger was an intimidating sight. His swarthy features grew even darker. His eyes glittered, hot and brilliant. The jerk of his breathing delineated a powerful upper body beneath the hug of his wet shirt. Big hands clenched at his side could easily prove his threat. And Gena took a hasty step back, her voice small and anxious.

"I'm sorry, Scott. They startled me. I should have known. I shouldn't have yelled like that. I didn't mean to—"

He took a few long strides forward, out to meet her in the middle of the stream. The rough compression of his arms literally crushed the rest of the words from her. He felt the sudden stiffening of her objection and overrode it with sheer, impassioned force. He hugged her hard to the pounding panic of his heart, letting the feel of her against him calm his fright. She was trembling. He was quaking. Inside and out. With his cheek pressed to the damp hair at her temple, Scott squeezed his eyes shut and tried to flush all the horrible images the sound of her cries had drawn. She was safe and he was shaken to the soul.

"I'm sorry, Scott," she said again, more strongly because she was no longer afraid within his embrace. "I was foolish. It was a mistake. It won't happen again."

"No," he murmured huskily, still tormented by what he might have found. "No, it won't. Because I'm sending you back to Boston."

She wrenched back out of his arms. "What?" Her wide eyes searched his frantically. His gaze was impassive, firm in its decision.

"As soon as possible."

"Because of this?" she demanded shrilly, a bit hysterically, unwilling to believe he could be so unforgiving of her error in judgment.

"Yes, partly, and because it made me realize that you don't belong out here. If something had happened—"

"Nothing did, Scott. Nothing did. I just had a bit of a fright. There was no harm done."

No harm? If she could only feel the express train tearing through his chest. The horrible sinking emptiness of blame. She was his responsibility. If anything had happened . . .

"Gena, things are harsh out here, cruel even. You're just not prepared to deal with them. It's not your fault, and I don't think any less of you."

Didn't he? Didn't he really?

"I'm putting you on the first train east," he continued with a determined finality. "I should never have let you stay on. I'm sending you home where you belong."

"I'm not going."

It was his turn to be taken aback. Then he scowled. "Yes, you are."

There was nothing coy or pleading about her expression. It was positively mulish. "No I am not!"

"Gena, you don't understand—"

"No. No, I don't, and I never will perched in some stuffy Boston parlor a half a continent away. I'm your fiancée. Being here, with you, is where I belong."

Looking bewildered and angry, as if a delicate flower he'd been tending had suddenly jabbed him with vicious thorns, Scott seized her by the arm, thinking to literally shake some sense into her. The change in Gena was immediate and alarming. Her tenacious manner fled as quickly as her color. She pulled against his grasp, shrinking away, plainly terrified.

"Scott, don't."

Confusion increased his irritation. He refused to release her or give before this new, disturbing ploy for sympathy. "You are going. I can't be here to watch over you all the time. I can't be responsible for you every minute of the day. I have things I have to do here. I can't take you with me and I won't sit home all day to see you don't get into trouble."

"I will."

Scott and Gena both looked in surprise to Aurora Prescott. The older woman gripped her son's hand,

218

plucking it from Gena's arm. Then, she put her own around the girl's shivering shoulders.

"I'll see to her. And she'll be just fine."

Scott stood dumbfounded as his mother squired Gena to the bank of the stream where she helped her into the dry gown. He was distracted from the incredible sight when Ethan thrust his boots and hat at him.

"Scotty, you ever hit that little girl?"

"What?" Scott glanced up at his stepfather, stunned by the low menace in his tone. "No. No, of course not. I would never—"

His protest trailed off as he stared after his fiancée. Wondering, with sudden dawning horror, who might have.

"Why?"

"Why what?"

Gena looked at the woman walking beside her with a grateful curiosity. "Why would you stand up for me? I realize you think I'm foolish and fluffy-headed and without any . . ." she reached back for the exact words and concluded, "spark of passion. I know you think I'm totally wrong for Scott, that I wouldn't make him any kind of wife. So why? If you honestly believe all those things, Mrs. Prescott, why would you take my side?"

Aurora was silent for a moment, composing her thoughts. She had seen how the meek Miss Trowbridge had raced after Scott when she thought him in danger, regardless of her own well-being. And she'd seen the naked emotion carved upon her son's features when he held the young woman in his arms. It hadn't changed her mind but it had given her pause.

"Let's just say, Miss Trowbridge, that I want the very best for my son. I've not decided whether or not that is you. Convince me."

Feeling more confident and determined than ever, Gena vowed, "I shall do my best, Mrs. Prescott."

"Good." Without glancing to her side, she said, "And you may call me Aurora."

"I hope we can become friends — Aurora," Gena murmured softly. "Because, you see, I happen to love Scott very much and I'm going to marry him. And I don't care what he is, what he does, or who his father was."

That brought Aurora up short. She studied the young woman's frail features and pale eyes and found in them, yes, a spark. And she smiled prudently.

"Perhaps we will be friends, Miss Trowbridge. But be warned, I will be more generous with my friendship than with my son."

Gena smiled, too, and it was not without a twist of respect. "Thank you for the warning. And it's Gena."

Chapter Fourteen

The next morning, Aurora took Gena into Crowe Creek to buy some practical clothes. On the drive there, Gena had her first lesson at the reins. According to the redhead, such knowledge was vital in the west, where one could not very well hail a cab outside the front door. A person was responsible for getting herself wherever she wanted to go, and unless Gena wanted to spend the entire summer on the Prescotts' porch, she'd best take some initiative. After some hesitancy, Gena surprised herself by taking competent control of their buggy. There was a sense of accomplishment and independence in holding the reins, as if for the first time she was taking part in the steering of her destiny. And she liked the feeling. And she found she liked the brash Aurora Prescott for encouraging her.

The young easterner wasn't as shocked as she once might have been by the primitive town and its rough inhabitants. Much of her innocence had been stripped away in her first three weeks in South Dakota. It was not Boston. But it was not the Cheyenne River reservation, either. Aurora seemed to know everyone, and their walk from the buggy to the first of several shops was interrupted at least a dozen times by greetings and introductions. For the most part, these were not the elite citizens she'd met at the Bar K. These were the wives of area farmers and shopkeepers, the women who sewed shot into the hems of their gowns to maintain decorum on the windy Plains rather than the latest styles from the east. They were common and direct and as faded in looks as the weather-beaten buildings, but there was a vim and vinegar to them that Gena found unique and appealing. They wasted no time conversing on meaningless pleasantries. Their talk was abrupt and to the point, as if they had no use for idle minutes. Different. Bracing. Refreshing.

Gena's gown was the center of much interest, all parties agreeing it was a glorious creation but quite unsuitable for daily wear. She understood them completely the minute she tried on a simple shirtwaist and skirt at McElroy's. It was like casting off shackles. The lightness of the fabric and freedom of movement was so delicious, she had her proper eastern attire wrapped up in preference of her new garb. Several utilitarian outfits were selected and even a doeskin split skirt, at Aurora's insistence. All women in the west knew how to ride. Astraddle. That shocked but also intrigued, like everything else in the wide, rugged country.

As they were coming out of McElroy's, Aurora was waylaid by the owner of the livery, who told her that the wagon they had in for repairs would be ready later that afternoon as well as the team, which was being reshod. It was both blessing and annoyance. Ethan needed the wagon the next morning, but it also meant another trip back into Crowe Creek to pick it up.

Gena, who had her attention drawn to a solitary figure at the edge of town, came up with a quick and ready solution.

"If you would like to wait and drive the wagon home yourself, I'm sure I could manage the buggy. I don't see how I could possibly get lost on the way back to the Lone Star."

Getting lost wasn't the problem. Aurora looked over her son's fiancée, seeing a pretty, fragile temptation. But then she considered the extra trip and the wasted time. "Why don't you wait with me, Gena, and we can go back together."

Gena glanced impatiently down the street, then back at her. "I'd really rather be on my way now, Aurora. I'd like to get a hem run in my new skirts. Please don't worry about me. I'm sure I won't have any trouble with the horse."

"Do you know anything about guns?"

"Oh, yes," Gena said eagerly. About as much as she did about doing laundry. And that hadn't proved too difficult.

"There's a scattergun under the seat. Any critters try to tangle with you on the road, just showing them the barrel should do the trick."

Critters? Bears? Wolves? She wondered if such predators would be discouraged by the brandishing of a rifle. But she didn't have the time to ponder it. She was already hurrying toward the buggy, calling over her shoulder, "And don't you worry. I'll get dinner started."

Dinner wasn't Aurora's concern. She began to frown. If anything happened to Gena Trowbridge, she hated to think how that might affect her relationship with her son. She was about to shout after her, to tell her she decided not to wait after all. However, the proprietor of the feed and grain chose that moment to come up to her with the details of a new mix he thought Ethan would be interested in. And by the time she could break away, the buggy was already gone.

* * *

Gena wasn't completely sure until she drew the buggy up alongside the woman toting her heavy burden down the road. Obsidian eyes regarded her impassively.

"Morning Song, isn't it?"

The beautiful Indian woman gave a brief nod, then recognition lightened her features. "You are Lone Wolf's woman."

"Yes," Gena claimed with unaccustomed haughtiness. Almost at once, she felt ashamed of her snappish reaction. She had no way of knowing for sure that this woman was a threat. Perhaps she was just the sister of Scott's childhood friend. Then, she took in the smoothly chiseled cheekbones, full lips, lush figure. Perhaps not. A jealous misery throbbed inside. How could Scott fail to be attracted to the lovely Morning Song, who was possessed of every confidence she lacked as a woman. But it wasn't envy, it was curiosity that made her linger. Curiosity about Scott Prescott's life as Lone Wolf, grandson of a Lakota chief. Unless she understood that side of him, she had no chance of holding to the rest of him. And she was willing to do anything to keep him.

Morning Song was lugging a basket of clothes upon one shapely hip. A remindful ache in her own shoulders recalled her to how weighty a stack of clothes could be.

"Might I give you a lift somewhere? That's an awful heavy burden to carry any distance."

Morning Song hoisted her chin to proudly say, "It is no burden and I am not going far."

Gena looked about her. "There's nothing for miles. Please. You can put the basket in the back."

Coaxed by her genuine smile, Morning Song relented. The day was hot and she was tired and faced with an afternoon of toil. And she was just as curious about Lone Wolf's white woman. On the surface, she could not see what attracted him unless it was the corn-silk hair.

The pale, spindly *wasichu* woman looked not to have the strength to hold his house and bear his children. Or maintain his passions. Not like Wadutah, his mother, who was said to have the power and courage of their finest warriors. This pale one, she was probably like the woman whose clothes she washed: frail, sickly, useless for all but complaining. That Lone Wolf would prefer her was a mystery edging on insult.

With the stoic Lakota maiden beside her, Gena urged the horse on.

"Where are you going?"

"To the Cheyenne where I will meet my brother."

"High Hawk."

Dark eyes canted her way. "You know of my brother?"

Gena's color deepened, but all she would say was, "We met yesterday at the Lone Star." Pushing that embarrassment aside, she said, "This will work out quite well. Scott — Lone Wolf went to the reservation this morning. Perhaps, I shall see him there."

"Perhaps."

There was a long silence, as quiet and cloudy as the whorls of dust rising in their wake. Finally, Gena ventured, "Lone Wolf tells me you grew up together."

"Yes."

Gena waited but no more was offered. "He says he and your brother were good friends. What happened to change that?"

Morning Song glanced sharply at the woman who asked such private questions. "Time and distance. Lone Wolf went away and my brother stayed behind."

"Why does he resent Scott trying to help him? They fought over the horse yesterday."

"I guessed as much," came the inflectionless reply. "My people have reason to be wary of the white man and his help."

"But surely you don't think Scott —"

"No. I do not. I think he can do great good for my family and others at the Cheyenne. But those, like my brother, who cannot see clearly through the hate, will not listen."

"Perhaps someday everyone will listen and have a voice."

Surprised by the intensity of those quiet words, Morning Song studied the woman beside her. And she was suspicious. "Why do you care what happens to my people?"

"Because they are Scott's people and he cares."

Gena's honesty impressed her.

"In the east, I belonged to committees who thought they were doing good for the Indian. After seeing the Cheyenne, I think the only good we were doing was to our own consciences. I wish they could see what I have seen."

Upon saying those words, Gena fell silent and thoughtful, an idea beginning to brew.

"That is where you met Lone — Scott?"

"In Boston. His mother's cousin introduced us. We will return there at the end of the summer and marry. He has a job waiting with my father."

Morning Song digested this without comment, and Gena began to feel that in her want to prove her own the superior claim, she had said too much. Indeed, the conversation was over. Morning Song ended it with one last revelation.

"Had he not gone to the east, I would have been Lone Wolf's woman."

To that, there was nothing Gena could reply.

"*Takoja,* this you might find more interesting than that book."

226

Scott glanced up at his grandfather, then followed his directing nod. And stared. At Gena Trowbridge and Morning Song together in the same buggy. They were dusky eve and silvery moon. The two of them, together. A punch of startled anxiety caught beneath his ribs, slamming the breath from him. He stumbled to his feet as both women whose kisses he'd enjoyed looked to him with smiles of greeting. And seated at his feet, Yellow Bear chuckled.

"One wonders what they found to talk about on so long a journey," the old man mused.

Scott was afraid he had a fairly good idea. Wisely, he stood his ground and let them come to him.

Morning Song bound lithely from the buggy. In three half-running steps, she had her arms around him in an affectionate hug.

"Lone Wolf," she murmured happily. "How good to see you here among friends and family. As it should be."

Scott was careful not to move as her supple body pressed close. His gaze was on Gena, who approached with a smile stiffening on her lips. She looked different somehow and it took him a second to figure why. The clothes. He liked the relaxed way they outlined her figure. But more than that. Something in her eyes when they sought and held his. Something deep, searching, asking. Angry. He lifted his arms around Morning Song, not to embrace but to gently discourage. When she came away from him, he spoke softly, in her native tongue. She looked uncomfortable with his words and stepped farther back, out of Gena's way.

Scott looked different to Gena, too. By degrees, she had seen him change from the man she'd fallen in love with in Boston. The civilized trappings had disappeared, one by one, until, today, he was stripped down to the man. To Lone Wolf rather than Scott Prescott. Had it happened all at once, she would have been terrified. But the gradual transformation, layer by layer, drew her with a fascination. Each stage was just a little bit more dangerous, a little bit more foreign. More exciting.

He had been sitting beneath a blanket canopy, talking with Yellow Bear and reading through a thick ledger. He was wearing crisp dark blue jeans. And nothing else. Bare feet protruded at the hem. Above, there seemed to be miles and miles of blatantly bare male. Gena had never seen a man's chest before, except for renderings on pugilistic posters. The comparison was lost upon her. She hadn't been prepared for how very — hard a man's body was, like a wall of stone or steel. And so dark. Stretched over the mass of muscle, his skin was taut and brown, as copper as a museum cast. As she approached, cautiously now, her gaze absorbed each magnificently etched detail: the broad range of shoulders veeing down to the valley of his throat, the separate swells and sinewy ridges of his arms, the pull of bronze flesh across the plain of his chest and the flat lands of his belly. Rugged, forbidding terrain. Her eyes traveled it all. And the journey left her breathless.

Scott watched her expression. He looked beyond the awkward blush of color to the way her gaze took in each contour of his upper body. He could tell she was shocked by the way her pupils widened. But she didn't look away. Her attention, the way her eyes devoured him inch by inch, was as potent as a caress and his unbidden response to it was immediate. In return, he saw her the way she was in the stream, all damp and deliciously delineated, dark-crested breasts hugged by wet cotton, pantalets wrapped about sweetly curved hips and slender thighs. The image that kept him awake most of the night. And stirred a similar urgency now.

When her stare reached his navel, Scott snatched up

his shirt and shrugged into it. He buttoned the bottom buttons so his shirttails swaddled his hips. No sense in presenting her innocent exploration with more territory than it was prepared to chart.

"Gena, this is a surprise." His voice was as thick as the hot sensations settling in his loins. "A pleasant one."

Gena swallowed and worked her lips against each other, as if they were as parched as his felt. "Yes," came her soft agreement.

She stopped just outside of arm's reach, made skittish by all that golden flesh and by the sudden dark hunger in Scott's regard. How she would have liked to cast herself upon him the way Morning Song had. To feel for herself the warm, taut skin, the hard flow of muscle. Propriety restrained her. That and a curious panic. Of what enticed and repelled her in an impossible confusion. The impersonal distance was better, easier to control. Even across the space between them, she could feel the charge, alive with a sensual current.

Watching the interplay, Morning Song was goaded by a mix of envy and remorse to intervene. "Have you found anything that will help my father?"

Scott's attention was torn away from Gena with reluctance and relief. He gestured to the ledger. "Some of Garrick's records. Ones he was willing to let me see, so I assume they won't tell me anything. I'm hoping I can read between the lines enough to get some direction."

"I am sorry for what my brother did."

Scott nodded, accepting her quiet apology without comment.

"I should go now." The dark eyes touched upon Gena in begrudging thanks. The blonde woman inclined her head in recognition, then watched as the young Indian went to claim her basket from the buggy. Such smooth, gliding sensuality. Gena bit down hard on the bitterness

229

of resentment and glanced to Scott to see if he was appreciating the dance of calico around bared calves. But he was looking at her, apparently oblivious to the Lakota's charm. And Gena felt her heart somersault.

"You drove out here, alone?"

Gena found herself pricked by Scott's disbelief. It was hard to check the crackling reproof that sprang to her lips. How helpless he must think her. Instead, she made herself bestow a mild smile. "No. I brought Morning Song." She briefly explained the happenings in town, pleased by the growing admiration in her fiancé's gaze. And pleased by her own sense of independence. The Gena Trowbridge of Boston would never have attempted anything so adventurous. Scott must have been thinking the same thing.

"Well, I can see you're busy so I won't detain you."

"He may be busy but I would welcome the company of a pretty face."

Gena smiled down at the old man. "Chief Yellow Bear, I would be delighted."

"You will have to come down to me. I am afraid I am not as nimble as I once was." When the old chief shifted on his blanket, she could see the strain upon his face.

"Are you ill, Yellow Bear?" she asked in concern as she settled upon the ground with her skirt wrapped modestly about her legs.

"If old age is an illness, or old wounds."

With eyes shiny and round, she looked at him in wonder. In innocence, she asked, "Were you wounded in battle?" Her thoughts were taken with the incredibly romantic image of Yellow Bear as a young man, astride a great horse, his face unlined and painted for war.

"In a battle without honor, New Waw. At a place called Wounded Knee."

Gena gasped. She'd read accounts of it. Some called it

retribution. Some, a massacre. But this old man had survived, one of the few. His story was a piece of history few would ever hear spoken.

"Will you tell me?"

Scott came down beside her, his expression tight with warning. "Gena—"

Yellow Bear waved off his objection. That same hand lightly captured Gena's chin. "It is all right, *takoja*. One should ask as a child in order to learn. One needs to hear in order to gain wisdom." The ancient chief looked to the past with sadness and, beside her, Scott tensed as if in pain.

"It began with a vision. At the time of the dark sun, a Paiute named Wovoka was carried to heaven where he learned the new Messiah was coming back to earth. He would be the savior of the red man, sent by the Great Spirit to drive the white invaders away and to restore the wilderness, the buffalo, and our many dead. Upon hearing of this, our people began to dance with the spirit of the old days. We fasted and steamed in our sweat lodges, praying that the secret of gunpowder be taken away so it wouldn't burn the red man, praying that soon soil five times the height of a man would bury our enemy." He smiled gently at Gena's look of disbelief. "I know that sounds silly and superstitious to you, but we were starving, we were hungry for our freedom, our dignity. We were ready to believe. We were ready for a miracle."

Scott had gone very still. Remembering that he had not danced, had not starved, had not prayed for his father's people. Because he couldn't bear the thought of his mother, Ethan, and Rory buried beneath the new soil. It had been a selfish fear, an unworthy one, considering what others sacrificed. Sensing that guilt now, just as he had then, Yellow Bear reached out to draw two fingers from forehead to chin down his grandson's somber face. It was a gesture he'd used when a young Lone Wolf's attention wandered or he became frustrated with his inability to learn as fast as he thought he should. A quieting gesture.

"Not all looked to this miracle. Many were too Christian or thought themselves too intelligent. Still, thirty thousand believed. The Eastern papers called it the Ghost Dance and said we were making dark and bloody plots against them. The leaders in Washington grew afraid and ignored wise counsel to let it pass. They stationed troops and ordered Sitting Bull's arrest.

"Here on the Cheyenne, Big Foot was a great chief. Many followed him into the wilderness where the dance continued. My wife, Oesedah, and I went with them."

Gena listened as the last proud days of the Sioux unfolded at Yellow Bear's telling. He spoke of the approach of winter. Of how Big Foot and his band were camped five miles above the mouth of the Cherry huddling in canvas tents and close to starving. They were armed with old shotguns and small game rifles, hardly a fearsome group contemplating the war path. While councils met to decide what to do, word came that Sitting Bull had been killed. The sacred Ghost Shirt proved no protection against the bullets of the enemy. A detachment from Bennett had been dispatched to take them into custody. The chiefs voted to head for the Pine Ridge reservation, some 150 miles to the south where the great chief, Red Cloud, would help them make talk with the government.

"We fled into the Place-Where-the-Hills-Look-at-Each-Other, the place you call the Badlands. It was a march of great suffering. Babies were starving at their mother's milkless breasts. Finally, our hunters brought down a steer to put hunger at bay, but in the end, we had to kill several yearling colts for food, which caused us much grief. But there was no going back.

232

"Big Foot contracted pneumonia but continued to guide and encourage our band. All were burdened by cold, hunger, and fatigue. Then, as we neared the outskirts of Pine Ridge, soldiers converged upon us, riding up from the south rather than as expected from the north. Thinking of his weary people, Big Foot ordered white flags flown, hoping that the government would at least feed us. It was then we learned the soldiers were of the Seventh Cavalry unit which had been assigned to Pine Ridge. Custer's old unit."

He paused then, filled with the picture of a group of gaunt warriors, half-starved mothers, and bewildered children marching despondently with heads bowed and expressions subdued to a place called Wounded Knee Creek where they were met by the rest of the army. There they would camp before going on to Pine Ridge in the morning. His words softened, building the suspense, the terror of what was to come.

"We were given small rations to partially ease our hunger, and with the hope of more food in the morning, most enjoyed a peaceful night's sleep under the protection of the government. Big Foot was gravely ill. We, his chiefs, held our own council. We could not sleep to the sound of the guards in our camp. We were uneasy with the memories of Crazy Horse and Sitting Bull and feared for the life of Big Foot. But there was nothing we could do.

"The morning was cool and clear. The soldiers' music woke us and we began to break camp, eager to finish our long journey. We were called to deposit all arms, which were few and poor, and this we did. Then the soldiers insulted us by searching our belongings. Our women, too, were rudely handled until there was much confusion and anger among us. We were under a flag of truce, yet they acted as if they would provoke us to fight.

"White man's history says one of our braves resisted

233

the search and fired upon a soldier. It did not happen that way. None were armed. But it did not matter once the shooting started."

The old man's voice faltered as he retold the facts that Gena had heard, made more frightening because she could feel them happening through him. Big Foot's people were caught in a deadly crossfire. Four Hotchkiss guns standing as if at ready on the surrounding hills poured down two-pound shells at a rate of fifty per minute. The discharge from infantry and cavalry joined in the melee to leave 90 warriors, 200 women and children, and 60 soldiers dead. A handful escaped that first barrage and fled in panic to the shelter of ravines.

"They hunted us down like animals. Young girls knelt in the snow and covered their faces with their shawls so they would not see the troopers who came up to shoot them. Some of us fled into the ravines to hide. Some of the women, my Oesedah among them, were pursued as far as three miles before being caught and killed. That day saw their Custer avenged. The dead and wounded soldiers were attended, but not so the Sioux. The soldiers returned to Pine Ridge where they gloated over their whiskey about how they put down an uprising. We, the survivors, were left in that blizzard for three days before they came back for us. We were allowed to return to the battlefield to search for our loved ones. Then the soldiers dumped them, over 200 bodies, into a single trench to be buried without ceremony or prayer. Even the Pine Ridge missionaries who wanted to come were not allowed to give services. Colonel Forsythe, who commanded at Wounded Knee, ordered no burial be given to those 'savages and Red devils'. 'Let them go to hell without a prayer,' he said."

"And was nothing done?" Gena asked in quiet horror.
"Colonel Forsythe was later court-martialed. But the

government refused to admit any crime had been committed along the Wounded Knee.

"Custer's defeat ended the wars on the plains," Yellow Bear concluded softly. "By winning, the Indians lost, for we were pursued without mercy after that. I bear the scars of five wounds from that day. The woman standing beside me survived with fourteen. But the one that pains me the most was that I could not bury my wife on the Wa-Jo-La with honor and respect. That is the wound that will bleed until I join her."

Sometime during the tragic story, Gena's hand sought and found Scott's. She took comfort in that warm, tight grasp as tears slipped quietly down her cheeks. A similar wetness gilded the old chief's withered face until at last the tale was told and he could wipe them away. Only Scott didn't cry. He sat tall and silent, features as still as stone. But the fingers laced through Gena's were cold and crushing.

Thoughts of death and despair were scattered by the renewed pattern of life. Released from the reservation day school, brown-skinned children dashed with abandoned joy through the encampment as though just freed from prison. Wildly yapping dogs raced at their flying heels. A smile shifted the downward flow of lines upon Chief Yellow Bear's cheeks as he watched them. Four of the freshly scrubbed youngsters separated from the others and came to wriggle like small excited puppies at the old man's feet. They cast shy glances at Gena and ones of curious admiration toward Scott. They were Morning Song's brothers and sisters. Scott snatched up the youngest boy and wrestled playfully with him before settling him upon his lap in a loose embrace. His smile was bittersweet, his thoughts recalled to sitting before Yellow Bear with High Hawk at about the same age clamoring for a story.

"Tell us. Tell us," the energetic gathering pestered in the Lakota tongue.

Yellow Bear put a fond hand atop one of the girls's glossy braids. "What is it to be? A just-for-fun or a legend?"

"*Ohunkankan!*"

"*Wicooyake!*"

"First, because we have a guest, you must remember your English." That brought a chorus of moans, but Scott murmured something that made them laugh and look at Gena with small smiles. "Have you all done your lessons for tomorrow?" The groans sounded again.

The oldest boy spoke up sullenly. "It is white man's history. Why must we learn such things of no importance to our people?"

"All learning is important to our people," Scott instructed quietly. "Especially about the white man. One cannot conquer what one cannot understand. If we are to survive in this white man's world, we must know them, for there is strength and power in knowledge."

"So we can become white men and forget what it is to be Lakota?" the boy challenged.

"No. What you are, you carry here." He tapped his chest. Then he smiled. "A wise man once told me to learn in order to bring hope to the people, to restore their dignity and their pride. That is what each of you must do."

Yellow Bear remembered and he nodded to his grandson.

"But the white man's knowledge is difficult," one of the girls complained. "We try to understand, but when we ask questions, our teacher beats us."

The old chief scowled. "A man should beat his horse, not his women or children. In this, the white man has always been confused."

"What lesson are you to learn today?" Gena asked suddenly, and the dark eyes turned to her timidly.

"It is the story of Christopher Columbus," the other girl murmured. "He is said to have discovered America. How is that, when we were already here?"

Gena laughed softly. "I understand your confusion. I have an idea. I will tell you the story of Columbus if you will tell me one of your stories."

It took the children a scant second to warm to that idea. They huddled around Gena, eager faces upturned, fear forgotten.

Scott sat back and allowed himself to be thoroughly mesmerized by the sight of Miss Gena Trowbridge of Boston, sitting on a tattered blanket with an Indian child tucked beneath each arm. There was not a trace of stiff propriety as she thrust herself wholeheartedly into her storytelling. There was no sign of icy reserve as her fingers toyed with a little girl's black braid. It was a moment of mellow contentment and Scott found himself as enchanted as the children. She looked so pale and ethereal next to the dark earthiness of her pupils. But not helpless, not frail. And something indefinable stirred inside Scott Prescott as he watched and listened. A tension began to build around his chest that refused to go away. It was ridiculous, really, being that out of breath from sitting crosslegged, listening to the story of Columbus. But the pressure wouldn't ease. He laid his cheek against the boy's sleek black hair and found himself wondering if Gena would someday have their children gathered around her feet. And the distress around his heart grew crushing. He sat silent, hugging the little boy, wondering in a wild panic what was happening to him.

Yellow Bear, looking between his grandson and the fair New Waw, smiled.

He knew.

237

Chapter Fifteen

"Come on. Let's get a move on. I don't want to keep any of them sweet young things waiting."

"The only sweet things you know won't be out until dark."

Ignoring his brother's dry comment, Rory whisked their mother up and two-stepped her energetically out onto the porch. Aurora laughed at his foolishness and looked young and pretty with her skirts twirling and cheeks flushed as they kicked up a dust around the yard.

"Boy, you're doing that all wrong." Ethan cut in, taking his wife in his arms. "You want to dance with a woman, you do it like this."

From the doorway, Gena followed their movements as they waltzed. She remembered watching her parents at a society cotillion. They had moved together with only their fingertips touching. With the Prescotts, everything was touching. It was less a dance and more a prelude to other, more private intimacies. They were smiling at one another, those looks promising what the shifting of the dance suggested. Only Gena appeared embarrassed.

"Well, hellfire, Daddy," Rory grumbled. "You surely

can't expect me to go a-dancing with my own mama that-a-way." His dark eyes canted mischievously up to the porch. "Now, then, if Miss Gena was willing . . ."

"Save it for your own sweet things, little brother."

Rory grinned. Scott, too, was smiling but his hand had risen to rest lightly at Gena's waist. In a subtle possession only a blind man would miss.

"Let's get a-going," the redhead cried, impatient once again. "Day's a-wasting."

"Mrs. Prescott, shall we continue this later?"

Aurora looked up at the big Texan, her golden eyes smoldering. "I think you can count on it, Mr. Prescott."

"Come on, you two. Quit mooning like a pair of lovesick calves."

"You've got no romance in your soul, Rory Prescott," his mother scolded.

"What I ain't got is money in my pocket and I'm meaning to win fifty dollars from Hank Durbin for riding that bronc of his. I tell you, Scotty, you ain't never seen a horse so cussed hard-jawed. Why, last year, he gave me a toss that nearly busted my a—behind. Not this year. I mean to ride him and be the richer for it. Yessir."

With Rory nipping at their heels like a dog tending sheep, the wagon was loaded and everything readied for the trip into Crowe Creek. Ethan and Aurora sat on the plank seat and Scott helped Gena up into the bed. She wasn't dressed for a ride on a straw bale. Her Parisian gown was of pale blue crepe de chine with black chenille polka dots and a deep flounce of lace at the overlapping hem. A double bow of mousseline was knotted high under her chin, tilting her head at the proper angle to show off a round little hat of blue tulle and black chenille dots with a bobbing black bird-of-paradise plume. Seeing her hesitate, Scott threw down a blanket and raised a dark questioning brow.

"I could hitch up the buggy if you like, but I thought it would be kind of nice to go all together."

Gena looked at the blanket with its straw ticking and smiled sportingly. Nothing was going to spoil this day. Not bits of straw. Not the hot sun. Not a jouncing ride. She was looking forward to this Fourth of July celebration for two reasons. One, she'd been isolated at the Lone Star for almost two weeks and she found the prospect of the festival exciting. Two, she'd had almost no time with Scott since that day with Yellow Bear. He was up and gone early each day, in Crowe Creek, at the Bar K or on the reservation, shuttling his attentions between Garth Kincaid and White Cloud. Over dinner, if he was there, he was distracted at best. In the evenings, he had his books spread out on the dining-room table while filling page after page with rapidly scrawled notes. There were times when she would catch him looking at her with an intensity of expression that set her pulse thrumming, but then he'd smile blandly and return to his books. Gena vowed not to complain, not to whine for attention as she'd seen Beth and Caroline do when they thought themselves ignored. She had only to remind herself that he'd not asked her to stay.

She couldn't complain of being idle. Aurora took it upon herself to acquaint her son's fiancée with every detail of western homemaking. Gena never thought to wonder why. It was not as though she was going to set up a home in the Dakotas, and she wouldn't need such knowledge in Boston. There, a woman was measured by the state of her home; not by how much of it she accomplished, but by how well her husband could afford to have it done for her. Monday there was the abominable laundry, followed by the pressing on Tuesday with coarse and polishing irons. Tuesday, Thursday, and Saturday were bake days and the heat from the cast-iron stoves was wilting. Monday and Friday, the floors were swept. And every evening, there was sewing to do. The men's work clothes were in constant need of repair. Aurora made most of their shirts, her own blouses, bonnets and undergarments, towels and handkerchiefs and knitted socks and stockings. A sewing machine would have cut the time for assembling a man's shirt from fifteen hours to an hour and a quarter, but Aurora said philosophically that she was in no hurry to get the work done. So in the evening, the two women stitched, Ethan shaped wood, and Scott read with only the lonesome cry of the coyote to punctuate the silence. Time passed quietly and companionably.

But as Scott settled beside her on the bale of covered straw, Gena was aware of her mounting anticipation. And she could well understand why such gatherings were a high point of the summer. The wagon started out with a jerk, rolling out into the shimmering heat haze where the prairie grasses were as sharp and bitter as an inhaled tonic. Rory rode his painted horse alongside, galloping circles around them and showing off to the extent of his mother's patience. Yes, it was going to be a glorious day. Gena knew it. And when Scott reached for her hand, she clasped it happily atop one silken knee, oblivious to the sudden tightening of his features.

A Dakota Fourth was noisy, raucous, and unrestrained. A tent town was thrown up on the outskirts of Crowe Creek to host the revelry. Gena was as anxious as a child at the thought of the bands, the speeches, the parades, the contests, the sideshows, and the after-dark fireworks. She wrung Scott's hand mercilessly as the first staccato pop of firecrackers reached them. Though it was ticking off the first minutes past nine, the area was crowded with wagons and buggies and the sound of merrymaking. The high spirits were infectious.

Gena found herself with a Prescott son on either arm. Much to Scott's chagrin, Rory decided to attach himself to them, at least until something better caught his eye. Then, when his brother's sense of the ridiculous kept Gena flushed and happy, Scott felt ashamed of himself. He'd never seen her so animated. It did funny things in the pit of his belly. It made his tongue bond to the roof of his mouth, prohibiting speech while Rory rattled on and on. All he could do was manage a painfully thin smile and stare at the woman on his arm.

She was beautiful. Not in the same porcelain way she'd been in Boston. There, she'd had a frail, fashionably tubercular pallor accentuating her small bones and big eyes. There, she'd appeared easily bruised and untouchable. Here, today, it was as if she wasn't the same woman. The absence of a shadowed parlor and exposure to the warm Dakota sun had kissed her cheeks with a peachlike blush of color. When she laughed at Rory's silliness, her blue eyes sparkled with life. Instead of walking docilely between them, she was dragging them from booth to booth, wanting to see everything, wanting to do everything. So did he. But he wanted to see and do it all with Gena Trowbridge — alone. If he could have made the crowds and his affable brother disappear with a wish, he would have spoken it. If he could fulfill that wish, it would be to have Gena in his arms, looking the way she had in the stream with only her clingy underthings on. Staring up at him through eyes that invited. That image had made the past days—and nights—unbearable. To sit in the same room trying to concentrate on his books when so aware of the way the firelight reflected in a silvery haze upon the fair head bent over needlework. To lie awake at night, knowing she was just across the hall. And when he thought he'd lost control over his want of her, memory slammed him hard and cruelly.

The look of terror on her face.

Scott, don't.

Never, he promised, never would he give her reason to fear him. Someone had put that glaze of panic in her eyes. Knowing that made him angry and helpless. It held him at bay better than all her proper Victorian reluctance.

While she laughed and hugged his arm, he wished he'd never seen her vulnerability. Then, maybe he could enjoy her as freely as Rory did. Then maybe he could return her smiles and make foolish conversation. Then, maybe he could look forward to the darkness and the thought of stolen kisses.

Scott, don't.

Against whomever had hurt her in the past, he swore revenge. And never, never would he force that pain upon her again. These dark oaths he took in the bright July sunshine with a pretty woman clinging to his arm. And they cast a cold pall over his enjoyment of the day.

But Gena was having the time of her life.

It was all so new. So exciting. From the sideshow attractions to the lightness she felt inside. Rory made her laugh until she thought her corset would pop. And just Scott's presence beside her set a whole shiver of sensations loose. This wasn't Boston. These people weren't sticklers for the proper. They could care less if she laughed a bit too loudly or if her happiness put a skip in her step or if she held a tad too tightly to her fiancé's arm. And so she wouldn't care either. She felt deliciously naughty. And wondrously free. To enjoy. To experience. To explore. Like a child toting along two indulgent chaperones.

Rory was delightful. He made everything fun. He won her a monkey on a stick at the shooting gallery and bought her sea-foam candy. He goaded her into seeing the bearded lady and the sword swallower and teased when she wouldn't have her fortune read. She knew the future she wanted. He was walking rather silently at her other side. If that wasn't the future meant to be, she didn't want to know it now, not when everything else was so perfect.

When the sun reached its zenith, the crowds left the midway attractions to open food baskets on big linen tablecloths. She and Aurora had packed fried chicken, new potatoes and garden peas, ham, baked beans, beet and cucumber pickles, lemonade, and pie. It had seemed so much that morning, but it disappeared beneath that cloudless Dakota sky like a drop of water upon parched ground. Sated and lazy, they leaned back to listen to the pleasing cacophony; the excited voices of children, a band playing "Yankee Doodle," hawkers luring in anyone with a pocketful of change.

"So," Scott asked, possessing himself of her hand, "what do you want to see this afternoon? A production of 'Ten Nights in a Bar Room,' a debate on 'Resolved: Farming does not pay,' a lecture on free love?"

His thumb was charting the ridge of her knuckles like a cartographer exploring Badland buttes. Gena experienced a thrill of longing. His touch was gentle, but his assessing golden gaze was as hot as butter sizzling in the sun. The contrast quite unbalanced her. He was so handsome, sitting cross-legged on the blanket, Stetson resting beside him so no shadow fell on his dark features. He was dressed western formal in boots, denims, and coat over white shirt and tie. Easy but not relaxed. Smiling yet still tense. The son of Aurora Prescott, who would fit in with the enveloping revelry. Son of Far Winds, who would not. A knot of love rose in her throat, delaying her response. Then, before she could speak, Rory answered for her.

"She's coming to watch me win fifty dollars. Why, that old bone-breaker is probably so tuckered out by now it'll be like straddling a hobbyhorse."

"Don't go breaking anything I can't fix," Ethan warned lazily.

"Like your fool head," his mother added.

"Don't worry none, Mama. There ain't much up there that'd come to harm." He reached down and hauled Gena up. "Come on, Sis, I'm going to treat you to some sheerly spectacular horsemanship."

"This I gotta see," Scott muttered.

Any time more than two cowmen gathered with a horse between them, a riding competition was sure to follow. With prime horseflesh always in demand and critical to their work, they had an appreciation for anything four-legged and reliable. Breaking a spirited animal into a capable mount was a prized skill among men on the range, and being a cowboy went hand in hand with a love of showing off. Bronc riding, when not a necessity, was a sought-after diversion, especially when cash money and an audience were involved. For the last two years, Hank Durbin had been cleaning out their pockets with his cross-grained stew-bald. Not a man had been able to sit the ornery Tumbleweed for ten seconds, and Durbin considered his fifty dollars safe.

Gena looked with consternation at the black-and-white-spotted brute. The animal had been ridden by four luckless souls already and it was lathered and wild-eyed. She put a staying hand on the redhead's arm.

"Rory, are you sure you want to do this?"

"Shucks, sweet thing, I eat horses like this for breakfast. What do you think, Scotty?"

Scott looked over every dangerous inch of the animal and shook his head. "I think you best hang on to your ten dollars and keep what little sense you have."

Rory snorted and passed Gena a gold eagle. "You hang onto that for me jus' in case." Then he ducked under the corral rail and shouted, "Durbin, you salty ole thing, get ready to divest some of that coin."

Having never seen a wild horse broken, Gena clung to Scott anxiously. "He won't get hurt, will he?"

"Naw, don't you worry about Rory. He's no virgin when it comes to horses."

She was too upset to blush at the comparison. "I meant the horse."

Scott laughed out loud, a booming, boisterous sound that made her heart buck sharply. "I think they're both too stupid to come to any harm."

Gena wasn't convinced. She held her breath as Rory approached the pawing animal. Two brawny men stood at the bridle, wrestling its head down. The redhead fit his boot in the stirrup and swung aboard. At his nod, the wranglers leaped away. And Tumbleweed exploded.

"Stick to him, Rory," Scott hollered as Gena hugged the top rail. He silently coached his brother to grip with his knees and snap with the vicious stiff-legged hops. "Thataboy! You got him!"

And then, he saw it coming.

Gena heard Scott's harsh draw of breath. Even as

she turned toward him, he was ducking under the rail, shouting at the top of his lungs.

"Rory, get off there. He's going over!"

Rory had ridden enough broncs to know what that sudden weightless feeling foretold. The horse, maddened by the sound of the crowd and the feel of man, was falling over backward, trying to crush him in the process. Frantically, he kicked free of the stirrups and jumped, hitting stunningly hard. He felt the animal land close enough to shower him with dirt. Saw its slashing hooves flailing with the power to maim. Then, the ground was moving under him as he was dragged by the shirt collar to safety.

"Rory? Can you move?"

He saw Scott and Gena bending over him next to swirling sky. He sucked hard for adequate air. "I think—I broke my—pride." Then the pressure eased, allowing a full sweet pull of breath. "Gimme a hand up, Scotty. I'm gonna go 'er again."

"The hell you say," Scott argued as his brother swayed dizzily within his grip. "Guess you've got to have sense to get it knocked out of you."

Durbin swaggered over, grinning. "Brush off the dust and pay up, Prescott. That's ten dollars a ride. And you saw plenty of daylight on that one."

Rory passed the ten-dollar piece from Gena to Durbin and fished in his pocket for another. When he would give it to the hawker, Scott snatched it from his palm and gave it to the man himself.

"I'll take the next ride," he said quietly.

Durbin grinned wider. He was new to these parts. He saw a stranger in shiny new denims and an unbroken Stetson with a society lady on his arm. He saw easy winnings. "Sure thing, city boy. He's all yours."

"Scott?"

He smiled in the face of Gena's worries. It was a grim smile. "I'll be fine."

"He'll be more than fine," Rory gushed, having recovered his wind. "He's the best dang horse breaker in the Dakotas."

Durbin's grin slacked.

"Take his head for me, would you, Rory?"

"You bet, Scotty."

It took only a minute for the spectators to realize they weren't going to see the regular routine of bone-jarring saddle-slapping. They hushed to a one and watched in awed wonder. Rory chased the others from the corral and took the animal's bridle firmly, standing inches from the huge bared teeth and flaring nostrils. Scott slipped out of his coat and whipped it over the horse's white-rimmed eyes. Then he uncinched the saddle and tossed it out of the way. With the long trailing rein ends, he made a loop around one the animal's back hocks and drew it up tight to its belly. Thusly trussed on three legs, the horse couldn't rear up. It stood blinded and trembling. Scott began rubbing over the lather-flecked hide, first with his palms then with the saddle blanket, crooning softly. Ears that had been flattened began to rise and twitch. The blanket was settled upon flinching withers, and when the horse was still, Scott leaned upon its back, letting it sample his weight. The moment the animal shied, he slid down. He did that several times until at last he was accepted. Carefully, he let down the back leg. The horse stomped a few times then was still. From the right side, Scott gripped a handful of mane and rolled up onto the bared back. After rocking his weight and murmuring low for several minutes, he motioned for Rory to remove the blindfold.

The bronc stood, stunned by the light and quivering for several long seconds. Then someone, probably Durbin, hollered and the animal lunged forward. Instead of hauling back on the reins, Scott gave the horse its head, encouraging it forward with the brush of his boot heels. After a couple of shimmying jumps, Tumbleweed broke into a canter, guided by Scott's easy hand around the circumference of the corral. When the reins were taken up firmly, the stallion rose once to paw the air, then came down and trotted aggressively from side to side. By that time, the animal had carried its rider a full two minutes and no one could question who was in charge.

"Whooee, Scotty," Rory called out proudly, but the others gathered around the corral were more guarded with their praise. They'd heard of Injun-gentling a horse, but none had ever seen it done. Until now. The fact that Scott swung down on the right instead of the left made those murmurs strengthen. Hearing the mutters, Durbin seized at the means of saving money on his now useless horse.

As Scott slipped on his coat, Durbin stalked up, his face set in angry lines.

"What kind of trick you playing? That ain't no kind of bronc riding."

Rory shoved out his hand, fingers beckoning. "Riding's riding. Pay the man."

"I ain't paying him nothing."

"Why, you chiseling, stinking, low-down cheat. He rode your damn basket-tail. Now pay him."

"I ain't paying for no thieving Injun magic. This here contest was for decent folk, not the likes of him." The grumbling of the crowd, especially those who'd lost money that morning, backed him.

Scott said nothing. He stood rigid, staring down the weaseling Durbin with a glare that made him unconsciously reach for his hair. He was aware of the attention drawn to them, of Rory seething at his side, spoiling for a fight, of Durbin's mounting confidence that he would get away with it. He spoke softly, with gritty sincerity. "You owe me, Durbin. I rode the animal fair. Pay me now or pay me later." That last trailed off with menace.

"You two should be ashamed of yourselves."

Scott and Rory both started with surprise when Gena stepped between them, claiming an arm on either side.

"I swear all this fuss and bother over a smelly old horse while I'm simply perishing for a want of something cool. Scott, dear, don't be a bore. Let the nasty man give you back your ten dollars and forget the rest. You promised to take me to the tent shows and the best ones have already started. I declare, I will not wait another minute out in this heat. Are you coming?"

Gena waited, breath suspended, praying he would take the opportunity to back down gracefully. Scott was staring at her. She could see his confusion. She'd never acted the demanding coquette with him, but she'd seen Caroline play the part enough to give a fair imitation. Her fingers squeezed his arm. *Please, Scott.*

Then, he smiled, a tight, teeth-baring smile that made Durbin think uncomfortably of the death's-head on a bottle of rat poison. "I am sorry, my sweet. Of course, we can go. With the ten dollars."

Durbin extended it gladly. Scott wouldn't take it, so Gena put out her hand. When she began to walk away, neither man was ungentlemanly enough to balk but came along, compliant and sullen at least until they were alone. Then, Rory pulled away, sulky and furious and in no mood to change.

"I'm going to get drunk," he growled, and stalked off toward the closest batwings.

Scott had his emotions under control, at least outwardly. Inside, he raged and cursed. But because he had embarrassed Gena enough for one day, he adopted a stoic front. She was probably shamed to the soul for the way he'd carried on, showing off, drawing attention to his past, nearly brawling at a public affair. Dragging her down with him. When she said his name quietly, he was sure she was going to ask him to take her home, away from the whispers and the ugly stares. He couldn't blame her for wanting to hide. He'd done the same thing in Boston.

So when she detained with that hushed tone, he expected a subtle censure or mild reproach. Something along the line of what she'd dished out for the benefits of the others. What he hadn't planned on was the look in her eyes when they lifted to his. Those great shimmering blue pools of compassion.

"Scott, I'm so sorry. How unfair of them to treat you that way. How wrong of them." The injustice of it made her voice tremble. The knowledge that they'd hurt him quickened an unfamiliar fury. "I apologize for how I behaved. It was the only way I could think of to keep you from rightly murdering that horrid man."

The quirk of a smile softened his hard features. A thaw of feeling melted through his insides. It welled up into an incredible font of tenderness for this unlikely heroine who thought to rescue him from the pain of truth.

"We can leave if you want to," he offered impassively.

"Leave? I don't want to leave. Just because of them? They don't matter, Scott." Her hand came up to rest over his heart. It beat hard and sure against her palm.

251

It made her bold. "I've developed a great respect for your mother. I think Aurora Prescott would say, 'To hell with them.' I'm saying it, too. To hell with them."

With the utmost care, he raised her hand to his lips and pressed a scorching kiss upon her palm. Then he tucked it into the bend of his arm and agreed, "To hell with them."

Chapter Sixteen

It was hard pretending it didn't matter, but for Scott, she did her best. She strolled along at his side, her head held high, ignoring all the pointed stares, the hissing words. Half-breed. Indian. She knew he heard them. She could feel the tension in his arm even when there was no sign of it in his expression. But then he'd had a lot of years of practice and it was new to her. She would learn. For his sake, she would learn. To keep the anger, the tears, inside. So this was how it would be, here, perhaps in Boston, too. How could they judge so harshly? So unreasonably? She blinked back the sting of anguish in her eyes and repressed the want to slap the next gawking face silly. Couldn't they just take the magnificent measure of the man inside?

And he was magnificent.

And she was so proud. Of him. Of being with him. Of the things he was trying to do here in the Dakotas. Of the dark, dangerous beauty of him when he'd sat that wild horse. And she felt breathless all over again. It wasn't enough to convey that sense of pride by flaunting it for strangers. She wanted him to know. She intuited his need to know. The image of his isolated silhouette at the Bar K party made her heartbreakingly aware of his loneliness.

He wasn't alone any more and it was time she let him know it.

As they danced to one of that day's surprisingly fine orchestras beneath a canopy of stars, Gena struggled with a set of inbred rules. *No unnecessary contact. No public displays of affection. No encouraging the prurient nature of mankind.* Then she weighed those rigid standards against the need Scott kept behind an inscrutable expression. What was she to do? What had Aurora Prescott done while dancing in her husband's arms?

Gingerly, as if expecting censure upon every inch, Gena swayed closer and closer to her partner, until her hem swept his boots, until her bosom brushed his coat. If Scott was surprised, his features didn't register it. His arm tightened around her waist like a good cowboy taking up slack. He stared down at her, gaze intense, questioning. It was far easier to go a step further and rest her head upon his shoulder than to manage an explanation. She could feel the pressure of his hand upon the small of her back but, because of the binding corset, not the actual touch of his fingers. And she wanted that touch, that closeness the day's strictures wouldn't allow. What was so wrong in what she was doing? The feel of him against her, moving in time to the music, was ever so much more satisfying than an impersonal arm's length away. There was a sense of oneness, a flow of rhythm from him to her that gave the movements an incredible depth. An enticing meaning.

That was it, then, the thing the censors feared. The seducing pleasure of bodies moving in time to one another. The disturbing friction of cloth over flesh. The heat that penetrated both. And it did feel wicked. And wonderful. Did he feel it, too? Gena turned her head to lean upon the opposite cheek. She could see his strong brown throat and the sharp line of his jaw but little of his expression. But there was a fast and furious pulse throbbing above his collar, an impatience in his rapid swallowing. Yes, she was quite sure he felt it, too. There was something excitingly forbidden in sharing such knowledge in the midst of others.

Scott had stopped the measured one-two-three of steps and was simply holding her, shifting slightly from side to side. He'd brought their laced hands up tight against his breast and she thought of the taut, bronzed skin beneath his starched shirt. How would it feel beneath her palm? It had looked hard and hot and smooth that day at the reservation. She'd been fascinated then, compelled by a sensory need to know. His cheek rubbed over hers. His was warm and rough. She wanted to touch him there, to explore the lean contours of his face, of his lips, but there were too many people and she knew she mustn't. It was a sharp frustration, the closeness, the distance, the wanting, the restraint.

"Scott."

She was surprised by the sound of her own voice. It was low, vibrating with the yearning coursing through her.

His lips parted. She could hear his breathing, suddenly loud and raspy.

"Let's walk."

His husky suggestion woke a shiver but no objection. Hand in hand, they wove through the crowd of couples and left the faint spill of lanternlight in search of private shadow. The grass sighed and bent beneath their feet. The way Gena's will sighed and bent.

When they'd become lost at the edge of darkness, still within the sound of merrymaking, Scott stopped them. He slipped out of his coat and spread it over the grass, then encouraged her to sit beside him. They weren't touching but Gena was overwhelmed by him, as smothered by the feel of him as she was by the night's blackness. Scared, but at the same time alive with anticipation. Silence thickened like the heavy evening air. Both made her

255

breathing race and labor. Her hands clasped together in her lap as a thousand words of warning pricked her conscience. By being here with him, alone and available in the dark, she was giving him the opportunity to make good on each one of them.

She gave a start as a loud hiss streaked skyward. With a dramatic boom, the first rocket bloomed into sparkles of color. A second followed, filling the dark heavens with a myriad of new stars. She'd seen fireworks before but never against such a vast canopy. The effect was spectacular and she oohed and ohed like a child.

Scott's fingers touched her wrist. "Lie back. It's easier to watch them."

Stretched out on Scott's coat with her knees bent and her head pillowed on her arms, Gena was fully captivated by the burst and blossom of lights. The distant band had begun to play a repertoire of patriotic songs and the sound of enthusiastic singing reached them. A wonderful gladness filled her heart, then the brush of Scott's fingertips along her cheek sent it ramming against her ribs.

His first kiss missed her mouth by miscalculation or design. Lips grazed her along the line of her jaw, trailing warm breath and hot sensation. Unthinkingly, she fit a palm to his cheek to correct his course. It was a tentative touch, achingly sweet, hesitant, yet guided by an uncontrolled longing. He let her steer him to the soft, ready contours of her mouth and lingered there at her command, gently shaping, subtly tasting her unexpected and inexperienced passions. He took his time, leading her, tempting her. With flirting kisses, with tiny nips of his teeth, with provocative flickers of his tongue. Coaxing her to open for him, to explore without reserve, to return the same tantalizing favors. And slowly, cautiously, she did.

She let her fingertips learn the angles of his face. She could feel his smile when creases deepened at the corners of his mouth and his cheek swelled. Her touch skimmed along the seam of his lips which remained maddeningly closed. She reached up, trying to part them with the pressure of her own, then finally used the tip of her tongue to melt the invisible seal that kept her out. His mouth opened and she paused, only for the briefest second, before proceeding with a shaky bravado. She traced the hard, smooth curve of his teeth and slipped beyond. He waited, forcing her to be the aggressor, making her come to him. And she did, in innocent timidity. And it was all he could do to hold still for the silky invasion.

A stunning explosion from above brought her away from the brink of total abandon. She fell back, panting and alarmed by what she'd done. By what they might do. Scott gave her the time to recover, watching the fireworks above then turning his attention back to the heavenly beauty below. Her eyes were wide, uncertain. He could see the twinkling lights reflected there, bright, fleeting, like the moment he would hold to a while longer.

"Thank you for staying on at the Lone Star, Gena. I know it's not how you expected things to be and I'm sorry," he told her softly.

"I'm not disappointed, Scott. Not with anything." *Not with you,* said the light stroke of her palm along his jaw.

"I'm glad you're here."

He lowered gradually, giving her the chance to refuse him. Instead, he found her lips moist and parted in welcome. This time, he was more persistent, his head moving, angling from side to side, his kiss opening wider, delving deeper. Melting beneath his heat, she lifted her arms, holding safely to his shoulders at first, then drawn inexorably to the tempting terrain of his chest. The restless movement of her hands loosened his tie. Her thumbs rubbed impatiently at the edge of his collar until one, two, three buttons of his shirt somehow gave way. She couldn't quite believe that she'd opened them. But in the dark, where no eyes could see, it was an invitation too alluring to resist.

She was surprised by the contrast, the tone of hard sinew, the sleek softness of skin stretched warm across it. Powerful. Sculpted muscle. It was easy to forget how strong he was when all that potent evidence was properly concealed. Confronted by it, she felt a tremor of vulnerability. He was a rugged, able-bodied man who could take with authority rather than coax with tenderness. He could conquer with force instead of persuade with passion. Knowing that, she felt helpless yet curiously in control. For when her hands caressed him, he moaned against her mouth as if she were molding him with her touch instead of just the opposite. The sound incited a quivering response in her and her heart thundered with a rush of forbidden feeling.

"No." She tore her mouth away. "Scott, no. This is wrong."

He trapped one of her trembling hands against his bare skin until her palm felt seared. "Does it feel wrong, Gena?"

No. It felt wonderfully right. And that was the problem. She couldn't muster the proper resistance. She wanted what he wanted, for the exploration to go on and on to its dangerous conclusion. She had to stop him now because she feared if they continued, she would no longer wish to.

"We shouldn't . . ."

"But we are."

"We cannot . . ."

"But we will. Eventually. If not tonight, then on another. God, Gena, I've been trying to behave but you're just so damned — tempting."

His claim shook her to the soul.

"Maybe we should go back."

258

He deliberately misunderstood her. "I don't think we can."

"I'm afraid . . ."

"Don't be. I won't hurt you, Gena." His voice was warm, rough velvet. Because someone had and he couldn't bear the thought.

He didn't understand. She wasn't afraid of him. She was afraid of herself, of her own lack of resolve. It was slipping, failing her. And she didn't care. She didn't care. That terrified her.

"Scott . . ."

"Shhh. Don't talk. Just feel."

And she did. Exquisitely. To the point of agony. Sensation so new and compelling she was lost to it. Beautiful, poignant feelings. Hot, scintillating sensation.

He was kissing her again and the emotions swelled and ripened inside her. She shivered and his hands soothed her. She tried to pull away and he quieted her with a whispered word. The way he had the maverick; gentling her, sapping her want to rebel. Until she accepted him, blinded to her objections by his patient mastery.

His hands were at her throat, tugging at the bow, turning back her bodice. The night brushed cool against her skin, bringing a shiver. And then his mouth burned hot against that same spot. Her back arched, instinctively offering more of that slender column. He kissed her throat, her chin, her mouth, until she was panting for precious air and precarious reason. He'd eased his torso over her, supporting his weight on his forearms so he could gently bracket her breasts with his wide palms. He felt her body buck in shock, and distracted her with enticing sworls of his tongue across her lips. The moment her tension eased, he began charting the snug curves of silk, drowning out her protest with the deep plunge of his kisses.

The fit of her corset thrust her bosom high and full to fill the cup of his hands, enhancing his possession. The

259

repetitive stroke of his thumbs created a hard pucker of response and Gena moaned, first in surprise then in soft awareness. His knee pushed up between spraddled legs. She could feel the prick of grass blades on the back of her calves. Then the seducing movement of his hand on stockinged knee.

"Scott —"

He groaned in lusty pleasure and his hand rode farther up one smooth thigh, his fingers kneading soft flesh, inspiring a flood of unknown expectations.

"Let me make love to you, Gena," he rasped out urgently, reaching higher beneath her rucked skirts.

Amazingly, she could think of no reason to deny him. Her fingers clenched in the short black satin of his hair as his face nuzzled between her breasts. Overhead, a thousand brilliants shimmered in starburst designs. Illuminating their entwined silhouettes. Permitting fate to intrude.

"Scotty, there you are!"

Scott was gripped by the shirt collar and hauled to his feet, giving Gena scant opportunity to cover what a moment of immodesty had bared. Seeing incredible opportunity dashed, he swung around, furious and frustrated.

"Dad blame it, Rory, I'm kind of busy here."

His brother regarded him blankly for a moment, then lowered his drink-glazed gaze. He grinned. "Well, howdy, Miss Gena. Didn't see you down there. I'm gonna borrow Scotty for a little bit but I'll bring him right back. Promise."

"I'm not going anywhere with you."

But Scott's protest was choked off by an arm looped about his neck, tightening with overzealous affection. He didn't have much choice except to stumble along at his brother's side, not if he wanted to go on breathing. He cast an apologetic glance back at what he was walking away from. Gena sprawled and available in the green

Dakota grass. And he would have groaned if he'd had enough air. As it was, he could only sputter. And wish his brother off the face of the earth.

Gena closed her eyes, feeling limp and emotionally drained. Inside, the fires Scott had kindled with his touch snuffled out like the sparks above, leaving her cold and dark. And guilty.

How could she? Not only had she allowed him liberties, she'd encouraged them. And if Rory hadn't stumbled along . . . It was wrong. Scott could soothe her conscience with his honeyed words and heavenly kisses, but it was wrong. She knew it right down to the heavy lump of shame settling in her belly. She couldn't blame Scott. He was a man and that was the way of man: to want, to demand, to take without a thought beyond satisfying their own primitive needs. He couldn't be expected to tame that bestial nature inherent in the male species. That was why she'd been raised to be strong. That's why there were strict rules of conduct to govern what went on between men and women. That was the problem. Here, what few rules they had were relaxed and easily bent. There was no rigid social structure, no guardian of innocence beyond one's conscience. And hers had failed her. Miserably.

She hadn't known she'd be so tempted. She hadn't realized how seducing the pleasures of the flesh could be. He'd swept her nearly to the brink of disaster and she hadn't tried to stop him. She hadn't wanted to. She had no business encouraging him while they danced. She had no business walking with him into the darkness. Or sitting with him. Or touching him. Or wanting him.

What was wrong with her?

She knew better. What she was doing was dangerous. The type of prolonged intimacy she'd invited by staying under the same roof had dire consequence. The type of petting she'd allowed would lead to sexual involvement.

261

And pregnancy.

Suddenly chilled, Gena sat up and quickly retied the bow beneath her chin. She made it tight, as if she could knot in all her impure notions, as if she could choke out all improper passions. Standing, she shook out her suspiciously rumpled skirt and brushed blades of grass from Scott's coat. She held that dark garment to her breast, hugging it as if he were still inside it. She hurried toward the light, toward the protection of the people gathered there. Wondering frantically as she did how she was ever going to withstand the seductive potential of what they'd started beneath a blaze of fireworks.

Ethan and Aurora were packing up the wagon when she found them. It was late. The family crowd was beginning to disperse and the men to drift toward the tinkling pianos and black-gartered gals found in Crowe Creek's many saloons.

"Where's Scott?" Aurora's shrewd gaze assessed the younger woman's high color, the wisps of blue gamma tucked in her neat coif, and the wrinkled jacket crushed in her arms.

"He and Rory went off somewhere," she murmured softly, evading the insightful eyes.

Ethan sighed. "Well, if that's the case, there's no use waiting. I'll tie off Rory's horse and they can find their way home." Ethan paused to consider Gena's pinched features. "Lessen you want to wait awhile," he added kindly.

Gena glanced toward the lights of the main street. She thought of the long silent ride to the Bar K, wreathed in darkness in the back of the wagon. With Scott.

"No," she said resolutely. "Let them enjoy themselves."

Then, she huddled alone in the back of the wagon bed with only Scott's coat to fill her arms and her shame to serve cold company.

"All right, Rory. Suppose you tell me what's so all-fired important."

His brother's anger made no dent in the redhead's high-spirited humor. He put a finger to his lips to quiet him, then said loudly, "You want your fifty dollars, don't you. Well, just so happens I caught a glimpse of Hank Durbin at the livery, tying off his basket-tail to his wagon. Thought you might like to make a little talk with him afore he left town. With your money."

Scott should have brushed off the suggestion. He would have in a saner moment. But his blood was thick and hot and his frustrations cried for venting. Durbin had cheated and shamed him in front of everyone. In front of Gena. And that didn't sit well with his pride. There would be no ladies around, no surly crowd. Just he and the narrow-thinking Durbin. And his fifty dollars. Before rational thought could interfere, he was striding toward the livery with Rory sauntering gleefully at his side.

Durbin's rig was in the side wagonyard with the stewbald tethered behind it. There was no sign of Durbin. Scott approached the barn warily, entering where the large sliding door had been left slightly open. The interior was dark. There were sounds of shuffling hooves and the shifting of restless horseflesh. The usual scents of straw, leather, and manure were diluted by a sharper, more pungent odor. Something hot. Scott drew up by the shadowed office. His senses tingled a warning. Things weren't right. He scanned what he could of the cavernous space, making out the shapes of twelve stalls, a large grain bin, and an open tack room. Nothing unusual there. Overhead, the hay loft was black and undisturbed. So where was Durbin?

Rory pushed past him and went to poke his head in the office. "Durbin!" he bellowed with all the subtlety of a bull moose. He turned back to Scott and shrugged. "Should be here. Wouldn't have left his gear all strung and gone off somewheres." He began to walk along the row of stalls. "Less the son of a skunk is in here sleeping it off."

"Rory," Scott called softly. "Let's go." He began backing toward the door. His gaze darted from shadow to shadow. His scalp tightened. "I don't like this. Come on."

Rory continued down the line of stalls, but he looked over his shoulder to call back a taunt. "What's got you pussy-footing? Scotty, you know it makes my skin crawl when you go all Injun-queer like that."

He turned. Then fireworks burst inside his head.

It sounded like a rake handle breaking. A sharp crack, then the muffled thump of something heavy dropping in the straw.

"Rory?"

Alarm made him forget caution. Scott took several running steps and realized his mistake. The livery door rolled shut, sealing the big room in darkness. He heard shuffling sounds, but before he could get his bearings, he heard a warning whistle of air. The fist caught him on the cheekbone, splitting skin, sending him reeling. Hands grabbed at his arms, pinning them as another punishing blow took him in the midsection. Laced hands slammed him beneath the chin. His head snapped back with enough force to clack his teeth together. Dizzy from the first punch, he tried to shrug off the hands and jerk free, but his movements were ineffective. From somewhere close, he heard a laugh.

"You might's well relax, boy. You're gonna take a beating and there ain't nothing you can do to stop it."

Scott shifted his weight abruptly to one side, upsetting the balance and giving him an opening to send back a hard jab from his elbow. There was a satisfying grunt of pain. Before he could take advantage of the slackened grip, a shaft of agony shattered through his ribs at the smack of a well-placed ax handle. He went down hard on hands and knees, sucking for air and breathing in pain. A swift kick to the same spot pierced him with splinters of fire. Clutching his side, feeling as though everything inside him had been broken, Scott toppled and let consciousness wan.

"You ain't supposed to kill him, fool."

The words were growled above him from what seemed like miles away.

"Be the better way, iffen you was to ask me."

"Well, nobody is and you ain't paid to do the thinking. Get me a light. Me and the 'breed's gonna parley some."

Scott set his teeth against the waves of hurt and forced eyes to open. Through the watery blur of his vision, he could make out the shapes of his assailants. Four men with kerchiefs covering the lower halves of their faces and hats pulled low. Trail dress. No help there. In the distance, he could see the unmoving bottoms of Rory's boot soles. *Rory.* He groaned with the monumental effort of gathering his knees under him and wobbled there in the straw like a newly foaled colt. A nudge from one scuff-toed boot sent him sprawling again. This time, he stayed down.

One of the masked men hunkered down beside him. Torch light glinted off the silver disks studding his gunbelt. His voice was low and rough. "You listen to me, half-breed. You listen good. You're sticking your nose in where it don't belong. Won't be long afore someone's gonna shoot it off. Consider this here a friendly warning. Leave things be. Take your fancy piece and head on back east. We don't want your kind strutting around here a-stirring up trouble. You ain't gonna pass for no white man no matter how many fine college degrees your grandpappy buys for you. Best you just skeedaddle."

Scott scarcely had the breath to breathe, but still he

managed a sneering defiance. "Go — to hell."

He clamped his jaw down against the want to cry out as a vicious kick struck him near the kidney.

"Here now, that ain't necessary," the spokesman chastised as he stood. "I think our half-breed friend gets the idea. Least wise he will when he gets a chance to think on it. Let's be sure he has plenty to remember, boys."

Scott heard a ripping sound and something white floated down from above. Feathers?

Then, in one gut-wrenching instant, he recognized the hot smell.

It was tar.

It was like trying to fight his way from underwater with someone's foot planted squarely on the back of his neck.

Rory moaned and managed to flop over onto his back. His eyes flickered open to see rafters soaring overhead. Church? That would figure in with the clanging in his ears. But he could smell horse and hay and the whiskey on his breath. He wasn't sure where he was, but it sure as hell wasn't church!

Muttering and nursing the back of his throbbing head with an unsteady hand, he rolled up to his feet and gingerly straightened. The livery. He must have tied on a real sweet one to have stumbled in here. Then, his fingers encountered a shotglass-sized swelling and the stickiness of his own blood.

Durbin. They'd come looking for Durbin. Then Scotty had gone all squirrelly on him.

Scott.

"Scotty?" The call echoed through his head like cannon fire. He lowered his voice to a hoarse whisper. "Scott?"

Walking set off the clamor again, like call-to-meeting bells gone mad. He moved slowly back into the main body of the stable. There, a shaft of light trickled in from the street through the partially opened door. Illuminating an outstretched hand.

"Scotty?"

He shuffled toward that ominous shape, squinting hard to adjust his vision. Then he drew up short, chest heaving, wishing he couldn't see quite so clearly. "Son of a bitch. Son of a bitch." He was cursing and crying, falling heavily onto his knees at his brother's side. "Look what they've gone and done to you."

Scott had managed to protect most of his head by crossing his arms over it. His shirtsleeves and back had taken most of the hot black abuse. Goose feathers stuck obscenely to the sticky mass they'd poured over him in an age-old statement of warning. Shaken, outraged, Rory tried to roll him over. And unintentionally woke him to a hellish awareness.

"Ahhh! God, don't."

Rory sat back on his heels, hands clenched helplessly into fists atop his thighs. For the first time, he could see the lumpy swellings on his brother's face. "They bust you up pretty good?"

"Think a couple — ribs — broke."

"You jus' stay still. I'll go fetch Daddy."

Scott's hand flashed out, gripping Rory's forearm with a staying strength. "No," he wheezed. "I don't want them to know — anything about this. You promise me, Rory. You promise me."

Rory's hand clapped down over his, squeezing hard. "I won't say nothing, Scotty. I won't say nothing." He took a deep draw of air and wiped his eyes and nose on his other sleeve. "I'll see to you the best I can. Let's get you cleaned up and home."

And that proved harder than anything he could ever imagine.

The sound of voices woke Gena from her uneasy slumber.

"What the hell have you two gotten yourselves into?"

"Scotty got himself busted up bad, Daddy."

"Get me some light, Ora. You boys been fighting in some saloon?"

"No sir, Daddy."

"Dear God!" That was Aurora, her words stricken and strained. "His face!"

"Ora, give me some room."

"Is he all right?"

"I'll know that as soon as you let me close enough to see."

Gena rushed down the stairs on silent bare feet, jerking to a halt at the sight of the four of them huddled at the table. Scott was slumped, bare-chested, in one of the chairs. He was barely recognizable through the swellings at cheek, jaw, and temple. But what gave her horrified pause was the discoloration mottling his ribs. Stunned, she sank down on the stairs, knowing she'd just be in the way if she went to hover over him. Aurora was doing enough of that for the both of them.

"Rory," Ethan growled. "Plant your mother down and see she stays there. Sit on her if you have to."

Pale and anxious, Aurora assumed a chair, perching on its edge. Rory stood behind her, his big hands kneading her shoulders through a spill of blazing hair.

Ethan began a gentle inquiry, counting ribs, pressing lightly until Scott winced. One more down and he groaned. Another and his boot heels scraped the floor.

"I count three pretty banged up but not broken. I'll bind 'em to give you a degree of comfort till they mend. Get kicked by a mule, pard?"

Scott's teeth were set against the pain, not allowing an answer to escape.

268

"Rory, you want to tell me about it, son?" Ethan looked up briefly, then started to wind an elasticized bandage about the battered midsection.

Scott was pulling in quick, shallow breaths. His gaze met Rory's over their mother's head. Calling him on his vow.

Aurora twisted in her chair. "Rory? If it wasn't fighting, what exactly was it? And don't tell me he fell off your horse."

"Not off the horse, Mama," he muttered. "Down some stairs."

"Whose stairs?"

He shifted uncomfortably, eyes evasive. "I'd rather not say."

"You'd better be saying."

"Outside Miss Elly's," he mumbled tactfully, as if trying to spare her the undignified truth.

"The whorehouse?" She all but shrieked it. "What were the two of you doing at a place like that? And where's your brother's shirt?"

Fabricating desperately as he went along, Rory hung his head and confessed, "Well, we'd been drinking, Mama, and things just sorta got outta hand. We had to leave real sudden like and Scotty, he don't hold his liquor so good. He took a tumble down the steps. It weren't in our best interest to go back after the rest of his things so I jus' brung him here."

Gena didn't need to hear any more. She had a very clear picture of what had happened in Crowe Creek drawn out for her. And it hurt. Numb, breathing as if her own ribs had been shattered, she dragged herself upright, drawing Scott and Rory's notice. Her tragic gaze met that of her fiancé. He looked as though he was about to call to her when Ethan pulled his bindings tight. By the time he could manage a decent breath again, she'd fled upstairs.

Rory refused to meet Scott's accusing gaze. Instead, he mumbled something about having to get back to the Bar K. Aurora saw him to his horse, leaving Ethan to finish his doctoring.

Ethan was nobody's fool. He knew on first glance that no roll down a flight of stairs would leave the kind of contusions Scott sported. He'd been beaten, and for some reason, he and Rory were keeping the truth secret. More than likely it had to do with the smell of kerosene and strong soap that the whiskey couldn't disguise. And the way Scott's collar-length hair had been chopped to the nape in back, leaving a patch of raw and reddened skin.

Somberly, he dabbed the ruin of his stepson's face with antiseptic, asking as he did, "You want to tell me about it?"

"Tell you what, Daddy?" He wouldn't look at him until Ethan gripped his chin and angled it up. Stubborn. So damned stubborn.

"You know who did it? Or why?"

Scott's jaw gripped. If he knew, he wasn't saying. Ethan sighed.

"All right. Take care of it your own way." He started to put his things away.

"Daddy? You won't say anything to Mama, will you?"

Ethan jerked his head toward the stairs. "Your mama ain't the one you have to explain things to. And you'd better make it good."

Chapter Seventeen

Gena wept until her whole body hurt, wrapped tight upon her bed in silent wretchedness. How could he? How could he go so thoughtlessly from her arms into another's embrace? Into some harlot's bed? Miserably, the answer came. Because there he found what she would not give him. A warm, willing woman to slack his lusts upon.

With the ten dollars she'd gotten back for him!

While smothering the great shuddering sobs that wracked her, she tried to make excuses for why he would hurt her so. He was a man. Her mother would say that was reason enough. She had explained that even the most decent of the masculine persuasion were driven by insatiable needs, desires that reduced a superior intellect to a base, rutting mentality. Conscious of one goal. Satisfaction. A true gentleman would not subject his wife to this aberrant behavior more than twelve times a year, for sex without procreation was immoral. And it was the wife's duty to guard her husband's soul. And his brain. Retained reproductive fluid was reabsorbed into the blood to stimulate mental powers. Gena remembered hearing these things, being mortified by the personal nature of them, but her mother had insisted that she not be naive about the true nature of marriage. So she had listened and cringed inside.

It was her fault. She had led him to last night's sexual sin. By encouraging him, then failing to provide. She was guilty of pushing him beyond the boundaries of control. She'd allowed his kisses and caresses. No, she'd wanted them. She'd been as eager and greedy as he. By succumbing, she broke her mother's most cardinal rule: a woman was to display little passion and was to touch her husband without a particle of sexual desire. Now, she knew why. Because once that spiraling urgency began, there was no halt. The only end was in the completion of the act. And she'd not finished what she so foolishly started.

Someone else had.

Knotted on her lonely bed of despair, Gena agonized over her situation. How was she ever to be a proper wife? How was she to pretend she didn't burn with longing for the man she loved? How was she to forever deny him the very touches she craved? Scott was not yet her husband. It was disgraceful for her to yearn for the forbidden. That was meant for the wedding night. How was he to respect her when she showed such weak judgment? How was he to behave responsibly when she disregarded dignity? She was supposed to be morally stronger, yet she caved in with the slightest simmering glance. It was her fault.

No.

As she lay staring at the darkened ceiling, tears lending it a sheen of stars, a deep, resentful fury arose. Subtle at first, then gaining a forceful resistance to her mother's teachings. Why was she to blame for Scott's indiscretion? She had responded warmly, even wantonly, to his desires. She hadn't discouraged him. The night had been ripe with promise. She hadn't rejected him.

She'd given him no reason to seek out another. She hadn't pushed him into the harlot's bed. He'd walked there on his own two feet. If anyone was to blame, it was Scott Prescott. He had failed to keep himself for her. They weren't man and wife but they were betrothed. He owed her his allegiance. And had proven himself disloyal. With some painted floozie.

And with Morning Song?

Why had he looked elsewhere? She couldn't keep the anguish from returning to her door. What was so lacking within her that he would look for it in another? Had her kisses been unfulfilling? Had her response been inadequate? In her inexperience, she could find no answer. She had given him everything she held inside and would have given all if they'd not been interrupted. Right there in the grass. Right under the stars. Without the benefit of his name. Why hadn't it been enough to sustain him?

Scott, what am I doing wrong?

What was she going to do?

She wanted so badly to believe Scott was different. She wanted to hold to the memory of his soft-spoken court. To his kindness toward her. To cling to the promises he'd made for their future together. She wanted to disprove the warning that a lover's devotion seldom survived the placement of a second ring. The ring that would bind her into a life of submission. That would forbid her from saying "no" or "don't." That would force her to comply with those ugly, sweaty things that went on behind the closed doors of wedlock. She wanted to thrust aside her fears and believe him when he swore, "I won't hurt you." And she prayed she would not discover that Scott Prescott was no different than—him.

One of the hardest things Gena had ever had to do was leave her room the following morning. The part of her that made it impossible to sleep in the throes of torturing humiliation urged her to keep to the numbing privacy of her own quarters. But the flinty spark of anger that made her hope Scott Prescott tossed and turned all night in agony insisted she wash her face, put on a pretty dress, and brazen it out.

She dressed with care. Each pale tress was curled and secured to perfection. Her lacy gown was feminine to the extreme. Without guilt, she applied a touch of color to wan cheeks to overset the shadowed circles beneath her eyes. What did he find lacking? She studied her image with critical intent. She saw no glaring faults, nothing to displease a man. Her skin was translucent and without flaw. Her eyes were large and clear. Her mouth soft, yielding. Though she wasn't possessed of bounteous proportions, there was nothing wrong with her form. Nicely rounded breasts shaped her bodice. No corset was needed to inspire a trim waist. Something deeper, then, something not in appearance but in manner.

Dispassionately, she took stock of her virtues and found they were many. She had no vices, no unappealing habits. She was the epitome of an eastern society woman. And more. Here, under Aurora's tutelage, she'd learned the ways of a western woman as well. For Scott. To please him.

What would it take? What did she have to do? How could she get him to love her enough to forsake all others?

But then, he'd never said he loved her at all.

All he'd said was he would marry her.

And at that moment, in the tattered recesses of her heart, she realized she would rather have the former than claim to the latter.

It was a terrible day, fraught with tense evasion.

Ethan and Aurora went out of their way to act as though nothing was amiss. Too far out of their way. They treated her gently, as if she was something to be pitied and protected. When Scott finally hobbled downstairs, she couldn't bring herself to look at him. Or to speak other than in the briefest terms. She made sure they were not alone, too uncertain of her own emotions to risk a confrontation. If he tried to apologize, she feared she would dissolve into tears. If he did not, she was afraid she'd lash out like the veriest shrew.

Covertly, she watched him move about the house, his gait stiff, his breathing harsh with effort. Part of her wanted to offer tender aid. The other part delighted in the evidence of his misery. As they sat at the supper table, she stole glimpses of him. His features made her wince. And when she thought of those golden eyes fired with desire for another, of those lips tasting passion while hers were parched, she was sorely and meanly tempted to add to the bruises he'd already accumulated. She was appalled by her vengeful spirit, yet at the same time, it felt wonderfully vindicating. He'd made a fool of her in front of his family, and now she was expected to meekly sit at the table and accept it. No. No, she wouldn't.

Ethan had gone out on the porch to smoke his pipe and Aurora was in the kitchen waiting for her to bring in the rest of the dishes. And Scott sat at the table, watching her. Gena reached in front of him, taking up his plate. When he caught her arm, her body snapped rigid.

"Gena—"

"Don't!" Her tone was low and venomous. The intensity of anger surprised them both. She tried to twist free but his fingers tightened.

"Please. Let me explain about last night."

She saw red.

Her glare stabbed at him with an icy dignity. "Explain? Surely you don't think that I am so stupid as to require one." She wrenched her arm back causing him to suck a quick gasp of discomfort. "Excuse me."

With the rest of the plates stacked precariously, she stormed off to the kitchen.

Groaning, Scott dragged himself up from the table and shuffled like an old man to one of the fireside chairs. He hurt. His head ached mercilessly, pounding to match the steady throb of his face. He hadn't quite gotten up the courage to survey the damage in a mirror. It felt as though his features had been ground through his mama's coffee mill, then rearranged in a different, ill-fitting pattern. The pain in his side was exquisite. Breathing hurt. Moving hurt. Sitting hurt. Talking hurt. Hurting hurt. Bruised, maybe a hairline crack, Ethan had said, and he believed him. But that didn't stop it from feeling mashed to pulp and strained through broken glass.

Worse than his own pains, more relentless than his own physical torment, was the way he suffered Gena's distress. Rory's thoughtlessly concocted story had wounded her. Deeply. And he didn't know how to go about repairing the tear in her trust. The truth would cause her to worry over his safety, but could it be worse then the anguish she already carried?

And he had other reasons, more selfish ones, for wishing to keep her in the dark. If she learned how far he'd gone in the offer of help to his father's people, would she still believe he meant to honor his vows to her? He'd kept his involvement quiet, unwilling to share his confusion about the future. To explore the great satisfaction he received when he could benefit the Lakotas with his knowledge. It felt good to be a part of them, to belong. Would Gena understand that or would she be threatened by the part of him she couldn't hold? Could he blame her if she was? The bond was so strong, so ingrained upon his heart, he wasn't sure he could pull away and return east without forever regretting that he'd walked away. But if he didn't go, he would be dishonoring another promise he'd made.

He tried to keep his thoughts upon Sal Garrick and the men paid to discourage him. There had to be some way to prove the connection, some way to tie Garrick's illicit doings down. He must be close or they wouldn't be quite so blunt in their message. Yet every time he tried to concentrate, his mind was distracted with disturbing results. Gena in her clingy underthings rushing to his rescue in the creek. Gena telling the story of Columbus to White Cloud's children. Gena saying staunchly, "To hell with them." Gena dissolving beneath him in a wash of passion that left him stunned and breathless. Every day, the thought of marriage to her became less an obligation and more an anticipation. And every night it became harder to stay on his side of the hall.

He hadn't meant for things to get so far out of hand the night before. He had a deep respect for her virtue and he hadn't knowingly set out to compromise it. But, God, she was sweet. So innocent. So eager. And he knew she would be loving if she just allowed herself the chance. He wanted that love. He basked in the admiration glowing in her eyes. And he returned it. He had to marvel at the determination she'd shown by remaining with him. And conquering his mother had been no easy feat. She had changed since Boston. He watched the evolution with mounting wonder. There, she had regarded him with a shy devotion. Here, she'd displayed passion and possession. She was trying so hard to fit into his world, how could he tell her he wasn't sure just where that was? How could he guarantee her a place when he had none of his own?

"Looking mighty low there, big brother. Brought you something for the miseries."

Smiling was out of the question, so Scott grimaced up at Rory, who shot a quick glance toward the kitchen before slipping him the bottle he carried. Hoping it would ease some of his physical and mental sufferings, Scott took a long drink. The bottle was cool in his hand and felt good pressed to his aching cheek.

"Hey, I didn't bring that over so's you could use it for an ice pack."

Obligingly, Scott passed it back, and Rory took a big swallow before sinking into the opposite chair.

"You holding up all right, Scotty? You look like hell."

Scott took another drink and let the fire burn down. Instead of answering, he asked, "How's your head?"

Rory rubbed the back of his neck ruefully. "Lucky there ain't much up there to damage."

"Got that right. A whorehouse!" He hissed the accusation, careful so no one would overhear them. "For God's sake, what made you say something like that?"

"I'm plumb sorry about that, Scotty. I ain't got your quick thinking. It was all I could come up with. I come over tonight to set things right between you and Miss Gena."

"No."

"But you don't want her to go on a-thinking that you was with some—"

"I said no. Leave it alone. It's complicated."

"It's stupid. That's what it is. But it's your business," he relented as he watched his brother take down another hefty swallow. He saw him wince and absently rub at

278

the swelling on his jaw. Rory's tensed and his mood darkened. "You got any ideas 'bout who bushwhacked us? Whoever it was must have paid Durbin to make himself scarce. Thought I might make a little talk with him tomorrow." He smiled. It was a humorless gesture, one that reflected the fury and helpless horror of having to scrub his brother down with kerosene to get the tacky tar off his skin. Of following it with the sting of harsh soap. Of cutting the worst of it out of his hair. Of suffering Scott's misery in silence on the long ride home. And now. "Hang it, Scotty, somebody's gonna pay dear for this."

"Let it alone, Rory. I'll handle it. It's got nothing to do with you."

"Nothing?" He tried to close off his memory to the horrible sounds of his brother's pain as he'd dragged him out of the barn to the watering trough behind the livery where he'd had to cut him out of his shirt. "You're dead wrong there."

"Just don't do anything till I'm on my feet. You give me your word, Rory."

Grudgingly, he gave it.

"They wore masks," Scott recalled. "But one of them had a real fancy concho-studded rig. Not the kind of thing you'd forget." He took several gulps from the bottle and blinked against the tear of the liquor. In doing so, he missed the shock of surprise on his younger brother's face. And the daze of disbelief that followed.

Gena had been watching them from the kitchen doorway, seeing the exchange of whiskey and man-talk. When Rory glanced over and saw her there, he clambered up with hat in hand and approached like a repentant pup.

"Miss Gena, I'm right sorry 'bout the other night. I gots as much grace as a three-legged steer and I

279

wouldn't blame you none if you was mad enough to spit."

He looked up hopefully, expression mournful. She was sure he'd been using it to melt his mother's temper for years. And suspecting it didn't protect hers from that same fate.

"Mr. Prescott, a lady does not spit."

His hug was quick and unexpected, sweeping her up in a bearlike embrace. She clung to him for a moment, fighting the tears that threatened. His rumbling words made the battle more difficult.

"Scotty's one lucky feller." He felt her stiffen and added, softly up next to her ear, "You go easy on him, Sis. He's hurting bad."

And I'm not?

Anger overcoming that pain, Gena pulled back. Before he would let her go, Rory bussed her cheek with a light kiss and left her with the enigmatic vow of, "Things ain't always what they seem."

As he sat hugging his bandaged side, Scott observed the two of them sourly. Rory got a hug and her forgiveness. He got a cool, reproaching glance as she passed by on the way to the stairs. He sighed and took comfort from a suck of whiskey.

Rory frowned at him. "You sure you don't want me to make things right with her?"

"I think you've done more than enough."

There was no excuse for the cutting remark. But then, it shouldn't have caused the degree of misery that came into his brother's dark eyes.

"Guess I'll be going."

"Rory?"

"What?"

"Thanks." That was all inclusive.

Rory's smile was thin and strained. "Sure, Scotty." He

280

lingered an awkward second as if there was more that needed saying, then he merely nodded and, clapping his hat on his bright head, strode for the door.

"Rory?"

Aurora came from the kitchen, a dishtowel fluttering in her hands. She drew up short when her younger son turned toward her. It was as if she could see his heart breaking in his eyes. She took a panicked breath. *What is it? What could be so awful?* She didn't have the chance to ask.

"Gotta go, Mama. 'Night."

Aurora stood silent for a long moment, stunned by the anguish she'd seen in Rory's gaze. Then, she looked to Scott. What weren't they telling her? She knew Scott was hiding something, but it didn't seem nearly as devastating a secret as the one her other boy carried. Or perhaps Scott was just more adept at deception. She walked up behind the chair where Scott sat staring moodily into space. She let her hands rest on his shoulders, her fingers kneading gently.

"Release your troubles, *cinksi,*" she murmured softly.

Scott had only heard her use that Lakota name for son once or twice in his life. Hearing her say it now brought him perilously close to blurting out the entire truth. But he didn't.

"They are many, *Ina,* and not easily spoken."

"And you brought them upon yourself."

From her sharpened tone, he knew she was referring to Rory's damning lie. "I hurt her, Mama, and I don't know how to fix it. If Daddy had done the same thing, what would you want to hear from him?"

"His prayers. Because I'd kill him if he ever stepped out on me with some two-bit piece of flash. You're lucky Miss Trowbridge is of a gentler nature."

281

"I don't know, Mama. I could feel her eyes cutting off chunks of me all evening."

"From all the appropriate places, I hope." She didn't sound at all sympathetic.

"How long do you think she'll stay mad at me?"

"She might not be staying at all."

His mother's words settled deep and dark like the heavy evening hours. He considered them long after the house lay in silent shadow. *Might not be staying.* She wouldn't really think to leave him, would she? Over some stupid tale his brother concocted? But then, she didn't know that. She had no reason not to believe it. And he couldn't reassure her without giving all away — his involvement with the legal woes of his father's people, the beating he'd received to warn him away. His increasing reluctance to return to Boston. She wouldn't actually go, would she? Back to where Horace Billings waited. A world away when he'd come to treasure her presence at his side. How could she think he would seek out another when the image of her in the stream burned inside him? How could she believe he'd want another after discovering the promise of paradise in her arms?

He wasn't a fickle man, nor did he let his lusts rule him. As a rule. As a Lakota, he valued restraint. As a gentleman, he valued an honorable code. But as a man, he reacted to Gena Trowbridge as if she were heat lightning, shocking his senses from a course of reason, jolting him beyond thoughts of control. He hadn't believed she could spark such a frenzy of desire within him. Cool, proper Gena Trowbridge. Corseted and coseted. Weaned on weakness and unwavering reserve. What kind of magic had she used upon him? In his head, he was too intelligent to believe in such things as magic. But in his Lakota soul, he respected his grandfather's stories. Could Gena be like the mystic deer-woman who

282

would lure a lone warrior upon the prairie with her seducing scent, casting a spell upon his sensibilities until all he could think of was making love to her? And when that act was completed, would she flee him like that mythical deer spirit, leaving him to a life of wandering madness?

His scalp suddenly prickled. The hair on his arms stirred like summer wheat in a wind. And from the darkness floated a pale vision. Superstition flung his heart up into his throat, choking back his startled cry. When he was able to swallow it down, a wondering warmth replaced it.

She appeared like an angel from his Christian heritage rather than a spirit of the Lakota netherworld. Her gown was white and flowing. Her starlight-colored hair shimmered in soft waves, accented with a glowing halo by the kitchen lamp. Gliding on silent bare feet, she crossed the puncheon floor with scarcely a ripple to her lacy bedclothes. His quick pull of breath sounded unnaturally loud and hoarse as she sank like a pale mist beside his chair. For a long, suspended moment, they neither spoke nor moved but melted, blue to gold, into one another's stares. Then Gena's hand rose. Her fingertips traced the crescent-shaped bruise along his cheek with an almost healing tenderness. And the breath shuddered from him. His hand covered her smaller one, guiding it to his lips then to his chest to feel the accelerated longing in his heart's hurried beats. His gilded gaze probed hers, looking for forgiveness, looking for an affirmation of her love. All he could see was an intense reflection of what shone in his own eyes. Yearning. Urgent, unrequited need.

"Gena." Her name rasped from the sudden tightness of his throat. "Gena, last night, I didn't — "

Mean to hurt you? Her fingers halted the rest of what

she expected him to say. No, he probably hadn't. She didn't want to hear his confession. She didn't want to listen to his apology. Not now.

When she leaned forward, her unbound hair spilled over him like silvery moonlight. He caught some of it in his hand, twining that silk-spun magic through his fingers as if he could hold to its elusive light. Her cool palms cradled his battered face between them, anchoring him with a breathless anticipation for the sweetness of her kiss. His eyes closed as the soft luxury of her mouth conformed to the shape of his and molded his emotions with every subtle shift. When he sought to deepen the union, she drew away, going only far enough to pillow her head on his shoulder. Her slender arms wound about his neck with a convulsive tightening. He felt the hot dampness against his neck at the same time he noticed her body's quiet tremors.

She was crying.

Guilt and overwhelming tenderness paralyzed him.

"Gena," he moaned. "Don't, please. I'm sorry. God, I'm so sor—"

The fierceness of her kiss silenced him. The aggressive stab of her tongue between his lips inflamed him. And while he was yet stunned, she said, "Don't tell me, Scott. Show me. Now."

She stood and, without a backward glance, moved to the stairs. It took him a full ten seconds to realize the nature of her demand. And by then, she'd disappeared into the darkness overhead. He started up from the chair to be struck both barrels by the pain in his side and the dizziness in his head. He reeled. He cursed low and impatiently. If he had to drag himself up the steps, he would. And he did, clumsily, noisily, determinedly. He knew a moment's confusion and a monumental disappointment when he paused in the upper hall. The door to her room was closed. And then, he saw that his was open and an inviting light beckoned from within.

Gena stood with her back to the door, her arms hugged about herself in an effort to hold to her resolve. She would see it through. To have him. To win him from the welcoming arms of the town harlots and seductive promise of Morning Song. If it was the physical bonding that meant more to him than emotional ties, she would supply it. He hadn't said he loved her. But he did want her. And once he'd taken her, there would be no going back, no altering their planned course. She would have him.

And that meant more than the hurt of his betrayal.

More than the fear of what was to come.

Or so she wanted to believe, until she heard his unsteady step in the hall.

Then both those things flew up to flutter about her heart in crazy palpitations. And clutched tight when his large warm hands closed about her arms. Turning her toward him. Pulling her against him. She stiffened but forced herself to be still, not to resist him as his mouth came down upon hers. She could taste the whiskey, stronger than before, because his kiss was wet and wide. The flavor, the fumes, swirled about her senses. Instead of soothing, they incited a remembered panic and a will to fight against the inevitable end of what she'd started.

"Scott." Terror weakened her voice into a pitiful plea. One he mistook for passion, for immediately his arms engulfed her and his kiss grew plunging. Pinned to his unyielding chest, she couldn't struggle. She could only drown in the mewling horror of the moment. Finally, she was able to tear her face away and gasp for courage.

"S-Scott, make love to me," she beseeched desperately. "Like last night." If he could stir her with those same sweet feelings, she could stand it. She knew she could.

"It will be," he promised.

But already, it was different. His voice was low and gritty, a stranger's voice. His hands were hard and hurtful on the tender flesh of her arms. She didn't know he was hanging onto her for dear life, trying to stay on his feet when all around him whirled. His kisses weren't sensitive and stirring but rather deep, devouring. And she didn't like it. Any of it. His hands stroked recklessly over her body, encouraged by the freedom to move over an unfettered form. Her gentle curves enticed him to greater boldness, and she gasped in startled shame as her delicate gown was pulled down from her shoulders.

"Ah, God," he groaned as his hot tawny eyes raked over her. "You're so beautiful." His palms rasped over her bared breasts and his dark head dipped down.

Thinking to slow him, she pushed away and started along the buttons of his shirt, but he wouldn't wait.

In a quick move, he snatched her up in his arms. She was light, but even so, his side rebelled with tearing agony. And what began as the romantic whisking of her into his bed became in reality a stagger and tumble on top of her. System shocked into immobility, he crushed her to the mattress and struggled not to swoon dead away from the pain. He should have given up the whole idea right then, but drink had blurred his head and passion fired him beyond thoughts of retreat. And she'd asked for him. He'd be damned if he'd disappoint her.

Slowly, Scott levered himself up on elbows and knees. Gena lay still and barely breathing beneath him. At the lifting of his weight, her eyelids flickered. She looked up at him through huge round eyes and her breath panted out lightly against his throat.

"Love me, Scott," she pleaded softly.

This once, she would have rather heard it spoken, but he couldn't have known that. So he showed her all the full, fearsome expressions of care she'd woken within him over the past weeks. He kissed her mouth, her cheeks, her neck, working downward in a wet, sultry trail to the untried peak of one quivering breast. She made a small sound far removed from one of pleasure, then roughly dragged him back up with a cry of, "No. No, Scott. Kiss me." Then her mouth ground against his.

Kiss me, Scott. Kiss me senseless, mindless, until the fear is no more.

But he was drawing back, wincing from the pressure of her palms upon the miseries of his face.

"Gena, maybe we should wait . . ." Something was wrong. For all of her insistence, he was aware of a reluctance, too.

"No," she cried as if stricken. "Now, Scott. Make love to me now." She wasn't sure she could ever find the bravery to come so far again. She kissed him passionately and his hesitation fled. "Now, Scott," she urged into that openmouthed exchange. "It has to be now."

Her eagerness and the smooth, soft feel of her nakedness combined in a potent combination. He started to shuck out of his denims, forgetting to take off his boots first and ending with hopeless tangle about his ankles. The hurt started to swell again, pounding against his ribs and through his head. Just as need pounded in his loins. He forgot about the twist of blue jeans and concentrated on the stretch of her warm skin. He heard her sharp draw of breath when his impatient manhood prodded her clenched thighs.

"Easy," he murmured into a kiss. "Relax, Gena." His lips moved persuasively and he felt her begin to loosen in response. She parted for him, then just as quickly stiffened as he settled intimately between her knees. "Just relax, Gena. I won't hurt you."

She wanted to believe him. Desperately, she wanted to believe him. Frantically, she recalled his gentleness, his kindness. No, he wouldn't hurt her. He wouldn't. She had nothing to fear. She let herself be seduced by the promise he made in both word and tender touch. The first shimmerings of desire warmed through her. She said his name softly, rapturously, beginning to believe herself safe.

Until that first invading thrust of him tore through her.

Scott smothered her cry of surprise with his well-intentioned kiss. He held himself still for a moment so she could get used to the feel of him inside her. For him, it was ecstasy. And agony. It wasn't at all how he'd planned it to be on this, their first time together. He'd wanted to make it so good for her. All the tender little nuances he'd meant to employ to ease her way into womanhood were beyond his power. It was all he could do to keep from passing out. Her feeble struggles stopped and he forced himself to move. Each stroke was heaven and hell. The exquisite burn of sensation was met with stabs of crippling hurt. He labored over her for several long, torturous minutes, trying to settle on a rhythm they could both enjoy. But it was impossible. She lay rigid and tense, defying his attempts to bring her pleasure. Her arms had fallen limply to her sides and her eyes were closed in abject surrender. Or was it merely endurance? Pain from his cracked ribs shot out like tongues of fire with every flex of his hips. He ground his teeth until sweat bathed his face. The harder he pushed toward satisfaction, the more illusive it seemed and the more determined his efforts became. The more he wanted it to succeed, the more it was an obvious failure.

Finally, when he was nearly out of breath and hanging to the last tenuous thread of consciousness, the need for release began to curl hot and tight inside him. He groaned with the effort of increasing his tempo. At once, even in her inexperience, Gena felt the difference in him. Her eyes flew open and she said in a rush of panic, "Scott, please, I don't want a baby."

Had she waited one second longer, it would have been too late. She felt him jerk back from the brink and then come a spurt of warm dampness across her belly. She sagged in relief. He collapsed with a noisy moan. After a time, he was able to stir, dragging himself off her to drop heavily on his back with knees updrawn to ease the stitch in his side. His breathing filled the dim room, a harsh, scraping sound.

Scott fought against the swamping pull of darkness. He needed to talk to Gena. He'd hurt her and she'd gotten no pleasure from their brusque union. Using that aching tenderness he felt for her to hold the pain at bay, he was able to murmur, "I'm sorry, Gena. The first time's never very good. Next time I promise I'll make it better for—"

He heard the sound of his door closing softly.

He was alone.

Anxious to make it up to her, or at least to try, he meant to go after her. Standing was hard enough, but battling the tangle of denims proved too much. He went down, hard and full-length on the floor, sprawling into oblivion. And there, he spent the night.

Chapter Eighteen

" 'Morning, sleepyhead," Aurora called over her shoulder. She took one look at her son and raised a curious brow. Scott wasn't the type to drag about in the morning clinging to the last vestiges of sleep. He was usually awake in an instant and charged with life. This morning, in the pure midday light of the kitchen, he looked positively gray with fatigue and as crumpled as a discarded sock. "Coffee's hot. Help yourself."

He muttered something indistinguishable and shuffled to the range. Pouring with eyes closed, he used the rising heat in the cup to tell when it was full, then slunk back to the table and dropped with a moan. After he'd sat there for several full minutes warming his face in the steam lifting from the dark brew, Aurora smiled sympathetically.

"Want me to put some of the hair of the dog that bit you in that?"

Scott's groan was heartfelt.

She chuckled and came to stand beside him. "Guess I don't need to ask how you're feeling this morning, do I?"

He groaned again and shifted so that his head rested against her trim waist. Her hands were gentle as they stroked his raggedly cut hair and bruised features. He sighed like an old hound when she began a light manipulation of his neck and shoulder muscles. It brought a whisper of peace to his troubled soul.

"Gena outside?" he asked at last.

Aurora frowned. The tentative quality of his voice gave away volumes. Softly, she replied, "She's gone."

"Gone?"

Scott jerked upright, surprise smacking him into full awareness. A desperate terror came into his eyes, momentarily giving his mother pause. He looked as though he were choking on his heart.

"She rode over to the Cheyenne River with Ethan. He wanted to check on that little boy with the broken leg and Gena asked to go along. They'll be back for supper."

She watched as Scott suddenly went boneless. "Maybe I'll ride on out after them." He started up, weaving and wobbling and cradling his side.

"Maybe you can make it as far as the front porch. Now go on out and plant yourself there. The fresh air will do you good. And Scotty"—she paused to gain his attention—"give it time to heal."

His shoulders slumped. "All right, Mama."

She fingered the colorful lump on his jaw with a tender consideration. "And after a hundred years or so, she might just forget all about it."

His smile was as weak as winter sunshine, and as fleeting. Cup in unsteady hand, he eased his way out onto the porch, then took a good full minute to lower himself into one of the chairs. His body ached. His head ached. His conscience ached. And together, they made for a miserable day of anxious waiting.

With his eyes on the horizon, he sipped the coffee and began to watch for their return.

* * *

"May I see?"

"Not yet. I'm almost finished."

Gena added the last few lines to the drawing on her lap, then shyly extended it to the old chief. He considered the likeness for a time, then nodded.

"You have much talent."

The pronouncement made Gena blush. She'd always loved the serenity that came with artistic creation. Her watercolors and charcoals were fine enough to hang in the most discriminating parlor. One dream had been to take courses in oil renderings but it had been discouraged. Proper ladies followed amateur pursuits; handicrafts, watercolor landscapes, sketchings. Anything more than dabbling was a trespass. The realm of fine art was reserved for men.

"I look like a winter apple withering on the tree. But you have made each fold of skin a map toward wisdom. I am pleased."

"You may keep it if you like."

"No. You. To remember me by once you return to the east."

Gena's smile faded as she took her drawing pad back. Back to the east. Back home. Though it hardly seemed so now. She flipped through the drawings she'd done that morning; of the camp, of Red Bird, of the children. None seemed foreign to her anymore. No more so than the split skirt and simply tucked shirtwaist she wore.

"When will you take him?"

Gena's fair brow furrowed, not understanding.

"Lone Wolf. When do you take him away?"

How strangely the old chief phrased things. "I'm not taking him away. We're going together to resume the life we'd plan to lead once we're married."

Why did he nod as if he didn't believe her? Why did she feel compelled to explain?

"It's his choice. He has a job waiting with my father."

"Yes. An important job," the old Sioux murmured.

Important? Gena fell silent. Pushing papers for her father? Bending over a desk in some dark, crowded room every day for the rest of his life? Traitorously, she recalled the look on his face as he regarded the clear Dakota heavens. He would suffocate in Boston. Why did she have to have that crystal-clear revelation just now? It was true. She'd known it long before they'd gotten off the train and he'd breathed in his first intoxicating draught of Dakota air. She'd heard it in his voice every time he spoke of it, of his Hills, of his family, of his freedom. He didn't want to go back to Boston. He was going for her sake, not of his will.

Where was the sense of victory? He had chosen her over the most valuable things in his life. To be with her, to go with her, to honor his vow to her. With heartfelt reluctance. There was no pleasure in tearing him from his preferred land, from his preferred people.

"I'm not forcing him to go," was her last feeble protest, and Yellow Bear quickly cut it down.

"If not for you, would he go?"

No. No, of course not. But she had trapped him well. By his vow. By what had passed between them in the night. She was his choice, not of heart and soul, but of the stronger, passionless ties of duty. That was cold satisfaction. Obligation gave no comfort. How well she knew. Throughout her childhood, she would have gladly traded all the expensive gifts and fancy frills for just one hug of affection. And now she would leave one barren existence for another.

"What should I do?" It was a question directed inward. She was surprised to find she'd spoken it aloud. She didn't want Scott's grandfather to think she was weak and wavering in her love of his grandson, but his smile said she need not explain.

"Follow your heart, New Waw. Sometimes the greatest love is not in the fight to hold on but in the strength to let go."

Was he saying she should walk away and leave Scott to his precious Hills?

"You don't think I'll make a good wife for him."

"That is not for me to say. Some things are not meant to be, no matter how much you want them. Lone Wolf is not of the cities. The part of him that is white can walk that path, but the soul of him is of the Lakota and it cannot be made to heel. His heart is here. Would you break it for your own purpose?"

That's not fair! she wanted to shout at him. But his benign gaze told her he knew it was not. Yellow Bear and his people knew all about the cruelty of fate. And while he could sympathize with her, he would do nothing to lessen that moment of misery.

The old man's gaze lifted suddenly and looked beyond her. She'd heard no one approach. Therefore, when she twisted to follow his stare, she was startled to see Scott standing so close he couldn't have not overheard. Never had Gena felt so naked, not just to the skin but to the very bone, beneath his penetrating golden eyes. He could see her doubts, her fear, her terrible anxiety over the time they'd spent nearly naked in his bed. Her mouth went dry, her complexion as pale as milk. And seeing the sudden jump of terror in her wide blue eyes, Scott recoiled as if she'd struck him. His body went tense. The angles of his face stood out like the harsh spine of Black Hills beneath the taut pull of his bruised and bronze flesh. He didn't speak. The power of words deserted him. He'd done the unforgivable. He'd broken his

294

promise. He'd hurt her and he'd made her afraid.

"*Takoja,* come, sit."

Scott's gaze never left Gena. "Another time, Grandfather. I've come to take Miss Gena home."

Gena's pulse leapt. The thought of the ride back to the Lone Star with this intense and vaguely threatening Scott Prescott left her quaking. Everything had changed between them. The emotions were raw. Her thoughts felt exposed. She'd needed time to compose them before being forced to confront them. And him.

"Your father—"

"Knows the way home," he finished for her. "And I know he took his own horse so he won't need the buggy." He put down his hand to her.

She stared at the callused palm, remembering the feel of it on her body. Her throat worked convulsively. And even as she struggled for some excuse, she saw her own hand lift to meet his. His grasp was firm, controlling, drawing her up on strengthless legs until they stood toe to toe, nearly touching. She didn't have to touch him to remember the feel. The hot, heavy feel of him, crushing her . . . hurting her. She took a quick step back and reached down for her sketchbook. Tangled in the web of her own making, she murmured a farewell to the impassive Chief Yellow Bear and let Scott steer her toward the buggy. She'd forced the issue of intimacy upon them and now she felt its strain. She'd tried to block it from her mind, for to dwell upon such matters was as indecent as the very act had been immoral. But she couldn't ignore it. She couldn't pretend she hadn't given her virginity to Scott Prescott any more than she could pretend the entire incident hadn't left her shaken and distressed.

When his hand slipped to the small of her back, an icy rebellion stiffened her spine and her flesh fairly crept beneath that light touch. And the fact that she felt such

295

revulsion, such overwhelmingly helpless panic at the hands of the man she loved, made her want to weep and wail. *What was wrong with her?* Or was this the way it was between men and women and she was too naive to accept it? Had she been foolish to dream of more? Hadn't her mother given her fair warning? He'd said "trust me" and she had. And now she felt angry and betrayed and inadequate. Endure, her mother said. But she'd never taught her how. She berated herself for her cowardly shrinking at his touch. *Don't let him guess how much you hated it. How much the thought of it happening again fills you with dread.* Accept it with passivity. With dignity. But she couldn't. She was sick inside and Scott, whom she loved, who had represented kindness and safety and escape, put a consuming terror into her heart.

"Are you all right?"

His question took her unaware. Her answer was guileless in its evasion. "I'm fine. How are you?"

His fingertips stroked the nape of her neck and a shiver rushed the length of her. He felt it. His lips tightened. "Gena, I'm sorry about last night."

How repetitive that sounded. A hysterical laugh quivered inside her. She fought it down to ask with an edge of dire consequence, "Are you sorry that it happened?"

"No," was his gentle reply. She trembled. "I just wish it had been better."

Gena felt her poise snap. The sting of it brought tears, the way the bowstring had when it slapped against her arm. She bit her lip hard, then managed to say in a brittle voice, "I'm sorry if I lacked the finesse of your other . . . paramours."

His hand curled about her upper arm, yanking her up short. She wouldn't look at him and he found himself arguing with the back of her neatly woven blonde head.

296

"That's not what I meant and you know it."

"And just how would I know that? I haven't the experience of those — those town hussies."

"Gena." He tried to turn her. She put up an admirable resistance.

"Don't." That word cracked. She blocked his attempted embrace with her forearms the way one would ward off an unwelcomed attack. Her gaze was angry. Scared.

"If you don't like it when I touch you, why were you so eager for me last night?"

She flinched. It was an awful thing to say and he regretted the words. But he had to know. Suddenly, he had to know. They'd reached the buggy. When she tried to climb up, he held her at his side. He was stronger, and she knew it was useless to fight. So she surrendered. The same spiritless way she had beneath him.

"Why, Gena?"

She lifted her tear-streaked face in supplication. "You won't leave me, will you, Scott? You won't forget your promise to come to Boston, to marry me?"

His expression stilled. And turned to stone. "That's what it was about? Making sure I went with you to Boston?"

"You are, aren't you?" It was a frantic question. Her hands reached out for him then drew back. He remarked upon the move with a slow twist of his narrowed lips.

"Yes. I'll go back with you, Gena."

The relief in her face was an arrow through the heart. It had all been a trick. Her passion, pretended. Her eagerness, feigned. She hadn't desired him at all. She'd done it to snare him with one of the oldest traps in the world. And he'd never suspected a thing.

And now, she had the incredible insensitivity to gloat.

297

Pride and painful disappointment prompted his blunt response.

"I would have gone anyway, Gena. Your sacrifice was quite unnecessary. And not as compelling as my vow."

She stared up at his rigid features, stunned and stricken. How could he be so cruel as to make sport of what she'd given him? As if it meant nothing? As if he cared nothing at all about her? She swallowed hard, nearly strangling on her tears. "Well, you needn't have b-bothered with the effort, S-Scott. I release you from it. Take your precious Indians and your cozy whores."

She lashed out at him in her need to get away. One flailing fist caught him in the ribs with unintended force. He cried out and clutched at his side, giving her the chance to jump up into the buggy and slap the reins down. He stood, doubled over, gagging on her dust and cursing them both in two languages.

Gena let the horse run. She couldn't have guided it through her blur of weeping anyway. She clung to the edge of the seat and sobbed. Despair wracked her. She'd lost him. She'd thrown her only chance away because he'd chided her for her awkward lovemaking. And he'd had every right to. What a coward she was. Cringing then, running now.

That prodded her enough to reach for control of the reins, for control of her feelings. What had he expected? A seasoned lover? An unbridled wanton? Why hadn't he made it nice, the way he had in the tall Dakota grasses? Why did he have to lie to her, then rend her with the truth? Why did she want so much to please him only to bear the disgrace of failure?

He couldn't love her and now he wouldn't even want her.

And she'd let him go.

Wiping her eyes on her sleeve, she cleared her vision

298

enough to see a man's white shirt lying alongside the road. Had she taken a second longer to wipe her eyes, she never would have seen it. That first white shirt, then a harum-scarum trail of laundry leading into a dense copse of cottonwoods. Puzzled, she drew in the horse.

Then, she heard it.

The sound was unmistakable. It had haunted her dreams for years, a relentless, chilling nightmare that Scott had brought to life upon his bed. She could hear it even upon covering her ears, as she'd done as a child. She could see the images even upon closing her eyes for they were burned upon her memory.

Her father lurching up the stairs. Reeking of liquor. His face florid and dangerous. His big hand imprisoning her mother's wrist as he dragged her up the steps. She'd been six years old, too young to understand. She'd huddled in the shadow of one of their big potted palms, quivering with terror. Part of her demanded she do something to help her mother, but she couldn't seem to move. The tableau was frightening. Fascinating. Her proper businesslike father in a whiskey- and sweat-stained shirt. Her regally reserved mother with her hair knocked askew and her bodice ripped open. She remembered the trail of seed pearls it had left on the stairs. Like a trail of tears.

You frigid bitch. I've given you all my money. Now you give me what I want. It's not like it isn't bought and paid for.

The door to their room slammed. Then the sounds began. Horrible. Indelible. The growls and grunts of an animal. Her mother's frail pleadings and whimpers of pain. The loud rhythmic creaking as if they were jumping upon the bed. Petrified and powerless, she'd crept along the hall and cowered outside that closed door, finally garnering the courage to peek inside. Just to make sure her mother was all right.

They were upon the bed. Her mother and father. Naked. Entwined. The sight confused her with its violence.

And then her mother had turned her head and had seen her standing at the door. And she had fled. The next day, Margaret Trowbridge was as cool and proper as ever as she poured her husband's coffee. They said nothing of the matter. Not directly. Subtly, casually, after that night, Gena began to learn of the ways of men and women from her mother. Of sex. Of how its denial brought dignity and power. And surrender meant disgrace and punishing illness. Gena was afraid of sickness. And she grew to be terrified of men.

Until Scott.

And then he had proved her mother right.

The sounds brought it back to her. A woman's frightened moans. A man's lusty mutterings. Then laughter, coarse male laughter. From more than one man.

She sat frozen on the seat. Instinct urged her to continue on, to pretend she'd heard nothing. But she sat, staring at that spew of laundry, and a fierce, primal rage began to build. Toward the kind of man who would make a weaker woman cry. Toward her father. Toward Scott.

"Help me!"

It was a faint cry. A futile cry. One that galvanized Gena with fury. Before she could think of the consequences, she grabbed beneath the seat for the scattergun and followed the path of clothing. Into thick brush. Into possible danger.

The sounds were clearer. She could make out words, ugly, intimidating words.

"Stop fighting. You know you like it. Jus' remember, iffen your pappy don't give heed, we'll be looking up your little sister."

300

"Get offen her. Save some fer the rest of us."

Then the woman's cries, shrill, panicked yet still defiant.

Morning Song.

Gena burst into the small clearing. She took in everything with a single glance. The four men, masked with bandannas. Morning Song flat on her back, her blouse torn, her skirt thrown up over her belly. With one man holding her hands above her head and one pinning either leg at a wide angle. And the fourth atop her, his fleshy buttocks pumping with obscene vigor.

Stunned, then maddened beyond clear thought, Gena hauled up the scattergun and squeezed the trigger. The kick of it knocked her back in a reel but not before she saw the Indian woman's violator plucked off her by a peppering of birdshot to the behind.

"She shot me! Goddammit! The bitch shot me! Get her!"

The three men scrambled up, leaving the fourth to wrestle up his britches over the oozing holes in his backside. Gena tried to fire again and found, to her dismay, that she'd discharged both barrels. Recognizing her own peril, she whirled and began to run for the buggy. She'd get help. She'd get Scott.

She could hear them, crashing after her, but not having their bulk, she was faster. Seeing the buggy, she sucked a last big breath and sprinted for all she was worth, leaping toward the seat. Only to be caught about the waist in one beefy arm.

"No!"

It was a scream of objection that echoed back over the years. Strengthened by her helplessness as a child, sparked by her frustrations as a woman. She fought. Wildly. With heels and hands and nails. Scratching. Even biting. Shrieking as she did, "No! You pig. You won't do that to me. Let me go!"

Her curled fingers clawed at his face, tearing flesh, pulling down the triangle of cloth. Unmasking him.

"Right sorry you did that, little gal," the man growled, struggling to contain her. " 'Cause now I'm gonna have to kill you."

One look into his soulless eyes told her the truth of it. And she knew she was dead. It was a cold, clear certainty. Then, his gaze canted down to her surging breasts. And something worse than killing came into his gaze.

"But maybe not right away."

At first she thought it was a vision born of desperation. Then he heard the hoofbeats, too, and looked up to see Scott Prescott bearing down on them full bore. His grip eased for only a second, long enough for Gena to jerk free. To begin to run toward the rider. Hearing no sounds of pursuit, Gena thought herself safe. Until a searing heat spun her into darkness.

From an impossible distance, Scott saw Gena struggling in the arms of a burly man. She broke loose and started racing to him, her long blonde hair free and billowing behind her like rays of the sun. Horror-stricken, he saw a pistol drawn and leveled. He didn't even have time to shout a warning before she crumpled there on the side of the road. A sound tore from him, from deep inside. A raw, wail of anguish so vast, so terrible it might have been made with the gutting blade of a James Black Bowie knife. He didn't see the shootist flee for the safety of the woods and the horse his friends had waiting. He didn't remember dismounting from a full gallop or flinging himself down in the dirt to scoop the limp figure up into his arms. All he could see through eyes skewed with tears, was her face. Pale. Her hair. Paler. Streaked with strings of crimson.

"Gena? Gena! Oh, God. *Wakan Tanka* have mercy. Please, God, be all right. I love you, Gena. You can't d-die. You can't leave me." He cradled her in his arms, brushing the wet strands of hair away from the crease along her temple. His hand shook. If he'd listened to his mother and stayed home . . . If he hadn't said those ugly, hurtful things . . . If he'd stifled his pride and started after her just seconds sooner . . .

Then, he felt her stir and it was as if his life started up again. His breath came quick and easy. He scrubbed his damp face on his sleeve and held her gently.

"Gena?"

Her eyes opened, blue, wildm and sightless. Her cry chilled the blood in his veins.

"No! Don't! I won't let you!" Her hands flew up and braced against his chest. Pushing. Heaving frantically.

"Gena, it's Scott."

He knew the instant she recognized him. Her gaze widened. But the fear didn't leave them. Not totally. Nor did she cease her struggle. The pressure of her hands was less frenzied but no less determined.

"Gena?" His thumb grazed her cheek and she trembled.

"No." It was a weak, pitiful plea. And it finished the earlier upward stroke of pain from belly to heart.

She wasn't strong. He could have retained her without effort. However, something in her shadowed eyes drained the power from his limbs. She was able to roll off his lap and stagger to her feet with no interference from him. Until she began to walk in a drunken sort of reel off the road and toward the trees.

"Gena?" He struggled to stand, pushing his elbow hard against his tortured side. He followed, sure the injury had dazed her. "Gena."

She jerked away from the light hand he placed on her

arm. Her gaze was disoriented but still determined. The wobbling strides didn't alter speed or direction.

"Gena, come back to the buggy. You've been hurt."

She ignored his soothing persuasion and began to work her way through the dense cluster of brush. He dodged the backward snap of a branch and frowned his exasperation.

"Dammit, Gena. Stop."

Unable to shake off his new grasp, she looked up at him, beseechingly. "No. Mustn't stop me. Have to help Morning Song."

Surprise slackened his fingers and she forged on, pushing her way back to that tiny clearing. Scott went along with her, this time aiding instead of arguing. Then, he pulled up in shock and stared.

Morning Song had managed to gain her feet. Her face was puffy and yet wet with her panicked tears, but her eyes were dry when they beheld him. There could be no mistaking the tattering of her clothes, the tangling of grass in her snarled hair, the bruises on her arms, the blood streaking her long, slender legs where they were exposed by the rent in her skirt.

She'd been raped.

Gena stumbled to her and without any hesitation embraced the other woman. Morning Song stood stiffly for a moment, as if she would refuse the comfort. Her lovely features worked with the effort of clinging to control.

"I'm so sorry," Gena moaned. "I'm so sorry."

And Morning Song sagged upon her shoulder in quiet sobs.

It was then Scott made sense of the rest of it. The strewn laundry Morning Song must have been carrying alongside the road when she was attacked. The discarded scattergun Gena had dropped when her unwise defense failed. Gena had come to the Sioux woman's rescue, charging in with a near useless weapon to fend off a number greater than her own. And had almost paid for it with her life.

Respect and love for his fair Gena knotted about Scott's heart and squeezed with desperate fingers.

Slowly, he approached the two weeping women and began to steer them back toward the buggy. He helped them climb up; Morning Song in the center, Gena on the outside, then he tethered his horse in the rear. When he took up the reins, Morning Song spoke up for the first time.

"Take me home, Lone Wolf. No one must know of this shame."

"Shame?" The word tumbled from Gena and her arms seized tight about the other's shoulders. "You have nothing to be ashamed of. Nothing. You did nothing wrong."

As the buggy began to move, the Indian woman caught sight of the line of forgotten wash.

"The clothes . . ."

"To hell with them," Gena concluded firmly.

No one needed to tell White Cloud what had happened. One look at his daughter's state and her stricken face told him all. She went silently into his arms. Ashen and angry, he looked over her head at Scott and Gena.

"Who did this?" Before they could answer, he did so himself. "Never mind. I know." That was affirmed when Morning Song blurted out the warning she was given in their native tongue. She was shifted to her mother's embrace and White Cloud motioned for his two guests to join him outside along with a stoic High Hawk who had yet to speak.

305

"You must cease your work on our behalf, Lone Wolf," the older man said slowly, sadly. He could not meet Scott's eyes. "I have brought this pain to my family. It must not go farther. I will give them what they want."

"No!"

All looked to Gena in surprise. She was a ghastly sight with her blood-matted hair and colorless cheeks. But there was a hot fire in her eyes.

"Then what happened to Morning Song will go unpunished."

White Cloud said nothing. His shoulders bowed as if beneath a great weight, the weight of his people's bondage.

"You have to do something," she cried in outrage.

"Enough has been done," High Hawk said at last. His black stare stabbed into Scott's. "Resistance has brought us this disgrace to bear."

"Disgrace?" Gena was appalled. And furious. "You make it sound as though you're guilty of something. Your daughter, your sister, was raped. Aren't you going to do something? What was done to her is a crime. Those men need to be hunted down and destroyed like the animals they are. You can't let them get away with it. Scott? Scott, do something."

High Hawk sneered at his former half-caste friend. "It is what he has done already that made us pay this price. Fine words. White man's words. Go back to your people, *wagluhe*. You bring a curse upon us."

Amazingly, Scott took Gena's arm and urged softly, "Come on, Gena."

She looked up at him through wide, disbelieving eyes. "You're going to do nothing? You're going to walk away as if nothing happened? What if it had been me?"

With a broken cry, she fled them and hauled herself

up into the buggy. Silently, Scott joined her there and turned the horse toward the Lone Star. His hands were clenched on the reins. His profile was uncompromising. Gena kept to her side of the seat, her arms hugging themselves, her gaze straight ahead. Blaming with her silence. Damning with her distance.

Chapter Nineteen

The Prescotts reacted with outrage and admiration to Gena's story. She was hurried up to bed where Aurora rinsed the gore from her hair and Ethan gently tended the furrow along her brow. Not life threatening, he pronounced, but good for one hell of a hangover. That was no surprise to Gena, who was already feeling the grumbling buildup of pain as it mounted into a storm.

She was banked up on her bed pillows, sipping hot tea, when she noticed him lingering in the doorway. So handsome he took her breath away. She almost forgot the words that had passed between them. Almost.

"May I come in?"

It was a quiet request. One she was too weary to deny. For that would mean dealing with all the confusions of her heart and she hadn't the strength.

She watched him approach on those light cat-feet, moving hesitantly because of his own injuries and because of the uncertainties that lay between them. He was unsmiling. His intense gaze skewered hers, looking straight to the soul.

"How do you feel?"

What an enormous question. How to answer.

"Fine," was her reply.

When he stopped at the edge of the bed, she sidled over uncomfortably to put a safe distance between them. He mistook it for an invitation and settled on the side of the mattress. Feeling the dip of his weight brought back a surge of memory. Gena swallowed hard. Her head was pounding. Her heart was pounding. She wished he would just go away.

Gently, he took up one of the hands resting on the coverlet, her right hand. Thoughtfully, he twisted the ring she wore with thumb and middle finger. He carried her hand to his lips for a whisper-soft kiss. Then he turned it and fit her palm to his cheek. His face was rough and warm and male. She felt the sigh of his breath against her wrist. Deliberately, she withdrew her hand, making it unavailable beneath the covers. Scott's jaw tensed. But he didn't pursue it.

"Gena, I want you to go back to Boston."

She should have expected it but his words took her like a fist to the chest. They knocked the breath from her.

Scott spoke slowly, carefully, phrasing each thought with the utmost delicacy. "It's best that you go. I can't do what I must unless I know you're safe. You're my responsibility. I gave that promise to your parents and to you."

And broke it. Her lips trembled.

"Things are going to get . . . complicated. I don't want you in the middle of them."

"I see," she murmured, and he wondered if she really did.

I don't want you. Her heart clutched miserably. Yes, it was better that she go. She couldn't bear the anguish of seeing him slip from her by degrees. He was being kind. He was offering her a way to salvage her dignity. She should take it. She should.

309

"I'll make the arrangements whenever you think you're fit to travel."

Gena drew a strengthening breath. "Tomorrow. I can be ready tomorrow."

"Tomorrow." He echoed the word softly. With regret or relief? She couldn't tell. Through dazed eyes he watched her hands appear, wringing together.

"Perhaps it's best we settle things now."

In explanation of her words, she began to remove his ring.

"No!"

His hands surrounded hers, tightening into a fist of protest. For a moment, his golden eyes took on an unnatural sheen. Then they closed. Upon opening, the betraying shimmer was gone.

"Wait, Gena. Please."

"Why?"

Her question tore at his soul. It was so forlorn. So hopeless. So resigned.

"Please," he repeated. "Until I finish here."

Her nod was slight but an agreement no less. It was the best he could hope for. With a small smile, he pressed a kiss upon her knuckles, then stood.

"I'd better let you get some rest."

He retained her hand for a long minute, kneading it between his with a restless agitation. He stared down at her wan features, at the stark strip of white where his father had bandaged her wound, at the demure muslin bedgown so like the one he'd eased off her shoulders just the night before. She appeared so frail and small yet was possessed of an incredibly brave spirit. Why hadn't he seen that in her before? Why hadn't he recognized his love until pushed to the brink of losing her? He wanted to sink down beside her, to enfold her in his arms, but her guarded gaze restrained him. She didn't want his

310

comfort. Not now. And he would have to accept that. When he let go, her hand thumped lifelessly atop the bedcovers.

Gena followed him with her gaze, with her heart, as he walked to the door. *Let him go. Let him go.*

"S-S-Scott?"

One glimpse of her ravaged expression brought him to her. Her arms snaked around his neck, winding tight, holding desperately. His embrace was fierce.

"Oh, Scott. I was s-so afraid."

"Shhh." His hand tangled in her loose braid the way her words tangled about his emotions. Meshing. Twisting. Hurting. His voice was hoarse with all the raw feelings he was struggling to repress. "You're all right, Gena. No one will ever make you afraid like that again. I won't let any one hurt you." His mouth moved against her hair, along her wet cheek, to her soft lips. Claiming them with infinite tenderness. She didn't respond. Nor did she resist. When at last he drew back, he found her gaze upon him, vulnerable, stripped naked by despair.

"Gena?"

The abrupt cry shocked them apart.

Rory crossed the room in three giant strides to scoop her up in his bearlike hug. His expression was tragic, his words shaken. "Are you all right? God, I'm sorry. I'm sorry. I never thought something like this could happen."

Scott went still inside. The words sank with deep meaning. He stared at his brother, hoping, praying the cold trickle of intuition was wrong.

"You could have been killed," Rory was saying. "And it would have been my—" He choked off and sat back to study her. "Are you really all right?"

"Just a headache." Her smile was weak. Then her features firmed. "It's not me you should be concerned with.

311

I wasn't the one who suffered. And no one—*no one*—should have to accept such a foul wrong. No one should have to feel that helpless."

Scott gave her a sharp look. The pain she spoke of sounded so personal. Was that how she saw what had transpired between them? A rape of the helpless? Guilt and objection roiled inside him. She couldn't believe that, could she? Then the tormenting recall of her terrified eyes returned to him.

"There's nothing I can do, Gena," he said softly, and then he flinched when her stricken gaze disbelieved him. "I can't make a case if she's unwilling to pursue it."

"And what about me? What if I chose to stay and bring those animals to trial? They were going to kill me, Scott, but not before they—they did the same to me as they did to Morning Song."

She saw the muscles along his jaw jerk and go taut.

"I saw one of them, Scott. The man who shot me. I know what he looks like."

"What?" Rory's demand was like a brisk shake. "Describe him."

She closed her eyes. How could she forget? "He was tall, big. Dark hair. Long in back and worn behind the ears. He had blue eyes, a hooked nose, and thick lips. He was wearing a gun belt with these shiny disks like silver on it." Scott's sharp pull of breath brought her attention to him. For all the violence in that sound, his features were surprisingly composed. He gave her a reassuring smile and brushed the back of his hand along her cheek. She couldn't control her body's sudden shuddering. His smile stiffened.

"You rest, Gena. I'll take of things."

She searched his closed expression. His very calm was frightening, the still of the gathering storm. "All right, Scott. I'll try."

Scott saw her settled beneath the covers and the lamp turned low. Then he gripped his brother's arm and urged him toward the door. Neither of them spoke as they descended the stairs, nor did Rory balk in following Scott out onto the porch. He stood tensed and waiting.

"What aren't you telling me, Rory?" Scott hissed into the darkness.

The redhead was bowed. He was staring at his boots with hands shoved deep into his pockets. After a long silence, he mumbled thickly, "I'm real sorry about Miss Gena. You got to believe me, Scotty. If I'd had any idea something like this —"

Patience snapping beneath a craze of grief, Scott spun toward his brother and slammed him up against the wall. Rory put up no resistance, letting himself be manhandled.

"Dammit, Rory, you talk to me! What do you know about all this?"

The dark eyes rising to meet his were awash with sorrow and distress. "I wouldn't want Gena hurt for the world. You know that, Scotty."

"Tell me!"

"I know him. That feller at the livery, the one what shot Gena."

"Who?"

"Feller goes by the name Jake Spencer."

Scott's fingers twisted in the fabric of his brother's shirt, balling it up until his shaking fists met under Rory's chin. The collar wedged under his Adam's apple, nearly choking off his air. "Why the hell didn't you tell me this before? He could have killed Gena, you dumb son of a bitch! I ought to tear your heart out!"

Rory's features crumpled. He hung limp where Scott pinned him to the logs. "You are, Scotty," he moaned in

313

anguish. He closed his eyes to the sight of his brother's battered features, just as he'd tried to close his eyes to the terrible truth. "You don't understand."

"Understand what?"

"Spencer works for the major."

The significance hit him like a steam train.

"Grandfather ordered Spencer beat me up?" he asked in a constricted voice.

"I didn't want to believe it, Scotty. I didn't know what to do. I didn't know what to do. If anything had happened to Miss Gena . . ." He let that trail off in misery. When Scott released him, he continued to sag against the house, gulping for breath. He watched his brother pace the length of the porch in short savage strides. The violence, the agony in his face, was dark and terrible. "What are you going to do, Scotty?"

Scott raked his fingers through his hair. The gesture brought a twinge to his side, an incredibly bitter pain. "Where can I find Spencer? At the Bar K?"

"No. Most nights he hangs out with some whore named Ronnie outside of Crowe Creek."

Scott left the porch.

"Scotty . . ."

He paused but didn't turn.

"I'm sorry."

He resumed his step without comment.

High Hawk looked in dismay as the plum-stone dice were thrown from the wooden bowl. Usually his luck at *kansukutepi* was good enough to earn him the cost of a bottle. On this night, it was so bad he would have welcomed the distraction had it come from any other source.

He scowled up at his childhood friend. His defiance

was fueled by his own helplessness and self-pity and by the anger churning in his soul. When Lone Wolf made a motion, it was his wish to ignore it with a contemptuous arrogance. But something in the set of the other's face prompted him to uncurl from his cross-legged position amongst the other gamblers to follow the *iyeska* into the shadows.

"Is this how you think to restore your sister's honor?"

The hissing slur was like a slap. "What do you know of honor, *wagluhe?*"

"I know it's not found in whiskey."

"When I'm drunk is the only time I am free."

"That's not freedom, my friend. That is cowardice."

High Hawk's blade jabbed beneath Scott's chin, causing a well of blood to fill the indentation. "I am no coward."

Scott's stare was steady and without fear. "Then prove it to me. To yourself. Help me punish those responsible for your sister's humiliation and my woman's pain."

"With your white man's law?" He spat on the toes of Scott's boots.

"No. In the way of our people."

He reached up and put his hand over the one that held the knife, slowly bringing it down. Eyes black and eyes gold met and mingled with a long-ago flame. A flame of brotherhood.

"I will follow, Lone Wolf."

Two bronze figures squatted near the fire, stripped down to brief breechcloths. Neither spoke as they painted their bodies with bold designs. The presence of another interrupted their ritual.

"Scotty?"

"Who is the *wasichu?*" High Hawk asked.

315

"He is my mother's son."

Not *"my brother."* Rory didn't miss the significance. And hunkered down, bathed in uneven flame, Scott didn't look like the brother he'd grown up with. He looked hard and dangerous; Lone Wolf son of Far Winds, not Scott Prescott of the Lone Star Ranch. The young redhead hesitated. There was no welcome in the glittering golden eyes. They glowed hot like the coals. This was another world to him, one from which his mother had isolated him. He felt no animosity toward the Sioux but they made him nervous. They made him feel a foreign intruder. And at the moment, so did Scott.

"Send him away. He has no business here," the Lakota brave growled impatiently.

"Go home, Rory," Scott told him with a quiet authority. He dipped his first two fingers into a pot of white clay and drew parallel lines from brow to throat, bisecting the halves of his face. Even with the short hair and his mother's tawny eyes, he looked every inch an Indian.

"No. It is my business." He thought of Gena in the hands of Spencer and those like him. Of Scott, beaten and betrayed. Of his own part in it because of his confused silence. He smiled grimly. " 'Sides, I always wanted to play Injun with you, Scotty, but Mama wouldn't let me. She ain't here to stop me now." He squatted down and put a finger into the white clay. This time, Scott stopped him. Rory gave him a long imploring look, asking the chance to redeem himself.

Scott wiped the clay from Rory's fingers upon the grass. "You're white enough already." Then, with his own hand, he smeared a black residue across his brother's cheeks.

* * *

Jake Spencer stretched his big frame beneath the single sheet. His thick lips curled back from a satisfied smile. It had been good tonight. He'd made Ronnie moan and twitch like a tick on a hot plate. 'Course it wouldn't do to go telling her his energies were fired by another. That sweet little blonde gal from this afternoon. He got hard again just thinking of it. He felt bad about having to drawn down on her. Too bad he hadn't had the time to put it to her proper before killing her. Especially when he'd been denied his chance on the squaw. Sating himself on his favorite whore was small consolation until he thought of how poor ole Quint was paying for the privilege. He wouldn't be sitting a chair for a good long time.

He heard a shuffling in the cabin's only other room and called out, "Ronnie, honey, bring me another bottle. I feel another celebration coming on."

"Then I guess we arrived just in time."

The deadly purr of a masculine voice killed all interest in a carnal revelry. Spencer gasped as three shadows filled the door. The dim light returned golden off lengths of bronzed skin. Injuns! Cursing, he rolled naked from the bed to grab for his fancy holster. Hard fingers closed about his wrist, twisting, thrusting him back onto the mussed bedding. Squealing in terror, he tried to escape off the other side only to be knocked back with a forceful shove.

"What do you want? What do you want? I ain't got no money. All I got's right there on the table. Take it!"

"We don't want your blood money, Spencer."

"What then? What? Anything. Take anything!"

Teeth flashed white in the speaker's painted face as he cast a glance down at the quivering man's fear-shriveled genitals. "What do you take when an animal won't stop pestering what's not his to mount?"

317

Spencer opened his mouth to scream and found himself choking on his own filthy shirt. His eyes rolled white with horror as a long, wicked blade glittered meaningfully. His wrists were quickly lashed to the sides of the bedframe, leaving him helpless to whatever the savages had in mind. And he had a good idea what that might be. He'd heard Sioux vengeance was a terrible thing to behold, and he was guessing it would be even worse to endure. He writhed from side to side, cries for an undeserved mercy stifled by the makeshift gag.

"Have you ever known fear, white man? The kind you put into the eyes of the women you violate? Have you ever felt pain? The kind you inflict in the dark when your number is greater? You will know these things when we are through with you."

The razor-sharp blade drew a thin red line from breastbone to navel. The soft-spoken words were salt in that wound.

"Have you ever seen an animal gutted and hung up until all the blood drains from its body? How long do you think a man could live with his belly slit open and his entrails exposed? I would think every minute would seem an eternity, a living hell. A fitting death for a man who abuses women and sneaks in the darkness with the rest of the craven coyotes. The Lakota have ways to prolong life long after a man begs for it to end. We have all night, white man. Shall we celebrate together?"

Spencer flopped wildly on the bed, straining against his bonds. Tears leaked from his eyes and spittle from the corners of his stuffed mouth.

"Or perhaps being the coward you are, you would prefer to talk to us about the things you know."

Spencer's head jerked up and down frantically. He was sobbing when the gag came out. "Anything. What do you want to know?"

318

"Who do you work for?"

"Major Kincaid. I do jobs for him."

There was a moment of taut silence.

"And was one of those jobs working over his grandson?"

"We was supposed to scare him off. Only being part Kincaid and part Injun, the damn fool wouldn't scare. We weren't gonna kill him. Me and the boys got carried away some."

"And the Indian woman? Were you ordered to do that, too?" The question was a lethal hiss, like a rattler in the coil.

"Not by Kincaid."

"Who?"

"By Garrick. He wanted the family's land. We works for him sometimes, too." Spencer lay panting in a pool of his own sweat, his frenzied gaze darting between the three silent figures. "You ain't gonna do nothing now that I tole you everything, are you? Are you?"

The knife blade trembled, then stilled. The quiet speaker leaned down close and vowed fiercely, "You pig. I am going to skin you alive and enjoy the sound of your screams."

The man's eyes were ablaze, glowing like the devil's and Spencer had no doubts that he was about to die horribly at his hands. Then one of the others reached down and grabbed his torturer's wrist, holding firm, twisting slightly until the blade was surrendered into his other hand. Before Spencer could breathe a sigh of relief, his rescuer struck him a tooth-loosening blow to the face. Then another and another. Finally, he was the one who had to be restrained.

The soft-spoken one leaned down again and gave him a sinister promise. "We will be back. We know your name. If you want to keep your yellow hide, you will go

319

to the *iyeska* lawyer, Prescott, and tell him what you have told us. You will answer all his questions in a white man's court. If you fail, we will hunt you down and hang you up in the sun to cure. The only escape you have from us is truth or death. You choose."

Then the three of them were gone, and Spencer began to weep.

Wiping the black stuff from his face, Rory Prescott looked to his brother who was resheathing his knife. "You weren't really going to use that thing, were you?"

Scott met his gaze and smiled, a quick expressionless baring of the teeth. "No, of course not. I'm too civilized."

Rory studied him for another second and then kept his doubts to himself. Better he not know the answer.

"You are troubled, *takoja*. We will smoke the pipe and talk."

Scott waited respectfully for his grandfather to settle himself and light the sacred *ptehincala cannunpa*. While it was passed between them in silence, the old man observed the younger through knowing eyes.

"It is time." Yellow Bear said simply.

Scott nodded. "I must choose a path. I can no longer walk between my two worlds. My heart is heavy. No matter what I decide, I must leave behind those I love. Either I stay to help my father's people or I go to the east to live as a white man. How am I to decide when my soul is so divided?"

The old chief sighed. "In the days of my youth, a man dreamed of the horse he would capture, of the feathers he would wear, of the enemy he would slay, of the pattern on his shield and paint of his face, of the woman he would marry and the way he would die. The white man

320

has made it a crime for us to seek the wisdom of the Great Mystery through dreams and visions." He pointed to the scars upon his sunken chest. "I, too, sought truth when in your years. A truth I have followed all my days. You must seek your own truth. In two days' time, I will pray for such wisdom to be visited upon you. I will dance one last time and give my vision to you."

Scott sat up, his features taut. *"Tunkasila,* I cannot ask this of you. I will not allow it."

Yellow Bear raised a haughty brow. "You think I am too old? I must be, for my ears have just betrayed me with words of disrespect."

"Forgive me, Grandfather." He mouthed the apology but his gaze was still stricken with worry. Yellow Bear was old, burdened by immeasurable hardships, weakened by foes of the body and spirit. He couldn't help being alarmed by the prospect of what his beloved mentor thought to do. "If you dance, so will I."

Secretly, the old Lakota chief was pleased, but aloud, he said, "This I cannot allow. I gave a vow to your mother, Wadutah, that I would not permit you to seek your path in the old way. I promised her that your flesh would not be torn. I am sorry, Lone Wolf."

"I do not walk in my mother's shadow," Scott told him softly. "I am a man, and as a man, I will find my own way and seek my own dreams in the way of my father. I will go with you, Grandfather, but to honor your vow, I will not seek my vision in blood."

The old chief nodded, satisfied and proud beyond words. Solemnly, he passed the pipe brought to their people by the White Buffalo Calf Woman to the man his grandson had become.

* * *

Her dreams were fevered and restless. In them, she saw her attacker's face, hardened with lust and intent. She tried to cry out but the sound would not come. She tried to run but her legs would not support her. Then, through that swirl of panic came the soft soothing notes of a remembered song, a sound she had heard once before in another dream. And Scott was there. Standing at her bedside, bronze flesh bared in her imaginings, all sleek and sinewy.

"I love you, Gena. No one will ever, ever hurt you again."

Such wonderful words. She smiled in her sleep and let herself drift deeper into that comforting realm. Scott was with her, if only in her dreams, and she felt safe.

Chapter Twenty

And he was there when she awoke.

Only this was not the partially clad Lone Wolf of her dream. It was Scott Prescott dressed in denim and cotton. Sometime during the night, he'd drawn a chair up next to the bed where he'd sat in watch over her. Where he had fallen asleep, bent forward at the waist, head pillowed on folded arms atop her covers. And still slept.

Finding him there was both a comfort and a distress. She was glad not to have been alone, but the thought of him studying her while she was unaware and garbed in little more than thin lawn and lace brought a hot flush of color to her cheeks. Even after the intimacy they'd shared, she found it difficult to accept such familiarity. And then, there was the fact that he held her hand trapped in his own beneath the weight of his head. Carefully, she tried to withdraw it. Her knuckles slid beneath the rough stubble of his morning beard. His eyes came open and he was instantly and fully awake.

He straightened quickly, wincing and cradling his side. His face was without expression as he waited for her to speak.

"I'm sorry if I woke you," she said at last. "I was surprised to find you here."

His reply was neutral. "You were very restless when I

looked in on you last night. I was afraid you'd wake and—need someone."

"I didn't sleep very well, but you needn't have—"

"I wanted to."

She'd drawn the sheet up modestly to her chin, unaware of how it softly outlined her figure beneath it. Scott allowed a covert glance to detail each hill and valley, committing them to memory. When his gaze returned to hers, he found her watching him intently. It wasn't a defensive glare. It was steeped in misery. For this was the day he was going to send her away.

Gena took a resolute breath. She'd been framing the words in her mind for half the night before she'd fallen into an uneasy slumber. Saying them face to face was not as simple as rehearsing them.

"Scott, I'm not returning to Boston today," she began. When he displayed no reaction, she continued more boldly. "I'm going to stay and press charges against the man who shot me. If Morning Song can't or won't put up a fight, I intend to see her defilers come to justice. If you won't handle it, I'll find someone else who will."

The slightest of smiles quirked his generous mouth but it didn't temper his somber words. "There's no need. Spencer, the man who assaulted you, is turning himself in. He's going to inform on the others to save his cowardly neck."

"Oh." So there was no reason for her to stay. Her hopes plummeted. She fought to keep the despair from escaping. The last thing she wanted was to play upon his pity with tears.

"Gena," he continued gently, "there's much more involved here than you know. More than Morning Song. More than you. It's something deeper, buried beneath lies and treachery, and uncovering it is going to be very dangerous."

"To you?" Her eyes grew large.

"Perhaps."

She bit her lip to hold back the plea that he go with her, that he forget the intrigue and the danger and the responsibility to his people. But she knew what he would say. And when she thought of Morning Song pinned helpless beneath her captors, she realized, in her heart, it was what she'd want him to say.

"Be careful."

He smiled a bit more at that firm command. Then the reluctance came back into his eyes and she waited in dread for him to speak what was on his mind.

"Gena, I'm going to be gone for a few days. Don't ask questions and I don't want you to worry. I'll be fine. I just want — I just want you to be here when I get back. We can settle things then. Just don't leave before I get back. I've got to go now and see Spencer into the proper hands. I don't know if I'll have time to come back to say good-bye, so I'll say it now. Wait for me, Gena."

His voice, his eyes, were so intense. They frightened her. Doubts and fears crowded her throbbing head, but all she allowed herself to say was, "All right, Scott."

He leaned forward to touch his lips to her forehead. "I'll be back as soon as I know — as soon as I can."

She couldn't help it. As he began to straighten, her hands flew up to catch his healing face between them. He paused, delving into the confusion of her gaze, then he came back down to her, slowly, definitively. His kiss was food for the spirit; sweet, stirring, sensuous. And Gena responded in kind.

Wordlessly, he came away. With a thin smile, he left her with the taste of him upon her lips and unasked questions upon her mind.

The days that followed were longer than Gena could ever have imagined. There was no word from Scott, nor did anyone seem to know where he'd gone. She mended. On the second day, a deputy marshal brought a sullen Jake Spencer to the Lone Star for her to identify as the man who shot her. That night, she awoke from dark, terrifying dreams crying out for Scott. It had taken her hours to resign herself to the fact that he wasn't there. She'd finally fallen back to sleep hugging her pillow, pretending his strong arms were about her. It was a hollow comfort. Her gaze kept a constant vigil on the horizon, waiting, watching, praying. He would come back. To settle things, he'd said. She tried not to think too much about what that might mean. Her finger grew raw from the agitated twisting of his ring upon it. The waiting was hard. The not knowing was agony. Where was he?

"Where is he?"

Aurora Prescott echoed her sentiments. Gena could hear her on the porch below as she sat at the window, watching, waiting, as always for Scott's return.

"Ethan, you know, don't you." It was a testy accusation. "Why the secrecy? I want to know and I want to know now."

"The boy's all right, Ora. No need to get your dander up."

"Don't tell me when I can and can't get my dander up. I want to know where my son is. It's not like him to just go off. Is he in some kind of trouble? Ethan, tell me!"

"He's with Yellow Bear."

Gena and Aurora expressed relief at the same time. But Aurora knew her husband too well not to know when he was hiding something.

"Why the mystery, then?"

"You won't like it."

"Where is he?"

"At a Sun Dance celebration."

Obviously Aurora knew more about it than Gena because she sucked an anxious breath. "But the Commis-

326

sion of Indian Affairs made them illegal almost twenty years ago."

"But that doesn't mean they stopped holding them."

"That old bastard! He promised me. He gave me his word he'd never let Scott take part in it. Where are they?"

"I don't know. Honest to God, I don't know. Somewhere in the Hills. It's not something they go advertising to the average white man."

"How could he? After all we've given him. How could he take all the opportunities he's had and throw them away to become a — a heathen! Damn you, Scott, and damn your father!"

"Ora . . ."

"I've lost him, Ethan." It was a heartbroken lament.

"No. No, you haven't. You haven't lost him. He's just trying to find himself. Give him the chance. You keep on strangling him and he won't come back. Let him go. Let him find out what he wants for himself. You raised him to have pride and to stand on his own hind legs. Don't cripple him now or he'll never forgive you." He paused, then added softly, "I don't know if I could either."

Aurora gave a quiet sob and Gena heard the sound of her husband comforting her. But she, herself, could find no comfort upon hearing Aurora's final words.

"Oh, Ethan, I can't bear the thought of him suffering such torture."

Suffering? Torture? Gena's blood froze in her veins. Surely a man of Scott's intelligence wouldn't submit to barbarity of that level.

But he was Lakota.

And she spent another sleepless night.

The vision wouldn't come.

For days and nights he sat fasting and praying, waiting to receive guidance for his life's pattern. But the Great Mystery was silent.

He was to have taken his vision quest during his thirteenth year with the others in the tribe. With High Hawk. It was believed a man could not be a success without the Great Spirit's help, and the quest was every young man's journey to contact the Spirit's helpers. The vision shown them would then be expanded and clarified in dreams.

But Scott had been sent to Boston in that thirteenth year. And he had never learned the path he was to take.

He partook of the belated ritual with the utmost reverence. After purification in the sweat lodge, Yellow Bear took him to a high and sacred place, the place he, himself, had gone. There they had made the eight-foot pit with cottonwood branches set to mark the four corners. Bright cloth banners were tied to honor each corner of the earth; black for west, red for north, yellow for east, white for south. The string corralling them was adorned with colorful cloth packets containing tobacco, herbs, and quarter-inch flesh offerings.

He sat on Yellow Bear's buffalo robe with a second to cover his shoulders. All he wore was his trousers. Eagle feathers were stuck in his hair to call upon the power of the bird. He used the pipe to pray for the Sioux nation and unity for all people, then rested it on a rack between the red and black flags. And he waited. For cool nights and broiling days.

He knew why. It was because his white blood broke his discipline. It tormented him with images of the flesh when he sought visions of the spirit. The world would not release him from its troubles. He sat on that lonely hill, tortured by his grandfather's treachery. He thought of the way the major had embraced him, speaking false words of pride, and tears came to his eyes. He thought of that same man whom he'd respected and loved all his years, of how he'd sent hired thugs in the shadows to beat him into submission, and his soul cried out in pain. He thought of Gena, his beautiful Gena, recoiling from his touch in fear. *Don't.* Of the way she'd pretended passion for him just to lure him back to a world in which he didn't belong. Of her hair stained with blood and her face so still and pale. *I love you, Scott. Make love to me, Scott.* Things his heart yearned for struck down with a single word. *Don't.* Why could no one love him enough to embrace all that he was? Not Gena. Not his mother. Not his grandfather Kincaid. Not High Hawk, Morning Song, or even Rory. Not even Rory understood. Only Yellow Bear and Ethan.

Dizzy from deprivation and sick in spirit, he came down from the hill after the final day hoping the dance would heal him. The Mystery Hoop was ready. In its center was the Sacred Tree with its attached rawhide images of man and buffalo and a cherry-branch bundle. Morning Song had wept at losing her place at the erecting ceremony. Only virgins were allowed to help carry the Sun Pole. He had never seen the dance, but it lived in the stories his grandfather told. He'd heard how his father, Far Winds, swung suspended by the eagle claws in his chest. The muscles refused to yield. Finally, they had attached buffalo skulls, the added weight tearing him free. Scott had listened in awe but seeing the circle brought home the reality of sacrifice for the first time. Everything was as he'd imagined. West of the tree was the altar with its pipe rack and buffalo skull. At east, west, north, and south, flags fluttered. The shade was built around the circle to shelter the spectators with its main entrance facing at the east. Sweat lodges had been built for purification of the pledgers along with the tipi of preparation which housed the ceremonial items and where they would dress before the medicine man led the dancers into the circle. He knew what to expect and he was not afraid.

The first days were the worst. His throat was parched

and his eyes inflamed from staring sightlessly at the sun. The muscles of his legs screamed in torment, for though it was called a dance, the participants stood in one place, allowed only to rise up and down on their toes or to shuffle slightly. The eagle-bone whistle he held in his mouth sounded each weary breath like a death rattle. And every time he felt as if he could not endure another second, he had only to look to his right where Yellow Bear stood uncomplaining in a rapture of devotion.

Sight and sound melted beneath the merciless sun. His thoughts pooled hot and formless. There was no more pain. Only numbness and, oddly, a sense of peace. He could feel the blood moving through his veins, the oxygen flowing into his lungs. So near to collapse, he'd never felt more alive. And on that final day, his vision came.

Gena.

His swollen eyes drifted from the top of the central pole for a fleeting second and he saw her. She stood beneath the Shade Arbor between Morning Song and Red Bird. And even from the distance separating them, he could see quite clearly that her gaze held tears. And pride. Incredible, bolstering pride. It fed his spirit in lieu of food and water. It reinforced his strength in place of rest. She was here. Somehow, she was here. With him. Amongst his people. And at that moment, he knew he could endure anything. Because she cared enough to be there.

"Oh, Scott," Gena moaned softly when his reddened eyes left her. For just that instant, she allowed herself to weaken. Tremors ran through her. Nausea threatened. And when Morning Song lent her arm, she leaned gratefully.

When she'd gone to the Indian woman to coerce Scott's whereabouts, she had no idea what she'd find at the sacred Sioux ritual. She'd expected — well, she'd expected a dance, a celebration, not this gruesome self-inflicted tor-

330

ture of body and spirit. Now she understood Aurora's horror. Now she understood Morning Song's reluctance to bring her. This was at the heart of what kept them apart from one another, this difference, this whole other way of living, thinking, worshiping. This was the part of Scott that was Lakota, the part that frightened her, the part that fascinated her. It was primitive. It was mystical. It was savagely beautiful. And powerful, like the winds, the sky, the sun, the land, encompassing all in a timeless embrace. And while it horrified her, it held her spellbound.

She hadn't recognized him at first. Standing with the others around the pole, only the length of his hair set him apart. He was stripped down to a length of cloth looped between his legs and bound at the waist with a thong. The rest of him was gloriously bared muscle gilded in bronze. His calves, his thighs, his flanks—she blushed but didn't look away—all a rich copper color hewn in hard, sleek lines. Formed to masculine perfection. And hers. She felt an unfamiliar stirring deep inside herself, a feeling that lodged like a hot swelling ache. One look at his face crushed all thoughts of desire. It was there suffering etched its indelible signs. He looked half starved, gaunt, as lean and hungry as a timber wolf. After the merciless exposure to the sun, even his dark complexion showed a stain of burning. There was a dazed dreaminess to his expression—crazed, for lack of a better description. She'd seen her mother look like that when heavily dosed with her tonic. As if reality was as abstract as time and space. And that's what frightened her the most. What had they done to him? What had he done to himself?

Sensing her fear and confusion, Morning Song did her best to explain the history and purpose of the ceremony. The way she spoke, with such admiration and respect, conveyed its importance in their heritage, a

331

heritage the white man had tried to stamp out as heathenish and demonic. It was a test of courage and endurance for the men, a time to seek visions and fulfill promises made under duress. Women would make flesh offerings. Children had their ears pierced. And some, the bravest, sought to wring pity from the gods through blood and pain.

Watching him shuffle on unsteady feet, Gena couldn't see the dashing Harvard student upon his polo pony, or the man in an immaculately pressed suit reciting his proposal, or the properly awkward beau asking her father for her hand. He was none of those things. Perhaps he never had been. And she was suddenly very desperately afraid that in discovering who he really was, she had lost all claim to him.

The sun had reached its zenith. It was hot and airless in the shade of the arbor. It must have been excruciating for those dozen who danced. No clouds eased its intensity. No breath of a breeze disturbed its downward beat upon their unprotected heads.

And then Yellow Bear fell.

He collapsed silently, without warning, and Scott was immediately on his knees beside him.

"Tunkasila? Grandfather?"

The puckered lids fluttered and the old chief looked up. "I am too old. You were right, *takoja.* I was a fool to seek this last journey. I would not regret dying if I had heard what the Great Spirit would tell me."

"You're not going to die," Scott argued angrily. His eyes burned. He had no moisture left for tears.

The ancient warrior smiled sadly. "I will not see another sunrise."

"No." Scott seized his hand and chafed it between his as if the warming friction could restore the years he lacked to go on. By then, others had gathered, including Gena. He felt her at his back, smelled her lemony scent, enjoyed her light touch upon his shoulder. "I'll take you to the Lone Star, Grandfather. Ethan can make you well. I know he can. He is the *Wasichu Wakan*."

"You must finish the dance. You must have your vision. I can wait that long. New Waw can tend me."

"I will," she said softly.

Scott drew a shaky breath. His voice was hoarse from thirst. "Then I will continue. But I will finish your dance and see your vision through my eyes. It will be my gift to you."

Yellow Bear shook his head weakly. "I gave a vow to Wadutah."

"She will understand, Grandfather. She will understand that I do what I must. I release you from that vow. Now, we must continue." He looked up and asked that the old man be taken to a cool spot and made comfortable. Gena remained with him, kneeling at his side. Her gaze was tender with concern. She touched her fingertips to his cracked lips.

"Morning Song tells me you have fasted for nearly a week." Her words quivered. "Will you at least drink some water?"

"It's forbidden," he told her raspily, kindly, firmly.

"Scott—"

"No. Not until sunset."

"But that's hours away."

He shook his head stubbornly.

Gena sighed in upset. She couldn't bear to listen to him breathe. It sounded like the pull of a slow saw through dry wood. He wouldn't drink and she couldn't make him. But she could see he got the water he so desperately needed. She opened the canteen she carried and filled her mouth. Before Scott had any idea of what she planned, she leaned forward to kiss him, parting his lips with the thrust of her tongue and forcing him to take the precious liquid in. He made a hoarse noise of reluctance,

333

then a greedy moan. When he'd swallowed jerkily, she relaxed the pressure of her mouth to soothe his dry lips with the wet lath of her tongue. She dampened her palms and stroked them over his flaming cheeks, cooling them gently. Then she sat back to offer an apology.

"I'm sorry. That was not terribly fair of me."

Scott was panting shallowly. His tongue scrubbed over his lips to catch and savor the traces of moisture. He should have been angry at her for her interference, at himself for his weakness, but he wasn't. He caressed her with his gaze, letting her see his tremendous feelings for her. What she'd done was wrong and yet so wonderfully right.

"I love you, Gena."

His rough fingertips brushed her cheek as she pulled a surprised breath. Before she could respond, he stood and returned to the sacred circle. Morning Song lifted her by the arm, guiding her firmly back to their place in the arbor where Yellow Bear rested fitfully. The Sioux maiden regarded her with a resigned smile.

"You are very lucky to have the love of such a man as Lone Wolf. And now, you must be very brave for him."

I love you, Gena.

She reeled as if she had a touch of sun madness. He loved her. At last he loved her. She could survive anything bravely with the strength of that knowledge. Or so she thought until she observed in horror the reason the Sun Dance was forced to go underground.

To dance looking at the sun and to cut the tiny patches of skin in a flesh offering were the mildest forms of earning the gods' favor. The final phase of the dance was the piercing. Only three of the pledgers took that last step; Scott and two others. The three of them were laid down upon the trampled earth. An awl was then thrust under and through the flesh and muscle of the chest above each breast and threaded with a skewer. That was then tied to a rope secured to the Sacred Tree.

"My god," Gena moaned as they set Scott back upon his feet. Thick rivulets of blood streaked his chest, but his features betrayed no trace of pain. She felt Morning Song's hand pinch her arm. That sudden sharp twinge drew her back from the brink of losing all control.

"You must not show your distress," the Lakota woman warned. "You bring him honor by your courage. Do not fail him. He and the others must pull on the rope until the flesh gives away and the sticks break free. It is the ultimate test of manhood. You should be proud of him. Let him see it. Let them all see it. Be strong for him."

Gena's hands clenched into fists at her sides. Her nails punctured small red crescents in her palms even as Scott strained away from the central pole. While sickness and horror roiled in her stomach, she fought to maintain a composed front. Scott loved her. He needed her. Even if she didn't understand the significance of his suffering, she would respect his right to it. Even as her emotions wailed and wept within, the only sign she allowed to shape her features was that of an intense pride. She breathed in time to the sharp sound of his whistle, willing him all her strength, all her support, all her prayers. Only once did she look away from the taut contours of his face, only for that fleeting instant when he lunged back against the ropes. She couldn't witness that raptured agony. She hadn't the Lakota belief to sustain her.

When she opened her eyes, she saw him pinwheeling backward, free-falling hard to the ground. She started forward but Morning Song gripped her tight.

"No. Do not disturb him. He dreams."

With the heavens swirling above and the sound of his own blood thundering like the long-dead buffalo through his head, Scott received his vision. He watched, not trying to understand the images, awed by them, by the sweeping panorama flashing before his eyes. At one

335

point, he cried out in dismay. And then it was gone, leaving only heat and pain and exhaustion. And Gena. She knelt beside him, her tears dropping like treasured rain upon his parched skin. She was smiling. Her words praised and comforted. And for that moment, everything in his soul was at peace.

"Grandfather."

"He's resting, Scott. Let me see to your—wounds."

"No. Not until sunset."

And when that sun pooled in a blaze of glory behind the sacred Hills, Yellow Bear was eased into the back of the Prescott wagon, his ancient head pillowed on Scott's lap. Red Bird remained behind, weeping at the decision to take her beloved husband to the white miracle man but not interfering with his grandson's right to decide. Gena handled the horses, struggling with the reins and her tears on the long ride to the Lone Star.

At Gena's frantic summoning, Ethan raced from the house to the wagon bed. Scott looked up at him, his features tragically set.

"Save him, Daddy. You can, can't you?"

Ethan saw the taint of death on the old man's withered face, but kindly, he said, "I'll do what I can, son." He gathered the frail figure into his arms and carried him into the house, to his own bed where Aurora had turned up the lamps. "Keep him out of here, Ora."

Scott walked into the house under his own flagging power. He was barefooted with only his jeans and an unbuttoned shirt on. His mother drew up sharply at the ravaged sight of him. Her gaze took in the terrible lacerations on his chest and her expression stiffened.

"Mama . . ."

"Ethan said to wait here," she told him flatly. Her eyes were riveted to his parted shirt. Finally, she said gruffly, "I'll fix you something to eat." Without another word or expression of sympathy, she strode into the kitchen.

Scott's shoulders sagged. He wobbled to the front window and leaned there, sucking air, fighting his body's weakness. Praying to every god and God. Gena resisted the want to fuss over him with her own concerns. She sat silently, watching him, waiting with him. Aurora brought him a watery broth and weak tea and he took some of both. No one spoke.

Some hours later, Ethan emerged from the room, offering no hope with his somber gaze.

"He's comfortable and awake. He wants to speak to you, Son."

Scott approached the sunken figure on the bed with a quivering in his heart. He managed a smile when the old chief turned to him, and Scott took up the birdlike hand in his own. The evidence of his grandfather's frailty shocked him. He was going to die.

"*Tunkasila*, you can't —"

"Hush, *takoja*. I haven't time to argue. I would hear of your vision. Tell me."

Scott swallowed back his grief and relayed what he had seen. A great grizzly rising up on its haunches, striking down a pack of snarling dogs until only one remained; a white wolf. As the two of them communed, the spirit of the bear was lifted, soaring to become that of an eagle. For a time, the wolf circled the still body that remained, sniffing, whining. Then, it ate its fill from the carcass and set out on its own, trotting through the middle of the Sioux village. Instead of crying out in fear, the Lakota children followed the animal into a field where corn grew thick and high. And there, they disappeared.

"Do you know what it means?" Scott asked quietly.

"We both know, Lone Wolf. I must fall and you must rise to lead our people to their survival. My wisdom will be visited upon you. It is a good dream. Will you follow where it takes you?"

"Yes, Grandfather." In saying so, his path was set.

337

"I am pleased. You will be a great man amongst the People. They will look to you for guidance. Show them the way into the future so they might flourish. And there is one thing I would ask of you."

"Anything." A constriction was forming about his chest, making it difficult to control the tremors of emotion. But he stayed still and listened.

"New Waw. Take her to you in the old way and be blessed."

"I will."

The old man nodded, satisfied. "Now go. I would speak my peace to your mother."

Scott gulped hard. "You can't die. I'll take you to the Hills where the tears of the Great Spirit flow. The waters will heal you—"

"No, *takoja*. I trust your white father's medicine. My soul is at rest. Accept what you must. Now, I would see Wadutah."

Scott swayed to his feet, letting go of the thin hand with reluctance and regret. "I love you, Grandfather."

"And you have brought me great joy, Son of My Son."

While Scott sat in the main room allowing Ethan to tend his torn chest, Aurora slipped in to sit with her old nemesis.

"Come closer, Wadutah."

She came to perch on the edge of the bed, showing the old man an impassive face. As always, she failed to display *wistelkiciyapi*, the expected shy respect for one's father-in-law. Her gaze was bold, challenging even unto the end.

"You and I have not been friends, Wadutah. We are strong spirits, both sure of our own will. There has never been anything we have agreed upon except one. That your son have a good life. He has the strength of both our worlds, and on this night, he has chosen in which he would walk. I would ask you as a dying wish that you

338

abide by his choice."

"The Lakotas," she said quietly.

"Yes. He could do great things. He will need you like never before. You and *Wasichu Wakan* have been his guides. Do not forsake him now."

"I love my son. I would never do that."

The old man nodded. "I go to join Far Winds. Would you have me tell him anything?"

Aurora's chin canted upward. "Tell him I have raised a son of whom he can be proud."

"As I am proud."

Aurora reached out and took up the wizened hand. She smiled softly. "Go in peace, Yellow Bear. All will be well here."

"Sit with me for a time, Wadutah, so we might enjoy this moment of friendship a while longer."

An hour later, Aurora left the bedroom and went to embrace her stoic son. She felt his strength buckle for an instant as she whispered, "He's gone, Scott."

Chapter Twenty-one

Scott stepped away from his mother. His expression was filled with solemn purpose.

"I must prepare him and make the Wa-Jo-La to hold his spirit up to the heavens."

"I'll ready him for the journey," Aurora offered.

"It must be done with loving hands."

"It will be."

He looked at her, searching out the sincerity in her eyes. Then he nodded. "Thank you, Mama." Her knuckles grazed his cheek gently. When she returned to the bedroom, he stood at a loss. The need to mourn in the Lakota way rose up hot and choking, but he couldn't release the grief there in his parents' house. As he had when the news of the Wounded Knee Massacre reached him, he began to push the raw feelings down, smothering them with a denying, numbing emptiness. He looked blankly at his stepfather when a big hand closed upon his shoulder.

"He was a good man, Yellow Bear," Ethan stated fondly. Then he said with unerring empathy, "Go on outside, Scotty. Walk it off."

A look of understanding passed between the two who could have been father and son. Ethan's fingers pressed tight, then pushed, propelling Scott toward the door.

The night was cool. It made him aware of how beaten and baked his body was. Slowly, like a sleepwalker, he made his way to the winding stream. There, on its mossy bank, he gingerly shucked out of his clothes and waded out into the glassy water. The cold gave a reviving snap to his system. He sank down in it, letting the pores of his skin open to the moisture like arid ground. He plunged his head under the surface so it could shock a sense of clarity back to his fatigue-fogged brain. He drank from his hands, greedily, until his stomach cramped in protest. Then, he simply sat, slumped over, letting the waters soothe him, letting the evening's quiet melodies sing to him. He rocked himself slowly in time to that basic rhythm of nature, hugging his knees to relieve the banding pain in his ribs. He hurt clear through, inside and out. Anguish swelled, pinching his throat and nose, stinging his dry eyes. He clutched his knees tighter as the grief continued to build. It started as minute shivers in his belly and gradually, inexorably, grew to a feverish shaking.

A small sound escaped the hot compression of his vocal cords, the merest whimper of sorrow. That tiny expression gave way to a wild bursting of emotion. It was the way of his father's people to greet death with a magnificent display of mourning. He let it overtake him, let it roar through him, savaging him with noisy laments wailed to the silent heavens. He let it wring the howling sobs from his soul, hard, wracking spasms that tore through him like cleansing fire, burning his eyes, his nose, his throat, his lungs, until he could barely breathe. He beat the water with fists and scored the flesh of his arms with taloned fingers. He'd raised his hands to rip at the skin on his face, when his wrists were gently caught and restrained.

"No," a soft voice chastened.

He looked up through red, bewildered eyes to see

Gena kneeling beside him in the stream. She was fully dressed. Her skirt billowed up to ripple on the water's surface like a reflection of pale moonlight. Her gaze was steeped in tender sympathy. He sat panting and gulping, then finally allowed her to draw him to her shoulder where he was lost to a more conventional weeping.

She'd been afraid to approach him at first, stunned by the unchecked violence of his despair. Then, she'd been moved by his desolation, by the sight of him, shivering, naked, and vulnerable in the scant two feet of water. The abject misery in his face touched upon all the love in her sheltered soul and she couldn't wait to take him into her arms to give him solace.

It took a long while for his grieving to run its course. Slowly, the jerking sobs eased to a heartsick moan and he leaned, limp and drained, against her. Gena held him, unaware that sharing his soul-baring vulnerability had stripped away the last of her own reserve. Her palms moved freely across the wet planes of his back and shoulders. She smoothed back the slick black satin of his hair and pressed her lips to the faint bruise at his temple. Then to the spot where his firm jaw met his ear. Then down to drink from the damp hollow of his shoulderblade. By then, his breathing had quieted to a rapid whisper. His hands came up to cup her elbows, rubbing them, climbing higher, to shoulders, to throat, to cradle her face between them.

Then he was kissing her, deeply, soulfully, without hurry, without impatience. His mouth parted at the flickering dance of her tongue, then widened for her exploration. She gave beneath his gradual pressure and direction, gliding backward in the shallows, easing up partway onto the bank so only their legs trailed in the stream, going down with him upon the cool, grassy bank. He moved over the top of her, leisurely, suggestively, until her hands were busy helping his push up her wet skirts and down the damp cling of her drawers. She felt him pulse hotly between her thighs but was so caught up in the lingering seduction of his kiss, she never formed an objection. Her knees parted, her hips lifted, and just like that, he was fully, snugly, inside her.

She went very still, waiting, anticipating the pain. Nothing. Nothing but the calming brush of the water against her bared thighs and the warmth of him within.

"Scott . . ." she breathed in wonder.

"I love you, Gena," he whispered in reply.

He rocked in time to the lap and ebb of the current, in and out, in and out, slowly, sensuously stroking, stoking. Gena tried lying submissively beneath him, the way she thought she was supposed to, returning nothing beyond his languid kisses, but a sudden restlessness shivered along her limbs. A longing, a needing. But before she had a chance to experience where it might lead, she heard his breathing alter and felt an urgent stiffening race along his form.

"Scott," she cried out in alarm.

Anticipating her protest, he pulled away, kissing her, holding her tight as his body harmlessly spent its pleasure.

They lay entwined along the cool bank until Scott began to shiver in earnest with a chill of delayed shock and weariness. Finally, he crawled up into the grass and wriggled wet legs into his Levi Strausses. Gena came up, too, surprised to discover she was soaked clear through. Wordlessly, Scott laced his fingers through hers and led her back toward the house. When they entered the yard and could see the warm glow of the interior, he hung back, expression going stiff and tense.

"I don't want to go inside. Not just yet."

"All right," she said softly.

He looked about, then tugged gently in the direction of the barn. It was warm and welcoming inside the dark

343

cavern. He threw a blanket down upon a bed of fresh straw and lowered himself gingerly to stretch out on his back. Gena hesitated at the opening of the stall. But having come so far with him, how could she retreat now?

"Take off your wet things and lay them out to dry on the rail. It shouldn't take long."

Because she couldn't see him down amongst the shadows, Gena assumed herself concealed. She began unbuttoning her bodice, unaware that she was outlined quite clearly in a wash of moonlight. She stepped out of her gown and draped it carefully over the partition wall. Her underthings were unpleasantly cold and close. After a quick struggle with a proper conscience, she peeled them from her skin. Standing naked in the evening air, she began to tremble, with anxiety, with excitement. Until he called softly, "Gena, come down here with me. I'll keep you warm."

The blanket was coarse and scratchy. Bits of straw poked through it to prick her tender skin as she warily lay down upon it. Casually, Scott extended his arm, coaxing her to pillow her head near his shoulder. When she complied, his elbow bent, drawing her up until she was flush against him. Securing her there to share body heat and heartbeats. It was an incredibly personal comfort, one he gave easily, one she took cautiously. He hitched a blue denim-clad leg over hers and let his free hand tuck about the curve of her waist. Holding her. Just holding her.

Gradually, Gena was able to relax and let her reservations go. Her mother was wrong. She marveled over that with some amazement. He hadn't hurt her. He hadn't used her body cruelly. She felt no lingering sense of disgust at knowing he'd taken his pleasure upon her. His spirit had been wounded and she'd given it ease. No sacrifice, considering what he'd endured that day. What was so wrong in what she'd done? What was so terrible about supplying her betrothed with

344

the kind of comfort only a woman could?

She touched her palm to his slow moving chest, letting it settle there hesitantly, then contentedly. The first stirrings of purely female accomplishment warmed through her. Even in her awkward inexperience, she'd completed him. And now, cuddled snugly into his side, she felt a sense of happy relief. He murmured something into the tousled crown of her curls. When she tipped her head up to question him, she was struck by the heavy sadness in his features. Sadness, fatigue, pain. And yet, when he saw her tender gaze, he smiled.

"I'll never forget all that you've done for me today. I'll love you for it for the rest of my days. That will not change no matter what else might happen. I will never stop loving you."

Those were the words she'd longed for, yet the way he spoke them, with such gravity, with such intensity, gave her a chill of foreboding. For what he wasn't saying. Was it good-bye? No. No, not after confessing his love. But the more he said, the more that horrible feeling grew inside. She listened to him in a wordless panic, praying she was wrong and desperately afraid that she was not.

"The things I must do, you will not understand. You may even hate me for them. Some vows are not made to be kept. I've tried. God, I've tried. I can't change what I am, Gena, any more than you can change who you are."

She ducked her head beneath his chin so he might not see the gathering misery in her eyes. His hand moved gently through her hair.

"The last thing I ever meant to do was to disappoint you, Gena. Please believe that. I truly thought I could be happy with the plans we made and I thought I could make you happy. I'm sorry. I just can't."

"I know," she said softly, trying even in her own despair to lessen his. "Yellow Bear told me. And I'm not disappointed. Not in you." And she would try to make that true. Though her heart might break, she would try to forgive him.

Silence settled as deep and tender as the night. Huddled close in defiance of what the next day might bring, neither of them expected sleep to find them. But it did, seeping in to calm the restless yearnings for what could not be.

He jerked awake in the predawn darkness, unaware of what had startled him. Then he felt Gena stir and his tension eased. Somewhat. The press of her soft bosom into his ribs defied total relaxation. He closed his eyes and tried to seek out slumber, but his body and mind were already fully roused.

Yellow Bear was dead. That struck him anew with its devastation. There would be no filling the void of the old man's presence in his life. There was no one else who understood without words the workings of his heart and soul. The aloneness that knowledge held was terrible. It wasn't the same between him and Ethan. Empathy wasn't understanding. And Ethan wasn't Lakota. He never pretended to take Far Wind's place, nor could he fill Yellow Bear's, and Scott's love for him didn't lessen because of that inability. All he had to rely on was the wisdom the old chief had given him over the years. And the power of his vision. Which meant severing one half of his life completely.

The magnitude of his choice shook him. But there could be no compromise. Garth Kincaid would have to be dealt with. And if that meant hurting Rory and his mother, he would have to harden his heart to their pain. And his own. There could be no half measures, no favoritism that would weaken his stand. They would either understand or . . . Or he would lose his family.

A quiet sigh from beside him pulled his heart in another direction. Gena. What was he going to do about Gena?

How was he to have guessed that loving a woman could take such a toll? She was a consuming fever in his blood, burning out of control. He could face all the trials of torture the Great Mystery put before him without the slightest fear, but the thought of Gena Trowbridge's tears reduced him to a panicked quivering. His courage took a terrible tumble at the thought of her coming to harm. Of all the vows he'd taken, others might herald more importance but none rested so close to his heart as the one he'd made to protect her. And how could he, once he started down the path he was to take?

In some ways, she was so brave, so strong of heart. She believed so completely in what was right and fair. She suffered not the slightest qualm at thrusting herself in the path of wrongdoing, as she'd done for him at the Fourth of July celebration. As she'd done with Morning Song. And in that single-minded strength was her greatest vulnerability. She was naive enough to think by crying "Stop" or "Don't" all things bad would come to heel. He knew better. They would run right over her without compunction, crushing her in the process. This was not Boston, where one could shout support for an unpopular cause. Here, a loud voice could be quickly silenced. Even as the calendar turned toward a new century, the old ways clung with tenacious fervor. And savage consequence.

Gena would support him. That knowledge both thrilled and terrified him. If she took up his cause, she would be marked by the same bigotry he suffered. She would be shunned. Or worse. There would be no hefty fees to be made taking on the plight of the Sioux. He could provide her with none of the luxuries and with damn few necessities. There'd be no fine home, no stylish clothes, no influential friends. Just poverty and peril. And how, loving her as he did, could he bring her down to that? He'd be resigning her children to the same half-life he led. How could he, a man of pride, offer less than the best to the woman he loved? He'd promised her a life of comfort, of affluence, a husband who was a respected lawyer, son of a rich Dakota rancher. What a cruel trick to play upon her trust. The truth was far less glamorous. The half-breed son of an Indian and his captive white squaw. A man with scant means to protect or provide for her. A husband who would jerk her from plenty to poverty, alienating her from family and friends. What kind of man would do that? A selfish, uncaring one. He was not that man. He clung to Yellow Bear's wisdom. In loving was the strength to let go.

To let go.

He touched a strand of silken moonlight that strayed across his chest. So soft. So fine. He followed that pale tress up to the gentle curve of her cheek and let his fingertips linger there to learn each sweet contour all over again. So smooth and warm. As the pad of his thumb traced her mouth, she stirred contentedly. Her lips parted and the enticement was too great to ignore. His were drawn to them, damning resolve, oversetting reason, for that brief promise of heaven. Hers gave a slow, sleepy response, and in an instant, he was lost.

There was something unbearably sensual about having her wake beneath his kiss, beneath his touch. Her movements were languid, liquid, lethal to his convictions. Let her go? God, how could he? She shifted like a supple cat as his palm stroked down her back. Her spine arched, pressing her breasts into him, rubbing her hips against the taut crotch of his Levi's as her thigh rode between his.

"Ummm, Scott." It was a languorous purr. Her hands began to move, roving over his back, urging in needy little circles all the way down to his hip pockets, kneading the hard muscles through heavy denim. Her face nuzzled his neck, blowing warm breaths there, then up to his ear to insight excited shivers. Unable to withstand any further provocation, he turned his head, seizing her lips in a wide, tongue-tangling kiss.

A wonderful dream, Gena mused groggily. Deliciously free, decidedly wicked and indecently passionate. Everything from the rough restlessness of Scott Prescott's hands to the hot, salty taste of skin was exquisitely prurient. Wouldn't Margaret Trowbridge just die. Gena smiled into Scott's kiss and fenced lazily with his tongue. Improper, it might be. Immoral, it probably was. But oh, so indescribably perfect. There was just enough drugging lethargy to numb her thoughts to all but immediate pleasure. And such pleasure it was. Dazing, dreamy enjoyment of each caress, each kiss. A state in which reality could not intrude. She let herself be lifted and teased by sensation. She allowed it to race hot and heavy in her veins. So that when he moaned into one of his desire-drenched kisses, "Gena, I need you . . . I want you . . . let me love you," all she could answer was, "Yes, oh yes, please."

In a second, he'd rucked out of his jeans and met her torso to toe with warm, willing flesh. She welcomed him with a wondering little gasp, and when he began to move, she just couldn't pretend indifference. He was streaking her nerves with fire. He was drowning her in a flood of feeling. She didn't want to wait. She wanted to pursue the same intense pleasure, to join him in the same wild ride. Her first attempts were awkward, then, sensing her need, Scott caught her hips and showed her the motion, taught her the tempo until they paced perfectly, matching thrust for thrust, beat for beat, breath for breath. And when his began to accelerate, hers followed. Building the same taut, sweet spirals to an explosive promise.

And at the last moment, when he tried to pull away, Gena clutched his hips, refusing to let him go. Not when she was on the shuddering brink of an unknown. Hearing her cry out his name, he committed himself with that final plunge, to carrying her with him. Into ecstasy.

Filled with him, body and soul, Gena lay still and marvelously sated. When he shifted above her, she tightened her arms and legs into passion's bonds, holding to him a while longer. Enjoying his heat and heaviness. Enjoying the happiness in her heart.

Finally, she allowed him to leave her, but only as far as rolling off to her side. There, she was pampered by his engulfing embrace and satisfied to settle wearily in his arms.

"Oh, Scott, I love you so," she murmured sleepily. "My mother was very mistaken."

Before he could ask her to explain that odd remark, she was fast asleep.

It seemed like minutes but must have been hours. Scott leaned over her, touching his mouth lightly atop hers. Without opening her eyes, she flung up an arm to catch him about the neck and was confused by the feel of his shirt collar.

"I have to go, Gena," he told her quietly.

He was dressed, smelling of clean shaving soap, and he was leaving.

She was about to protest when he indulged her in the luxury of a long, breath-stealing kiss.

"Thank you for last night. I will love you forever."

Gena drifted on that sultry sentiment, in no immediate hurry to move once he'd gone. Loving Scott Prescott forever was indeed a pleasant prospect worth a daydream or two. The persistent tickle of a piece of straw against the back of her leg finally made her aware of her situation; she was stretched out naked in the Prescott barn. Her eyes snapped open to discover the first pastel of dawn shimmering silver on the motes floating overhead. Gracious, it was daylight! She sat up, clutching the blanket.

When certain she was alone, she scrambled up and squirmed into her clothes of the night before. To her dismay, she found her shoes and stockings gone. She must have left them at the creek when she and Scott . . .

Crimsoning all over, she trotted barefoot to the house, praying no one would be about in the early hour. The moment she slipped in the door, she knew it to be a futile wish.

"Gena?" Aurora called out. "Is that you?"

Swallowing her shame, she crept into the big kitchen where Aurora was washing the last of the breakfast dishes. Astute amber eyes touched on muddied hem, indelible wrinkles, and bits of straw. Aurora raised a curious brow but made no comment about it.

"There are some leftovers on the range and coffee. Help yourself."

Blushing fiercely, Gena forced herself to ask, "Has Scott eaten yet?"

Aurora turned back to the sink. "A little while ago. But not as much as I would have liked him to. He and Ethan went to bury Yellow Bear this morning. He wanted to do it alone, but he didn't have the strength to lift him atop the Wa-Jo-La."

"The what?"

Aurora's apron fluttered up to dab at her eyes. "The Sioux bury their dead above the ground. They place them on platforms six feet in the air and, for two weeks, return each sunrise and sunset to chant prayers to the Creator. After that, the body is laid to rest in a vault of stone with its feet pointing west. Scott sees it as his duty to help his grandfather into the Netherworld. He loved that arrogant old man."

"So did I," Gena added softly.

Aurora looked to her abruptly. "I'm glad Scott had you to turn to last night. He's never let anyone close to him before. No one should feel as alone as he's allowed himself to be. Don't let him grieve too long."

"I won't," she promised, averting her eyes. Did his mother know exactly what she'd done to ease his pain? If so, it would seem she approved.

"Oh, Gena, a message came for you yesterday. From your parents, I think. It's on the table in the other room."

Something cold and terrible clutched about Gena's heart, as if they had reached all the way from Boston to snatch the joy from her life. Woodenly, she walked into the main room. There, she saw it. A plain envelope with the power to destroy her future. She lifted it, weighed it in her hand. The writing on the outside was her father's. Her hopes plummeted. Her mother attended to all the cordial correspondence. Her father handled the unpleasant business aspects.

She turned the missive in her palm then hurriedly broke the seal. Something fell out onto the tabletop. She looked at it for a long, devastated moment. A train ticket to Boston. For one, one way.

Hands shaking, she unfolded the curt note. No flowery preamble. How like her father to get right to the point.

Will be awaiting you at the station. Expect you to have sensibly ended things with Prescott before arrival. Can no longer in good conscience accept the match for reasons you undoubtedly already know and have, unwisely, decided to keep from us. Will discuss when you get home. Your devoted parents.

Who told them? Horace? Caroline? A well-meaning Beth? It didn't matter. They knew. They knew about Scott and they would never permit them to marry.

The letter crumpled in the convulsive tightening of her hands.

What was she going to do?

Her mood of panic was broken by a frantic pounding at the door. She was surprised to see Morning Song on the porch. As she approached, the Lakota woman cried out, "I must see Lone Wolf."

"He's not here. He's gone to bury his grandfather. What's wrong?"

"Men from the BIA agent have come to force us from our land. They have guns. I am afraid for my father."

"Where is your brother?"

"He did not come home last night. I do not know where he is. I do not know what to do. I had hoped Lone Wolf would come, that he would stop them."

"I'll come with you. I'll stop them."

Morning Song stared at her with such trust, with such admiring awe, that she couldn't very well go back on her word. Scott would be gone for hours. By that time, White Cloud's family would be homeless, his children without a roof above their heads. If she could just slow down the process until Scott arrived.

"Aurora, I'm going to visit White Cloud," she called into the kitchen. "Have Scott meet me there as soon as he can." She spoke the words without a tremor and strode to the fireplace. Above it, placed in honorary brackets was an old Henry repeater and a heavy Sharps. She took them both down and checked them as she'd seen Ethan do. Both were loaded. With a rifle under each arm, she followed Morning Song outside. "Do you know how to harness a buggy?"

The Indian woman looked at her blankly.

"No, of course you don't. I suppose we'll have to ride."

Gena had never been on the back of a horse. Morning Song made it look easy. She shoved the bridle bit into a horse's mouth and quickly buckled the pieces together. Gena did the same, wary of the animal's huge yellowed teeth. Then the Lakota gripped a handful of mane and vaulted up onto its back. After much consideration, Gena led her mount to the corral rail and climbed on via its rungs. With her dress wadded up between her legs, juggling the rifles and trying to stifle her terror, she nudged the creature into a jarring trot. By the time they'd crested the first hill, Gena decided it would be a miracle if they arrived without her shooting the horse, herself, or them both. And so it was. Never had she felt such relief as in approaching the humble farm. Nor such anger.

A group of riders were milling in the yard. Their horses purposefully trampled over the spindly stalks of corn. Their lariats dropped over fence posts and jerked them to the ground. She didn't see White Cloud or his family and presumed they were hiding inside the inadequate shelter of the house. Several of the riders held torches, and it was only a matter of time before they would put the walls to flame.

"Damn them," she muttered fiercely. Bracing a wooden stock upon either hip, she brought both weapons to full cock. Gripping her legs about the animal's barrel chest, Gena kicked it forward, racing down in defense of the helpless, clinging for dear life.

Chapter Twenty-two

"Hey, Scotty! Danged if you don't look like you was dragged every which a-way through a stampede of longhorns."

"The old man inside?" he asked as his brother fell in step beside him in the yard.

Rory gave him a sharp look, sensing trouble. He could feel it, the way he did when a storm was building on the other side of the Hills and a restless tension got the herd to milling. "He's in the study going over the payroll. What's on your mind?"

"Plenty. Make yourself scarce for a while."

Studying the angles of his brother's face, Rory murmured, "Thank you just the same, I think I'll stick around." He held the door open to the house and waited for Scott to stalk through. Yep, helluva storm coming in. The snap of it fairly crackled in the air. "Ruth, could you bring us some coffee into the major's office, please, and see we ain't bothered."

Scott paused outside the double doors. Tension worked at his features. "Rory, I don't want you in the middle of this."

"Can't help where I'm standing, big brother," was his offhand reply. He knocked twice and swung open the heavy doors. "Major, Scotty's here to make some talk with you."

Garth Kincaid looked up impassively from his paper-strewn desk. He took in the ragged appearance of his grandson, from the yellowish reminders of the beating he'd taken to the subtle hitch in his gait. His expression didn't change. "Have some word on those lobbyist proposals, do you, boy?"

"Not yet. I expect to by the end of the week." Scott drew up beside one of the big chairs facing the Bar K patriarch and waited for the invitation to sit. Though he nearly shook with weakness and fatigue, he stood stiff and tall. And his grandfather kept him standing.

"Good. That's good. You've done a fine job for me, Scott. I knew we could work well together."

You son of a bitch. Scott smiled grimly.

Ruth came in with the coffee service. She gave Scott a startled look, but, aware of the fierce undercurrents in the room, said nothing before withdrawing.

Kincaid took his time in pouring from the silver pot. "A shame you're going back east. The three of us could have made quite a team; you, me, and your brother. With all the things the Bar K's involved in, we could have kept you busy."

"Oh, I agree there, and there's a good chance you will. I've decided to stay on and start up a practice here."

When he reached out for his coffee cup, it rattled noisily in his unsteady hand.

"For God's sake, Scotty. Sit down before you fall down," Rory insisted. He gave his brother a push in that direction, not liking the plays of power between him and their grandfather. Restlessly, he paced the width of the room, trying to find a neutral stance. And failing. Finally, he gave up and went to stare gloomily out the window, bracing for the blow.

"Why, that's grand news, isn't it, Rory?"

"Yessir," he mumbled without turning.

Kincaid bestowed a charitable smile upon the man sitting opposite. "You can count on me to help you get things going for you. Once I put out the word, I can guarantee you'll be representing the interests of most of the folks around here."

"Yes," Scott agreed softly. "Yes, I will. I've already got my first case and I know it'll lead to lots more. I'm representing George White Cloud against the greedy, corrupt, land-grabbers who think they can twist the system to suit themselves."

From the window, Rory uttered a soft expletive.

Kincaid's smile dropped by degrees into a thin, hard line. "I don't know if I'd consider that a wise first career move, boy. You go sticking up for the Indians and no decent white man's going to trust you to do his dealings."

"I mean to do more than stick up for them. I aim to be their voice at the Court of Indian Offenses."

Kincaid took in that information without a flicker of betraying emotion. "Son, let me wake you up to a little truth. Sal Garrick pretty much owns the judges. You don't stand a snowball's chance in hell in going up against them."

"That's why I mean to take Garrick down first. Cut off the head of the snake, there's not much of a bite."

"I admire you for your ambitions, Scott, but you're on a fool's errand."

"I've been on them before," Scott said quietly. "I think I can recognize the difference now."

The major smiled. It was a deceptive gesture, one hinting at goodwill, one that meant quite the opposite. He tented his fingers atop his desk and tapped them together. "So, you're going to take on Garrick. You got yourself some kind of plan, do you?"

"Scotty," Rory warned softly.

Kincaid turned on his young foreman with a deadly

357

hiss. "You stay out of this, hear. Lessen you want to pull up stakes and stand behind him. That what you want?"

"Nossir." The redhead dipped down as he began to study his boots.

"Well?" the old man snapped at his other grandson. "Just how are you planning to take the bull by the horns?"

"I'm not. I'm going right for the throat. Garrick's been terrorizing folks to get their land leases and he's been pocketing the profits on both sides. That's a mite illegal."

"You got proof?"

"Enough. And I'll get more. Garrick's just the start. When he falls, he'll take down the rest with him; all those who thought they could profit off a bad system and an unscrupulous man."

"You'll be stepping on some mighty powerful toes."

"And I mean to step hard," he promised coldly.

"No matter who it hurts?"

"The law's the law. Those who break them deserve to pay for it."

Kincaid's gaze narrowed. "When I came out here, I was the law. When I spoke, the ground trembled and things happened. I can still make things happen. I don't think you quite got an understanding on that."

Scott came up out of his chair to plant his palms wide on the big desk. He leaned across it to drawl menacingly, "Oh, I think I understand. You might say I had the light beat into me very thoroughly. If you don't give a damn about whose blood you spill, why should I? I'm not going to stand aside and let men like you stomp the life out of anyone who gets in your way."

"You ungrateful little whelp!" Garth Kincaid rose up in a towering fury and came down, nose to nose and hackled like a hound. "I let your mother bring you into my house, the mewling little bastard brat of the savage who raped her. I could have drowned you right then and nobody would have faulted me for it. But your mother and that fool, Prescott, thought you were worth saving and they almost had me believing it. I took you from a half-breed snot and gave you the best a man could ever hope for. My money and my influence bought you into the best school in our country because I thought you could make a man of yourself there. And what do you do? You come back here and spit in my face. And you do it with the very education I gave you. I was willing to treat you like my own. I would have seen you to the very top. And you, you arrogant, ignorant fool, you throw it all away for the sake of some dirty blanket Indians who are going to hate you for the misery you're going to bring down on them."

A blunt finger jabbed Scott between the eyes.

"You got one chance, boy. You tuck your tail and hie on back to Boston. But you try and tangle with things here and you'll end up a lot worse than on your belly in some barn with the stuffing kicked out of you. You'll be going home to your mother stretched out over a saddle. You think and you think hard before you stir up any trouble with the Sioux. Who's going to protect them after your family's through crying over you?"

"And I suppose you'll be shedding tears right beside them."

The slap delivered to the side of his face packed enough force to send Scott sprawling along the desktop. Rory was instantly at his back, gripping his elbows, assisting him up.

"Dang it, Scotty. Let it go," he mourned in an anguish of twisting loyalties.

Scott shook him off to square up once more against the powerful rancher. "You black-hearted bastard. Don't pretend you ever gave a damn about me. I know why you paid for my schooling. It was to get me as far away as possible, so you wouldn't have to claim me as a Kincaid. To think I actually admired you, that I would have done near to anything to please you. But you didn't want to be proud of me. You wanted to use me for your best interest. Well, sir, I'm not going to back off, because, as my daddy would say, I'm a Kincaid. And I'm a Lakota. And I'll be damned if I'm going to apologize for either. You do your worst, but you'd better be ready to paint for war."

"Get out of my house! You're going to regret —"

"No, you are. I'm going to make you pay for every scrap of misery you caused my father's people."

"Rory, get him out of here!"

"Come on, Scotty."

Scott threw off his hand to splay his fingers on the desk. "I'm going to take you down. I'm going to pry into your books. I'm going to track down every pound of beef you supposedly sold to the government for annuities the Lakotas never saw. I'm going to investigate every inch of grass your cattle graze on and God help you if you didn't get it fair and square. If my mama's going to cry, it's going to be over you when you come begging to her door for your next meal!"

"Get him out!"

Rory's arms banded his heaving chest, but he dug in his heels for one last promise. "You better sleep with one eye open, because you won't hear me coming."

Rory gave a quick jerk to knock him off balance, then towed him to the door. Once in the hall, Scott struggled free with a growl of, "Get your hands off me. I don't need one of the major's trained dogs to show me to the door."

Rory's hands dropped heavily. "There it is, Scotty. You help yourself."

"I will," he snarled, and strode fiercely out onto the porch. Feeling the strength collapsing in his knees, he grabbed for one of the porch supports and clung there for a long minute, shaking with weakness and fury. He cursed the numbness in his legs and the dampness on his face, denying both angrily, when he heard the door opening.

"That weren't exactly the smartest thing I've ever seen done." The door shut behind Rory. His boot heels clunked across the boards, growing silent at his brother's side.

"And you know smart when you see it, do you?" He pushed away from the post and scrubbed his eyes on his sleeve.

"I know stupid, and riling the major like that ain't got no other word to describe it. You put a scare into him, Scotty, and that's gonna make him mighty mean."

Scott rubbed the side of his face ruefully. He could still feel the imprint of his grandfather's temper upon it. "Oh yeah, got him shaking in his boots. He will be. When I'm finished, he will be. Rory, you go over the books with him, don't you?"

"Sure," he admitted cautiously.

"Then you could get me the proof I need. Payoffs to Garrick, false stock counts—"

"The hell I will!"

Scott looked up at him in surprise to find Rory scowling. "Are you telling me no?" He was incredulous. Of all the people he knew, he trusted Rory more implicitly than the rest of them put together. If he needed to count on someone, that person was his brother. The last place he'd expected to run up against interference was with the exuberant redhead. But Rory's boot heels were planted as firm as brick wall.

"That's exactly what I'm telling you."

"I don't believe this! You don't care what he's doing? That he's stealing from defenseless people, snatching their homes, taking their food, as good as killing them just so he can feed a few more cows."

"And I'm right sorry about that. But they're not my people. They don't mean nothing to me. The time of the

361

Sioux is past, Scott. Now, I didn't have nothing to do with that being the way things are. They just is."

"And that's that. That's good enough for you?"

"Yeah, it is."

"You dumb cowboy." He started angrily off the porch only to have the front of his shirt caught up in a grip that turned him and lifted him onto his toes in one powerful move.

"I ain't dumb and I ain't blind. You open your eyes, Scott. What you're doing is gonna tear things apart."

"Starting with your nice cozy job. That what you're afraid of? Let me go."

Rory let him go, with enough force in the motion to send him careening backward off the porch and into the dirt. Scott lay there, sucking air painfully and trying to move and not being particularly successful in either as his brother stomped down the steps to stand over him.

"Don't you go sneering at me, Mr. Fancy-Pants College Man. You're the smart one, the one things come quick and easy for, the one who goes off to some fine and high-faluting school where's you wear pressed suits and pointy shoes and trot around with pretty little gals on your arm. The one who can be somebody. The one I've always been so proud of I could right up and bust my buttons. That don't give you the right to come sashaying back here to thumb your nose at everything that means something to me. I ain't smart. I don't got no big college edge-u-cation. But I'm doing what I want to do and I'm damn good at it. I work my ass day and night to get the respect of the men who work for me. Everything you can see in any direction you look is gonna be mine some day and I earned it. Now, you expect me to just let you go and cut the legs out from under every dream I've ever had. Well, forgive me for breathing but I ain't that stupid!"

He kicked at Scott's feet and walked in a tight, agitated circle. Finally, he pulled up and wagged a furious finger.

"Do you know what the trouble is?"

Hugging his side and struggling to sit up, Scott groaned, "I'm sure you're going to tell me."

"You're just like him. Yes, you are. The two a you; narrow-sighted, selfish-minded, and all-fired certain that God gave you the right to decide how things should be for everybody else. You don't give a hang about folks any more than he does. You just charge on in and plow under everything that don't get out of the way. You jus' can't stand not having it all your way. The major, he looks at them Injuns and sees 'em taking up valuable grazing land. You look at the ranchers and see folks who snub their noses at you and you want to make 'em pay for it. He won't give up the old ways and you won't make use of the new. Danged if I gots any patience left for either of you." He stuck down his hand. "Go on, git on your horse and git outta here before I decides to whack the bejesus outta you."

Scott clasped his hand and let himself be hauled up. "Rory, I—"

His brother shook off his hand and glowered. "Go on and git. I ain't got time to waste on you. I gots work to do." He wheeled away and stomped across the yard toward the bunkhouse, leaving Scott to look after him, stunned and speechless.

By the time he reached the Lone Star, Scott had no ambitions beyond crawling into his bed to shut out the rest of the world. At least until an hour before sunset, when he would have to go pray for the spirit of Yellow Bear. Several long hours of sweet oblivion were just what he needed to flush the pain of the old chief's death and the betraying sting of his grandfather's and brother's words. As he rolled down out of the saddle, he was vaguely aware of his mother on the porch.

"Scott?"

363

He groaned, recognizing the tone. "Mama, can it wait?" he mumbled as he shuffled toward the house. "I feel like the bottom of an old pair a boots, all scuffed and full of holes."

"Scott, there was some trouble out at White Cloud's. Gena rode out there. I don't have all the details, but from what I've heard, Garrick's got her in jail."

"What?" He was already turning, heading back for his horse.

"Scott?" Aurora came after him. "This came for her."

He looked blankly at the ticket to Boston his mother pressed into his hand. And everything collapsed in on him.

"I'll take care of it, Mama. I'll take care of all of it."

Gena came up off the flour barrel she'd been sitting on and rushed to the door of the storage room. Scott! Now they'd be sorry! Now they'd pay for locking her up in a damp, smelly old room where unspeakable things scurried in the corner shadows, for treating her like a common criminal.

She launched herself upon him the moment the door was opened. He stumbled back a few steps. In her enthusiasm, she didn't notice how stiffly he held himself or that he made no move to return the embrace.

"Are you all right?"

"Oh, Scott, it was awful. They were trampling down the corn and they had torches—"

"Are you hurt?"

The curtness of his tone finally penetrated. She uncurled her arms from about his neck and eased back in uncertainty. His features were stony.

"Did they hurt you?" he repeated.

"Not physically, no. But they put me in this dirty little room and—"

"Come on."

She stood, openmouthed, in the middle of her grievances. Then blinked. He was angry. At her. No, that was too mild. He was enraged. He didn't want to hear about her travails. He didn't want to offer sympathy and enact proper vengeance. He caught her wrist and began dragging her toward the door as if fighting against the urge to soundly beat her. When she caught sight of the thin, hawk-faced man who had shoved her into the storeroom like a naughty child, she applied her heels rebelliously.

"Scott, that man, he—"

"Shut up, Gena."

She was so stunned she offered no further resistance, even as Sal Garrick sidled up with an ingratiating smile.

"I shore am sorry 'bout the inconvenience to you, Mr. Prescott. And to the lady. I didn't rightly know what else to do with her. Didn't want to get the law involved, knowing she was your woman and all. And what with her a-carrying on and shooting things up, I couldn't very well—"

"I understand," Scott gritted out. "I understand completely. I'll make sure it doesn't happen again."

Garrick tipped his battered hat, displaying a shiny pate. "It was nice to meet you, Miss Trowbridge."

If Gena hadn't been so totally flabbergasted, she would have laughed hysterically. Because a lady didn't spit.

"Oh, and here's the lady's armaments."

Scott stared at his father's rifles for a moment, then snatched them up furiously. He continued toward the door in short proddy strides, jerking Gena along behind him the way he would a disobedient pup on a lead. She cringed beneath the bright slap of sunlight that struck her the moment they stepped outside. So, at first, she didn't see the crowd gathered silently about the porch of the reservation agent's office.

"Scott, let go. This is really not necessary. Scott, you're hurting me."

That brought him up beside her. His grip on her wrist eased, but not so the intensity of his expression. His words ground out in a low, threatening rumble.

"If not for your admiring audience, I would take you over my knees and switch the hide off you."

She wasn't sure which startled her more, the group of curious Indian faces or the dark vehemence in Scott's.

"Do you know what they're calling you? The *witkowin*, the 'crazy woman,' and I can't say I disagree with them. Now, you walk with me like a right proper lady over there to the horses, and on the way home, you best be praying that when we get there, I'm not too tired to forget that I'm half-white and too civilized to beat a woman."

For a moment, Gena quelled beneath his intimidation. Then a starchy anger served as a stiffener. "I would like to know why you are behaving like this. As if I were the one at fault. All I did—"

"Was go charging in to something you know nothing about like a goddamn Annie Oakley." He glanced about at the amused onlookers and snapped, "We're not going to discuss this here."

"Well, I'm not taking another step until we do. Someone had to do something," she cried in her own defense.

"Someone was," he drawled back icily. "I was. But you destroyed all that this afternoon."

Gena hesitated. She'd done something terrible. She could feel it in the waves of frustrated fury emanating from him. Her defiance slipped a trepidant notch. "I thought you'd be proud of me."

He drew a quick, shaky breath. His hands balled at his sides. "What I am is mad enough to wring your neck. You have no idea what you've done. I should have let Garrick keep you. At least you would have been safe from me."

Tears of fright and fury stung her eyes. "Then why didn't you?"

He moved so fast, she hadn't the time to gasp. His big hands clamped behind her head to propel her forward, nearly lifting her off her feet. His kiss was punishing, possessing, driven by panic. By the awful image of her struggling in Spencer's grip, of her sprawled seemingly lifeless at the side of the road. Proud? God, yes, he was proud, but he was also petrified by her heedless bravado. If they'd fired back . . . If they'd decided not to bring her back to Garrick as a tool of leverage . . . His tongue stabbed deep into her mouth to thrust those horrible visions from his head.

Released abruptly, Gena staggered. Her senses were dazed by his potent answer. She braced her wobbling knees as he strode away from her, and as soon as she could, she hurried after him. The Indians clustered in front of Garrick's office, chuckled amongst themselves, and quietly dispersed.

Scott had already swung up onto his horse and sat waiting impatiently. Tethered at the bar next to his was the unsaddled animal that had caused such irrevocable bruising to Gena's backside. She eyed it with disfavor, unconsciously rubbing her sore flanks.

"I am not getting back on that ungainly stack of bones," she declared.

Scott reached down to untie the reins, and looped them over his saddle horn. He stared down at her, rankled by the haughty tip of her chin, by the petulant pucker of lips still moist from his, by the expectant way she assessed the spot behind him, anticipating the offer. She was wearing the same gown he remembered from the day before. What a vision she'd appeared to his sun-swollen eyes. He recalled the needy desperation in the way he'd pushed up her skirt in the soft creek bed and the way she'd slowly removed it in the barn. If a soiled hank of material could stir him so effectively, he hated to imagine what the coil of her arms about his middle would do on the long ride back to the ranch.

"A good Lakota squaw can put in a day's walk behind her man," he mentioned provokingly.

Gena's brows soared. "Well, I'm not walking in anyone's dust."

He sat his saddle, watching her stalk away in an agitated twitch of skirts. He almost smiled. Then, he nudged his horse and held it at a lazy pace just behind her heels. She didn't look back at him, but her stiff carriage said volumes as they made their way in an odd procession through the Lakota camp. She wasn't wearing footgear appropriate to the rocky soil, nor was the twenty-pound pull of petticoats and fabric making her obstinate trek any easier. By the time she hobbled out onto the road leading to the Lone Star, his surly humor was appeased. He drew up alongside her and said her name softly.

Gena looked up at his proffered hand and her lips set mulishly. His expression was galling; aggravated, assertive, awaiting her submission.

Well, he could wait.

She continued down the road afoot, pride carrying her onward when she feared her legs were no longer capable of the task. Scott kept his horse at an easy lope, patiently waiting for her to admit defeat. She wouldn't have. She didn't until a misstep snapped the heel off her dainty leather half-boots. Even then, she maintained a stubborn limping until finally he turned the horse sharply to block her path.

"Give me your hand," he growled unpleasantly.

To argue would have been pointless. She was too weary to take another step. And the look in his eyes said clearly that if she refused, he meant to drag her up anyway. With as much dignity as she could muster, she lifted her hand and fit her foot into the stirrup he freed for her. After a bit of awkward maneuvering of bulky material and aggrieved limbs, she settled astride behind him. There was no way to tug her skirt down to decently cover her legs. They swung bare of all but stockings from above the knee to ankle, hugging to the outside of his when he nudged the horse into an easy canter. The motion forced her to hold to him about the waist, though she vowed to take no enjoyment from it. Not when he sat rigid and incommunicative. Terrorizing her with his silence.

What had she done?

The rolling movement of the horse brought them in constant brushing contact. A rhythmic bumping so suggestive of the way their bodies had touched while making love. Better she hold tight to him than be tortured by the insinuating friction. She was drained in body and spirit. It was easy to seek rest against the unyielding wall of his back and pretend he was the same caring lover he'd been the night before. He wasn't unaffected either. When he steered the horse off the road to go cross-country, he gripped just behind her knee to hold her on as the animal surged up a steep embankment. And his hand remained, rubbing seditiously to test the tone of her thigh, hiking her skirt until it was pushed nearly to her hip. Then, as if angry with what he'd found himself doing and thinking, he jerked down the material and returned both hands to the reins.

The afternoon was all but gone when they rode up to the Prescott porch. Without dismounting himself, Scott reached around to ease Gena to the ground. As he straightened, his features took on a glaze of impossible distance. Gena looked between the two brothers, sensing the trouble there like a palpable pain. Offering not so much as a nod of greeting, Scott urged the horse toward the barn where he met Ethan coming out.

"Your mama's got supper ready. Don't worry about putting him away dry. I'll tend it after we eat."

"Jus' as soon do it now, myself."

"Scott—"

"I said I'll take care of it."

Rory frowned in their direction, then gave Gena his dazzling grin. "Howdy, Sis. How you feeling?"

"Better."

"Good, 'cause you look like somebody mucked out a stable with you." But that didn't stop him from coming close enough to buss her cheek with a quick kiss. His gaze went back to the barn. Gena had never seen him look so unhappy. "How's he doing?"

"I wouldn't prod him with a stick if I was in striking distance."

"One thing about ole Scotty, he do tend to get a poisonous bite on him when he gets riled. Best tell Mama to get the first aid ready."

Chapter Twenty-three

Gena took extraordinary care with her appearance for dinner. She was fresh and crisp from the skin outward. Her gown was of mignonette green cashmere trimmed in black ruching of mousseline. Its skirt was carefully fitted and the bodice bloused gracefully at the waist. Tight sleeves rose to a fullness beneath double caps, and a high neck cradled her chin. Not at all like Annie Oakley or a stable swabber. She'd worn it the first night Scott had come to call on her in Boston. They'd gone with Beth and Merle to hear a lecture. She couldn't remember what the topic had been, but she could recall clearly every unsettling little shiver she'd felt in his company. It seemed like an eternity ago, a moment snipped from the lifetime of two strangers. Would he remember?

Obviously not, since he scarcely lifted his eyes from his plate. And when he did, his covert glances were made toward his brother, who sat just as grimly silent across the table. Aurora and Ethan weren't quite sure what to make of the dissension between their sons and they were offering no hints. Just close-clipped replies to direct questions they couldn't avoid. Conversation was approached as carefully as a baited trap.

"How are your parents, Gena?"

Gena jumped in her seat and sat with her insides quivering like a tuning fork. "They're fine," she murmured in response to Aurora's question. And hundreds of miles away, they suddenly seemed to be in the same room with her.

"They must miss you terribly. I know we did Scott when he was away. Is that why they sent you the return ticket early?"

Gena swallowed. What could she tell Scott's mother? That her pristine parents had insisted she break her engagement with their son because he was unsuitable? Never, ever could she hurt them with that truth.

"I suppose they felt I had imposed upon your hospitality long enough."

"Oh, nonsense. We've enjoyed having you here. Besides, it can get quite lonely with just these surly men for company. It's been nice having another woman to talk to."

"And to share the work with," Ethan interjected laconically.

"Ethan, really. You make it sound as though I've been using her as a slave. If you would bring plumbing into the house, we could have both been sitting around like ladies of leisure."

"Maybe this fall."

"It's been this fall for the last five years."

"Then it'll be electricity and a telephone. Woman, you just can't be satisfied." He thought about that for a second, then indulged in a smug smile. "Well, at least in some areas."

Gena had to lift her hand to her mouth to catch her smile. She'd almost laughed. And surprisingly, it was not an embarrassed gesture. It felt good, the earthy sparring between man and wife. Natural. Wholesome.

Her mother would have succumbed to a swoon had her father ever expressed himself so candidly. Almost at once, her expression began to stiffen. No, there was no spontaneity in the Trowbridge household. To speak of such subjects aloud was as forbidden as laughing uproariously in church. The atmosphere in her home was as different from the Prescotts' as winter from warm summer. It was no wonder she'd never had the chance to grow.

And what did it matter if she returned in one week or five weeks? She was going back. Because Scott had never once suggested that she stay.

Would she? Would she consent to a life so far removed from everything she knew and understood? She canted a glance to the man beside her.

Yes. Oh, yes.

Because everything she loved was here.

"And are you going to Boston with Gena, Scott?" Aurora approached that delicately, trying and failing to sound neutral.

"He's staying on, Mama," Rory put in flatly. "Didn't he tell you his plans?"

Scott's jaw tightened with annoyance, but he didn't oblige his brother with a look.

"Scott?"

"I'm going to be working through the CFR at the Cheyenne."

Noticing Gena's start of surprise, his mother prompted, "For the rest of the summer, you mean."

"No, that's what I'm going to do with my fine Kincaid bought-and-paid-for edge-u-cation. It's a danged sight more responsible than finding legal loopholes for a bunch of thieves."

Gena paled.

Rory stiffened.

Ethan leaned back in his chair, remarking silently on the sudden surge of tension, before drawling quietly, "That's a mighty respectable calling. Won't put much in the way of a roof over your head, though."

"I won't need much. I know how to live light and lean. I can take care of myself."

Alone.

He didn't say it. Gena didn't need to hear it. She knew. A terrible lightness swirled giddily in her head. It was what he'd been working up to. Subtly. Surely. Easing her out of his life. How long had he known he wasn't going to take the job with her father? How long had he been making plans for a solitary move into a Cheyenne River tipi? When he'd made love to her the first time? Last night when he'd spilled himself inside her?

She could be pregnant.

How could she go home not knowing? How could she face her parents? The thought of admitting to her mother that she was broken and breeding was enough to cause the evening's meal to roil in her belly.

What had she been thinking of to lie with him without the security of his name? How could she have so blithely discarded all her mother's wisdom and warnings? If she had listened, she wouldn't be facing possible disgrace.

If she had listened, she would have never known the splendor of loving Scott Prescott.

She wanted to look at him again but she didn't quite dare. Her emotions were too fragile, too close to collapse. He said he loved her. And she had thought that would solve everything. Because she loved him, too, and wanted to believe it.

"Does that old Henry of mine still pull to the right?"

Realizing that Ethan was speaking to her, Gena

374

gazed up at him rather blankly. "What?"

"I haven't had those old rifles down for a lot of years. Did you hit anything with them?"

Gena blushed uncomfortably. "A fence post and a tree, I think. Neither was fatal."

"What's this?" Rory spoke up curiously.

Aurora answered with relish. "Our little Gena led a one-woman campaign on a group of marauders threatening an Indian family."

"With Daddy's guns?" He stared at her, trying to picture the lovely socialite before him in the commission of such an act.

"And bareback," his mother added. "The first time she'd ever sat a horse."

"Hot damn! Did you put the fear of God into 'em, Sis?"

Growing acutely aware of Scott's displeasure, she murmured, "I think I was the only one praying. I had my eyes closed the whole time."

Scott's hands slapped down on the tabletop. Silverware hopped on the cloth. The four of them hopped in their seats. "I'm glad you all think it's so funny. White Cloud and his family aren't going to be as amused when Garrick goes in tomorrow and has them evicted."

"But I stopped them—"

"You didn't stop anything. You started it. They were just a bunch of hoorahing toughs paid to put a scare into them. That's all they could do. I saw to it that Garrick didn't have grounds to lease the land out from under them. Until you rode in guns blasting. You gave him all the reason he needed. Assault with deadly force and intent to commit murder. He'll have it built up to look like they had guns and were ready to go on the warpath. And if I try to step in, he'll have you arrested. You wanted to know what you did? You made it im-

375

possible for me to save those people. You tied my hands, Gena."

In the face of all his vibrant fury, all she could offer was a faint, "I didn't know—"

"Did you ask?" he shouted at her. "Do you ever ask? No. Hell, no. You don't have the slightest idea of what life's about out here. It's not Boston. You can't just go around butting in where you don't belong. Good intentions get innocent people killed. Stay out of things that are none of your business."

Her cheeks as white as Aurora's table linen, Gena rose and very quietly, with great composure, left the room in favor of her own overhead.

"Scotty, there was no call—"

Scott's anger turned on his brother with the force of a blow. "I'm surprised to hear you say that. I'd think you and the major would be in high clover planning on how you're going to use that land you stole from them."

"What is going on between the two of you?" Aurora demanded.

"Nothing, Mama."

"Nothing, my ass."

"Scott!" Ethan's tone gave notice he would brook no more. "I won't tolerate that at your mama's table. I know you're grieving. We're your family—"

His chair shrieked back across the floorboards on two legs as he propelled himself up from it. "I buried my family this morning."

"Son—"

"I'm not your son." Angry and distressed, he shot out of the house, banging the door behind him.

There was silence. Then Ethan started up.

"I'm going to plant my boot so hard on that boy he's gonna have to say 'Ahh' so I can take it off."

"Ethan."

His wife's voice, so soft and anguished, settled him back into the chair with a mumbled, "Sorry, Ora. I know he's hurting."

And he wasn't alone.

From her window, Gena saw Scott ride out, a sleek, low silhouette against the deepening plum-colored horizon. Bareback and wild. Like an Indian.

Hurt piled upon hurt, stinging, throbbing, becoming an avalanche of misery. She leaned her cheek against the sun-warmed pane and wept. Tears streaked the window like threads of summer rain. The clear glass fogged from her heavy, chugging breaths. How was she going to leave all this behind? The embracing affection of the Prescott family for the chill propriety of her own? The bolstering support of Rory's hugs and the promise of Morning Song's friendship for the shallow discourse with those like Caroline Davies? Aurora's tolerant tutelage for her mother's sharp reprimands? And Scott. That was a pain too deep to dwell on.

She reeled away from the window and went to stand sightlessly before the mirror. Methodically, she began to pluck all eighteen prodding hair pins from the coil of pale tresses until her hair hung loose and thick past her shoulders. She closed her eyes, feeling Scott's fingers tangling through them. Why had she ever feared the tender fire of his touch? Now, she feared she could not live without it.

She'd been so careful to guard herself against his passions, she'd neglected to protect herself against her own. He'd been the first to wake her from the sheltered slumber of her existence, coaxing her to life with the soft, drawling cadence of his voice, encouraging with the simmering admiration in his eyes, inciting with the passionate persuasion of his touch. She wanted him. God help her. She did. Hungrily, greedily, desperately.

377

Without boundary, without control. And the sheer magnitude of those feelings shook her to the core. For though her mother taught her meticulously how a lady was to behave, she never explained to her how one was to feel. She had no idea how to curb the pound of emotions within her breast. To say "Stop" or "This is wrong" was not enough. Because she didn't want to stop and it felt so very right. Why hadn't her mother cared more for the state of her heart than the state of her posture?

Mother, why didn't you tell me about love?

Perhaps because Margaret Trowbridge knew nothing about it.

She'd spoken volumes about the carnal nature of sex but not one word on the tender stirrings of devotion. She'd been a fount of knowledge on the dangers but dry as a Dakota desert when it came to the delights. To protect her daughter or herself? Because her own existence was so miserable she wanted to spare her only child from that same pain?

Gena looked back upon the barrenness of her childhood. She had been reared in a stranglehold of restraint. A child's corset was a daily part of her female dress. She went immediately from infant to mini-adult, impressed with social expectations and drilled with habits of industry. Her entire world — social, moral, domestic, and sexual — was controlled by the rigid Margaret Trowbridge, to whom cleanliness and order were moral imperatives in home and body. While yet a child, Margaret instilled a strict pattern for her life: get fresh air; avoid excitement and intimate activity; refrain from too much tea, from playing cards, and from engaging in excessive mental labor. The sheer excitement of life was enough to bring on dire maladies. And diseases of the mind. Hysteria. That was her mother's diagnosis of her every nonconformity. It caused her capricious character, her whimsical conduct, her excitability, her impatience, her obstinacy. To cure her of her intemperate habits, excitants were removed from her food and novel reading was prohibited, especially those of a romantic tone which provoked the bodily organs and created morbid mental stresses. And when she transgressed, she was quickly and effectively subdued by a dose of paregoric.

As a girl, Gena lived in constant terror of those vague threatening illnesses. She was on a continual watch for their insidious signs: insomnia, depression, dyspepsia, timidity, palpitations, headaches, chills, morbid fears, dry skin, dilated pupils, and sweaty hands. She almost laughed aloud. Was love some terrible disease, then? Worrying over them as an impressionable child was enough to bring on the symptoms. And that brought a greater fear: the cure.

When she was eight, her parents had a terrible disagreement. Their shouts had her cowering under her covers. The next morning her father called for their physician, who had her mother's aberrant behavior diagnosed as neurasthenia. The treatment was severe: low-voltage electricity and tonics tainted with opium and up to forty percent alcohol. For weeks, Margaret Trowbridge languished in a stupor until her father deemed her sufficiently restored to a proper balance of passivity. The lesson was etched indelibly upon the young girl's mind. A show of individual spirit would be swiftly and effectively broken. Meekness was what a man desired in a woman. Submission was a treasured virtue. Unchecked emotion was dangerous. Those things she firmly believed. Until Scott Prescott undid the fastenings of her restraint.

The freedom he introduced her to was intoxicating.

The freedom to think, to act, to touch, to express. And now that she'd succumbed to the temptation of delight, how was she to return to what she was before? To the tyranny of her father? To the domination of her mother? Scott had promised to be her savior. He'd vowed his lifelong protection with the gift of his ring. There was to be no eternity with Scott Prescott. That was the crushing truth of it. But had he left her something in lieu of his name?

His child?

She clutched her flat midriff. How could she have been so careless? To lie with him. To do so without precautions. She had learned about contraception by overhearing talk between their cook and laundress. Though discussing sex was strictly taboo, not so information on pregnancy, childbirth, and the prevention of both. Some of the methods sounded so bizarre they must be true. Rock salt, rhythm, nursing, a cone of melted cocoa butter, boric acid, Vaseline, because "a greased egg cannot hatch." The washerwoman had claimed "voluptuous spasms" would interfere with conception or even contribute to sterility. Gena had had no idea what "voluptuous spasms" might be. Now she understood and could only pray that the concluding passion she experienced with Scott had been enough to prohibit fertility. The only sure way she knew of birth control was avoidance of intimacy. And that shouldn't be too difficult.

Because in two days' time, the temptation would be gone forever.

Sitting with Yellow Bear had returned a calm to his spirit. As the frustration and anger cooled atop the high shadow-drenched hill, Scott recognized the foolishness of his behavior. It had been the madness of the moment, the driving despair of his own futility. The most precious thing he could claim was the love of his family. He was grateful for the faith that it would survive the lash of his tantrum. Still, that didn't lighten his mood as he rode back to the Lone Star and stabled his horse for the night. The need for forgiveness weighted his heart as the uncertainty of direction weighed upon his soul. His feet dragged the distance from the barn to the house, his worries succumbing to a down-to-the-bone weariness. He'd planted his foot on the bottom step and hesitated. Blunted senses finally alerted him to the fact that he wasn't alone. A solitary figure separated from the shadows. He caught a flash of red.

"I thought you'd have gone back to the Bar K by now."

Rory stepped aside to give his brother plenty of room to mount the stairs and pass. He reached out to touch tentative fingertips atop one slumped shoulder, then drew back and mumbled, "I'm right sorry about the old chief. I didn't know, else I wouldn't have torn into you like I did earlier. I know you thought the world of him."

The dark head nodded simply and Rory shuffled his feet awkwardly.

"I brung you these and wanted to hang around long enough to give 'em to you."

Scott took the pages and gave them a look. His fatigue-blurred eyes couldn't focus on the rows of figures well enough to decipher them. "What is this?"

"Copies of the major's ledger sheets showing the number of cattle he sold to Garrick and the price he got for 'em. Could be it's considerable different than what he's got listed on the government record. And there's some agreements there leasing allotment land, showing Garrick's cut in the doings. You do whatever you thinks right with 'em."

381

Scott whispered a stunned expletive and looked dazedly from the papers to his brother. "You sure?"

"Seems iffen I need my butt covered, I know one damn fine lawyer to look for loopholes."

Scott swallowed noisily. "I'll try my best to keep you out of it," he said in a thickening voice.

"I know you will, Scotty. And you take care, you hear. You watch your back. You need me to see to it, you just call out. I'll be there for you." His voice gave a sudden hitch. "If I have to bring you home to Mama for burying, it's gonna plumb break my heart."

In the time it took for each to take a step, they were locked in a fierce, choking embrace. When the need for a decent breath made it slacken, they continued to lean, one into the other.

"Scott, what the major said, don't take it too personal."

"I didn't know it could be taken any other way."

"You listen to me?"

"All right. Arguing sure didn't get me anywhere."

"He's scared, Scotty. All the ranchers are. We can't bring back the profits of ten years ago any more than you can bring back the buffalo. He's just looking for the means to survive. We all are. The big outfits have been failing. It's a fight just to hang on. You go stirring up all sorts of legal trouble and they're gonna go under. Scott, you'll be killing our neighbors."

"What am I going to do?"

"You asking me?" He sounded stunned.

"Yeah, I'm asking you."

"Well, seems to me like you're going at it all wrong. You got to start higher up. It ain't the men that are bad, it's the system a doing things. You show a feller a way to keep from drowning and he ain't gonna give it two thoughts. You give a man like the major a choice a

382

doing right or wrong, and he'll pick right 'lessen wrong's the only way to get things done. Give 'em a choice, Scotty. Go after Garrick and men like him that prey on folks that's weaker. You want to pay him a visit, I'll be more than happy to play Injun with you." He straightened, grinning and wiping his face on his sleeve.

"How'd you get so smart?"

"Must be the Prescott in me. We ain't quick, but we sure as hell are surefooted."

For the first time in a week, Scott felt like laughing. "You know, Rory, when I left, you were nothing but a runny-nosed little kid. I sure am proud of how you turned out."

"Shucks, Scotty. You go shining me on like that and I'm like to commence blubbering like a baby. I gotta head on out." He slapped his palm lightly against his brother's cheek. He sobered to speak man to man. "You be careful now. You need something, you come to me. Might surprise you to find I ain't without influence of my own."

"I'm not surprised at all," Scott told him with a quiet honesty. He stood, smiling into the night as the sounds of his brother riding hell-bent-for-leather receded over the rise. Then he heard a soft step.

"You boys get things set right between you?"

"Yessir."

"You done acting like a damn fool?"

"Yessir."

"Anything I can do for you, pard?"

"Just be there for me, Daddy."

"Always have been. Always will be. You know that."

"I know that."

"Then go on inside and give your mama a kiss good night."

"Yessir."

"Scotty, I delivered you. You took your first breath right here in my two hands." He set them firmly on Scott's shoulders and squeezed. "I changed you when you was a baby. I sat up with you when you were ailing. I set you on your first horse and gave you your first whipping. And I did the same for your brother. You and Rory are my sons. I wouldn't have let you call yourself a Prescott otherwise. Now, if that name ain't good enough for you—"

"Prescott's fine, Daddy. Always has been. Always will be. You know that."

"Do now. Go tell it to your mama. And it wouldn't hurt to sweet-talk her some so she won't go fretting at me all night."

"Yessir."

Music. Soft, poignant music from the soul calling to her heart. It was impossible not to answer. Gena slipped a cotton wrapper over her nightgown and was tying the satin waist sash as she ventured down the stairs. There was a faint light burning in the lamp on the table but no one was about. The soft mournful tune lured her to the door and onto the moon-washed porch. The notes came to an abrupt end as Scott looked up from the chair he was sprawled in.

"Please. Go on," she urged softly.

He wet his lips slightly and brought the wooden recorder back to them. He didn't glance up as his fingers worked the chords from five small bores. The song floated on the night, as mysterious and melancholy as any drifting up on the sultry breeze. And when it was done, silence settled like a midnight curtain of calm about them.

"That's beautiful. I've heard you play it before. At

the Bar K." He didn't deny it. "Where did you learn it?"

"It's something I made up." His eyes lifted then, glowing soft and golden. "For you."

"Oh?" A disquieting pleasure rippled through her. "Are there words?"

He brought the flute up to rest over his heart. "In here," he told her simply, then looked away, far out into the night. "We went to listen to a reading of Oscar Wilde. His *Ballad of Reading Gaol* had just been published and you were trying to pretend you weren't crying. You were so shy I was afraid to let you see me looking at you. And so beautiful."

"When was this?" she asked softly.

"The night you wore that green dress. The first time you agreed to let me court you."

He remembered. His wistful reminiscence struck the breath from her.

"You were so delicate, so fair. I spent half the night looking at your hands, wondering if I held them if I would somehow break them."

Oh, Scott, not now. Please, don't do this to me now.

But he went on, expression one of incredible sadness, voice as hushed as the melody he played. "I wanted to be everything for you, Gena. I wanted to give you all you deserved and more. I'm sorry."

But he was. And he had. Couldn't he understand that? He was everything good and honorable in her eyes. His quiet intensity, the deep sensitivity he held for the way of the world around him, the still passions that burned inside him, his anguish for and commitment to his father's people. She so admired those things and wanted to share them with him. If he would let her.

He heaved a great, heavy sigh. "This has been the worst day of my life."

385

"What would make it better?"

"Someone coming over here to put their arms around me to tell me that they love me." His gaze touched hers again, wearily and so heartsore everything inside her just melted. She couldn't even maintain enough dignity to hesitate. She went right into his arms.

"Oh, Scott, I do so love you. And I'm so very, very sorry about what happened today."

He gathered her up on his lap like a child seeking comfort, tucking her beneath his chin in a small, tight ball of misery.

"I didn't know it would cause so much trouble," she moaned wretchedly. "I didn't mean—"

"Shhh. It's all right. I know you didn't." He pressed his lips to the top of her head, to the nape of her neck, rocking her upon his chest. "You did a brave thing, Gena. Stupid, but incredibly brave."

"But those c-c-children w-won't have a home, now, and it's my fault." She buried her face in the folds of his shirt and began a plaintive weeping.

"They'll be all right. They'll be taken in by family and friends. No one goes without amongst the Lakotas." He rubbed his cheek against her moonlit pale hair and, unbidden, he smiled. He was thinking of his Gena, a bareback Annie Oakley toting his daddy's rifles. It was quite an image. She was quite a woman. "Gena, did you put the fear of God in them?"

It took her a moment to catch the reference, then she gave a low, sniffling chuckle and confessed, "I was so scared I fired both the guns at once. The kick knocked me right off the back of the horse. I guess you can say I scared them into submission. They were afraid I'd broken my fool neck. So much for being a daring crusader."

His fingers spanned the back of that fool neck to massage gently. His smile faded. He considered that slender column. How easily broken. He considered the soft movement of her breathing. How easily stilled. By a fall from a horse. By a careless bullet. By a cruel hand. All her bravery and beauty crushed out in a moment.

"Scott?"

Her soft call made him aware of how his fingers tightened, biting into soft flesh. He relaxed them immediately, but his anxiety knew no slackening.

"When will you move over to the Cheyenne?"

"I don't know. Soon. Red Bird's offered me my grandfather's lodge. She'll need someone to provide for her. I need to be there, among the People so that they might trust me. Those who leave and return educated keep themselves to the white world and ways, keeping to their house and comforts, losing their Indian values. I don't want them to see me in that way. I want them to know the sight of me so that they might bring me their troubles, so I might become more to them than an *iyeska* playing at good deeds."

She nodded, understanding the reason and wisdom in all he said. He would have to do those things to accomplish what he had to. He would have to live as Lone Wolf so that they would accept his counsel. And there was no place for a Boston bride in that world. What argument could she offer? She loved him for what he was doing, something of more impact and importance than juggling numbers for her father. It was what he wanted, a dream he was capable of achieving, a dream she respected. What could she say to sway him from a people who needed him? That she needed him, too? Somehow, in the face of all she'd learned since coming to the Dakotas, her own wants were minuscule compared to the despair of the Sioux. If Scott could do some good for White Cloud, for High Hawk and Morning Song, for the children, how could she force him to consider her instead?

And so she hid her breaking heart to speak to him of the future he would have without her.

"You can do good for them, Scott. I know you can."

She rode with his sigh. "It's just so frustrating. There's one set of rules that apply specifically to Indian issues and a different set to law in general and the judges can choose which they want to apply. Then there's the mess of jurisdiction between state and federal law on allotment lands. The Indian courts are staffed by judges who serve the agent rather than the community. There are no doctrines to rely on. The government thinks of the severalty law as the solution instead of the first step while the Indian is lost in political busywork."

"But you can help change that."

Her confidence gave strength to his reply. "Yes. The system is failing. The government pretends to let us govern ourselves yet denies us the liberty. They break down our laws, customs, and religion inherited from our fathers. They exclude us from fair trade, from civilization and equal representation under the law, and make us puppets to the tyranny of politicians. It must be changed for us to survive."

"You will." She sat up and looked with an admiring certainty down into his eyes. "You will."

And hearing her speak it, in seeing her faith, he believed it possible. Her trust was the cornerstone of his conviction. The unwavering assurance in her gaze made him powerful, invincible, determined. Sure he could do all things with her behind him.

But she wouldn't be there.

"God, I love you, Gena."

His voice throbbed with the truth of it, with the impossibility of it. That raw, candid claim snagged her emotions, bringing back the ache of tears. She didn't trust herself to words through that sudden thickening, so she touched his face with a speaking caress, letting her fingertips chart each noble line. He leaned into her palm, eyes closing, surrendering himself to the exquisite anguish of the moment. Her hand began to tremble, so he put his over it, bolstering her support of his cheek. She drew a ragged breath and let it out slow so it wouldn't sound like a sob. It had to be said.

"What are we going to do, Scott?"

He studied her with an agonized intensity. "I want to wake up like I did this morning every day for the rest of my life, with you there beside me but—" His voice fractured painfully. What could he offer her? There were no guarantees he would even live that long. He didn't delude himself about the danger of what he was doing, but he couldn't confide that to her. The important thing was she would be safe, that if Rory brought him home over a saddle, it wouldn't be to her door. She'd wept enough tears over him. That if Garrick sought vengeance, she wouldn't be his tool. If somehow his love was to bring her harm—he couldn't live with that thought.

"But you can't," she finished for him. "I know."

"Your folks will take care of you. I'm sure they've missed you, and you, them. I know you'll be glad to get home."

Her jaw shivered. She almost laughed. Oh, Scott, now who was being naive. Not all families were like the Prescotts. Not all families were steeped in the kind of love that could heal a broken heart. She knew the moment she stepped off the train in Boston, all hope would be torn from her soul. Her parents would never allow him back into her life. There was no use pretending otherwise. The ticket was for one way. She took a deep breath. "I want — I want —" The words caught.

"You want . . . what?" he nudged gently. Kindly. With unfailing tenderness. She loved that about him. That and so many, many other things.

"I want to be brave for you."

That broke him.

Wordlessly, he pulled her down to fill the hollow of his shoulder, hugging her there so she wouldn't see the desolation etched upon his face. She didn't cry. And somehow, that made it worse, all those terrible, tearing feelings damming up, swelling up with no release. He held her in arms that couldn't bear to let her go long into the hours of the night. For nothing could fill their emptiness when she was gone.

Chapter Twenty-four

Gena hadn't expected it to be just like any other morning. This was the first of the last two she would spend beneath the Prescott roof, and somehow, she thought things would be different. But they weren't. Everything was agonizingly familiar. While Aurora gathered eggs in her apron, she diced potatoes and Ethan ground coffee. From the small kitchen window, she could see Scott standing at the end of the back porch, shaving. His back was to her, so she had to imagine what the motions suggested: lathering, scraping, washing, toweling dry. He performed the task with unconscious ease, but to her, it was an incredibly intimate act. She'd never watched a man ply his facial hair with a straightedge before, and it seemed an interesting personal accomplishment that resulted in smooth skin without a single nick. A bittersweet act because it was unlikely she would ever witness it again.

She gave a soft gasp as the knife she held scored a shallow cut in her thumb. She was sucking on that aggrieved member when he came in looking as slick and fresh as early morning. He drew up at the sight of her, a smile tugging the corners of his mouth wide.

" 'Morning."

The scant hours of sleep he'd managed between the time they'd parted in the hall and sunup when he'd risen to visit Yellow Bear had done wonders. The stamp of fatigue was gone from his features and his eyes were a clear Dakota gold. Molten now that they touched on her, like the sun rising warm and blazing over the plains. She felt the heat. Clear across the kitchen, she felt it.

"No coffee yet?"

"If you was in that big a hurry, you should have put some on yourself before you begun your primping," Ethan rumbled as he put the pot on to perk.

Scott rubbed his fresh-shaven chin. "Not everyone wants to look like a mangy ole grizzly in the morning, Daddy. How does Mama put up with all that fur on your face?"

"She puts up with it just fine," Aurora drawled in her Texas best as she came in to lay the eggs out on the counter. "Now you good ole boys amble on outta here so we can get food on the table."

Once the two of them were left alone, Gena could sense Aurora's questions and blessed her for her silence. They worked side by side in a companionable efficiency, whipping up a big western breakfast to serve to their men. Which was summarily devoured in short order.

Scott pushed back from the table to pat his flat middle as if it had suddenly expanded over his waistband. He looked marvelously fit and rested, like the son of a prosperous Dakota rancher in his bib-fronted cotton shirt and blue denims instead of like the lean and hungry grandson of a Sioux chief abusing his body to appease his people's superstitions. It was a hard juxtaposition to make in the Prescotts' homey cabin.

"I'm riding out to the Cheyenne," he announced,

then his gaze cut to Gena's with a snaring intensity. "You want to head on over with me?"

They had made a more-or-less-unspoken decision on the porch the night before that they would not speak of the coming day, of their inevitable parting. *Please,* was what his eyes conveyed across the empty plates and platters. *There's not much time left. I want you with me.* So how could she refuse? She, too, wanted to fill her every second with him.

She almost fled up the stairs to return minutes later clad in the sensible split skirt and puckered shirtwaist. She wore her hair down in a thick flaxen braid that swung saucily along her shoulders with every step. His look was approving though he didn't say as much. In fact, he said little, even when she announced her intention to ride alongside him to the reservation. She gritted her teeth as she settled her bruised posterior into the contoured saddle, reminding herself of her intentions. On this day, she would be everything Scott Prescott could possibly desire in a woman. That was how she wanted him to remember her. She would throw off every delicate disposition to conform to his rugged country home. She wanted to soak up the freedom, the adventure, the excitement, the way someone going blind would absorb every treasured sight before being plunged into blackness. She would live this day, hour by hour, as she would have had she become Mrs. Scott Prescott. Because this was as close as she would ever get.

His transformation was subtle but complete. The moment they rode onto government land, Scott began to change. He slipped off his black Stetson and let it dangle by its tie strings from the saddle horn. His feet kicked out of the stirrups to hang down naturally over the curve of the horse's belly. His words went easily from English to Teton as he exchanged greetings with those they passed. And watching him made for a fascinating study.

Red Bird welcomed them at the strangely empty lodge. Yellow Bear's strong shadow still cast itself over all. Such a strong spirit, an irreplaceable one within the hearts of those who knew him. Scott saw Gena situated beneath the canopy shade while he presented his grandmother with gifts from Aurora's kitchen. He spoke to her softly in the strange gutturals of their people, gesturing frequently toward where Gena sat. The Sioux woman was nodding and smiling with the sadness of a wife still caught up in a deep mourning.

"What was all that?" Gena asked as he came to crouch down in front of her.

"Red Bird will see to you while I'm gone." He lifted a quick hand to silence her objection. "Just for a little while. I have some business. It won't take long. Will you be all right?" *Will you stay out of trouble?* That's what he meant. He was smiling, but the tension behind it gave him away. He was walking into a dangerous shadow. And he was asking her not to add to his worries.

"I'll be fine," she assured him, touching a hand to his bent knee. Her fingers wanted to linger there on that taut stretch of denim, but she made herself release him. To do what he had to do. Her eyes followed hungrily as he walked away. And watched anxiously for his return.

She thought she'd have a quiet morning to fill her sketchbook with slices of memory. In the back of her thoughts was the want to capture the plight of the Lakota so it could be shown to those in the east, those who thought they understood but who were as blind as she had been. Perhaps in that way, she could be of some small help to Scott. Yet each time she looked up, one member or another of the Lakota clan arrived to pay their respects. Most didn't speak English. Some merely nodded, some gestured a formal welcome, some spoke to her with halting pleasantries. And she was thoroughly puzzled by the attention. In her past visits, she'd been regarded as a curiosity from an impartial distance. She felt a genuine warmth from those who approached on this day and she wondered over the difference. When she asked Red Bird to explain, the older woman summed it up simply.

"They come to pay you honor as the woman of Lone Wolf. They have heard of your courage and wish to show respect."

"Oh," was all she could manage, quite bewildered that actions stripping a family of its home could be viewed as heroic.

But the perplexing homage continued throughout the morning as she awaited Scott's return.

Disheartened by his failure to accomplish anything with Garrick, Scott's return to Yellow Bear's tipi was unhurried. He had hoped to glean something from the records that would jar with what Rory provided him, but so far, nothing. The man was careful. He would probably have another set of ledgers somewhere to suit the viewer. But how to get them within the limit of the law?

His scuffling footsteps stopped. For a moment, he was totally off-balance by what he saw. Gena, like a fair island in a red Lakota sea. She was still sitting beneath the canopy where he'd left her, but sharing her blanket were White Cloud's children and a dozen others. Hanging back with a bit more reserve were the older ones and the young women, even some men. Including High Hawk. He could hear Gena's clear voice and listened long enough to recognize the story of the Boston Tea Party. The Lakotas were chuckling over the image of white men on the warpath disguising themselves as Indians. He, himself, smiled. It struck him strangely, that tide of acceptance, tightening where it oughtn't have, softening where he would remain firm. *Dammit, Gena, I can't leave you alone for a minute, can I?*

The Indian must be rubbing off on me, Gena thought. She knew the moment Scott came up behind her. It wasn't as if he made any sound, it was a sensation that crept over her. A completing warmth. She arched her neck slightly as he lifted the heavy braid and brushed its ends along her jaw, then she looked up at him. With his swarthy features and solid build, he presented a wholly masculine picture. One that might once have incurred a trembling of fright in her breast. The only stirring she was aware of now was a deep liquid heat pooling down from the drenching gold of his eyes.

He came down in a crouch behind her so his knees spraddled on either side of her shoulders, hugging her loosely between the vee of his thighs. His cheek was close enough for her to smell the trace of shaving soap upon it, and she was taken by the urge to sample its smoothness in her palm or to even steal a taste. But not with so many watching.

"Are you opening a new missionary school?" he wanted to know. He continued to playfully tickle her beneath the chin with the tip of her braid. His mood was an appealing mix of tease and temptation.

"Well, it started innocently enough with just the four children, and the rest came along to listen. I don't think half of them even understand what I'm saying."

"The Lakotas love stories. And beautiful story-tellers." His smile was slow and seducing and she was willing to be cajoled by his quixotic charm.

And then the youngest in her audience began to chant, *"Wicooyake. Wicooyake. Wicooyake."*

"Finish your legend," he murmured softly. "I have more patience than these small ones."

As he straightened, her heart soared up right along with him and remained suspended even after he went to answer the summons of High Hawk's nod.

"She has a generous heart, your woman," the Lakota brave noted. "It is an interesting tale she tells, of white men fighting a faraway chief to claim land that was already ours. She makes them sound like great warriors. I have not seen many *washachu* who have more than the courage of a coyote. They must travel in a pack to get their bravery. Except *Wasichu Wakan*. He is yet talked of at council fires."

Scott accepted the compliment for Ethan with a nod. "There are good and brave men in both the white world and the Lakota. If the belief is strong, the heart will follow."

"New Waw, your woman, is strong in her belief. She has put shame upon me. She came to take my place when my family called for help. The debt I owe her is great. You have done well in your choice, Lone Wolf. She will bring much joy, much pride. She will make you great sons."

Scott experienced a wash of bittersweet pain as he looked back toward the fair head bent near so many dark ones. All his friend said was true. Gena would have done all that. For a moment, his longing for it to be so was plain upon his face. Then, his friend from childhood, the man who was like his brother, surprised him.

"Both you and New Waw will need family for the *okiciyuze*. I offer mine if it would please you."

Scott stared at him, staggered. He managed a soft,

"It would," through the sudden tight paralysis that caught his throat. He swallowed hard. "Tonight. It must be tonight." Yes. His thoughts seized upon the idea with a determined clarity. Yes, of course. It would honor Yellow Bear's last request. And it would be a bond his heart could hold to forever.

"I will see things ready," High Hawk told him, amused by his friend's impatience. Even the lone wolf needed a mate.

"And your family, are they well?" Scott asked, tearing his thoughts from Gena.

High Hawk sobered. "Agency men come tomorrow to take our land. Then we will become *tuwe otakuye k'eyas,* anybody's relative."

The brave's bitterness sat heavy with Scott, too. The image of White Cloud and his family going from place to place begging food until their welcome was worn raw aggrieved him.

"If only I had found what I needed to rid us of Garrick," he muttered fiercely.

"And what would do that miracle?"

The proud Lakota, still smarting from his failure to protect his family, listened, and stared thoughtfully in the direction of the agency office.

The day was hot yet still filled with industry. Gena watched with saddened interest as White Cloud and his family erected a canvas-covered tipi. She couldn't shake the weight of responsibility that settled cold in her belly. Her impulsiveness had brought them back to the reservation from their attempt toward pride and freedom. The family's lack of resentment increased her guilt. Every kindness they showed her twisted her self-blame tighter until it was a nearly crushing band about her heart.

Morning Song and her mother and Red Bird sat with her chattering in the flowing Teton tongue while they stitched and quilled upon pieces of pale butter-soft hide. Deer, Morning Song told her. Five skins were needed for the tradition garment they fashioned. They politely refused her offer of help, so she settled for sketching the three of them bent over their beadwork. Morning Song explained that the lizard motif was used because it resembled the *t'elanuwe*. The serpentine umbilical cord was said to protect against feminine disorders. Gena smiled. Superstition not unlike the odd cures of the east.

Throughout that sultry afternoon, Scott hovered close-by but didn't approach. She was ever aware of his hot, glowing stare upon her. When she'd look up, he'd smile slightly and a flare of yearning would ignite between them. He'd traded his boots for a pair of soft moccasins and bared his body from the waist up in the Lakota way. As he crouched down beside White Cloud to speak to him in earnest, Gena worked to capture that essence of him on paper. The way his powerful thighs swelled snugly within the confines of tight denim. The way he balanced effortlessly on the balls of his feet with forearms braced on his knees and hands dangling between them. She wished she had oils so she could represent the deep tawny sheen of his shoulders and the raven black of his short hair. By now, he was as dark as any of his Dakota brethren, though more brown in hue than copper. She detailed the sculpted angles of his face with a loving hand, remembering as she did how each had felt beneath her touch; the jut of cheekbones, the curve of lip, the slant of eyelids, the scoring smile lines. And she depicted the badges of bravery scarring his broad chest with the same pride as he bore them. Signs to all who would see that he, Lone

Wolf, was worthy to be among them.

Gena put aside her drawings when Red Bird asked her to bring water from a nearby stream. She needed to start the preparations for the evening meal. There was to be a celebration, she told the young white girl with a wistful smile. Wondering if they would be able to stay that long, Gena made her way through the village. The prospect was exciting. Another slice of a very different kind of life she could take with her on the train tomorrow.

Tomorrow.

She'd tried hard not to think of it. When surrounded by the happy children and contented women, it was easy to feel at home among them. As if she would be staying forever. Such an odd thought. Why would she consider resigning herself to the miserable life they led when she could have the comforts of Boston? Why would she think an existence of poverty, of baking in the sun, of going without the simplest necessities, held any charm for Miss Gena Trowbridge of Boston? Because, she realized, even in their desperate straits, they were family. She'd witnessed it all day, that oneness, that belonging. The way the women, total strangers, had come up to her to touch her fair hair and nod. The way the children had run up to her to tug on her hands, trying to entice her into one of their playful games. The way they brought things with a casual generosity to share with Red Bird because she had lost her man. One close, caring unit in which each looked after the other. They embraced her, a foreigner, and Scott, a man of mixed blood. And it felt good. She could understand his desire to remain here over the impersonal chill of the east. For when one was loved, it was easy to endure the hardships of life.

But who would she have to love her when she

returned home?

Home. Home was the Prescotts' kitchen filled with the yeasty scent of baking. Home was the endless stretch of green and gold that carried the eye and soul forever. Home was in Scott Prescott's smile. She would be leaving the only home she'd ever known behind her.

She blinked at the dampness gathering in her eyes, but it was persistent. She didn't want to think about these things now. She didn't want anything to spoil this last day. But the more she willed them away, the more determined her tears became. Stinging. Seeping. Blinding. She stumbled, and dashed angrily at her eyes with her sleeve. Something struck her, then, just a small thump between the shoulder blades. She continued her walk until another pebble glanced off her arm. Thinking one of the children was pestering her with a game, she turned to admonish the youngster. And found herself confronting Scott.

She drew a ragged breath. He looked so wonderfully inviting, leaning up against a cottonwood with a half-smile teasing upon his handsome face. Offering everything she could dream of in that softly glowing gaze.

She resumed her walk toward the stream, pace brisk and purposeful. Behind her, she heard him say her name in surprise and his light footfalls on the path.

"I didn't mean to startle you," came his caressing voice close to her ear.

"You didn't. Go away. I have to get water for Red Bird." How peevish she sounded. She walked faster, fighting the thickening of tears in her throat.

"I'll help."

"No."

But he'd taken the handle of the bucket. Her fingers tightened, refusing to let go. For a moment, they pulled it back and forth between them. He finally released his end to stare at her incomprehensibly.

"Gena? What's wrong? Did someone upset you?"

The bucket dropped. With a small wounded sound, she was in his arms. His skin was warm beneath her cheek, beneath her palms, hot from absorbing the sun, heated by the man within. She squeezed her eyes closed, wanting to remember the feel of him. Exquisitely male. Protective. Safe. She could hear his heart accelerate as if it had been provoked into sudden flight, and felt a slight tremor race along the strong arms that held her. His breath rushed unsteadily through the wisps of hair at her temple. And then he calmed.

"Are you all right?" he asked softly. At her nod, he asked, "Do you want to go back home?"

"No," she moaned with all the meaning in the world.

Pretending to miss the significance of her words, he said, "We don't have to stay. I just thought — it looked as though you were enjoying yourself with the others."

"I was. I am," she sniffled. She pushed away from him and picked up the bucket. "I was getting water. Red Bird is going to teach me some Lakota cooking. They're having some sort of celebration tonight. Do you think we could stay?"

His knuckles grazed her jaw. "If you'd like. These things go on pretty late."

"I'll have plenty of time to — to pack in the morning."

His hand stilled, then turned to cup her cheek. He bent down. His kiss was incredibly delicate. "I'll tell them we're going to stay. You've made good friends here, Gena."

"I like them, too. I would never have imagined such a thing two months ago. Funny, isn't it? I used to be so afraid of them, but now they're almost like family."

"I love you," he told her in a hushed voice. As he bent to kiss her again, she drew back and held up the bucket

402

between them. There was only so much of the sweet torment she could withstand.

"I'd better get the water."

He let her go, watching her hurry along the path as if pursued by demons. Maybe she was.

"I love you," he said again, softer this time, as if the words were wrung from his soul.

To Gena, the rest of the afternoon flashed by too rapidly. She wanted to hold to each second, to cherish and savor each moment, but, too quickly, they became hours. Just before sunset, Scott and Red Bird somberly went to hold their vigil with Yellow Bear. Morning Song and her mother tugged her inside the new tipi that would be their home and surprised her with a gift of the garments they'd been laboring over all day. Touched beyond words, Gena slipped out of her own things, feeling modest when Morning Song insisted she strip completely. But when the deerskin dress settled next to her skin, it was so wonderfully soft and supple, she forgot her objections. The hem was slashed so ribbons of fringe brushed along her calves. A brightly beaded belt molded it to her figure. The yoke of the dress was surprisingly heavy with its extensive design of quillwork and beads. White Cloud's wife insisted she sit so a pair of buckskin moccasins could be fitted to her feet. Behind her, Morning Song loosened then rebraided her hair, weaving strands of colorful beads through the pale tresses.

"Like white man's wheat," the Lakota woman murmured as she nimbly twined the sections together. "You are very beautiful. Tonight, Lone Wolf will be impatient to have you."

Gena blushed hot at the woman's candid prediction.

403

Inside, she flushed hotter, hoping it was true.

"You are lucky woman, White Swan. He is handsome man. He will be good to you. He will fill your nights with pleasure." Morning Song's fingers stopped their flickering movement in her hair. "One time I had hoped . . . But it is plain to see how much Lone Wolf loves you. You are good woman of strong heart. You will make him happy."

Gena drew a pained breath. Oh, if only she could. If only she had the chance to make it so.

As if in answer to her ardent wish, the first poignant tones of a flute carried in from the night. Her song. Gena stood, aquiver with the sweet yearning contained in the simple melody.

"You know the sound of your man's *siyotanka*." Morning Song sighed. "Go out to him, New Waw."

Scott, no, it was Lone Wolf, waiting for her outside the tipi. His swarthy features were cast even more in the Lakota mold by the headdress of antelope horns he wore. In the darkness, his eyes glittered, almost black. They moved over her like a lingering caress. Slowly, he opened the woven blanket he had wrapped about his shoulders, lifting it above his head and curving it in a wide circle that encompassed them both.

"What are you doing?" Gena whispered.

"*Sina ao pemni inajinpi.* Standing in the blanket so we can be alone."

The notion struck her as ridiculous, as if by engulfing themselves in Red Bird's blanket, no one in the busy village would know they stood toe to toe, nearly nose to nose beneath it.

As if he read her thoughts, Scott crooned quietly, "So no one will intrude when I tell you how beautiful you look to me and how I can't wait to kiss you."

Remembering Morning Song's words brought an

404

urgent expectancy. She leaned up against him, lips parted, welcoming the eager plunder of his mouth the way she hoped to welcome him more intimately when they were truly alone. He drew on her lower lip, biting it lightly, then gave a husky chuckle.

"What?"

"I shall have to tell the shaman his medicine was good." He touched the bag he wore around his neck. "Elk medicine made from the heart and inside gristle from the fetlock. The elk is our symbol of masculine virility, virtue, and charm. He guaranteed it would render you helpless."

Gena's fingertips grazed his chest. "Did you think you would need it?" she teased.

Scott was suddenly quiet. "I wasn't sure." He lowered the blanket. The air beneath it had grown humid from their combined heat. In contrast, the night felt cool. Gena was surprised to see him looking somber and vaguely uncertain.

"So you have wooed me with your love song and enchanted me with the spirit of the elk. What next?"

He smiled, some of his playfulness returning. He produced a small mirror from his pants pocket and held it so she might see herself. "Now I have captured your reflection in my glass so I might have power over your will."

She smiled, too. "Yes, you do."

"Then come. We will enjoy the music and the feast."

He took her hand and led her to a large gathering. The crowd parted to let them into the very center where food was plentifully arranged. He coaxed her to sit beside him and partake in the meal, then, afterward, reclaimed her hand. He held it loosely between his while they watched a lively and quite sensual dance performed in which young men and women moved clockwise in a circle, frequently hugging each other in expressions of joy. Drums beat in three-quarter time and a group of men seated in the center of the dance circle began a low singing chant. The pulse of the music was vibrant, primitive and stirring. Gena felt as though her entire being throbbed in time to it. Nothing in the dance was overtly sexual, but watching it woke explicit sensations within Gena. Slowly, Scott lifted her hand, pressing her palm to his chest so she might feel the thud of his heart. The tempo was the same. Impatient. Passionate.

White Cloud and his family had come to sit beside Gena, and Red Bird took a seat on the other side of Scott. They began to talk in the monotonous Teton gutturals, not to her or Scott but, she sensed, about them. There was much nodding. All the while, Scott was watching her, his eyes glowing, his smile small and bewitching. Parcels were exchanged between White Cloud and Red Bird: fabrics, tobacco, a fine-honed cutting knife. Each item was examined and exclaimed over.

To appease Gena's curiosity, Scott told her quietly, "Gifts from my family to yours. It's a symbolic gesture. White Cloud has offered to represent your people. It is an honor, for they feel they owe you a debt of gratitude." He lifted one of the gifts, a weighty necklace of bone and shell, and fastened it about her throat. "These are elk teeth. They're very valuable, because only the two front ones are used. This was made from forty of them, brought down in the hunt by my grandfather, my father, and by me."

She touched it reverently. "It's beautiful, Scott. Thank you." She reached up to remove the jeweled combs she wore to hold back her hair and extended them to Red Bird. The old woman murmured in delight, turning them so they reflected the light from the central fire.

Scott was pleased by her gift. He told her, "I've given White Cloud four horses and he has accepted the *sawicayapi*, the bestowal of gifts. The exchange and acceptance of them has formed a *okiciyuze*, a joining-together of our families. All are satisfied. Come." He stood abruptly and lifted her beside him with a rather forceful grip on her elbow. Those around them began a lusty chuckling. Gena smiled, uncertain of the reason for their sly whispers and knowing smiles. Until Scott led her to the newly erected tipi. He threw up the door flap and waited for her to enter.

"I don't understand." Gena glanced back toward the fire, to where everyone seemed to be watching. "This is White Cloud's home."

"No," he disagreed huskily. He pointed to the designs the men had painted on the canvas. She hadn't paid them much attention before, but looking at them now, she could see the patterns were very distinct. A howling wolf. The figure of a man divided in half. Lone Wolf. "It's ours."

He propelled her inside, and the moment the door flap closed, bawdy shouts rose from those celebrating.

Scott lit the central fire. It added to the sweltering heat of the night but brought the interior into focus. It was much like Yellow Bear's tipi, with three sleeping platforms slung hammock fashion over which decorated curtains were hung to keep off water from the smoke hole. The sides were raised up several inches to allow a slight breeze to waft through. Their saddles rested at one side of the door. Scott removed the headdress he wore and placed it carefully beside them. Then he turned to her with that same expectant smile.

Gena swallowed uncomfortably. She could still hear

the whistles and shouts of his friends. When he reached for her, she skittered away.

"Gena?"

"Scott, they'll all think we came in here to—to—"

"Mate?" he supplied with a wicked grin. "I don't know about you, but that's sure what I had in mind." He caught at the belt to her dress but she jerked away, agitated and alarmed by his lack of concern. She put the fire pit between them and watched him warily.

"It's—it's not—"

"Proper? Is that the word you wanted? In Boston, no. Here, that's up to you. No one out there sees anything wrong with it. You're mine, Gena. They won't interfere. No one will take exception to anything we do between us." He came around the fire with a slow but purposeful step. Gena held her ground for a moment then began a hasty retreat. He stopped, looking perplexed then annoyed. "But you do. Don't you?"

She canted a nervous glance at him from beneath her downswept lashes. He looked so big, so bronze, so . . . bare. She felt horribly embarrassed. Everyone would know. All of them. How would she ever leave the tipi in the morning and face them with that knowledge?

He was watching her face, assessing her blushes, her obvious reluctance. His sudden fierce oath made her jump. "Forget it. Never mind. I'll take you back to the Lone Star." He strode angrily to the saddles and was reaching down for his when she said his name softly.

"Scott."

He turned his head toward her just as the heavy beaded belt she wore fell about her dainty feet. The significance struck him with a devastating force. He sucked in his breath and let it out noisily through his teeth. When he straightened, his hopes were clearly defined by the crowding strain of his Levi's. He approached her cautiously, as if she were a timid mare he meant to gentle. She quivered at the brush of his fingers along her cheek but she didn't withdraw.

"Are you sure you want to stay?" he asked quietly. "I was being a fool before. It's just that — it's just that I wanted everything tonight to be so perfect."

Gena swallowed down her misgivings and let herself become lost in the steeping passion of his gaze.

"It was," she assured him. "It will be."

Chapter Twenty-five

His kiss was little more than a whisper of breath upon her lips. He moved slowly, giving her time to respond, time to think, time to resist, if she wanted to. She didn't. He sketched her cheeks, her jaw, her temple, first with fingertips then with the brush of his mouth. She stood still and quiet, letting him. He pulled at the strips of rawhide that held the shoulders of her dress together, loosening them a stitch at a time. It was a slow, seducing dance, a mating ritual that no one had to teach them. As each lace gave, his lips caressed the exposed patch of fair skin until both shoulders were completely bare. With a nudge from him, the weight of bodice beading carried the garment to the ground. She was naked.

Scott stepped back. His gaze traveled the length of her in a leisurely stroke. At first, she thought to conceal herself from his avid stare, then a strange warming began inside at his intense admiration. And continued to grow. She reached out, hesitant then bold, for the waistband of his jeans, opening it. She tugged but they wouldn't budge. The increased volume within the snug fit of denim held them firm at his hips.

"Let me," he murmured gruffly, and between the two pair of impatient hands, his Levi's were peeled down and kicked off. Freed from the tight confines, his manhood sprang eagerly toward her and Gena jumped back with a tiny gasp. She stared at him with rounded eyes, wondering how a part of him that seemed so huge could fit so well inside her. She made a small sound, like the apprehensive giggle of a schoolgirl.

Scott's forefinger brushed under her chin, lifting it so she would meet his eyes. His stare was intense, almost anxious.

"Are you pleased with what you see, New Waw?" For all his proud male confidence, she could sense his need of her approval and gave it with a whispered, "Yes." Then proved it further by touching him.

She was surprised at first by the way he pulsed with life. Then intrigued. When her light exploration continued, Scott gave a ragged laugh and caught her hand. He lifted it up to press a hard kiss upon its palm.

"Later," he rumbled. "Elsewise, things will come to a rather quick conclusion. Later you can do whatever you want with me."

She wasn't sure she understood exactly what he meant, but his reaction to her timid caress fueled her with encouragement. A curious excitement budded. *Whatever you want.* Daring her. Coaxing her. Urging her to consider what she might like to do but had never, ever dared to dwell upon within the frame of her still rather virginal mind. The prospects made her fluttery. And at the same time, incredibly sure. He was hers to do with as she wanted.

Her hands lifted, palms pressing to the hot sleek flesh of his shoulders, revolving slowly then sliding over and down his back. His hand found the curve of her spine and drew her up against him. His mouth came down to hers, settling with familiarity, demanding with authority. His kiss was hurried and hungry and so were

411

his hands as they rubbed over her satiny skin until the chafe of longing was too much to bear. Then he scooped her up like a captured prize and strode with her to the sleeping mat. She was surprised when he sank down beside her instead of on top, and disappointed. But the disappointment didn't last.

While he kissed her, his hand skimmed down to one bared breast, charting first the perimeter like a careful scout then converging upon its crest in a conquering rush. She gasped then moaned as his deft fingers plucked and provoked her nipple to full arousal, preparing the way for the rasp of his tongue. Then his head moved lower, his mouth trailing down her jerking rib cage to lath wet circles on her belly. She wiggled restlessly and her fingers meshed in his hair. He thought for a moment about delving farther down, then changed his mind. It wouldn't do to shock her senseless while still breaking her in. Better to gentle her slow and easy. They had all night. No need to rush the ride.

He lifted back up on his elbow, and for a moment just looked down at her, at the fan of pale hair spun about her shoulders like January sunshine, at the well-kissed lips parting for more, into the blue eyes which had once shone with the light of innocence and now burnt with desire for him. When he'd seen her at the door of their tipi dressed in native costume, wonderful things, hopeful things had leapt inside him. As if she belonged to this place, to these people, to the man called Lone Wolf. The feeling of possessive pride shook him. So brave. So beautiful. Willing to accept all that he was in a timeless embrace of love. For this night, it was true. And tomorrow, the tomorrow he tried hard to forget, he would have to somehow find the courage to watch her leave.

But tonight, she was his.

Gena stirred in a marvelous languor. Scott's slow, satisfying forays drugged her with sensation. The drums yet sounding from the fire echoed the fierce pound of blood in her veins. It was a steady, hypnotic rhythm, pulsing along the sensitive points of her body to settle low in primal urgency at the junction of her thighs. As if drawn by that throbbing beat, Scott's hand moved across the gentle plains of her body in search of its most fertile valley, seeking to explore and conquer. But when he reached the swell of its downy foothills, he found access suddenly denied him. Her thighs were clenched tight. He patiently stroked those shapely limbs but they refused to limber or loosen.

"Gena?" he queried softly. "What is it? What's wrong?"

She couldn't look at him. Concentrating her attention on his brown throat, she whispered hoarsely, "This is wrong, Scott. The things you make me feel, the things we do. We shouldn't —"

"Why? They don't pleasure you?"

She looked up quickly and he saw her answer shimmering there in the great pools of blue. He saw her confusion, too. Her tender lips firmed and he heard her mother's prim voice speak from them. And he didn't like it.

"What we're doing is carnal and offensive in the sight of God. To surrender to lust like animals . . ."

He smiled and actually chuckled.

"Don't laugh at me!"

"You don't understand how truly foolish you sound," he said with a tender humor. "Like some old maid who couldn't get a man into her bloomers so she invents all sorts of reasons to convince herself she wouldn't like it anyway."

"Scott!" She started to rise up, incensed and mortified. He stopped her most effectively. With a deep, wet kiss. It went on and on until all the protest was drained from her and she slumped weakly against the mat. She had no argument against his kind of persuasion. She lay still, eyes closed, tears hot on her cheeks. He brushed them away with the soft cushion of his lips.

"Gena, the Great Mystery inbred in animals the need to mate and multiply," he explained quietly. As he spoke, his hand began a seducing massage upon the tense areas of her body. "It's a mindless thing, the urge to make more of their own kind. There is no choice involved. Man, he raised above the animals, at least most men. He gave man the right to choose, to refrain, the ability to love, the want to share. He placed in our hearts a need to bond, one man to one woman, and the gift to take joy from one another. There is nothing less animalistic than lovemaking. If it were bestial, it would be without control. Man would mate when and wherever the need struck. You would have found yourself spread across the breakfast table this morning with me tearing at your skirts. My mama and Ethan would have never accomplished anything these last twenty years outside of the bedroom."

Gena had to smile at that. The image of being sprawled out between the biscuit platter and coffeepot with Scott lost to a rutting frenzy between her knees was as absurd as it was exciting. He smiled, too, sharing that salacious vision. She had relaxed beneath the caress of his voice and kneading palm. Her aroused body rocked and arched subtly to meet his hand. And when he strayed low, he found the way open for him, waiting, willing, wanting.

"Pleasure is man's reward for caring, for enduring,"

he continued. His words grew husky, labored with love. "To give, to take, it is the most sacred of his gifts. It is a thing to be honored, cherished, upheld above all other things. I love you, Gena. You are the mate of my heart and soul and spirit. There is no shame in taking of the joy I give you. Or in wanting to give in return. It is the way of things, the way of man."

Gena's breath had grown ragged and strained. She listened and let herself be lost to the luxury of his touch. While he continued the coaxing circles with one hand, leading her on an upward spiral of delight, his other slipped beneath to show how he planned to enter her as soon as she'd climbed as high as he could take her. Then he bent down to place his mouth upon one yearning breast and sensation exploded through her. She clung to him in amazement, to this strange quixotic man who breathed life into her body, who spoke the wisdom of the heart. She cried out his name as if it was her answer to everything. He was. At that moment, he was.

He was above her and inside her before the last of her spasms quieted. Voluptuous spasms, she thought wildly. Yes, they were that. And as Scott began to move within her, matching the driving rhythm of the drums, she let go of the last of Miss Gena Trowbridge to become White Swan, woman of Lone Wolf. She gave voice to the pleasure he brought her, knowing no one could hear over the revelry outside — not caring if they did. She opened her eyes and was glad she had, for above her, she found he was smiling, his golden eyes lambent. She'd never seen a sight as beautifully breathtaking as the bronze angles of his face pulled taut and harsh with his passion for her. Her gaze drank boldly of his splendor, intoxicated by it. Their eyes met in a communion more expressive than words, and then hers closed to savor the quickening power of her release as it built and shuddered through her. His hands curved under her hips, lifting, tipping them to accept him more fully into the heart of her, so that when he spilled his seed of life with a ravaging groan, it was planted deep and sure.

And as they lay joined and replete, he petted her hair and spoke to her in the language of the Sioux. Low, throbbing sounds that Gena knew without understanding were the words to his love song. Spoken to her from the heart of Scott Lone Wolf.

It was still dark when his internal clock woke him, saying sunrise was near. Time to journey to his grandfather's resting place to pray for the safety of his soul. He wondered if the old man was nearing the Hereafter, if he was looking at the pocket watch to tell the Sun Spirit the white man's timepiece said it was time to shine. How he would have chuckled at that thought. Scott's insides tensed and trembled with the ache of missing him.

He shifted on the sleep mat and puzzled over what seemed so different. He was naked, but that was how he always slept. A heavy lethargy had settled in his limbs, defying his want to move them. He was sore. It felt as though he'd ridden bareback for an entire day.

Or throughout the night.

He grinned to himself as memory returned. Gena. He shifted onto his side to where she slumbered as if dead. As well she should, he thought with a smug self-satisfaction. How many times had they found mutual ecstasy over the passion-filled hours of the night? Enough for him to moan as if he'd been beaten. Enough for her to plead reluctant exhaustion in the middle of their last union, then begin to snore softly while he was yet inside her.

He reached out to brush a silvery strand of hair from her cheek. Contentment swelled inside him the way desire had the night before. He'd never expected his gentle Gena to become so voracious in his bed. Or so tenacious out of it. His respect for her knew no bounds. She was everything he could want in a life's mate. Everything. And yet a train was coming to take her away.

When he gathered her close, she gave a sleepy little mutter and burrowed into his shoulder. Trustingly. Lovingly. He fought not to crush her to him as the panic of separation settled. No Gena to quiet his spirit with her tenderness. No Gena to inflame his heart with her newly discovered sensuality. No friend, no helpmate, no lover, no mother for his children. O mighty *Wakan Tanka,* how was he to stand it?

But those were selfish reasons. In his mind he knew what his soul decried was the only and right thing to do. He knew it every time he saw her soft smile and imaged it twisted into a grimace of fear. He knew it every time he touched her soft flesh and pictured it bruised. He knew it each time he heard the music of her laugh and had it echo as weeping. She was his life, his light. How could he allow those things? He thought of Ethan's frail first wife, who had adapted to the wildness of the frontier by going quietly insane to the point of ending her life and that of their unborn child. Not Gena. Never Gena. He could never force her to endure the hardships ahead at the risk of her gentle spirit. Nor could he thrust the brutality of life into her face and cruelly demand that she accept it. But if she remained, she would have to, and he couldn't bear the thought of her disillusionment of life. Of him. He couldn't quite believe she could love him that much.

He stroked the sweet curve of her back and shoulders and let his fingers sift through her hair. And suddenly his heart seized up with a killing stroke, the kind that took the unwary who wandered about at night and suffered *wanagikte* from bumping into ghosts.

What if she forgot him?

What if, after returning to the east, his sweet Gena found another to love? After breaking her heart and sending her away, how could he expect her to remain true? She had found the joys of being with a man— dammit, he'd taught them to her! Could he expect her to swallow up that fresh excitement of life and lock it away in memory of what they'd shared? He would. He faced that reality stoically. There would never be another for him. But could he ask that of Gena? Could he expect it? He had only to envision her with another, someone like Horace Billings. He could imagine his cousin's hands upon her, stoking her desires to the flash point.

"No," he growled aloud, hugging her slack figure to him. "No, dammit, you're mine. Mine."

Almost as if she sought to prove him wrong, Gena muttered in her sleep and pushed away from him to roll to her opposite side. Closing him out. Abandoning him. He lay there staring up through the smoke hole into the lightening heavens, fury seething through him, dread making him tremble. It was madness. She'd filled him with her scent and was leaving him to perish from the emptiness inside.

He flung himself up off the mat and jerked on his jeans. He would pray. He would kneel beside the burying place of his grandfather and pray for wisdom to be visited upon him. Wisdom and strength. Because there was no way he'd be able to do what he had to do alone.

Scott was gone. Gena stirred and slit her eyes open against the pastel pales of dawn. It was yet warm, but she felt chilled without his heat pressed against her.

"Scott?"

She sat up and groaned at the chafe of excess. It was a glorious pain. The saddles were still by the door with Scott's shirt, boots, and hat resting upon them. He'd probably gone to be with Yellow Bear. Sighing softly, wearily, she sank back onto the willow bed and tried to return to sleep.

Tomorrow was here. She gasped in dismay. This was the day she would leave the Dakotas never to return. She found a blanket at the foot of the bed—the one Scott had held over their heads so he could kiss her—and pulled it up in an effort to still her shivering. It wasn't a cold from without. It was a deep, frigid vacuum within. She squeezed her eyes shut and tried to warm herself with the memories of their passion. How it had burned. Fierce. Consuming. Relentless. Surely he wouldn't send her away now. Not after that. Not after they'd shared their bodies with wild abandon and their souls with a poignant peace. He said he loved her. He'd proven it again and again with his hands, with his words, with his compelling thrusts. Surely he'd come to recognize how important she was to him. Surely he wouldn't put his career and his people before her in his heart and mind.

Oh, Scott, please don't make me go back there. I'll die. I will. I'll just die.

Did people die from loneliness, from despair? If not, she would be the first. He wouldn't want that on his conscience, would he? If he knew, if he understood how it was for her beneath her parents' roof, he wouldn't make her go. If she told him how her spirit had begun to flourish on his wide plains and beneath his soaring skies, he would understand and keep her with him. He would, wouldn't he?

Scott had never actually broken their engagement. The only solution seemed to marry here without the consent or knowledge of her parents. They would never allow it. If she returned home, they would break down the sacred bastion of her love with unholy zeal. *We'll discuss it,* her father's note threatened. Emmett Trowbridge never discussed anything. He made rules and others followed. He'd never struck her before. She'd never given him reason. She'd never gone against any of his commands. Until now. She loved Scott and she would have no other. She could imagine her father's fury. A half-breed Indian had taken her virginity. She could see it darkening his features, twisting them into something that yet haunted her dreams. He would bend her to his will. If not with verbal intimidation or physical force, then with the lulling narcotic balm he'd used to tame her mother. She curled into a tight ball and hugged the rough blanket to protect her from her fears.

Marry me, Scott. Marry me now.

Or was that no longer his plan?

Gena's terror became a living organism eating away her confidence one piece at a time. Why had he brought her west? He had to have known she would discover the truth about him. That the others would find out, too. Had he been hoping the news would reach her family's ears? Had he counted upon her father's repugnance for anything not up to social snuff to end their betrothal? Had he brought her to this wild country hoping she would be so overcome by it that she would flee for the safety of her seaboard home? He no

420

longer had to return to face her father's wrath. She had given him everything without the benefit of his name. Would he see it as necessary any more? Would he want her, a silly eastern girl with grand ideas, cluttering up his life? The plans they'd made together — all gone. Was their future, too? Was so much of him lost to Lone Wolf that he forgot the things that mattered to Scott Prescott? She had made him so angry when she tried to intercede with White Cloud and the agency. She'd been trying to help, because she loved him, because she cared for his people. It had been a disaster. Was he unable to forgive her for that blunder? Did he think she could never learn, could never fit in, the way he had never fit in while in Boston? She'd tried her best to show him yesterday. The Lakota accepted her. Aurora Prescott accepted her. Couldn't he?

She felt a disturbance in the air when the door flap was lifted. She never actually heard him enter but knew he was there. Gena lay still, waiting for him to join her on the mat. How desperately she needed to feel him near her. But he didn't approach the place where they had wallowed in sensual rapture for half the night. She could sense him waiting, watching. Finally, unable to stand the suspense, she rolled toward him.

Scott was hunkered down on the balls of his bare feet. He wore only his Levi's and his most impassive face.

"Good morning," she ventured quietly. She kept the blanket tugged up over her breasts, not feeling secure beneath the cool assessing eyes of the man across the cold fire.

"I didn't mean to wake you," he replied.

"You didn't. I've been up for a while. Thinking."

He nodded but didn't pursue it. He rose then and fetched her clothing. Not the deerskin gown but her

421

white clothes. He even turned his back while she dressed in anticipation of this morning's modesty. By the time he looked back, she was decently clad and trying to make sense out of her tousled hair.

"Let me do that."

Gena was startled but not displeased when Scott settled on his knees behind her. Very gently, he combed through the snarl of flaxen tresses with his fingers, working out the snags with scarcely a pull. Then, he began to braid it.

"You don't have to do that."

"It is something a man does on such a morning, *mitawicu*."

Did that mean "mistress"? she wondered glumly as he formed a neat, thick tail woven through with quilled hair strings that trailed eagle plumes. When he was finished, his hands lingered, stroking along her neck, then the slope of her shoulders.

"You brought me much happiness last night," he told her softly. His words were tinged with the low Lakota inflection she found so mesmerizing. "Was it so with you?"

Her voice failed. She could only nod.

"I thought as much. You were very loud."

He sounded pleased with that even as she blushed. His hands dipped down the front of her bodice, just brushing across the tips of her breasts. Then he stood.

"I'll saddle the horses. My folks will be wondering what happened to us."

What happened, Gena thought in a wild despair. Nothing had happened. Nothing had changed. He was sending her to Boston. Something died inside her. It was her spirit.

Scott returned to find Gena seated primly on one of the mats. Her folded hands rested in her lap and her head was bowed demurely. The deerskin dress and elkstooth necklace sat upon her knees. Only the stiffness of her shoulders betrayed her.

"Gena? Are you ready?"

She looked up slowly. Her gaze was dull and defeated. It gave him pause. He'd hurt her. After all his vows. He had to make her see it was the only way. Her expression didn't change as he came to kneel down before her. Her hands were cold when he lifted them into his own. He placed the ticket to Boston in one of them. She looked at it as if it were a live scorpion.

"I love you," he told her. No reaction. It put a frustration of panic within his breast. *How long would it take for her to fall out of love with him in Boston?* He didn't want to find out. His hands cupped her face, tipped it so she couldn't avoid his intense gaze. "Gena, could you be happy here with me?"

Animation sparked in her eyes. They shone like sunlight on water. "Yes. Oh, yes, Scott, I could."

He fought down the sudden leap of elation in his heart and continued cautiously. "I want you to think on it carefully. I'm not sure what kind of work I'll be doing. For a while, it will be here on the reservation. That'll mean no money, no luxuries. We'll probably live here in this tipi. It's beastly hot in the summer and frigid in the winter. There's never enough food."

"I don't care," she cried joyfully.

"You will," he warned. "There'll be no clean water for washing your hair. No fancy soirees. The folks in town will call you breed-lover. And worse. It's going to hurt and keep on hurting."

"I can stand it," she vowed.

He licked his lips. His mouth felt dry as dust, fueled by the blasting heat pumped from his heart. God, how he loved her. "Gena, I can't promise you'll have any of

423

the nice things I told you I'd provide. Times will be hard. Later, I mean to work my way up in the legal system. It might even mean going to Washington for a while. It'll be long hours and unpopular views. Gena, your own people will hate you for being with me. Remember how it was with Horace and Beth and Caroline. This will be worse. Please think on it. Don't agree to something you'll regret."

"How could I ever regret being with you?"

She said that so passionately, so sincerely, he began to believe, to really believe it possible. He smiled. She smiled back through her tears.

"And we can spend our nights like the last one and wake beside one another." He scooped her up into his arms, crushing her against him with a possessing passion, one she returned without reserve.

"Not every night," she protested faintly, and he chuckled, thinking he'd worn her ragged in his enthusiasm for her. "No proper lady of Boston would allow for more than twelve."

He was feeling better. She was pressed close, her arms around him. They were talking about their sleeping habits for the future. Things were going to be fine. "A week?"

She astounded him by saying quite sincerely, "A year."

His laugh boomed. "Well, that'd see us for the first week or so. What are we going to do for the other eleven and a half months? Can I borrow ahead? Maybe in about a hundred years or so I won't want to make love to you every night. Just every other."

She smiled at that, wondering how he could sound so impatient after the night they'd just spent together. And hoping at the same time that he would never lose that sense of urgent want. "We'll have to sleep apart," she teased happily. "Then the temptation won't be so great."

"Apart? Gena, you'll be sleeping in my arms until the day I die. In no time, you'll be full of my child. If I were a true Boston gentleman, then I supposed you could have your separate beds. If I was a full Lakota, I wouldn't be able to touch you for two years."

"Two years?" She gasped. She couldn't imagine it. She couldn't picture being under the same roof with him and not wanting him, not having him. Or him going without a woman. Her smile began to stiffen. "Then I suppose you'd be going back into Crowe Creek." There was no keeping the ache of distress from her quiet words.

"For what?" he asked innocently.

"For what you found there on the Fourth." Was that how it was to be? If she refused him, he would go elsewhere. To some whore. The image was there before she had the chance to block against it: Scott in the arms of another. Her mother and father on the stairs, struggling.

His arms tightened. He kissed her temple, her cheek, and tried for lips, but she evaded him. "Gena, listen to me. I wasn't with a woman that night. It was a lie Rory made up so you wouldn't know I'd been beaten up by Spencer. I've never, ever been unfaithful to our vow. Never. And I won't be."

She leaned back and peered at him through searching eyes. His were warm with love, glowing with truth. The doubts fell away in that instant and she believed. "And what do the Sioux men do for two whole years while their wives are breeding?" she couldn't resist asking.

Now he wished he'd kept his mouth shut. He made his reply as neutral as possible. "They're free to visit

425

the divorced or widowed women. Or in the old tradition, take a second wife. That's illegal now. Or they can use the *berdaches*."

"Who are they?" Was that the Lakota term for harlot? She scowled.

"You don't need to worry about me going to one of them." He wasn't sure an innocent like Gena Trowbridge was ready to hear about the men visited by dreams of the Double Woman. He was just white enough to be uncomfortable with the idea, though he held no malice for those who assumed female dress and behavior. "You don't need to worry about me going anywhere except our own bed. I mean to enjoy it well until it becomes dangerous for you and the child. When it's born, we can start over again. Like a honeymoon. Until we have four or five little Prescotts for Mama to spoil rotten."

"First things first, Mr. Prescott."

"Yes," he answered softly as her gentle teasing brought back the meaning of the moment. He sighed determinedly. "I'll come for you as soon as I can."

Her world caved in around her.

"What?"

"You have a good long visit with your folks and explain things to them. You might not be able to get back for a long time. When I set things right here, I'll bring Mama and Ethan and Rory with me. Heaven help Boston when Rory gets there." He grinned, thinking of it. It made the ache of their imminent parting easier to bear. He wouldn't think about missing her. He would look ahead to their reunion. "We'll do things up right, the way you wanted. We'll have flowers and ferny stuff all over the drawing room and bouquets of roses in the music room, clover blossoms on the dining-room sideboard and daisies on the parlor mantel. Just like a gar-

426

den. Just like you wanted. Your mama can play hymns on the piano and you can get yourself that dress, that one with all the silk and lace and pearls and—Gena? What's the matter? Isn't that what we talked about? Don't you want it anymore?"

"No," she moaned in horror. "No, there can't be a wedding." She could imagine the awful humiliation of it. Scott and his family; the beloved Prescotts shunned at her door. All the affection they held for her twisted by hurt and disdain. No, there would be no wedding to Scott Prescott son of Aurora Kincaid and the Lakota Far Winds in the Trowbridge parlor. Her father would see her locked away in a sanatorium first.

Scott froze. Something huge and choking rose to lodge in his throat. Disbelief. Or was it fear that what she said was true. No wedding? But they'd already— He tried to swallow. He tried to speak. He tried to think, but his mind was numb. *Wakan Tanka,* didn't she want to be his wife?

With a small sound of pain, Gena collapsed upon his chest. She clung to him, her fingers digging into the hard muscle of his shoulders, her face rooting into the hollow of his neck. She was confused by it all. That had to be the answer. He made himself grow calm of spirit. He touched her glorious hair and made soothing noises.

"Hush, hush, now, *mitawicu.* Don't cry. It will be however you want. And we'll be happy. As soon as I get things taken care of here, I'll bring you to the home we'll share. Unless you'd rather live at the Lone Star. Maybe that'd be best, me being gone so much of the time. And we can start on those four or five little Prescotts."

Gena had gone rigid in his arms. "No, Scott," she whispered.

427

He tried to smile, rubbing her hair with his cheek, smelling the tangy lemon verbena she used. "All right—three, then."

"No. There won't be any children."

He was sure he'd heard wrong. "Maybe not right away. But soon. I've seen you with them. They love you. You're wonderful with them." The cold began to settle about his heart again, making it difficult to breathe.

"You don't understand, Scott," she began with an ominous quiet. "There won't be any babies. Not for us."

He realized then that she was serious. Horribly serious. He jerked back to stare at her, bewildered. Then furious. "Is it anybody's babies you don't care to have or just mine? Are you afraid they won't be white enough to suit your family and friends? Is that it? Is that why you all of a sudden aren't so sure you want to marry me? Is it, Gena?"

He was shouting. She cringed back, chest jerking with silent sobs. Angrier than he could ever remember being and more scared, Scott gripped her by the arms. She cried out as if she feared he meant to break them. Mind reeling crazily, he made himself release her and she scuttled back, eyes rounded with terror.

"Gena—"

"Lone Wolf!"

He turned at that desperate cry and was surprised to see Morning Song slip inside his tipi. Her face was marred by distress. She'd been crying.

"Lone Wolf, you must help. High Hawk, he has been shot. The agent Garrick is dead. He killed him to get the books you said you needed. He was fired by the *witkowin's* story of the white man's tea party. He did not want to appear weak in comparison." She took several

428

deep swallows of air and looked at Gena. There was incredible hate on the face of her new friend. "What have you started? First, you cause my family to lose their home and now my brother may lose his life. Go away! Go back where you belong, white woman! Haven't you caused enough sorrow?"

Chapter Twenty-six

Gena recoiled from the vicious words. From the cruel truth of them.

Scott took Morning Song by the shoulders and turned her away from the source of her fury. "Morning Song, where is your brother now?"

"We have hidden him away. What are we to do, Lone Wolf? I am so afraid."

He gestured to the door. "Wait for me." When she'd gone, he looked to Gena. She was pale as parchment and shaking. He hated to leave so distraught with the uncertainty and anger of their own words hanging between them. But he had no choice. He reached out to touch her cheek. She flinched and he felt as though she'd cut him with a knife. He didn't attempt any other overtures except to quietly say, "Stay here, Gena. Wait here for me. All right? Please. Wait for me."

When he got no response, he sighed in frustration and followed Morning Song from the tent he and his woman had christened with their love.

Gena sat stunned for a long moment. Then she stood shakily to gather her things. She found her horse saddled outside the tipi, and without looking about, she quickly mounted. She could hear the commotion amongst the Sioux, a confusion of relief and worry. Their enemy was gone. He was dead. She might as well have killed him. He and High Hawk. Her heels slashed back, startling the horse into a brisk canter. Away from the Cheyenne River reservation. Away from Scott Prescott. Morning Song's words beat into her brain like the horse's hooves on hard-packed earth. Scott's were a tormenting echo.

You caused my family to lose their home and now my brother may lose his life. Go back where you belong . . . Haven't you caused enough sorrow?

You made it impossible for me to help those people. You don't have the slightest idea of what life's about out here. It's not Boston. You can't just go butting in where you don't belong. Good intentions get innocent people killed. Stay out of things that are none of your business.

White woman . . . get people killed . . . don't belong . . .

Gena clung to the saddle horn with both hands, flopping on the horse's back like loose blanket ends. Its gait jarred her insides, sending her tears spraying and working her remorse deeper.

Don't belong . . .

He was right. He was right. She didn't understand these people. She didn't understand the way they moved in his life. What had happened to her dream? To the somber-souled, kind-eyed law student from Harvard? To the happiness that was going to last forever? Where had she lost those things, or had she ever had them? When had she forgotten who she was and begun to live some crazy dream? She swayed on the back of the big horse as if a cutting wind had suddenly swooped out of the west to buffet her spiritless body. How foolish she'd been to think she and a man like Scott . . . A silly little eastern girl naive enough to

431

think she could help the world. And ended up getting people killed. As surely as she'd shot them with Ethan's booming Sharps. The way she would kill Scott's love for her in time. She'd didn't belong. It was time to go home and quit playing at Indians and Annie Oakley. She was neither. She was meek Miss Gena Trowbridge of Boston, afraid of her father's shadow, afraid of her mother's dire warnings. Afraid of life and what it would mean to live it with Scott Prescott.

"Scott? Gena?"

Aurora came out of the kitchen and stopped dead. With a soft, "Oh, my dear!" she crossed the room and enveloped a sagging Gena in her arms. She steered the young woman to the sofa and sank down upon it with her. The girl's heartsick sobs sent a shiver of terror through her. She patted the heavy braid and demanded softly, "Is it Scott? Has something happened to him? Is Scott all right?"

"We're not going to be married."

Aurora felt an instant of relief at knowing Scott safe, then was prodded by a sharp annoyance toward her son. She tightened her arms about the quaking figure and soothed, "Scott loves you, Gena. I'm sure you'll work things out between you."

"No. No, we won't. I'm going back to Boston where I belong. You were right, what you said at the Bar K. I'm not right for him. I'm not the woman he needs. I can't be."

"Of course you are," Aurora murmured gently, feeling a guilty twist over her own part in the young woman's pain. "You're just what Scott needs. You're smart and pretty and generous. And you get along with his mother." She hoped to make Gena smile with that observation, but the girl was too lost to misery.

"It's not enough. It doesn't change things."

Some of that sympathy chilled in suspicion. "Because Scott's part Indian?"

"Yes." How could she deny it? It was the one thing he couldn't change, the one thing she couldn't overcome. It placed a difference between them that had become insurmountable. No matter what either of them wanted.

Aurora had gone very still. Anger stirred inside her, a helplessness that came with wanting to believe in the young woman she'd embraced into their home, into their life. She straightened, putting Gena from her. Her gaze was cool and accusing. "You said you didn't care what he was. Isn't it a little late to decide you don't care for the color of his skin? Or for the blood of his father's people? Isn't it rather sudden of you to decide you don't want to pass that on to your children?"

Gena was silent for a long, stunned moment. She could imagine the children he would sire; of golden skin and golden eyes. She thought of the way he had held White Cloud's son upon his lap, of the joy and contentment she'd seen in his face. "The children he makes will be beautiful. With someone else." That truth tore through the weeping woman, torturing her anew. "I wish they could be mine. But they can't. Don't you see?"

"No. No, I don't."

"That's because you're strong. That's because you don't know what it's like to live your life in a shadow, in a cage of convention. Afraid to express an opinion. Afraid to draw a breath of air for fear that it contained some dire contagion. Afraid to do, say, or be anything less than what was acceptable."

Then Aurora understood. "This is about your parents, isn't it?"

"They would never, ever see Scott the way I do. They

433

would never accept our marriage or the fruit of that union. Ever. And if I go home to them, I won't be allowed to be with Scott again. My father will see to it. He has—ways of making sure his rules are obeyed. My mother tried to go against them and he crushed her spirit. The way he'll crush mine."

"The bastard," Aurora muttered fiercely. Then to Gena, who was limp and nearly lifeless upon the sofa, she asked, "Does Scott know any of this?"

Gena straightened, aghast. "How could I tell him? He'd hate me! I lied to him. I let him think I could be a good wife to him. I let him think I could be strong enough to bear the differences between us. And I tried. I did. I wanted to be a part of his world. I wanted to believe in him—in us. I thought if I could make him love me, if I could make him want me—" She broke off, flushing hotly. It was highly vulgar to be describing a son's tender lovemaking to his mother. But Aurora wasn't offended. What she was, was insistent.

"You have to tell him."

"No!"

"But, my dear, you must. How else is he to understand?"

"He won't," she sobbed miserably. "He'll hate me for being weak. He'll despise me for not standing up for what I know in my heart to be right. He'll think the fault is *his*, for being what he is instead of *mine* for being what I am. And in the end, that would hurt him more than my leaving now. Better I should leave him to the *berdaches*."

"To the what?" Aurora's head snapped back. She could not imagine her son visiting the effeminate males held sacred by the Sioux for the purposes prescribed. Surely the girl was confused.

"It wouldn't change things, him knowing. I'm not

right for him. I'm not strong, the way you are. I'm like my mother."

"Nonsense." Aurora took her arm and marched her over to a mirror. "Look at that woman. That is not the weak-spirited child my son brought here from Boston. In that glass is the woman who tried to save a Sioux woman from rape, who charged armed men on horseback, who watched her man suffer the Sun Dance. There is no more Miss Trowbridge."

Gena looked at the face reflected back. She saw features warmed to a healthy tan by the Dakota sun, ones no longer haunted by a tubercular pallor and timidity. She saw Lakota hair strings woven into a thick braid, not a fluffy hairstyle anchored by stabbing pins of propriety. She saw a woman who had known love and spectacular loving. But what had really changed? Not enough. Not the fear that kept her from giving herself freely to Scott Prescott. Not the repressive hand that reached half-way across a continent to snatch her hope of happiness away.

But Aurora wasn't finished. She hauled Gena into the bedroom she shared with Ethan, crossing to a beautiful maple cradle that sat in one corner. She knelt down and rocked it gently.

"Ethan made this for Scott. One day his children will sleep in it."

Gena regarded the baby cradle with a depthless despair. It was empty. She would never place a child of Scott's within it.

Aurora stroked the smooth wood, her fond gaze skimming back across the years. "Oh, Gena, dear, there is no shame in being afraid. Do you think I wasn't afraid when I was pregnant with Scott, knowing he was the child of a Lakota warrior, knowing my father would never accept him? Do you think it was

435

easy going against my father's will to marry Ethan when he would have had me wed to some proper easterner? Do you think I had all the answers then? That I knew all the right things to do?" She shook her head wistfully, thinking back on the panic of uncertainty, of the many mistakes she'd made. "I listened to my heart, not to those doubts or those fears. The sound of my son's first cry. The look on Ethan's face when he laid him in my arms. That made everything right, every sacrifice worthwhile. I knew from that moment that he would be special to me, my little son born to such dire circumstance. I vowed I would protect him from the hurts of the world, but of course, I couldn't. I made a promise that I would never allow a woman into his life unless I felt she was equal to the hardship of loving someone like him. I confess, I didn't think that was you. But I was wrong." She lifted her head and smiled up at the young woman. "I was very wrong. You are exactly what Scott needs. Don't abandon him over something the two of you can heal between you."

Gena wrested her troubled stare from the empty cradle. "It can't be healed, Aurora. The tear is too great. I can't become the wife he needs. I know you can't understand, but please try to forgive me. I have a train to catch."

"Does he know you're going?"

"He wants me to." That was a partial truth, the only one that mattered. He did want her gone even if he didn't realize it would be forever. She thought of his angry words and Morning Song's. *Don't belong.* The pain of it swelled inside her, strengthening her decision. "I can't stay and watch Scott grow to hate me for my weakness and naïveté. I don't belong, you see. He knows that. He's always known. It just took longer for me to believe it. I tried my best but it just wasn't

436

enough. He doesn't think I'm strong enough to stand beside him. Why else would he be sending me away the minute there's any trouble. He's right. I've made nothing but mistakes. I've given him no reason to be confident in me. And I can't go back among his people, to face their blame for my foolish interference, not now that Scott's made me his *mitawicu*."

"His what?"

"His mistress," she confessed glumly, unable to meet his mother's eyes.

"But Gena, *mitawicu* doesn't mean 'mistress'—"

"It doesn't matter," Gena interrupted lifelessly. "Don't you see, nothing matters now. I have to pack."

"Is Scott coming to see you to the train?" Aurora asked, still reeling from what she'd heard.

"No. He has business with his people. They need him. And my being here distracts him from his work." There was no bitterness, no resentment in that claim. Just a weary resignation.

"I can have Ethan drive you. If you're sure it's what you want."

"It's what has to be."

What has to be.

Mechanically, Gena began to lay her pretty eastern gowns upon Rory Prescott's bed. Soon, the expensive bits of cashmere, satin, lace, and silk would be hanging in her own wardrobe cupboard. Earthy split logs would be replaced by the flat beige walls of her own bedroom where no papering would torment her brain into a nervous irritability. She thought about that for a moment, then gave a strained little laugh. How utterly ridiculous it sounded. If anything, the lack of excitants was going to drive her to madness. When she got home, she would insist upon putting up wallpaper. Something in green or gold. Or maybe blue. Something that would remind her of the Dakotas. Something that would help her dream away the lonely days to come of this, God's most perfect place.

Wiping her eyes, she returned to the careful folding of her garments. How stiff they felt to hands that had caressed supple doeskin. She would forget the freedom of movement she'd enjoyed once cinched up again by social strictures. Tight laces, metal stays, heavy petticoats, scalp-piercing hair pins, high-heeled shoes a size too small, each restricting, each controlling in their own subtle way. Each would help her remember she was no longer in the Dakotas. Each would conform her into the rigid daughter of Emmett Trowbridge.

Snapping the catches on her trunk, she caught sight of the cover of her sketchpad. That, she could never leave behind. Upon its pages was the life she would live within her memory. She didn't really have the time for reminiscences. The train wouldn't wait. Still, she found herself flipping through it, smiling wistfully at the images trapped inside. Red Bird, Morning Song, and her mother beading the doeskin dress, the little nut-brown children, their faces whitened with clay as they played "White Man," Yellow Bear with his old, wise eyes. *How I wish you were here so I could go to you for counsel.*

Scott.

As impatient minutes ticked by, Gena sat on the edge of the bed, lost in her study of the drawing. Someday, she would have to pull out this picture, by then curled and yellow with age, so she could bring his face back to her memory. She would look with a shocked curiosity at the proudly bared body, at the arrogant strength of expression and wonder, from the dull confines of her eastern life, how she had ever given her heart to such a wild half-Indian man. How she had

438

ever survived the danger and emotional upheaval of living in his world. By then, it would be like a youthful dream; living, loving, laughing with Scott Lone Wolf on the endless Dakota plains. And she would be as dry and brittle inside as that piece of fragile paper from the past.

A drop of moisture fell onto the drawing, soaking and spreading. Quickly, Gena blotted at it, fearing it would blur even the most insignificant line. She would keep this memory clear in case the image of Scott Prescott faded in her heart.

In a hundred years or so.

I need you, Gena. I will love you forever.

"I'm sorry, Scott. I can't be that brave."

Scott was off his horse before its stop was complete. He never touched the stirrup irons as he vaulted to the porch.

"Gena?" he called out as he strode into the house. With a quick glance about, he headed for the stairs. He couldn't wait to tell her the way things had worked out. They had started grimly enough, with High Hawk surprised by Garrick as he was going through his papers. The Lakota brave had taken a bullet to the arm before Garrick fell as they grappled for the gun, striking his head with a killing blow. Between them, Scott and Morning Song had erased all evidence of struggle and saw the room reeked of whiskey. Garrick's intemperance was well known. It would look as though he had fallen in a drunken stupor to bring the onset of his own death. And Scott suffered no pangs of conscience in knowing otherwise. All that mattered was that the immediate threat was gone. White Cloud would not lose his chance in the white man's world. And Scott was possessed of enough information to see that another would not take Garrick's place in the plundering of his people.

"Gena," he shouted a second time as he bounded up the steps in his eagerness to grab her up in his arms. He would kiss her breathless and then they would celebrate. White Cloud asked that they be guests in his house and Morning Song was anxious to beg the forgiveness of her new friend for her harsh words. And he was anxious, too. Anxious to wipe away the confusion of feelings between them, to start over, to start here.

"Scott."

He paused, almost to the landing, and looked down at his mother. His smile stiffened and died at her expression.

"She's not up there."

In defiance of the truth he saw in her face, he continued up the steps with panic pounding in his heart. The door to Rory's room was open. And the room was empty.

Scott didn't remember turning away. His head and heart couldn't accept what his eyes told him. She couldn't be gone. Somehow, he made it back to the stairs and had nearly reached the bottom when his knees gave way. He sat hard on one of the steps, barely feeling the jar to his spine. "She left? God, I never thought she would. How—"

"She asked Ethan to take her to the station."

"The train." His mind began to function again, thoughts turning slow and labored, then gradually gathering momentous steam. "I lost track of the time. I asked her to wait for me. I never thought she'd go with so much unspoken between us." He ran unsteady fingers through his hair. He was still bareheaded, shirtless, and bootless. In his exuberance, he'd overlooked

440

his mother's rule to dress in a civilized manner before entering her house. She said nothing about it now. Her eyes were on the tragic set of his face. "Oh God, Mama, she's left me."

The truth of it was devastating. He closed his eyes, trying to clutch at the numbness, at anything that would hold his sorrow at bay. Nothing could stem the swamping tide of it as it engulfed his heart and drowned out all his hopes.

"She left some things for you on the table."

Scott focused his eyes on the small stack of her belongings. He could make out the doeskin dress and elkstooth necklace. What else had she left him with? he wondered dully. His ring? He couldn't quite gather the courage to look. Not yet. "Did she leave a note or anything?" he asked. God, how could he bear to read it in black and white, so permanent and proper, the severing of life blood to his heart.

"No."

That hurt. She would leave him without a good-bye.

"Maybe this will explain some of what's been bothering her for the last few days. I found it in her room."

Scott scanned the tearstained message from Emmett Trowbridge that his mother brought him. His hand crumpled it in one savage movement. "Damn them. She said it didn't matter to her and I believed her. God, how could I be so blind to think she'd want my half-breed children."

"Is that what she told you, Scott?"

"Not just like that, but that's what she meant."

"No. What she meant is she's scared to death of the thought of disappointing you."

"What? She's never—I never—"

"No, you never. You never told her you needed her. You never told her she had an important place in your life. You never let her prove to you and to herself that she could be of value."

He threw the offensive note across the room and growled, "I did tell her. She chose not to believe me." Hurt continued to swell into unchanneled anger. But Aurora Prescott had no intention of letting him focus it on Gena.

"Then why didn't you tell her that *mitawicu* means 'my wife' not 'my mistress'?"

Scott's jaw clamped tight.

"You married her in the eyes of the Lakota and you didn't even tell her? Scott, how could you do such a thing?"

He couldn't meet his mother's angry glare. "I made a promise to Yellow Bear that I would take her to me in the traditional way. She was going back to Boston, Mama. I wasn't sure when I'd see her again. If I'd see her. I wanted — I needed something stronger between us than just a piece of stone."

"And just when do you plan to tell her?"

"When she comes back," he admitted softly. "And if she doesn't, our laws won't be binding on her. Only on me. If she finds someone else —" He shrugged eloquently.

"Oh, Scott," Aurora moaned, exasperated by the one-dimensional thinking of the male species. "If you'd told her, she would never have even thought of leaving you."

His expression sobered into firm lines. "It's better that she did."

"Better, how?"

"This way she'll be safe."

"From what? Living?"

"From the things I'll be doing here. Mama, you of all people should know how hard this life is. It isn't

442

enough that we're so isolated, but the work I'll be doing for the Lakotas is enough to set a price on my head." *From men like your father.* He didn't say that aloud. He couldn't. "I didn't want her in the middle of that. She's not —"

"What?" his mother challenged. "Strong enough?"

"Mama, if something was to happen to her because of me, I'd just die. I would. At least back east, she'll be protected."

"Protected? What's to keep a streetcar from hitting her the minute she gets off the train? Who's to say she won't contract diphtheria? Would you consider yourself responsible if those things happen? You can't hide the people you love from the risks of living. If I've learned one thing in all these years it's that survival at any cost is better than surrender. My life would have been easier if I'd given you up, Scott. I could have gone east and married well. But I wouldn't have had you or Ethan or Rory. And to me, that was worth everything I might have had. And I don't regret one minute of hardship, one second of sacrifice. I'd do it all over again, and if I die tomorrow, I can say in all honesty that I haven't missed a thing. What will you and Gena be missing? Do you think she'll enjoy that nice safe life in Boston for the next sixty years any more than she'd cherish one or two years here with you? Did you ask her which would mean more to her, or did you just assume that being safe and miserably lonely amongst those who don't care about her is better than taking a risk beside someone she loves? Do you love her, Scott?"

"As much as Daddy loves you. As much as my father must have loved you."

"Then why don't you go ask her what she wants instead of making all the decisions for both of you."

Scott looked up at her incomprehensibly. Ask her?

443

How? Too late for that. She was gone. He got up off the step, dragging himself from the mire of misery to make himself walk to the table to see what Gena had left him. Unconsciously, he began to clench his gut for the punishing truth that she was truly gone. He touched the elkstooth necklace. At least she would always be his within his heart and soul. But that seemed such small comfort to him now. Anguish rose to form a knot within his chest, a heaviness that told him there was no purpose in a life without his love. Had he pushed her out of it with his good intentions. Or were they very selfish intentions after all? Just as Rory said. Would he end up like Garth Kincaid, a lonely, angry man with nothing but his ambitions? Or like his daddy, who knew how to appreciate the value of what he had.

He would go to Boston. He would take his unsuitable self to the Trowbridges' fine uptown home and give them a taste of the Lakota. He would teach them of the *wiinahme* and steal their daughter away. He would . . .

A small slip of paper protruded from beneath Gena's wedding garb. Thinking it was that final word of good-bye, Scott reached for it with reluctance. He glanced at it, then stared for a full, breathless minute.

"Mama?"

It was the one-way ticket to Boston.

Unused.

The water sighed and gurgled with its own mysterious laughter. It was cool, having trickled down from the heights of the sacred Hills. The tears of the gods. Healing. Soothing. In its lapping embrace, she'd known comfort, she'd found courage, and she'd discovered how beautiful love could be. The circle of shady cottonwoods through which the waters ran would always be her special corner of the earth. It was only nat-ural she go there to wait. And hope.

Something plucked at her sleeve. Then at her skirt. Frowning slightly, Gena brushed at them. Then, she saw a round shiny pebble land at her feet. Her head lifted. Her heart lifted.

"You looked miles away," Scott said softly. "I thought I was going to have to start pitching rocks to get your attention."

"And now that you have it?" she challenged with a matching quiet.

He didn't answer right away, but stood tossing the remaining pebbles he held in his hand one by one into the stream. When the last of the overlapping ripples stilled, he told her, "I'm sorry."

Gena dared not jump to any conclusions. She'd been in an absolute terror over what he might say, but now, she forced herself to calm her heart and wait for him to unburden his.

"I thought you'd gone. I thought you'd left me. I've never known such emptiness." He didn't look at her as he spoke, but, instead, studied the pattern of sunlight flickering golden upon the creek's surface. He didn't need to see her. He felt her in every pore of his body, beating within his blood, riding on each pull of his breath. How had he ever thought he could strip away that vital part of him and go on as if whole?

"I couldn't leave," Gena confessed. "I just couldn't find the courage to walk away from everything that matters to me. I'm sorry. I know I promised you I'd be brave."

He turned his gaze upon her then and his eyes glit-tered like that reflecting water. "It wouldn't have taken courage to go, Gena, but it's going to take a hell of a lot of it to stay. If that's what you want. Is it?"

"Yes. Where else would I be, *mihigna?*"

My husband.

He was staggered by emotions too profound to voice. In the end, what came out sounded more like an accusation.

"Mama told you. And all this was just to make me crazy?"

"Your mother thought you might need something to get you thinking. She said it would be best if you came to your conclusion on your own, the way I had to. I'm sorry. I know it was cruel." She was watching his face, trying to decipher the shifts of expression working the angular planes in tight, controlled spasms. She could read hurt there, the uncertain fear and anger. Would there be forgiveness?

"Where are your bags, all your things, if not on the way to Boston?"

"In your room."

The logic of it was stunningly direct. Where else? In his room, with his things. His woman. His wife.

He was silent for so long that Gena was forced to ask in a constricted little voice, "Scott, do you want me to stay?"

What else could he say but, "Gena, I never wanted you to go. I thought—I thought—I just thought too damn much. I should have been listening to my heart instead of my head, like Grandfather told me."

"Then listen now and stop talking so much."

He took a quick step. She came forward to meet him, rushing into his arms and completely conquering his spirit with the offer of her own.

Between the scattering of urgent kisses, Scott told her, "I have another ring to give you. A gold one."

She was touching his face, his hair, his chest, feeling the scars of his bravery, the beat of his love.

446

"I couldn't belong to you any more than I do now."

"We can still have flowers and family, but it will be at the Lone Star."

She kissed the sound of apology from his lips. "I always wanted to get married at home." And she was home. Deliriously happy, Gena couldn't seem to keep her hands from him, from charting each corded ridge of muscle, each flat plane and exciting swell. Hers to do with as she pleased. Oh, how she liked that idea. Even more so when her fingertips brushed across the hard denim-encased fact that he was getting some ideas of his own.

Contrary to the bold claim of his man's body, Scott's touch was achingly sweet. He pushed the straying tendrils of fair hair away from her lovely features and continued to hold her radiant face uplifted in the cup of his hands. His golden gaze caressed hers tenderly.

"We have a lot to talk about. Don't be afraid to speak to me of all that's in your heart. I love you, Gena. There's no fear that either of us carries that we can't lay to rest between us."

Gena smiled up at him, her eyes tearing with belief. Her fingers began to unbutton the band of his jeans. "We can and will talk later. But right now, words aren't what I want lying between us."

"Why, Miss Gena," he teased in mock astonishment. "Right here, in broad daylight!"

"I can't think of a better place than beneath God's canopy, can you?"

He couldn't. But because he wanted to slow the incredibly vivid shocks of sensation she was stirring with her not-so-innocent touch, he muttered, "What about your folks? We should send them some kind of word. A telegram or something. They'll be waiting for you to get off the train in Boston."

Gena mulled that over for a moment. She could see them plainly. Margaret Trowbridge with her pinched, pallid face, holding a handkerchief to her mouth so she wouldn't inhale any impure vapors. Emmett Trowbridge scowling and checking his watch, planning his chastisement of his wayward daughter who had the poor judgment to sully the family name.

And then she considered the man she loved, the man she was wed to in her soul of souls. And she smiled.

"To hell with them."

Slowly, his mouth lifted at the corners, curving into that tempting, heart-taming smile. His fingertips grazed her cheeks, marveling at the softness without, awed by the strength within. He spoke to her quietly, low, hushed words straight from his soul. She searched his face, seeking their meaning. And he smiled wider.

"I said, welcome home, White Swan, wife of Lone Wolf. Your place in my heart will be forever."

"And my place is beside you. Forever."

"I love you, Gena Prescott. Nothing else will matter."

And nothing would. For what else was there beyond the love of this man. To show him, to close the door forever on what was past and to begin upon the path of the future they would share, she used her kiss to lure him down to the warm Dakota ground. In the way of the Lakota. In the name of love.